CW00547413

The Devil Finds Work ...

John Ruttley

Non-fiction by John Ruttley

Prisoners in the North

Mowbray the people's Park

The Devil Finds Work...

ISBN No 0-9543366-2-3
© 2005 John Ruttley

The right of John Ruttley to be identified as the author of this work has been asserted by him in accordance with the Copyright, Designs and Patents Act 1988.

All right reserved. No part of this publication may be reproduced, stored in a retrieval system or transmitted, in any form or by any means without the prior written permission of the publisher, nor be otherwise circulated in any form of binding or cover other than that in which it is published and without a similar condition being imposed on the subsequent purchaser.

All characters and events in this publication are fictitious and any resemblance to actual events or real persons, living or dead, is purely coincidental.

The quote by Robert Byrnes is reproduced with the kind permission of Robert Byrnes.

Published by Holroyd Publications.

Printed by
Stonebrook Print & Design Services
Buddle Street
Wallsend
Tyne & Wear
NE28 6EH
01912633302

Foreword

If, like me, you've searched in vain for an authentic description of life in the shipyards of Britain, you need search no longer. This book gives you the smell, feel and taste of shipyard life. It portrays the camaraderie and the hardship endured by the men who made ships and gives an in-depth description of their family life. As the men and their women struggle to survive in a climate of industrial unrest and threats to their livelihood they are faced with a stark choice....to fight organised crime or go under. Add an intriguing plot to authentic detail and you have that most enjoyable of things, a damn good read.

Denise Robertson, October 2005

"In order to preserve your self-respect, it is sometimes necessary to lie and cheat."

Robert Byrne, American author.

1

Monday 5th November 1979

The barmaid smiled coyly at him as she pulled on the pump. "There you are, pet, a nice pint of Best Scotch beer," she said, placing the pint glass in front of him on the bar counter.

Trev paid her, then, pint in hand, he placed his foot on the dull, brass rail that surrounded the base of the bar counter. He took a long swallow of the dark beer as he looked around the grubby bar room, taking in the carpetless floor littered with cigarette stubs and the dirty yellow walls discoloured by years of tobacco smoke. The Cross Keys was an unpretentious pub, used mainly by shipyard workers. He noticed the four domino players huddled over the board in the corner in front of the large window. The black night sky, framed by the window, lit up periodically when fireworks exploded outside. He could see that they were playing partners by the significant looks, and not overly covert hand signals being sent across the board.

Next to the domino players sat a couple of men deep in conversation. They'd both had a lot to drink, and it showed. Trev knew that one of the men was drinking homebrew he'd brought into the bar in Newcastle Brown Ale bottles hidden under his coat. The homebrew was a lot stronger than that sold in the pub and much cheaper. The customer had bought one pint of beer when he came into the bar, and then furtively refilled the pint glass with his own brew at intervals. Up to now, it appeared that the landlord hadn't noticed, but he almost certainly would, and probably sooner rather than later. The empty Brown Ale bottles under the seat were a dead giveaway. There were another five men standing at the bar, near the door, but he didn't recognise any of them.

The four shipwrights came in through the door a few minutes later, bringing with them a blast of freezing cold air, and a whiff of acrid smoke from outside. They passed Trev and took up their customary positions at the end of the bar near the domino players. The four were dressed immaculately in heavy expensive overcoats, dark suits, coloured shirts and distinctive ties and all wore pungent aftershave. Trev envied them their tradesmen's high earnings, and the fact that they worked permanent day shift. They all nodded and spoke to him as they passed and he politely refused their offer of a drink when they ordered their own. As he paid for the round of drinks one of the shipwright motioned towards Trev's half-empty glass on the bar counter.

"You sure you don't want a pint?"

Trev shook his head. "No thanks, I'm expecting company."

"You still night shift?"

Trev nodded.

"You going in tonight then?" the shipwright asked.

"Aye. I'll have to. I lost two nights last week because of the welders' walkout, and I can't afford another shift off."

"Did you know that the welders walked out again this morning? We were all sent home at twelve o'clock, so you might be having another shift off tonight."

Trev's heart sank. That was the last thing he needed. Another short pay packet. He was finding it difficult to remember the last time he'd worked a full week and the car payment was due again, he couldn't miss another one and Christmas wasn't that far away.

The door opened, again admitting the acrid smell of burning. The newcomer was an overweight, red-faced, cheerful looking man, who looked about three times older than Trev's twenty-two years, but was in fact only in his early fifties. He was dressed in the same type of dark blue overalls and donkey jacket as the younger man, but wore a battered, flat cap, pulled down over his eyes, and carried a khaki haversack on his back. He'd worked in the yards all his life, first as a labourer and now as a crane driver.

"Pint of Scotch, Harry?"

"Can a fish swim? Why-aye I want a pint, I'm bloody parched, man. I had a hell of a good drink this afternoon. Started off in here and then went up to the club. It was a real good session but I'm paying for it now alright," he said, rubbing his forehead.

"What the hell have you got in there?" Trev asked, eyeing the bulky backpack.

"Some books I promised old Bob, the gateman."

"It's alright for some isn't it? I wish I could read during night shift and get paid for it," Trev said jokingly.

"Well, when you grow up and get a really responsible job like a gateman's or a crane driver's you just might get the chance," his friend answered with a smile. "You want to knock in for a game, they're playing Partners?" he asked, nodding towards the domino board.

Trev cast an evaluating eye at the large clock on the wall behind the bar.

Harry shook his head. "Doesn't matter anyway. Two of them are day shift labourers. They'll not play with me, they were in the holiday club," he explained defiantly, and then changed the subject. "You definitely going in tonight then?"

"From what that shipwright has just said, we could all be laid off again."

Trev repeated to his companion what the shipwright had told him.

"It's that Morgan, the welders' new shop steward. Ever since he got the job we've never had a full week in," Harry said, his lip turned down in disgust. "What's wrong with the bastard?" He shook his head in disbelief. "This is the wrong time to be having walkouts. The lads were saying up the club this afternoon that it looks like the yard is going to be taken over, and these unofficial stoppages don't help things at all."

"Taken over?" Trev repeated.

"Aye, the rumour is that some American syndicate is having talks with the management."

"That's all we need," Trev shook his head. "If the yard's taken over they'll sack most of us, you know that, don't you?"

"That's probably what'll happen alright, but what can we do about it? The whole bloody country is going to the dogs. Everybody seems to be on strike."

They sat down with their drinks on seats near to the domino players. Harry placed his heavy haversack on the floor. All the players acknowledged Trev's presence, but two of them pointedly ignored Harry.

"What with walkouts, and layoffs, I've been out more times than the gas this year. Mind you, night shift does have some advantages, like good afternoon sessions at the club, but I think I had a bit too much today," Harry said, rubbing his head again. "I'm surprised that you weren't up there."

"Skint," Trev explained.

"Skint? A single lad like you, skint? What do you do with your money then?"

"It's the car. The repayments are crippling me. There's always something to pay out for, tyres, or the battery, or exhaust or something. The big end's gone now."

"Well, I told you when you bought it that it was a bloody great drain, didn't I? You want to get rid of the thing, get it sold and give somebody else the problem," Harry said, pulling a battered old Golden Virginia tin from his overall pocket.

"No fear. I'm keeping it. Worth its weight in gold that car is. It's a right babe magnet. I've got to pull the birds off the car to get the doors open, man."

"Good-looking lad like you doesn't need a car to pull the lasses," Harry said, expertly constructing a cigarette between his nicotine-stained fingers. "You can have any girl you want." He nodded towards the bar. "That barmaid keeps giving you the eye, for one. If she bats her eyelashes at you any faster she'll start to hover." He licked the Rizla's gummed edge, rolled, then trimmed the ends of the cigarette and dropped the excess tobacco back into the tin. "You still going out with that posh dolly bird with the legs?"

"Tina? No."

"I'll bet she spent your money alright. It's about time you got yourself a decent lass and settled down."

"I want to try and make something of myself first, Harry. You know, be successful, maybe get into show business before I tie myself down and get married."

"Aye, that's not a bad idea, and mind you don't forget your old mate when you're a rich and famous singer," Harry said, lighting the roll-up, the few stray ends of tobacco flaring in the flame of the Swan Vesta.

"How's Olive?" Trev asked, changing the subject.

Harry shook his head and seemed to deflate before Trev's eyes; he blew thin blue smoke from his lips, his shoulders sagging.

"She still really ill then?" Trev asked quietly.

"Aye. That last dose of radium treatment has just about knocked her lights out. The hospital said that she's nearing the maximum treatment limit now anyway, and there's not much more she can have."

"Can't they give her anything else?"

"They said they'd take her in for chemotherapy or something in a week or so and that's it. After that there's nothing else they can do." He paused. "The chances are that Olive won't last much longer, so I've paid for Debbie to bring the grandchildren across from Australia for Christmas and New Year. There's no way that they can afford to pay for the trip, and her husband can't come because he can't get the time off work. He's still trying to build up his business and is having a hard time of it from all accounts. So Debbie and the kids are coming across in a few weeks. We've never seen the grandkids, you know. Oh, we've seen photos and spoke to them on the phone but we've never actually met them. It's costing a small fortune, but what's money compared to having your daughter and grandkids around you at a time like this?"

The conversation lapsed. Trev guessed that at least part of the money for the flights had come from the lads' holiday fund, but he understood his friend's motives.

A particularly loud explosion just outside the pub door made them both start involuntarily. Trev felt embarrassed talking about Olive's illness. He never knew what to say for the best, and generally avoided the subject unless Harry himself brought it up.

"Olive will be alright, I suppose. She's a real strong woman when it comes to anything like this, but goes off the deep end for the little unimportant things, you know? But they're all the same women, funny buggers, you just can't weigh them up, man, can you?" Harry said philosophically, swilling his beer around in his glass. He sat up straight and pulled himself to his full height in an effort to recover from the feeling of helplessness and regain control of his emotions. He drank the remains of his beer. "You ready for another?"

"Aye, go on then," Trev said, handing Harry his empty glass.

The bar was beginning to fill up and the noise level was rising. Harry made his way to the bar, bought the drinks and returned to his seat.

"Hey, I've just remembered, it's the annual work's trip to the races this weekend, I hope that you've got enough money for that, mind," Harry said placing a pint on the table in front of Trev.

"I'd forgotten about that," Trev said. "When is it? Next Saturday?"

"Aye, last flat race of the season. Olive says that I've got to go. She says if she sees much more of me she'll go crackers. And don't you worry. You won't need a lot of money anyway, just enough for a few pints."

"Just as well that we paid for the coach in the summer. It was cheap enough anyway, what with the yard subsiding the cost of the coach," Trev said.

"Well, sponsoring a race is good publicity, isn't it? And it costs them next to nothing, it'll be tax deductible."

"I'll be there. I'll get a few quid from somewhere. It should be a good day out. We could certainly do with one," Trev said. "Who else is going on this little outing then?"

"Well, a lot of the day shift labourers are going. They couldn't fill all the seats on the bus so there'll be half a dozen welders there as well. All the fore-end squad, Richie and Alan will be there..."

"That thieving bastard!" Trev interjected.

"... Joe's going and your mate Mickey. Is that right he's got a weekend job as a bouncer at one of the clubs in town? I suppose he's got to make up his money somehow, us being called out on strike every other day, and what with the kids' Christmas presents and what not, but I wouldn't have thought he'd go for something like that."

"That's right. Mickey's working weekends at the Blue Angel. But he'll not last long there. I don't think he's really suited to being a doorman at all. He's far too easygoing, no killer instinct, that's why he never turned pro. He can certainly handle himself, what with all the boxing he's done, but he's too much of a gentleman to be in that game. I'd forgotten about Mickey going. Aye, I'm looking forward to the trip now. It's a pity that toe-rag Alan's going as well."

"That young Richie's not so bad, he's just trying to imitate his cousin. He's easily led that's all," Harry said.

"Maybe you're right. But that Alan's an out and out bastard. I'm sure it was him that stole my pay packet the other week. A whole week's wages lost."

"It wouldn't surprise me at all if he'd done it, but proving it is another thing. I think that maybe you were a bit out of order accusing him like that in front of everybody, though," Harry said, remembering the confrontation that would have certainly ended in blows if the other lads hadn't stepped in between the pair.

"He was the only one anywhere near my jacket when the money went missing and you know how light-fingered he is. I was left with nothing to live on for a whole week. I don't know how I would have managed if you and the lads hadn't have had a whip round for me."

Trev took deep breaths to calm himself down. Just thinking of the recent loss of his week's wages made him angry. "Which race meeting are we going to again?" he asked to break the lengthening silence, and his mood.

"York. Nice little course it is. Been there lots of times. I always have a few winners there, it's a lucky course for me."

Harry was an incorrigible gambler, spending hours weighing up the racing form before placing his bets. He wasn't particularly successful at selecting winners on a regular basis, but pulled off some real good wins now and again.

The two pints that they'd each drunk had made them feel a lot better; warm, and content. The alcohol had relieved Harry's hangover symptoms from the lunchtime session, but neither of them was in the least inclined to venture out into the dark, cold night and start work. But they were going in. They'd lost too much work and too much money because of the unofficial walkouts over the last few weeks. They were desperately short of money and Christmas was on the horizon. If they were turned away at the gates there was not much they could do about it, but they were going to go down to the yard, and hopefully they would actually get the chance to work.

The homebrew drinker next to the domino board stood up unsteadily to go to the toilet and knocked over some of the empty bottles he'd deposited under his seat. They rolled noisily across the floor, causing customers to step over them. The landlord, suspicious, came from behind the bar to retrieve them.

The shipwrights in the corner ordered another round of drinks and the smiling barmaid obligingly pulled their pints. The domino players were arguing about some of the more blatant hand signals being made, and accusations of cheating filled the air.

The two men looked at each other and drank the remaining beer in their glasses. They stood up with resolution and walked to the door. Harry having difficulty placing the heavy haversack on his shoulder, and they left the warm, smokey, congenial atmosphere of the bar. Other night shift workers followed them out into the cold night air.

Bonfires raged in gardens and on waste ground right across the city. Rockets lit up the night sky with explosions and cascades of colour and light that flared briefly, and then faded sadly like children's cheap Christmas torches.

2

Half a mile from the yard, in a respectable residential area, stood a row of terraced cottages. In one of these small, double-fronted, single-storeyed cottages, identical to the thirty others in the street, a plump man, aged about thirty, stood in the bathroom extension, vomiting into the toilet bowl. He'd already evacuated most of the content of his stomach and was now bringing up only bile. He stood up gasping for breath as he made his way into the kitchen. "I knew that I shouldn't have had that meat pie for tea."

"Are you alright, Joe?" His wife said with concern, handing him a damp towel. "I shouldn't have given you anything greasy to eat, but you haven't had any trouble with your stomach for a while and I thought it would be alright. Anyway, it's more likely to be because the day shift has been sent home than anything you've had to eat. Your face went pale when you heard."

"It's not your fault, Brenda," he said, putting his hand on her shoulder. Every time he looked at his wife, Joe realised just how lucky he was. Brenda was a beautiful woman, had a tremendous figure and could easily have made a successful career as a model had she had the chance. She was intelligent and very attractive to men and Joe was always amazed that she loved him. "Like you say, I haven't had any trouble for weeks."

They walked into the small sitting room and sat down. Joe holding his hands over his stomach protectively. "Every time I think of the mortgage I get a pain in my stomach as if I've been punched." He shook his head. "I haven't had a full week's pay in months, and I don't know how we're going to pay the mortgage this month. We're two months in arrears already and liable to get repossessed if we miss any more payments. We should never have lumbered ourselves with this millstone of a mortgage. I said at the time that we'd never be able to manage the payments. We've had nothing but worry the whole five years we've been living here."

"Try not to worry, Joe. We'll manage somehow; we always have up to now, haven't we? I'll look out for some sort of part-time casual work so that I can still look after Sharon properly. There must be somewhere with hours that will suit."

At the mention of her name, a young girl turned her face away from the flickering television and her eyes searched the couple's faces, seeking reassurance. Both adults smiled and nodded at her encouragingly until, satisfied, she turned her attention back to the TV. The child, Sharon, Brenda's younger sister, was another real cause of worry for them both. She was sixteen years old, but had a mental age of about half that. Her mother had looked after her until her death six months ago.

Brenda had willingly taken on the responsibility of caring for her young sister, who was absolutely terrified of being placed in a residential home, but Sharon's social worker's attitude was that the child should be placed in an institution where she could be looked after by properly trained staff, and consequently the social services were unwilling to allow any financial assistance at all towards her keep.

Brenda had appealed against the decision, and this was in the process of crawling through a very lengthy and time taking appeals procedure. Providing the proper level of care had obliged Brenda to give up her full-time job in a clothing factory, and the couple's financial situation had deteriorated rapidly since then.

"I'll go straight on the sick if we're locked out for more than a couple of shifts," Joe said decisively. "Then at least we'll have some money coming in. I've still got my qualifying three days in, so I'll get paid from day one."

"Are you sure that the doctor will give you a sick note?"

"Oh aye, she'll give me a note without any problem. I've always exaggerated the problem with my stomach, and I've got to have that X-ray soon, so I've only got to ask," he said, with a confidence he didn't entirely feel, as he placed his packed sandwiches into his ex-army canvas backpack. In his overall pocket he carefully placed a packet of anti-acid tablets, a small bottle of aspirins and some prescription tranquilliser pills.

At the time Joe left the house, two young men passed the bottom of that same terraced street on the way to the yard. They watched the soaring rockets exploding in the inky black sky, the younger one now and then pointing out a particularly spectacular display to his companion. Although they were cousins, their mothers being sisters, and they both worked at the yard, the two were different in every way, physically and mentally.

The older and more muscular of the pair swaggered as he walked. He was a thief. A shifty-eyed, dyed-in-the-wool, confirmed criminal. His never still, aggressive eyes constantly searching for any advantage, seeking out other's weaknesses. He instinctively knew that the best form of defence is attack and would attack first without hesitation. He had a lengthy criminal record for theft and housebreaking despite his age of only twenty-two years.

He had a considerable chip on his shoulder, hated everyone in authority and considered that the average working man was a mug, working for buttons, and sweating to make someone else rich. His attitude to women was very similar to his attitude to work, and he considered that any man who allowed himself to be tied to a woman was daft, and deserved all he got. Alan was currently on bail awaiting trial for burglary. The magistrates had sent his case to Crown Court for trial because they considered a prison sentence might be appropriate, if he was found guilty. He had returned to work, in an attempt to impress the judge and escape a custodial sentence if he were convicted, which he thought was very likely.

His cousin, Richie, was a tall, gangly and bespectacled youth of eighteen years. He was courting steadily and planned to marry soon. Richie was very naïve and a bit slow in thought and movement. It was generally accepted that he wasn't exactly the Brain of Britain, and never would be; in fact he couldn't read or write properly, a fact that embarrassed him and which he tried to conceal. He was a decent enough lad who admired his older cousin, but he could never dare to fully emulate him in his criminal activities. He hero-worshipped Alan because his older cousin did the things that he knew he could never even think about doing himself.

Neither of them had heard about the welders' walkout and fully expected to work the shift that night.

"I don't know if this is worth the bother," Alan said disgustedly. "I could make more money in an hour than I'll earn all week in that stinking dump of a yard." Despite his regular pronouncements regarding his expertise, cleverness at crime, and his supposed association with big-time criminals, Alan's criminal career consisted entirely of petty theft. Although he was reluctant to admit it to himself he was afraid of getting into anything bigger or more serious, preferring to remain a small fish and keep out of the way of more serious criminal activity and the resulting penalties.

"But having a proper full-time job will help you with the Court won't it, Alan?" Richie said, peering at his cousin over the top of his specs, which were in their usual position, balanced precariously on the end of his nose.

"I suppose so, but I sometimes think that I'm just wasting my time. They'll send me down anyway. They have got it in for me and no mistake." He shrugged, and looking around furtively, lowered his voice conspiratorially. "I've got a big job in the pipeline. It's only at the planning stage now but if it comes off I'll be in clover. You won't see me for dust, Richie lad, and neither will the Court. Anyway, it's no great problem. If I do go down, I can do the time standing on my head."

Richie didn't like the thought of his hero not being seen for dust, or worse still, being in prison again. He changed the subject. "That right about your dad then?"

Alan hadn't been very old when his father had left them, and he couldn't even remember what he looked like. There were a few old photographs in the house that showed a thin, tall man smiling into the camera, but they portrayed nothing of the man's personality or presence. When he was a child, his mother had told him that his father was in the navy, and that's what he'd told the kids at school, but as he became older, he realised that this wasn't true and his mother had eventually told him that his father was in prison. He was arrested after years on the run and was being released soon, after a fourteen-year prison sentence, and coming home.

"Aye, that's right."

"It'll be a bit funny like won't it? You know, him being around again after all this time?"

Alan had very mixed emotions about his father's return. His memories of his father were very dim and shrouded in the fog of nostalgia. He had a natural affection for him, but it had been his mother who had brought him up and he knew she wasn't looking forward to her husband's release.

"You still going on this work's outing to York Races on Saturday then?" Richie asked, sensing that his cousin didn't want to talk about his father.

"I suppose so. You?"

"Oh aye. I've never been to the horse races. Still, it should be a good day out. All the other lads are going."

"That's just wonderful. Having to go with that crowd of losers." A thought suddenly struck Alan. Hey, your Julie okay about you going then, is she? I thought she'd be moaning that you should be saving every penny for the wedding?" Richie was silent. Alan looked at Richie closely. "She does know that you're going doesn't she? You have told her haven't you?"

"Er, not exactly. Not yet."

Alan sniggered. "Well, get her told, man. It's you who wears the trousers, isn't it? Start the way you mean to go on. Don't let her

14

dictate to you what you should be doing, or she'll have you right under her thumb."

Richie nodded silently and digested his cousin's advice.

Three miles away on a large sprawling council housing estate, identical rows of houses presented a bland front to the world. In the back garden of most of these houses bonfires burned and fireworks exploded.

In one such garden a man and his family were standing near to a small bonfire. The garden was divided equally along its length by a stone-flagged path that followed the course of a washing line strung between the house and a metal post at the end of the garden. One side of the path was a grassed play area for the kids, the other side being given over to the growing of various vegetables and contained a small greenhouse. Both the greenhouse and the vegetable patch were empty of plants and seeds at the moment.

The big man was trying to light a firework. He spent a minute or so trying to read the instructions, but the night was dark and the flickering bonfire in the garden gave off a shimmering and uneven light. He'd bought the fireworks from Alan who always seemed to be able to get anything cheaper than you could buy in the shops. Mickey knew that the fireworks were probably stolen, but he couldn't afford to buy proper ones, and he didn't want his children to be one of the few in the street that didn't have any fireworks on Guy Fawkes Night.

As a practising Catholic, buying stolen goods troubled Mickey's conscience, but there wasn't much else he could do. And anyway, he rationalised, he didn't know for certain that they were stolen, did he? The half-dozen that he'd let off previously had been more conventional, and less than half the size of this one, and had gone off without any problem. He gave up trying to read the small print on the firework. It was no good; he couldn't make any sense of the instructions. The print was very small and indistinct, red lettering on a black background, and anyway he thought that they might be printed in some foreign language. He placed the firework carefully onto the grass.

Making sure that his wife and the children were standing well back, and away from the big roman candle-like tube, he stepped forward and lit the blue touch paper. He retreated to the safety of the garden path and joined his wife Tracy, and young son and daughter who were waiting with ill-concealed impatience as they watched the blue paper burn down towards the main body of the firework. The flame disappeared. The little group waited in hushed and expectant silence. Nothing happened. "Blast," Mickey said under his breath and made to go forward.

"No, wait," Tracy said, wringing her hands nervously. "Give it a minute, Mickey, it might still go off if you go over there."

Mickey stayed where he was for about thirty seconds, then impatience won and he stepped forward to examine the dud firework.

Boom! The thing went off like a mortar bomb. It exploded with an ear-shattering bang. The garden was briefly illuminated with a brilliant white light, then smoke enveloped the whole area and for a few seconds nothing else was visible at all in the dense atmosphere. Mickey looked wildly around trying to see the kids and his wife in the gloom, and was relieved to make out their shadowy figures as the smoke slowly dispersed. The smaller child, his daughter, was crying inconsolably. Just as Mickey was beginning to calm down and his heart rate returning to normal, something heavy hit him on the top of his head. "Damn!" he exclaimed involuntarily, covering his head with his hands. "What was that?" He was hit again. Not so heavily this time, but enough to make him wince. It was earth. Sods of grass-covered soil were falling all around them.

The clumps of earth, dislodged from the garden by the explosion, were now falling back on the small group as they huddled together, their arms over their heads to protect them from the bombardment.

Using his coat as a makeshift shelter, Mickey protected their heads from the hail of now much smaller and lighter missiles still falling from the sky, spreading his large hands and arms over their heads to protect them from the debris. Finally the assault was over. They looked around as the smoke gradually cleared and drifted away assisted by a slight, cold breeze. The scene that was revealed to them was astounding. The spot on the lawn where Mickey had placed the firework was now a fair sized crater of about a foot deep and perhaps two feet across. He now knew that that was where the clumps of earth that had been bombarding them for the last ten seconds or so had come from. There were slight wisps of blue smoke still winding their way from the bottom of the crater and it had the appearance and smell he assumed a new bombsite would have.

They stood and tried to take in the scene of minor devastation. Mickey was absolutely speechless, and it took his wife a while to recover her normally vocal expressive velocity.

"I told you not to buy them off him, didn't I? He's no good that one. Everything he touches is rotten. I knew there was something wrong with those fireworks. I said that, didn't I?" his wife said loudly, her voice shrill and her face white with shock. Tracy was the opposite of her husband in appearance. She was agonizingly thin, never seemed to eat much of anything and lived on her nerves.

"Give it a rest, Tracy," Mickey said, wiggling his index fingers in his ears that were still ringing from the explosion.

"Oh God, look at the windows!" Tracy screamed.

Mickey looked around quickly. The debris from the explosion had peppered the whole of the house wall and windows. It didn't look as if any were actually cracked or broken, but they were certainly splattered and muddy.

"It's only soil, it'll wash off."

"Light another one, Dad," said young Paul. "Go on set another one off, please Dad. That was really good."

Mickey was half inclined to do just that, but one look at Tracy's face convinced him that it wasn't a good idea. "No, that's all for this year, son, you've had a couple of rockets, some bangers, and your sparklers, haven't you? Anyway, I've got to get ready for work, look at the time."

His daughter, Terri, clung to his leg in a vain attempt to keep him from going indoors. He picked the girl up and swung her easily up onto his muscular shoulders so that her legs dangled either side of his head. With his giggling daughter holding tightly to his ears, the gentle giant carefully lifted his son, who was hanging tightly on to his crooked arm, a foot from the ground and made his way into the house.

His huge frame filled the entrance and he bent almost double to make sure that the girl's head cleared the doorway, Paul still dangling from his arm. Tracy took a final, unhappy look around the devastated garden before following them inside.

Tracy made up her husband's sandwiches and a flask of tea. Although he could make tea at work she insisted that he take his own because she'd made it and it tasted better. She sent the children upstairs to get ready for bed, warning them not to misbehave and threatening to be up in a few minutes to tuck them in.

"You make sure that you get the money back off that bloody Alan," she insisted. "He must have known that they weren't proper fireworks. That thing exploding like that. It could have killed us all. Can you imagine what would have happened if you'd have gone back and picked it up like you were going to? It just doesn't bear thinking about; it would have taken your arm off. He's a wrong one that Alan, always in trouble with the police. The things were probably stolen anyway."

Mickey grunted noncommittally.

"Well, make sure that you do. We haven't got the money to waste on things like that, I don't know why you bought them."

Mickey thought about what she'd said then answered slowly and deliberately, "I bought them because it's bonfire night, and all the kids have fireworks on bonfire night, don't they?"

"All them that can afford them do," she said bitterly, slamming down the knife that she was buttering the bread with on the kitchen worktop. "All them that aren't laid off work because the welders haven't got enough time off to spend all their money, and walk out for any reason they can think of. Oh Mickey, why don't you try and get another job? Something that's more reliable than working in the yards? I never know from one week to the next how much money's coming in. I wish you had a bit more ambition."

Mickey took a deep breath and sat down at the kitchen table. This was a familiar topic and he knew what was coming next, but remained silent, waiting for her to finish her tirade. It was the tradesmen; if not the welders, then it would be the platers or the shipwrights who were out. One of the trades always seemed to be in dispute with the management about something or other. It was getting worse. Sometimes it seemed that everybody in the whole country was on strike. Not so long ago most factories had been working a three-day week so as to save electricity because the miners were on strike. Not that Mickey, who was a plater's labourer, minded what anyone did, or for how long they were out on strike, it was just that when one of the shipyard trades was out, the others couldn't work, and everybody lost work and money.

Most of the tradesmen were decent blokes just trying to make a living, and were sympathetic to the labourers' position, but they were highly paid and could better afford to lose money. Mickey didn't think that there were enough hours in the day for them to spend the astronomical amounts that they were rumoured to make. Some estimates were as high as £80 a week. To him, this amount of money was obscene. He took home a quarter of that when he was lucky enough to get a full week's work in, plus another ten hours overtime by working an extra shift on a Friday night.

He and his wife always seemed to lurch from one financial crisis to another. They managed somehow or other, but it was always a constant struggle and generally involved complex manipulation of the little money they had. Christmas and the kids' birthdays were nightmares of essential expense that had to be planned and calculated for months beforehand. Bonfire night fireworks' costs were minor compared to those, but still required some consideration so as not to deprive the kids of their enjoyment. Anyway, Mickey thought, Alan had provided the solution this year with his cheap fireworks, no matter where they'd come from, so that was one less problem to worry about.

"Look at that George that you used to work with. He's doing very well now as an insurance man," Tracy persisted.

Mickey shook his head. "I couldn't do anything like that Tracy. I'm not the type. You've got to be a good talker, a patter merchant, and be able to sell policies and stuff. Then there's a lot of bookwork as well."

"Well, there's all sorts of factory jobs advertised in the paper every week. They're crying out for machinists. Why don't you try one of those six-month training courses? Bobby Brown did that, and he's semi-skilled now. Works across the river somewhere, on good money, his wife was telling me. He makes components or something."

"I couldn't be a dilutee love," Mickey said quietly. "That's doing the time-served tradesmen out of their jobs. And anyway, you can't learn a skilled job in just six months, I don't care what they say."

What he said was true, but although he wouldn't admit it even to himself, there was another reason that he didn't want to leave his job. He was scared of trying to do something else, he liked working in the yards, knew the job inside out and didn't want to go elsewhere where he'd be forced to learn new skills. Besides, he'd been born near to the river, next to a shipyard gate in fact, and the moving crane jibs had been one of his earliest memories. All his friends had lived near him and had grown up with him before starting work at the same yard together. It was a very close-knit community, everyone knew everyone else, and all doors were open to the neighbours. He'd lived in that same house until the street was pulled down five years ago and the inhabitants moved to the new council estate.

Tracy turned away from him and threw the knife into the kitchen sink. "You're too bloody soft you are. What do you think the high-and-mighty tradesmen are doing to your jobs? Do you honestly think that they give a toss about you and all the other unskilled workers losing money because of them?" She started to sob uncontrollably.

"Just how in God's name am I supposed to feed and clothe the kids when there's no money coming into the house?"

Mickey stood up and crossed the room to stand behind her, putting his arms on her shoulders.

"Working in the yard is all I know, pet. I've been there since I left school. Anyway I don't want to work in a factory. I don't think that I could stand being inside all the time, doing piece-work, clock-watching and being chained to a machine for hours on end."

Tracy, turning to face him, dabbed her eyes with a handkerchief, sighed and conceded defeat on that front, but decided to try another approach. "What about asking to be moved to day shift then?" She sniffed. "The kids and me hardly see you, and working permanent nights can't be very good for you, can it? It'd be a lot better for you working proper hours during the day."

"Yes, it probably would. I've thought about that myself, but if I was on days I'd lose the shift allowance and I'd have to work three half-shifts and a Saturday morning as overtime, just to make the same money I'm on now. I'd have no time to workout, or do my road training, would I? I'd never be able to get to the church youth club to help out with the boys' coaching. I've promised Father Gallagher that I'll train these lads up to competition standard, and I will. The ABA trials are coming up soon and there are a couple of the lads showing some real potential. Then there's the North Eastern Boxing Championship in the summer. Anyway, if I was on day shift then you'd probably see a lot less of me than you do now."

"Maybe, but at least you'd be in bed with me every night."

"Don't you think that we've got enough kids, then?" he said, with a feeble attempt at humour, and kissed her forehead.

She shook her head and smiled weakly. "I suppose we'll manage somehow, as usual. I could get a job on the twilight shift at Jackson's if my mother could mind the kids for a few hours every night."

The kids were tucked up in bed when she saw him off at the front door with a kiss and a wave, and he set off as usual, to jog the three miles to work. But he and his workmates were wasting their time; the night shift was locked out that night, and every night for the rest of the week.

3

The night shift workers congregated outside the grey metal gates of the shipyard that Monday night. The dark shapes of the sheds and the ghostly towers of the cranes were just visible through the sea fret, the white freezing fog that had gradually seeped inland from the river. The yard had been operational since the early years of the nineteenth century, and had employed a lot of local workers during its existence. For most of the local population the yard was their mainstay, their only prospect of employment.

The waiting men were expecting to be sent home. They all knew by now that the yard had been closed during the day, and that any chance of them working that night was almost non-existent.

"Not good, lads, you can't work tonight," Skinner, the general manager, confirmed, standing in front of the firmly closed shipyard gates, his arms akimbo. Skinner was small in stature and slightly built, but his very presence proclaimed intransigence. His body stance and body language proclaimed that he was immovable. What he lacked in height, he more than made up for in pretentiousness, strutting when he walked and making extravagant gestures. There was a grumbling murmur from the crowd of thirty or so men.

"Look, there's nothing we can do about it. You know as well as I do that if the day shift hasn't been in then there isn't any work for the night shift to complete," Skinner said impatiently, striding to and fro before his audience. "Then there's the safety aspect. You don't want to be working outside in this weather, now do you?"

A man near the front of the crowd spoke up. "This is the sixth week running that we've lost time. I can't afford to lose work like this."

"Neither can anyone else," the manager replied.

"The welders can. That's the trouble. The money they are getting is enough for them to have a couple of days off every bloody week. They're always ready to walk out at the drop of a hat, and it's us that suffer. We don't get the sort of money that they do, and we find it hard to even manage on a full week's money, never mind short time. How are we expected to live like this?"

The men behind him voiced their agreement.

"Look, you all know as well as I do, that there's nothing at all we can do about the situation. The welders are holding a meeting tomorrow morning and they will decide then whether they are going back to work or not. Until they have their vote tomorrow there's nothing you can do but go home and wait. Come back down tomorrow night and if they've returned to work, then you will be back in tomorrow night," Skinner said.

"Can't you let us work sweeping up or something for tonight? At least we'd get paid," Joe asked, sucking an anti-acid tablet.

"No. I can't authorise that. Something like that raises all sorts of demarcation and safety issues. You wouldn't like other people doing your work now, would you?"

"What fucking work?" someone shouted from the back.

"Any sort of arrangement like that would have to be mutually agreed between the management and your union. You wouldn't want to cause a strike now, would you?" The manager's irony was lost on the angry men.

"Well, what about some sort of retaining payment? You know a flat-rate, one-off, payment to cover shifts lost through no fault of our own?" Joe asked.

"Oh yes, that's a really good idea, and the company buying every one of us a Christmas present is an even better one, but there's not much chance of it happening, is there? I couldn't see the directors agreeing to anything like that, could you?" Skinner said sarcastically. "But if some of you would like to propose it at the next union meeting," he went on, "then I'm sure that the shop stewards will put the idea forward to the convener to take to the management."

Skinner stood with his arms held out and his palms upwards in an exaggerated position of helplessness. "You'll just have to make the best of it and stop moaning, that's all. That's the system and there's nothing we can do about it."

There was a discontented murmuring from the men.

"Listen to me," Skinner went on, his voice breaking with annoyance. "You all know as well as I do that if I let you in here to work tonight, then the welders would stay out on strike tomorrow, because their Boilermakers Union has an agreement with the yard's management, that if the day shift is out, then the night shift doesn't work until the dispute has been resolved."

Realising that further argument was futile, most of the locked-out workers decided that they were wasting their time, and started to drift away from the gates in twos and threes.

The small group of fore-end labourers had a brief discussion amongst themselves. Mickey decided that he was going to use the unexpected spare time to do some training at the youth club. Joe went home as his stomach was playing up. The others, Trev, Harry, Alan and Richie decided to go and have a drink before going home. They only had enough money for about a pint each, and decided that they'd be better off buying beer with it as it wasn't enough to use for anything else.

Their group was the last of the night shift workers making their way up the bank away from the yard.

Harry suddenly stopped dead in his tracks. "Shit. I've still got these books for old Bob. I forgot to drop them in at the gatehouse, what with us being locked out and everything." He looked back in the direction of the shipyard gates, now entirely enveloped by the white mist.

"Give them here," Trev said, taking the backpack from Harry. "I'll nip down with them, otherwise we'll never get a pint, the speed you move at."

"Cheeky bugger," Harry said, but passed the pack to his younger friend with relief. "We'll see you in the pub," he said, resuming his slow trudge up the bank.

"Aye. I'll see you up there. It'll not take me long," Trev said, and set off briskly toward the yard.

After a few minutes the dark shape of the closed gates materialized out of the thickening freezing fog. Trev could now make out the dim light inside the gatehouse at the left side of the gates, and two shadowy figures moving around inside. As he approached the gatehouse he heard voices. Voices raised in anger. The door was open, spilling golden light out onto the mist. The sound carried well in the fog. He recognised the irritating nasal tone of Skinner's voice. He was arguing with someone out of Trev's sight at the back of the gatehouse.

Trev moved more slowly, and went to one side of the open door. A few steps further on and Trev could just make out some of what Skinner was saying.

"...keep them out for as long as you can. We don't want them back at work at all if possible, but you've got to keep them out at least until Christmas...that should do it."

The response from the other man was quick and muted, the words muffled and Trev couldn't catch anything of what the man had said in reply.

Stepping closer to the open door, Trev could now see that it was indeed Skinner standing in the gatehouse. The manager had his back to the door and was blocking Trev's view of the other occupant, who was standing well back inside the room.

The shadowy figure spoke again, and this time Trev caught some words.

"It'll do it alright...but the men aren't happy at all. I'm running out of excuses...them out. What about the cash? I'm sick of promises…I want the money."

The man was in shadow, and Trev couldn't see his face, but he thought that the voice was familiar, although he couldn't put a name to it.

Skinner looked at his watch impatiently. "You'd better get out of here now before the gatemen come back." He stood aside to let his companion leave by the door.

Trev just had time to leap back into the white folds of the fog, to avoid being seen, as the man left the gatehouse. The man didn't look right or left, but quickly strode away, a bulky figure melting into the mist like a ghost.

Trev stared after the mysterious figure. Like his voice, the man's build and gait was vaguely familiar, but remained tantalizingly elusive to Trev's memory.

"What do you think you're doing here?" It was more a demand than a question. Trev jumped at the unexpected voice. Skinner had left the gatehouse and walked up behind Trev without him realising it.

Mickey called in at home to let Tracy know that they were locked out yet again, before making his way to the parish youth club.

Tracy was so angry that she shook when she heard that he'd been locked out again due to no fault of his own. "Did you get your money back from that Alan?" she demanded, directing her anger at an obvious target.

"Er, no love, I didn't get much of a chance to have a word with anyone, what with the lockout and everything," Mickey answered evasively, cracking his knuckles, and itching to be away. "I thought that if I can't work, then I might as well call in the youth club and check on the lads' training."

"We really can't go on like this, Mickey. There's no money coming in and the bills are piling up, and the kids need clothes and Christmas is just around the corner. What are we going to do?" Tracy yelled shrilly, her voice taking on the edge of hysteria.

"Look pet, we'll manage somehow or other, we always have,

haven't we?" Mickey said unconvincingly. "Anyway, the doorman's job at the Blue Angel is bringing something in, isn't it?"

"I don't like you working there, Mickey. You're out until all hours of the morning and I can't sleep for worrying."

"I'm sick of telling you, Tracy, it's as safe as houses. Don't worry."

He unpacked his sandwiches from his bag and placed them on the kitchen table. "I'll have those for my supper when I get back." Relieved to have temporarily escaped his wife's ire, Mickey jogged off towards the boys' club.

Entering the wooden hut that passed for the club he joined Father Gallagher who was watching two teenagers spar in the ring.

"Is it laid off again you are then, Michael?" The priest said in a broad Irish brogue, turning to welcome the newcomer. "I don't know what this country's coming to and that's a fact. The world's gone mad. It seems as if everybody is out on strike at the same time. If it's not the miners then it's the car workers, the shipyards or someone else." He shook his head, but smiled. "Ah well, it's an ill-wind and all that. If the shipyard won't have you, then we certainly will. At least the boys will benefit from some extra tuition."

The two men watched the boxers in the ring. The boys sparred well, ducking, blocking and punching. Their footwork was good and Mickey was pleased that they were using their newly learned combination punches.

"Is that true about you getting yourself a part-time job then, Michael?" The priest asked, his manner suggesting that he already knew the answer.

"Er, yes, Father, that's right."

"Well, I'm sure that the money will be welcome, but you must be very careful working in a place like that."

"I'm always careful, Father."

"I'm sure that you are, but a nightclub like that must attract all sorts of unsavoury characters, what with all that drink there's sure to be trouble. You just be careful and take care of yourself. I wouldn't want you to get hurt, Michael, and we'd be lost without you here."

"Don't worry, Father, I've no intention of getting hurt."

"Your coaching is working wonders, Michael," the priest went on. "All the time and effort that you've put in is really paying off. Any one of these lads is a potential champion with your help."

"Well thanks, Father. But it's the lads themselves, you know, not me. I can't bring it out if they haven't already got it in them."

"Nonsense. You are much too modest, Michael. These lads will win the North Eastern championships next year and it's all down to you. Without you, half of them would be forever in trouble with the police and not doing any training at all. I'm hearing that there are more and more youngsters taking drugs now, smoking that marijuana, whatever they call it, that dope. Once they go down that path they're lost. No more healthy living and keeping fit. Sport goes out of the window. Believe me, they need a role model like you, someone they can respect. You are the mainstay of this club, Michael, and these lads look up to you and admire you."

Michael was pleased and flattered to be thought of so highly by the parish priest. His life revolved around the church and he was actively involved in a lot of parish activities, including raising money for the church and the school in various ways, but the youth club was his real interest. As always, any compliment caused him embarrassment and to cover his awkwardness he walked nearer to the ring and shouted advice to the sparring boxers.

Joe made his way home and sat watching television nursing a glass of milk. Both he and Brenda had been expecting the lockout, but that didn't make it any easier.

"Turn that down a bit Joe, Sharon's just gone off to sleep," Brenda said in a low voice.

"She alright?"

"Yes, she's worried, poor kid. She knows something is going on, what with that social worker shouting the odds and demanding she goes into a council home."

"Good old Miss Hagstone. She's well named and no mistake. She's nowt but an ugly, middle-aged, bag. She looks down her nose at us, and obviously thinks that the bairn couldn't be cared for properly by the likes of you and me. What she doesn't seem to realise is that Sharon doesn't want to be anywhere else but here, with us. Where else could she get the sort of love she gets here?"

"That's right, Joe, but I've got to admit that I got off on the wrong foot the first time Miss Hagstone called here. Remember I told you that she caught me unprepared and in the middle of decorating the kitchen? Sharon was helping, she likes to get involved with everything that I do." Brenda smiled at the thought. "Sharon managed to cover herself, and me, with loads of paint and thought it great fun to throw some over Miss Hagstone when she arrived. You should have seen the old girl's face. Hagstone was disgusted by my lack of control over the child and blew her top." She paused. "What I didn't tell you was that I lost my temper and a right shouting match followed. I said some things that I really shouldn't have said. But the damage was done. Hagstone put in her report and recommended that Sharon be placed in the care of the council."

"It'll turn out alright, love, you'll see. They'll okay her being here permanently and then they'll pay all the backdated benefits."

"You really think so?"

"Oh yes. And we're managing alright now anyway. I don't know how you do it sometimes, Brenda, you're a wonderful manager."

Trev caught up with Harry just as he reached the pub. He'd run all the way up the bank and was out of breath. The two men entered the smoke-filled bar and stood at the highly polished pub counter. The bar was still crowded, but the shipwrights had gone, so had the homebrew drinker and his empties, and there were four new players seated at the domino board.

The smiling barmaid made a point of serving them before other, already waiting customers, and they incurred a disapproving frown from an old woman standing at the hatch of the snug with an empty glass in her hand.

"Where are Alan and Richie?" Trev asked, looking around the room.

"They decided to go to the Mason's Arms. Alan must have something going on up there."

"He's probably casing the place."

"Get your sandwiches out. Come on, pass them around if you're not going in." The shout was from one of the domino players in the corner. Both Trev and Harry good-naturedly passed their sandwiches across to the players, who quickly opened, shared them out amongst themselves and ate them.

"Guess who was in the gatehouse when I took those books of yours down?" Trev asked, picking up his pint from the counter.

"I don't know, the Queen Mother?" Harry said flippantly, also picking up his pint.

"Don't be daft. Skinner was in the gatehouse talking to somebody who I think might have been Morgan." Trev drank from the pint glass, consuming about a quarter of the liquid.

"What do you mean, might have been Morgan, aren't you sure?"

"No. It was pretty foggy and I only got a glimpse of his back as he left, but it could have been him."

"So, Skinner was talking to Morgan. So what?" Harry said, replacing his pint glass on the counter, pulling his tobacco tin from his pocket and start to make a cigarette.

"It's what Skinner was saying. I think that he was telling the other guy to keep the lads out at least until Christmas."

"Keep them out? Who, the welders? On strike you mean?"

"Well, presumably. What I overheard was very patchy, but that's what it sounded like to me."

Harry shook his head. "But what possible motive could Skinner have for keeping the welders out on strike? He's the general manager, surely he'll be doing everything he can to get them back to work?"

"You'd think so wouldn't you?"

"You sure that you heard right?"

"I've told you, it was very patchy. Then this other guy comes out of the gatehouse and I step back so he won't see me, and watched him walk away. It was dark and foggy, I only saw the back of him, and he looked familiar, but I couldn't swear that it was Morgan."

"Is that all?" Harry asked, licking the gummed edge of the Rizla paper, interested now.

"Yes. Except that I'm stood there like a puddin' and Skinner comes up behind me and scares the life out of me. 'What are you doing here!' he yells right into my ear. Nearly crapped myself. The bastard."

"What did you say?"

"I just said I was dropping some stuff off for old Bob, left the haversack inside the gatehouse door, and got away as fast as I could." Trev drank more beer. "I could tell he was looking at me funny, you know, trying to gauge if I seen or heard anything, but I just played the innocent, said goodnight, politely like, and got away."

Harry lit up, inhaled the smoke, deep in thought. "Could you swear to what you heard Skinner saying?"

Trev shook his head.

"And you've already said you're not certain that it was Morgan."

Trev nodded. "But who else could it have been?"

"You probably thought of Morgan when you heard Skinner say strike, and keep them out, or whatever."

"You think I'm imagining things?"

"It could have been, and probably was, an entirely innocent conversation, whether Skinner was talking to Morgan or someone else. I think it's best if we don't say anything about this to anybody, mate. It could cause a lot more bother, and that's the last thing we need at the moment, we've got enough as it is."

4

The small group of men waited at the prearranged picking up point on Saturday morning. They'd got there early, which was a mistake, as the bus was late. Harry and Joe arrived together shortly after Trev and Mickey. Alan and Richie turned up five minutes afterwards and stood a short distance away from the others.

Waiting around for the bus was no fun at all. The sky was overcast and threatening rain or perhaps sleet, and the bitterly cold wind went right through the men's clothes. The freezing men coughed, complained, beat their arms violently against their bodies and stamped their feet in an effort to improve their blood circulation and keep warm.

The coach arrived at last. It was an old, battered, pre-war model and had seen a lot of better days. It shook and trembled like a dying animal as the driver turned off the engine. He stood up, leaned across and pulled open the doors manually.

"Come on, lads, get yourselves inside. We'll get going as soon as the engine cools down a bit," the driver said cheerfully. The grateful men clambered aboard. They'd waited for almost half an hour and were very cold.

"Where the hell have you been? We've been standing there for ages, man, and it's bloody brass monkey weather," Trev said rubbing his hands briskly together in an attempt to generate some heat. "Any chance of getting the heater going then?" he asked hopefully.

"The heater's knackered, son. So is the engine, it's overheating, that's why I've had to turn it off. We don't want it blowing up now, do we?"

"It can please itself. Get the thing ticking over, man, we'll all die of hypowhatsit."

The labourers were the first of the passengers onto the vehicle and claimed the long seats at the back of the bus. The upholstery was worn, faded and threadbare in some places, but the old seats were soft and comfortable. "They didn't waste too much money on the transport then," Joe joked.

The bus filled up quickly as men appeared at the door and boarded, blowing on their hands and complaining about the cold weather.

Although they had very little money, and certainly none to spare, they had all still decided to go on the trip because it was already paid for. The general consensus was, why waste the money already paid out?

The trip had been arranged some time ago, before the current disputes. The organiser, a labourer working with the aft-end squad, had plumped for York as the destination simply because it had always been a favourite drinking place of his since he'd done some courting there many years before. There were some very good pubs there, he'd promised them, and the racecourse had a number of bars and beer tents where, if the worst came to the worst, they could shelter from the rain and sleet that threatened to pour down from the dull grey sky.

"Look who's coming," Richie said, "it's that big-mouthed welder, the shop steward, the one that was going to belt Harry." The labourers watched as a group of men alighted from a car and walked to the coach.

"Morgan," Joe said quietly. "Just the man to make the day go with a swing."

The welders' shop steward and his three mates climbed onto the bus and took seats five or so rows from the back. They all seemed to be in a good mood and were laughing and joking. Morgan, the tallest, fattest, and noisiest of the group, stood up again, turned and looked around the bus at the other passengers with disdain, his small, piggy eyes minuscule in his large round face. "Right bunch of tossers we've got here, lads. Are you sure that we're on the right fucking bus. This lot looks like they're going to a fucking funeral." He saw Joe and Trev, who were visible from the aisle, but didn't see the others, who were hidden behind the seats. "Talking of fucking funerals, where's your thieving mate?"

No one answered.

"Probably sitting at home thinking up ways to rob his mates again, eh?" He laughed and the other welders joined in. "Fancy stealing money from your mates to take your missus on holiday. Just because she's sick doesn't make it right."

"I've told you that you'll all get every penny back," Harry said, sitting up.

"Aye? Well I'll not hold my fucking breath until that happens. We should have got the police in like I wanted to and got you locked up," Morgan said as he turned to sit down again, but he saw Alan, changed his mind and turned to face the rear again. "And there's the jailbird as well, out for the day are you? It's a right thieves' kitchen back there, lads," he said to his friends. "Thick as thieves that lot are, in fact if they weren't so fucking thick they might have been welders." This drew another wave of laughter from his friends.

"You mean welders aren't thick? That's funny, I can't remember the last time I saw a welder on University Challenge, can you?" Trev said loudly.

Morgan ignored the remark and counter-attacked, his face taking on a cunning appearance. "I'm surprised that there's so many labourers here mind, what with lay-offs and everything. Shouldn't have thought that they could afford it. I think they're getting paid too much money, what do you think, lads?" Again there was a chorus of laughter from his companions. Morgan looked back and suddenly became aware of Mickey's presence within the group at the back, and his attitude changed dramatically, he swallowed hard, shut up and quickly sat down.

"Big mouthed bastard," Trev said.

"Should I have a word with him?" Mickey asked quietly.

"No, don't do that, just ignore him," advised Harry. "He's just trying to wind us up."

The empty seats were soon all taken; the driver gunned the engine, which exploded gamely into life, and the old bus set off somewhat shakily. They'd only been travelling for a few minutes when the day shift labourer sitting in the seat in front of them produced a pack of battered cards and a borrowed domino board to use as a card table. He balanced the board across the aisle, resting it on the arms of the seats and invited them to play three-card brag. They agreed and soon the card school was in full swing. At almost the same time another two card schools appeared further down the coach.

Trev joined in, the others in the back seat being content to watch. After about ten minutes or so, Morgan swaggered back and watched the game. When it ended, he threw money into the middle like the others and was dealt three cards.

"I'll show you how to play properly," he sneered.

Trev was lucky and won the first three games straight off. It wasn't a lot of money, but he enjoyed playing, and especially enjoyed winning. The shaking of the bus added an extra element to the game, as the coins in the kitty gradually moved position on the wooden domino board, which was precariously balanced. Especially so when the bus unexpectedly turned a corner rather sharply and all the money slid into one of the player's lap, to the concern and alarm of the others.

Trev won a fair amount of money and the biggest loser was Morgan; the others either won or lost a little, but not enough to make much of a difference to them. Trev's winnings were gradually building up and were very welcome. It was more or less generally accepted that it was the player with the most money who won at brag, as at poker. But, others subscribe to the theory that it's a game of skill, and that it is possible to win even with a bad hand by bluffing or bragging, hence the name. Trev had never given these theories any thought at all; and if he had, he'd have dismissed them out of hand. He knew that it was a game of pure luck. He knew that for a fact because he was always lucky.

After a couple of hours on the road, they were almost at their destination and they knew that this was to be the last hand. The kitty had built up to a sizable amount, and each player was determined to win. They bid blind for quite a while and the kitty got even bigger. The players with the least money chickened out first and sneaked a look at the cards they had been dealt. They kept their hands over the cards, and held them very close to their chests so that only they could see them.

The players dropped out one by one until inevitably there were only two left, Trev and Morgan. The kitty had swollen to over ten pounds now. Both were still throwing money into the centre, blind, neither one having looked at their cards. Trev was playing at a disadvantage as his money was getting low, but, he didn't what to be the first to look at his cards as it would then cost him double to play.

"Just me and you left, bonny lad eh?" Morgan said. "Let's see, we'll make it a bit more interesting by upping the ante. Let's double it shall we?"

The question was rhetorical because under the rules of the game, a player that hadn't yet looked at his cards was perfectly entitled to increase the ante, but a player who had looked at his cards couldn't raise a man bidding blind.

Trev smiled, displaying a confidence that he didn't feel. His insides were as tight as a drum and he was far from relaxed. He knew that he only had two choices, he could go on throwing money into the kitty, and try to outbid Morgan, or he could fold now and cut his losses. He desperately wanted to win this hand and not just because of the money, welcome, as that would be. The last thing he wanted now was to have to back down and leave the kitty to the big-mouthed Morgan. The problem was that he had only a couple of pounds of his money left. Everything else, including his previous winnings had gone into the kitty.

Harry, sensing his uncertainty, leaned over and whispered in his ear, "Go on, Trev, I'll back you. I've got a fiver here."

Trev made up his mind immediately and played on. The kitty built even higher, and the game now attracted attention from some of the other passengers, as the bus had arrived at the destination and the engines shut down with a final, almost fatal-like, shudder.

All the money that Trev had in front of him was now gone and stood piled in the middle of the board with the rest. Trev felt a hand dip into his jacket pocket as Harry bent over him. Placing his own hand in the pocket he felt the folded crisp one-pound notes.

"Your money all gone then, bonny lad? You should have known better than to play with the big boys, shouldn't you?" Morgan said as he reached with both hands to rake in the kitty, a big smile on his lips.

"Just you hold it," Trev commanded, producing a pound note from his pocket like a conjurer. "Let's raise the ante, eh? Let's say a pound blind?"

"A pound blind?" Morgan repeated like a parrot. "A pound a fucking go? Blind? Here, you sure that you haven't looked at them cards?" he asked suspiciously, his small eyes narrowing even more.

"You know that I haven't, you've been watching me close enough."

Morgan was very suspicious. He hadn't expected this at all. He'd expected his opponent to fold his cards and drop out, overwhelmed by the amount of money that he'd have to pay to continue, but now, not only was he still playing, but he'd actually increased the ante. He knew Trev must be bluffing, and yet...

"Last of the big spenders eh? Alright then, go on, there's my pound," Morgan said as he nonchalantly threw a note into the middle.

Trev tried not to swallow too hard and appear nervous. He smiled and pushed a pound in towards the centre. Morgan threw another pound note in and so did Trev. Morgan hesitated; he didn't know how much money Trev had, and only knew that he was using a great deal of his own.

"Fuck this," the big welder said loudly, "we'll be here all fucking day." He picked up his cards and looked at them. Trev knew from the man's face that he had nothing. There was a sort of light that disappeared from his tiny eyes. An involuntary, momentary change, that was apparent, deep in the dark liquid depths. The telltale flicker was indescribable, but unmistakable to Trev. Morgan kept his face expressionless and did his best to cover up his disappointment. Now he could either fold or attempt to bluff it out until Trev looked at his cards.

Trev was down to the last borrowed pound, he smiled again and threw it in, then picked up his own cards, brought them as close to his eyes as he could, and then slowly fanned them open. Bollocks, he thought, king high that's all. He smiled even more broadly and carefully placed the cards face down on the board.

"You to go," he said to Morgan politely, as he pretended to reach for more money in his pocket.

Morgan hesitated, and looked at Trev suspiciously. "You playing on?"

"I sure am," Trev answered, and added cheekily, "bonny lad,"

"Let's see what you've got," Morgan demanded, throwing two crumpled pound notes into the centre.

Trev waited a couple of seconds before revealing his hand. "King high," he said, laying the three cards on the board face up.

The watchers gasped.

"I thought that he had three threes at least," one of them said.

Morgan sat and looked at the king with disbelief, the folds of his chins quivering. "Lucky bastard," he hissed, and throwing his cards down in disgust, turned and strode angrily along the bus towards his seat, followed by his friends.

Trev raked in the kitty with glee, reaching out and pulling the money to him with both hands.

"Let's see what the nice gentleman had then," Harry said and picked up the welder's discarded hand. "A queen that's all. Not good enough. Serves him right."

"That's right, not good enough," Trev said happily.

Trev repaid Harry his fiver with interest, and shared his winnings equally with his friends. He, Mickey, Joe and Harry elected to pool their money and decided to scrap their original plan to spend nothing during the day. There was no need now to keep their money back for buying a few drinks in the evening. Trev was ecstatic, as much for getting one over on Morgan who had made his obnoxious presence felt by the labourers more than once. Alan and Richie at first refused Trev's big hearted offer to share his winnings, and then changed their minds. Alan accepted his share gracelessly and without a word of thanks, not that Trev expected any.

They'd all brought homemade sandwiches for their lunches to cut down on the expense, but with Trev's winnings, together with their own money, they reckoned that they should have more than enough money for a meal and unlimited alcohol.

They arrived in the historic, walled city at about eleven o'clock and their spirits were sky high as a result of the card game. They soon found a café and ordered their lunches, having decided to keep their sandwiches for later. Joe stuck to a chicken salad because of his stomach, but the others each tucked into a large plate of mixed grill.

After eating, they felt a lot better and in the mood to explore the city. They toured the shops, having no intention at all of buying anything, but celebrated the fact that there were a number of department stores big enough to have ladies' underwear sections, where they could pay particular attention to the lingerie. The small group toured the famous Shambles open-air market, despite the freezing temperature. Here there was plenty to hold their attention and interest. A lot of the goods on sale were of good quality and were a great deal less expensive than in the shops. They spent some time there and almost lost their sense of time as they walked from stall to stall. They eventually covered them all and then made their way slowly back to where the coach was parked, to complete the last leg of the journey and travel to the racecourse itself.

Morgan, and the rest of the welders were already on board the coach and remained in a somewhat sullen and sombre mood for what remained of the journey.

The first race was not until 1.20, so the lads had plenty of time to walk around, and familiarise themselves with the course. The bookies were starting to set up their boards alongside the track, and the course was beginning to fill up with spectators, and the atmosphere building, despite the overcast weather. They found the bar, and settled in front of a large window to enjoy the spectacle. The hum of excitement increased as the runners in the first race were paraded around the ring, and the men walked down to have a look at the horses. Tipsters offered three guaranteed winners for half a crown, and Trev and Joe bought small envelopes containing tips from two separate touts. The six tipped horses turned out to be entirely different, so they were still at a loss as to what to back.

Harry had brought the Daily Mirror, and insisted on following the selections of his favourite racing tipster, Templegate. Unfortunately, none of the selections in his famous double was running at York that day. Harry had spent a bit of time with the formbook the night before and had a few selections, but the others couldn't agree on what to back. The going was hard and a lot of the runners had proved themselves over such going. The men hummed and hawed, and finally agreed to make their own selections, and to place their own bets.

They each bet on a different runner to win, and with six of them betting, and only eight horses in the first race they felt pretty confident that one of them would win. They didn't. Against the law of averages, they all lost money on the first race. They fared better on the second race, all backing the winner, a name that jumped out of the race card at them, Morgan's Folly. It came in at eight to one, and they were jubilant. Mickey and Trev picked the winner of the third race that romped home at five-to-two.

It was now mid-afternoon, and there were another three races to go. The weather began to close in, and the sky was dark and overcast. The group took refuge in the bar again; settling down to pit their wits against the bookies.

The next race was the yard's sponsored race, the Yule Shipbuilder's Handicap run over a mile and four furlongs, and they were determined to back the winner. Joe was having problems with his stomach, despite sticking to soft drinks and, borrowing Harry's newspaper, he took himself off to the toilet. The others had, by a concentrated group effort, narrowed the probable winner down to two possibilities out of the twelve runners. Harry strongly fancying the outsider, while most of the others wanted to opt for the lower priced second favourite. They were still debating the various runners' merits when Joe, returning from his trip to the lavatory, excitedly interrupted them in their deliberations.

"Listen to this, lads," he said urgently, "while I was in there, who should come in for a run-off but Morgan and guess who he was with? Skinner. Morgan has obviously been on the pop since he got here, 'cos he was stupid like, and talking daft…"

"So what's new? He always talks a load of shit," put in Alan.

"But listen to this," Joe insisted, his voice high with excitement. "There's something funny going on. Skinner was telling Morgan not to worry, the strike was working, and that the money for the pay-off was being sorted and everything was going ahead as agreed. Those were his exact words."

"You sure that's what he said?" Harry asked, leaning forward intently.

"I'm telling you that I heard him say it plain as day."

"Are you sure that's what he said?" Harry asked again, giving Trev a significant glance. "The strike is working and the pay-off is going ahead?"

"Certain," Joe said, fidgeting with the newspaper.

"And they didn't know you were in there?"

"No. I'd been there for a good ten minutes or so before they even came in. I'd read half the Daily Mirror in there."

"Alright then," Alan said reasonably. "You just tell us why Skinner would be saying that the strike was working and there is going to be a pay-off? It just doesn't make any sense at all."

"I don't know do I? But that's not all I overheard," said Joe, with a sense of mystery.

"Go on then, tell us."

"Well, Morgan wanted to know more about the pay-off, and Skinner tells him he'll get it when the deal goes through."

"They're taking the piss, man. They knew you were in there, and were winding you up, hoping that you'd bite," Alan maintained. "We'll all be getting paid off if this takeover goes ahead. Anyway, why would they meet here, where there is a good chance that they'd be seen by one of us?"

"How do I know? Here is as good as anywhere else. Skinner is here to present the winning horse's owner with the cup for the race isn't he?"

"They're pulling your pisser, man. They gave you an awful lot of info in a short time while they were in there, didn't they? It's a put-up job, they're trying to get us to bite," maintained Alan, still unconvinced.

"Well, let's say that you're right then, why would they want to go to all that trouble just to wind me up, eh? You tell me that," Joe asked.

"Are you sure they weren't talking about something else, Joe, and you misunderstood them?" Trev asked.

"No, they definitely said what I've just told you. Their exact words." He paused. "Hang on a minute, Skinner said something else. He said that the Yank would see them alright. The Yank."

"Now that's definitely a load of bollocks," Alan said, "there are no Yanks around here."

"An American has just bought the Blue Angel Club," Mickey said slowly.

Both Trev and Harry looked at each other. "The club where you're working?" Trev asked.

Mickey nodded.

"That's got to be it then." Trev said decisively. He quickly explained to the others what he'd overheard at the yard gates, and why he and Harry had decided to keep quiet about it.

"So, it looks like Skinner and Morgan are doing their level best to keep the welders out, for reasons best known to themselves, and if successful, then they're going to get a payment of some description from this Yank?" Joe stated.

Trev nodded. "That's what it looks like to me."

"What if this Yank is the front man for this American syndicate that's rumoured to be taking over the yard?" Harry said quietly.

"Now you're being just plain stupid," Alan said dismissively. "That's a bit far-fetched isn't it? We're getting into the realms of fantasy now."

"If there is something funny going on, then we should do something about it, shouldn't we?" Joe asked.

"Look lads, what about if we meet up at the allotment when we're all sober, and talk this whole thing out? I think it's best if we don't say anything about this for now, eh? We might have got the wrong end of the stick entirely, and we don't want to cause trouble now, do we?" Harry suggested.

The others agreed with Harry, most believing that Joe must have misheard the conversation.

"And, we're never going to get a bet on this race, they're off in two minutes," Harry said.

After a brief but fairly ferocious discussion it was agreed to place the princely sum of six pounds win on Harry's selection, Gold Digger. The men pooling a pound each, plus the tax payable on the bet. By paying the tax up front with the stake, they hoped to save money if the horse won, as the tax would then not be liable on the total winnings. Trev promptly set off to lodge the money with an appropriate bookie. The small group looked anxiously out of the window, following Trev's progress through the crowd, watching as he searched the bookies chalked boards for the best odds and placed the bet.

Trev returned to the bar with the news that he'd managed to get an impressive twelve-to-one for their selection. The excitement rose as the horses approached the starting line, and the lads crowded around the window overlooking the course with great anticipation. They all shouted and cheered with excitement as the runners raced past them to the finish line. All the runners were spaced out as they approached the line and Gold Digger romped home by a full length to win.

The lads jumped up and down with excitement as the horse sped past the winning post. The six pounds stake brought them in seventy-two pounds, plus their original stake making a grand total of seventy-eight pounds. The lads were ecstatically happy. They didn't win any more money on the last two races, but they didn't care, they were well up on the day, what with the share out of Trev's card winnings, and then their win on the horse, they were sure that their luck, and especially Trev's, was very definitely in.

5

It was still overcast and almost dark when they piled onto the bus laughing like excited children. The coach left the racecourse and drove to Harrogate, where they planned to stay for the evening and have a few drinks. Having disembarked, the group discovered that the first pub they came to in the town centre was to their liking.

The pub was cosy and had low, black, ceiling beams that looked authentic. The place was ideal and catered for all of their requirements. It was warm and dry, had plenty of vacant seats, sold good beer, and had an added and unexpected bonus, a blonde barmaid with obvious and highly visible charms.

"Has anybody ever told you that you look just like George Best?" she asked Trev.

"A few people have mentioned that, pet."

"You lads from the North East?" she asked, smiling at Trev, who was smiling right back as he ordered the drinks.

They all agreed that they were indeed from that part of the world, and Trev's smile got wider.

"Just here for the day, then?"

Again they affirmed that they were.

"You not working?"

"We're on strike, love. Well, not on strike exactly, locked out more like, because the welders are out on strike."

She nodded. "I heard about the walk-out on the news. I used to work up that way, in a big hotel near the coast. I really enjoyed it up there. The sandy beaches are just marvellous. I used to go to the coast every chance I got, never tired of it," she told them breathlessly.

"It's a nice place to live, pet."

"I just love your accents. I think they're really sexy."

When she said that, Richie nearly fell off the bar stool that he'd just climbed onto. The group all started to speak at the same time, just to prove that they all did have the accent that she found so sexy. She smiled as she took the money from Richie, who was having difficulty getting his mouth to produce any sort of sound at all. He was even more surprised when she gave him change for a tenner instead of the five-pound note that he'd proffered for the drinks. She gave him a knowing smile and winked as she handed over the money. "You lads must be feeling the pinch, what with Christmas coming up and everything."

"You can say that again," Trev agreed.

"I was wondering if one of you big strong lads could help me with some heavy boxes that need moving upstairs?" She said looking directly at Trev and smiling.

"Er, of course, I'll give you a hand, pet," Trev said eagerly, jumping down from the barstool.

"Oh thanks," she cooed. "Just wait for a few minutes until the manager goes out. He can't lift anything because of his bad back, you see. He doesn't like me talking to men," she explained hastily to the bewildered Trev.

"Sure pet, just shout when you want me, alright?" he said leaving the bar and joining the others at the seats near the big open real fire.

"Just shout when you want me, pet," Joe mimicked.

"I just want a big strong man," Harry joined in, imitating the barmaid's voice. "But, I suppose you'd do at a push, seeing as there aren't any big strong men around."

"You're right in there, Trev. Mind that you pace yourself, you don't want to let the side down now, do you?" Joe said.

"You can put my name down as first reserve if you like, Trev," Harry put in.

"Get lost," Trev said pleasantly. "She only got us that round in for nowt, didn't she, Richie?"

"Aye," Richie confirmed, showing them the change that he held in his hand.

"Always did like barmaids," Harry said wistfully. "I only wish that I was ten years younger."

"What? Fifty years younger you mean," Joe scoffed.

"Bugger off," Harry replied.

They sat and sipped at their drinks and were surprised when the barmaid came across ten minutes later with another tray full of replacements. "Here you are, lads, same again wasn't it?"

"Er yes, thank you," Trev said hesitantly, putting his hand in his pocket for the money.

"Oh, you can pay for these later. And the manager's just on his way out now," she waved to a large, powerfully built, middle-aged man who was walking toward the door. The man gave the group a decidedly unfriendly stare as he passed.

"He the manager, then?" asked Joe unnecessarily.

"Yes, he's my dad, actually."

Trev nearly choked on his drink. "That's your dad?"

"Yes. Can you come through and help me now?"

The others looked on silently as Trev followed the shapely, mini-skirted figure of the blonde through the elevated bar counter opening, and into the serving area behind.

"Cover the bar for me for a few minutes, Ada," she said to a bored looking, middle-aged woman who was polishing glasses in the almost deserted back room, where only two customers sat quietly at a table near the fire.

As soon as they were in the back room with the door safely shut behind them, she made if perfectly obvious that it wasn't the shifting of anything heavy that she had in mind, but perhaps some of Trev's bodily fluids.

She flung herself at him and nearly ripped the shirt from his back as she kissed him, and clawed at his clothes. They kissed feverishly and passionately as they groped each other's bodies with abandon. Just then the door opened and Ada put her head around it.

"You got any change in here, Mandy?" Ada asked in a broad, bored Yorkshire accent and stared at them without batting an eyelid, as if it was the most common thing in the world for her to come upon, the manager's daughter locked in a passionate embrace with a complete stranger who had just walked into the bar.

Mandy reluctantly disentangled herself from Trev, and readjusted her clothing as she walked to a large wall-safe visible in the corner of the room. She pulled open the heavy door, which wasn't locked, and putting her hand in came out with a number of small plastic bags full of various denominations of coins. These she passed to the still waiting Ada. Trev, during this brief interlude realised two things. One, that he hadn't known the girl's name until just now, and two, the fact that Ada hadn't turned a hair seeing them together was probably because she'd seen the same thing countless times before and it was nothing new to come across the landlord's pride and joy in a clinch with a man.

"Now then, where were we?" Mandy said as she got back to him, "oh yes, things were just getting interesting weren't they?"

Trev nodded his agreement, his mouth dry. "They sure were, Mandy."

"How did you find out my name? I still don't know yours."

"Trev," he said. "Pleased to meet you I'm sure."

She giggled. "Likewise. But how did you know my name?"

"I'm psychic."

"Are you? Really?"

"I sure am. For instance, I can tell you what you'll be doing exactly in 60 seconds time."

"What?" She asked intrigued.

"Use your imagination," he said, pulling her to him, and gripping her tightly.

To his surprise she pulled away from him. "We'd better go

upstairs. It's more comfortable up there, and warmer. Besides, it's more private, and we don't want Ada butting in again, now do we?"

He followed her upstairs quickly, eager to continue the encounter. He admired her apple-shaped backside as it wriggled temptingly just in front of his face as she climbed the stairs, and couldn't resist the urge to bite it. She giggled playfully and ran up the remaining stairs. At the top there were doors to the right and left and straight ahead. The door ahead was ajar and Trev could see the outline of a bed, but she took the left and taking his hand led him into a small sitting room with a large sofa that took up much of the floor space.

"In here," she said huskily. "We'll have to be quick because Dad will be back soon."

Trev wasted no time at all, and they were soon in another passionate embrace that left them both panting. She was soon parted from her little frilly panties, and had her short skirt hitched up around her waist. Pushing the sofa away from the wall, Trev stood behind it, his back against the wall. He preferred to be able to see the door in case anyone came in. Taking her in his arms, he lifted her up and sat her little bottom on the back of the sofa. The back of the sofa was just at the right height for him to enter her without him having to bend his knees. She gasped as he entered her, and writhed, gripping her arms and long shapely legs tight around him in ecstasy, moving her hips slowly in rhythm with his. Their passion was too intense to last long, and Trev was soon spent in more ways than one. He was exhausted as soon as he came, his knees went weak and he felt as if he was going to collapse. He had to support himself by leaning back slightly onto the wall.

Standing in front of her, and still deep inside her, his nerve endings tingling, he was more that a trifle surprised when, to his consternation, the door at the top of the landing opened and Mandy's father walked in. Trev stared at him in horror. Mandy was still wriggling in front of him, now slightly leaning back across the sofa at a dangerous angle, and making little noises of contentment. All the man had to do was to turn his head left to take the scene in, Trev thought with alarm. What his reaction was going to be when he saw his little daughter wrapped tightly around him was not something that Trev wanted to even think about. Holding his breath, Trev tried to keep Mandy still with both of his hands which were still gripped tightly on her beautifully rounded buttocks.

Trev's mind raced as his mouth tried to form some sort of suitable words to say to her father. He couldn't very well just say something conversational like good evening, or pleased to meet you. And he couldn't even try to disguise what they'd been up to because it was perfectly obvious to a half-blind man that they'd been shagging. In fact, Trev realised with horror, they still were. Well, Mandy was anyway. He tried desperately to hold her still, which only made her wriggle all the more. He just hoped that she wouldn't cry out again. Oh shit, Trev thought, her dad is going to go absolutely bananas. He'll kill me. I'm a dead man.

Still holding his breath, Trev nearly collapsed with relief when her dad turned right and disappeared through the door to the kitchen, without looking in their direction. "Quick, get up and straighten your clothes. Your dad's just gone into the kitchen." The tone of his voice told her that this was no joke, and he helped her down from the sofa.

"Go downstairs, quick," she whispered to him, pushing him towards the door. He saw her panties lying behind the door where they'd been thrown in their passion, and he scooped them from the floor and absentmindedly wiped the sweat from his brow with them before stuffing them into his top pocket as he tiptoed to the stairs and quickly disappeared down them, still fastening his trousers.

The lads were still sitting by the fire where he'd left them. They'd drunk almost all their beer, and his too, he noticed with annoyance. "I see you've seen mine off as well then?" he said accusingly.

"Aye, why we thought that you wouldn't mind. What with your mind being on other things like. How'd you get on, anyway?" Harry asked.

"He couldn't have got on all that well, man, he's only been gone for two minutes," Joe put in.

"So? Two minutes is enough, isn't it Trev? Why, some people can do it twice in two minutes," Harry said.

"I'm sure that you could," Joe joked.

"No, he's never ever done it twice, have you Harry?" Alan said.

"No. Well, not in the same week that is," Harry answered. They all laughed, including Trev.

"Come on, let's get out of here and try somewhere else," Trev said, looking around furtively, half-expecting Mandy's father to descend on him at any minute.

They visited a few other pubs before finishing up in a large, modern place that had a very loud jukebox and was absolutely packed to the rafters with customers. The pub was dimly lit and full of smoke. The group was all now well and truly drunk. It was only another hour to go before the bus was leaving, and most of the lads agreed they would be glad to get their heads down and sleep on the coach all the way back home.

Mickey nudged Trev, and nodded in the direction of a secluded corner near the door. "That's Morgan, isn't it?"

Trev peered through the darkness and the smokey atmosphere of the room, where a couple were sitting very close to each other in the corner, but he couldn't make out the identity of the man. He continued to watch and eventually the man got up and went to the bar, carrying two empty glasses. As the figure neared the bar, he became illuminated in the lights and Trev could now make out his features. It was definitely Morgan.

"Well, the son-of-a-gun," Trev said softly, "I'll bet he wouldn't like their lass to know about this." The group watched as Morgan came back from the bar with more drinks for him and the girl.

"She's on the gins," Joe said.

"Must be costing him a packet," offered Harry. "They can't be cheap in here."

"Wait here, I'll be back soon," Trev said, and disappeared into the crowd.

The lads decided that Morgan must have somehow separated from the company of his mates either by accident or design, and picked the girl up in one of the pubs that he'd been in during the evening. The lads couldn't be sure how long she'd been in Morgan's company, but from the look of her, she'd been drinking for quite a while. She laughed and giggled loudly, and before long had drained her glass again. This time he returned from the bar with two glasses of gin, doubles by the look of them. The girl seemed perfectly happy to be drinking the spirit that Morgan kept buying her. Joe estimated that he must have spent a fair bit of money on her and wondered how Morgan thought that he was going to get his money's worth. There wasn't much time to go before their coach left, and if she wasn't going to come across in the very near future then, it looked like it was money down the drain.

It appeared that Morgan was beginning to think along the same lines, and was whispering in the girl's ear. She giggled and shook her head. He tried again, and this time she seemed to be a lot more receptive to his suggestions, and smiled.

By now, it was not just the other fore-end lads who were watching the pair in the corner, but there were also quite a number of others from the coach who were taking a keen interest in the proceedings. This stemmed not only from the collective wish of the group to see their comrade do well, and secure the best possible return on his investment, the money he'd forked out for her drinks, but also because they also had a secondary interest in the outcome, namely that Trev had made it his business to tour the room and bet the others a pound each that Morgan wouldn't make it out of the bar with the girl.

It looked as if Trev was going to lose the bet, as the big welder and the girl were now getting really friendly, snuggling in to each other in the secluded corner, he even had his arm around her waist. Others were already mentally rubbing their hands in anticipation at their winnings, when Morgan stood up and made off for the toilet, casually looking through the coins he took from his coat pocket as he went.

"Looks like he's on a promise," Joe said.

"Aye, there's a condom machine in there alright," put in Richie.

The way to the girl now clear because of Morgan's temporary absence, Trev took the opportunity to make his move. He sat beside her and whispered something in her ear. She smiled and nodded eagerly, and the pair stood up and walked out of the bar immediately. Trev winked knowingly at Joe as he passed.

"Did you see that!" Richie said absolutely flabbergasted.

"Aye, he's a fast worker is Trev. Doesn't hang about like, does he?" Joe said with undisguised admiration.

Morgan returned soon after, his recent purchase safely secured in his inside pocket, and he was somewhat mortified to discover that the object of his lustful intentions had disappeared. That was bad enough, but when he learned that she'd left with Trev, he went crazy, launching into a tirade of insults aimed at the parentage and sexual improprieties of both of them.

The more he ranted and raved, the more the others laughed. Trev had pulled a number of real strokes on him today, and they all knew that the resentment he felt was not going to dissipate, but turn into real and vicious anger.

The group left the pub about half an hour later, and made their way to the bus depot, where they could see their coach standing at the curb. They were the first of the party to arrive, and stood smoking and talking as they waited for the driver to turn up and let them on board.

Mickey pointed to the rear windows of the bus. "There's somebody in there already, look. It must be the driver."

The men walked the few steps to the rear of the bus. There did indeed seem to be someone already ensconced on the back seats. They had to stand on their tiptoes to be able to see in properly, but there was no doubt that somebody was in there. The windows had misted up almost completely on the inside.

"Come on then. Looks as if the heater's working again, and if he's in there, we can get on as well, I'm not fucking freezing my balls off out here while he's asleep on the back seat," Morgan said, as he walked to the front of the vehicle and pushed at the door. It came open smoothly with a soft whooshing sound. The big welder, closely followed by the others, clambered aboard and made for the back seats.

Morgan, only a few steps from the back seats, stopped dead in his tracks. His halt was so sudden and unexpected that Joe, who was directly behind him, walked into the stationary man.

"Fuck me," Morgan said quietly, "it's Trev."

He was right, it was Trev, and lying under him on the back seat, her legs tightly wrapped around his neck, was none other than the girl he'd left the pub with thirty minutes earlier. The pair seemed to be totally oblivious of the intruders, being engrossed and entangled in each other.

"Come on, let's leave them to it," Joe said quietly, pulling at Morgan's shoulders. The group retreated back down the bus to the door and alighted.

"What's the matter?" Richie asked, as he was forced off the bus by the crush coming toward him.

"Just back off and let me get off this fucking bus," hissed Morgan. "I don't fucking believe this," he said as he strode up and down the pavement. They'd walked a short distance from the bus and were now standing freezing in the cold night air. To make things even worse it had started to rain. "We're stood out here like spare pricks at a wedding, and he's in there, in the warm, dry bus, fucking shagging." He shook his head in disbelief.

"He should be warm enough alright but I wouldn't have thought that he'd be very dry," Harry said. Most of the others laughed. Morgan didn't.

"Well, look at it this way," put in Joe, "if things had turned out differently that would be you in there now shagging your brains out now, wouldn't it?"

"So?" Morgan asked puzzled.

"So he's saved you all that bother. Look at the energy and effort you'd have had to use up to shag her. I mean it just wouldn't be worth the effort now, would it? Anyway, your lass would have been sure to find out, and then you'd have been right in it, wouldn't you?"

"Fuck off," Morgan said.

"You'd probably have to fuck her twice I'd think, a girl like that," Harry put in thoughtfully.

The whole group laughed again. Their laughter was silenced abruptly as the couple appeared at the open door of the coach and stepped out. The men watched as they embraced and kissed before she walked off with a wave of her hand.

Morgan was in a vile mood, he stood red-faced, clenching and unclenching his fists impotently as he stared at Trev. It was only the close presence of Mickey that stopped him physically attacking Trev. Finally, the welder spat on the ground and turned towards the coach. "Maybe we can get in out of this fucking rain now then?" Morgan demanded ill-temperedly as he marched towards the bus.

Trev stood by and let them all board while he lit a cigarette. "Have a good day then?" he asked as Joe stepped onto the coach.

"Yes, but not as good as you have," Joe answered, and slapped Trev on the shoulder.

"It hasn't been all that good. I lost ten bob on one of those horses, you know."

The return journey was uneventful and the terminally ill coach arrived back on time. After an initial attempt at singing, which soon died out, most of the passengers got their heads down and slept all the way back, leaving only a few diehards to resume their game of brag.

6

Joe's hospital appointment was the following Tuesday morning. Because of the lockout he'd been in bed the night before, but hadn't had a good night's sleep. He'd worried about going to the hospital, the places frightened him and he was worried about what the X-ray might reveal. He was also very concerned about Sharon. The Social Services had notified them by letter that the Area Manager would be calling to see them this morning regarding their case and Joe was worried what might happen in his absence. He'd almost cancelled his hospital visit but Brenda had insisted he attend after waiting so long for it.

Joe was nervous and sweating. He couldn't keep still and had a pain in his stomach. He felt like he'd been punched. He didn't like hospitals, never had. He'd taken off all his clothes in the cubicle and now sat naked except for the gown. He felt ridiculous wearing the hospital gown. The white, flimsy, starched covering was meant to be fastened at the back, but Joe found this all but impossible to achieve and the gown remained gaping open, leaving his back and buttocks in plain view. Naked except for his socks and shoes, which didn't do anything for his modesty or his feeling of well being, but actually added even more embarrassment to his farcical appearance.

He sat apprehensively in the cubicle, wiping his wet brow with the sleeve of the hospital gown until they called his name, and then walked quickly across the stark, green tiled, main corridor and tried to avoid the curious and amused stares of passers-by, as he made his way the few yards into the X-ray department.

He was given a small glass of a thick, white, fizzy liquid and told to drink it, which he did, finding it was easily swallowed. He assumed it was barium meal, or the equivalent, but had been expecting a huge glass of porridge–like, undrinkable glue, as this is what he'd been assured by his friends was the normal procedure.

He was told to lie on a machine by a nurse with an amused smile playing around her lips. He did as requested and was turned, twisted and manoeuvred into a variety of highly unusual positions while being X-rayed. The machine swung him through every degree of the spectrum like a gyroscope, and at one point he found himself actually standing upright. Turning his head, he could see a viewing window in the side of the machine and looking more closely he was shocked to find that he could see inside of his own chest cavity. He could plainly see his stomach wall and ribs. Quite giddy with the realisation, Joe was relieved to be assisted from the machine and told to go back to the cubicle and put on his clothes.

Walking awkwardly and unsteadily back into the main corridor, Joe turned and could see the nurse smiling at his retreating figure. "We'll send the results to your doctor," she said, still smiling sweetly.

Joe got the distinct impression that she would burst into uncontrollable laughter as soon as he was out of sight. He hurried across the main corridor and into the safety of the cubicle to retrieve his clothes.

He dressed hurriedly and made his way out of the antiseptic smelling building and was in such a hurry to get home and find out what the Area Manager had said, that he was still arranging his clothing as he ran for the bus.

Alan stood in the dock and stared up expressionlessly at the bewigged judge seated on the padded leather chair. The judge occupied the highest seat in the courtroom and had gained access to it from his own private quarters nearby. Behind his head hung the large and impressive monarch's seal of justice, its coat of arms proclaiming the court's majesty and might. The lion and the unicorn, helmet, crown and the Latin inscription Dieu et Mon Droit. All these trappings were meant to intimidate, and they certainly did, Alan thought, but he was trying determinedly not to show it.

The clerk read out the details of Alan's case and the judge examined him closely, peering over his nose, through half-moon spectacles with unfriendly eyes, as if he were inspecting some sort of curious specimen of insect.

Durham Crown Court was an imposing building both inside and out, and court number two even more so. Its windowless walls had witnessed some historic criminal cases over the years since its construction in 1826. Robbers, kidnappers and murderers had been tried here, some imprisoned and some even executed in the adjacent prison or outside the court building. The upstairs public gallery was visible to Alan from his position in the dock, but the rows of wooden benches were empty except for his mother and Richie, the only people curious or at all concerned about Alan's fate. Below, in the well of the court, were positioned the bewigged clerk of the court, barristers, other court officials and his probation officer.

The prosecution barrister gave an explicit account of Alan's alleged misdeeds, which, although biased, was, he thought, more or less correct.

Various witnesses were called, all for the prosecution.

Alan's barrister stood and gave his client's side of the story. Well, that is to say, he more or less rolled over and begged for mercy for his client, all the while studiously avoiding Alan's eye. The brief looked bored and ready to accept the inevitable.

The jury sat impassively in the raised wooden benches of the jury box. The twelve were tightly packed in, three women and nine men, crowded together shoulder to shoulder in the small space, four rows, three to each row. The three women all sat together in the back row. A fat man in the front row wearing a checked sports jacket, looked decidedly uncomfortable, his face was flushed and he was sweating profusely. They patiently heard all the evidence and then after a brief summing up by the judge, retired to the jury room to consider their verdict.

The court reassembled less than an hour later, and the foreman, the sweating fat man in the front row, pronounced Alan guilty.

The judge gathered a sheaf of typewritten papers into a folder and scanned the text quickly, his mouth a straight thin line of distaste. He glanced down at the prisoner in the dock from time to time as if in disgust. Finally, he looked up from the papers and cleared his throat to speak. "Anything known?"

The clerk read out a quite impressive list of Alan's previous convictions.

The wig bobbed up and down as the judge digested Alan's past transgressions, and his mouth got thinner and his eyes even less friendly.

Alan got the distinct impression that he was going to be sent to prison. He'd only once ever been inside and that was while on remand awaiting trial. That small taster he'd experienced wasn't too bad and he didn't worry about going back to prison. Ironically, now that his father was due home, he now had a very good reason to stay out, and wished he'd been more careful and not been caught.

The judge made a show of studying all the files before him before making up his mind. "The offence of which you have been found guilty, together with your previous criminal record warrants a prison sentence. However, I'm impressed that you have made the effort to find a permanent job and your probation officer is convinced that you are a reformed character and want to make something of your life. I understand that you are also apparently to be shortly reunited with your father, who perhaps might be able to exercise some sort of parental control and be a steadying influence on your behaviour." The way that he said this indicated that he thought it highly unlikely.

He paused for effect. "Therefore, I am not going to send you to prison today. I'm suspending your sentencing and calling for more probation reports. When I have those reports and have studied them I will be in a better-informed position to decide and pass an appropriate sentence." He looked down at Alan. "Do you understand?"

"Yes," Alan said, trying very hard to keep the relief out of his voice.

7

"Has he been?" Joe asked Brenda even before he'd closed the door.

Brenda nodded,

"Well, what did he say?" Joe demanded.

"Sit down, Joe."

Expecting the worst, Joe sat on the edge of a chair.

"Don't worry, Joe, he was a nice man. Reasonable, I could talk to him, you know? He said that they were still considering our case and were taking all aspects into consideration."

"Is that all? Is that all he said? We've been waiting months and they're still considering it?" Joe asked, searching his pockets for an anti-acid tablet.

"I explained to him about the social worker being nasty and he is going to look into it."

"Good, she's a right witch that one. What else?"

"Well, he explained that as we are applying to adopt Sharon, we'll have to be assessed just the same as anyone else would. Just as if we were strangers."

"But she's your sister."

"Yes, but they still have to satisfy themselves that we are fit and proper people to have responsibility for Sharon. He said that Sharon needs long term care, not just for her emotional, but also for her physical and mental needs. Being disabled. She needs trained carers who have special skills, the time and patience to look after her and the skills to identify and develop her educational needs. He said that my mother had been extremely brave to take on the task of caring for Sharon on her own, and it had undoubtedly taken a toll on her own health. He didn't actually say that it had killed her, but made it plain that he thought that it must have contributed to her early death."

Joe was silent, digesting what he'd been told. "That doesn't look good for us then does it?"

"Well, they are inclined to place special needs children with relatives if possible, but they have to be careful and make lots of checks before they commit themselves. Although they take the relatives' considerations into account, and they know that we want to be responsible for Sharon, it is the child's welfare that is paramount, not ours. That's what he said."

"So what happens now then?"

"They are still running checks on us. Our health, financial situation, is our relationship secure? Do we have a police records? Things like that. They have to satisfy themselves that we will maintain our sense of responsibility toward Sharon and not change our minds later on for any reason, that's the way he put it."

"We're not likely to do that are we?"

"No, of course not. But they don't know us, Joe, do they? They've got to make sure and satisfy themselves for Sharon's sake."

"If they make credit checks they'll find out about the mortgage arrears," Joe said.

"And your stomach trouble, if they get details of your medical records."

Joe shook his head. "You don't think that will affect our application, do you?"

"I don't know. We'll just have to wait and see, Joe. Anyway the manager said that Sharon could continue to stay with us until they've finished their investigations." She paused and looked at her husband. "They'll also want to know if we plan to have children of our own, and if so, how will it affect Sharon?"

Joe remained silent.

"We should both ask the doctor about having those tests done, Joe."

"Maybe next year, when things are back to normal at work."

"But why wait until then? Just having the tests won't automatically make me pregnant. There might be a medical reason why I can't conceive and if there is, I want find out about it as soon as possible."

"Look, I've seen enough of doctors and hospitals lately to last me quite a while. Let's just leave it for now, alright?"

Mickey pulled at the unaccustomed black bow tie. It felt tight around his neck and restricted his breathing. He rolled his shoulders back in an attempt to feel more comfortable.

"You'll get used to it, don't worry," his companion, the head doorman, said. "Just keep a close eye on these bastards tonight. We don't want the place kicking off when the new boss turns up for the first time do we? That wouldn't be a very good first impression now would it?"

Mickey felt like a stuffed monkey with the suit and tie on. The suit was a trifle small and felt like it still had the coat hanger in the shoulders, but it was the only spare at the club. The head doorman's words suddenly registered through his discomfort. "Er, this new boss, he's an American, isn't he?"

"Aye, that's right. His name's Lovell Chisholm. Lovell I ask you? He's got to be a Yank with a name like that, hasn't he?"

They stood and watched the customers queuing outside the club waiting to get in. Friday night was one of the busiest of the week and the queue moved slowly. Quite a few of the potential customers were loud and obviously drunk and the doormen watched them warily, already mentally selecting, and preparing to bar from entry, any likely troublemakers.

A large, black American car drew up at the curb. "That's got to be him," Mickey said.

"Yeah, that's him alright. He's worth a fortune from all accounts. They reckon he makes a mint supplying equipment to the rigs in the North Sea."

"What's he bought a club here for then?"

"Well, he obviously thinks that the Northeast is the place for night life. Got big plans for the place he has apparently."

The head doorman moved forward to open the door. The American stepped out onto the pavement and looked around. He was a tall, distinguished looking man wearing an expensive camelhair overcoat. He strode purposefully across the pavement towards the club, nodding to the doormen as he approached. As he neared the entrance, a group of lads who had been refused entry were turning away, not happy at all, and one of them deliberately pushed into the American. Another swung a fist at the American's head and caught him a solid smack on his jaw. The dull thud echoed as Chisholm staggered backwards into the head doorman, both of them falling onto the pavement.

Mickey sprang forward and grabbed the attacker just as he was about to kick the stunned man on the ground. Mickey swung the assailant around and pushed him hard into the brick wall of the club. The man's friends swarmed around Mickey, one jumped on his back as another two punched into him. Mickey swung the man on his back into the wall, hard, and he fell off with a grunt of pain. Turning his attention to the others, Mickey hit one lightly on the chin. Although Mickey had pulled the punch, the blow was hard enough to knock his attacker to the ground. As Mickey turned to face the other assailant, the man ran off, chased by two bouncers who had run from the club entrance to help.

The head doorman had by now regained his feet and was helping the American to regain his. The pair walked unsteadily across to Mickey.

"Thanks for that," Chisholm said in a slow drawl, as the head doorman fussily brushed a mark from the back of the American's overcoat.

"No problem," Mickey answered, cracking his knuckles as he

watched the two men he had felled get up from the ground and run away.

Chisholm nodded and entered the club. The doormen holding back the queue until he was safely inside.

The head doorman returned, straightening his tie and brushing off specks of dust from his suit. "That bastard caught me unawares or I would have floored him," he said bitterly.

Mickey nodded and said nothing.

The next hour or so passed quietly enough at the club, most of the queuing customers were allowed in, and were duly engaged in having a good time. Mickey was told to remain at the door with another employee and was waiting there when Chisholm emerged from the club. He nodded to Mickey and stepped outside just as a car came to a stop outside of the club. Mickey watched as the American got into the car and it swept away. There were two men already in the vehicle and their faces were partially illuminated by the streetlights. They looked familiar. Large and muscular men. Mickey had seen them somewhere before, but the memory was vague and just under the surface of his conscious. He worried away at the half-memory for a while before giving up. Then a few minutes later, bingo, the memory surfaced and he remembered who they were. They were twins. A pair of local hard cases and petty criminals called the McKennas. What would Chisholm be doing with those two? he wondered.

8

"It must be some sort of a special left-hand thread or something," old Bob said. He was puzzled, and shook his head sadly. "I've tried everything I can think of. All sorts, releasing oil, the lot and I still can't shift them." He indicated the pointers with the small screwdriver in his hand. "It really is a beautiful timepiece, really nice. You don't see many of these around nowadays. I worked on one exactly like this last year and didn't have any trouble with it at all. I stripped it right down without any problem and put it right. Those chimes are murder to reset in their proper sequence, mind." He looked at the timepiece mystified, "This one has me beat and no mistake. I've never seen anything like it. I can't even figure out how to remove the pointers, and until they're removed I can't take the face off and get at the workings behind the dial." He sipped his tea from the chipped old mug. "But it's not going to beat me. I'll figure it out one way or another. Give me another week and I'll have it fixed, don't you worry," he said without conviction. Bob wasn't as old as he looked, but with an untidy mop of grey hair, a large drooping moustache and a reeking old pipe permanently gripped between his blackened teeth, acquaintances could be forgiven their mistaken overestimate of his years.

Alan nodded. The timepiece had been his grandmother's, and it hadn't worked for years, not since shortly after she'd died. Recently his mother had got the impulse to get the thing repaired for some reason. It was a large, mahogany-cased, Westminster Chiming Clock, that when working, chimed every quarter hour, and on the hour. It had been his grandmother's pride and joy; she really had loved it, and was always polishing the casing. It was a fine piece of furniture and looked good on his mother's mantelpiece. It looked good, but didn't work. His mother had taken the clock to large, well-known jewellers in town, but they wanted an arm and a leg to fix it, so she'd abandoned that idea as being too expensive.

Then Alan had remembered old Bob. The old man worked at the yard as a gateman, and Alan had planned to take the clock into work to show Bob, but the lockout had forced him to alter his plans, so he'd taken it to the old man's home for him to look at.

Old Bob had taken off his false leg and leaned it against the wall. Not realising it was there, Alan had knocked it over when he'd placed the clock onto the kitchen tabletop.

"Don't worry about that, son, it's had worse knocks than that, and it doesn't hurt, you know." Bob had said as Alan picked it up from the floor. "I take it off every chance I get. Can't keep it on all the time 'cos it gets uncomfortable."

"How do you manage at work then? You're supposed to check the yard throughout the night, aren't you?" Alan asked, his eyes narrowing and mind racing.

"Oh, I wait until about twelve and then take it off for the night. I generally put it back on and show myself around the shed after five o'clock and then get back in the gatehouse for my breakfast."

Alan smiled, the beginnings of an idea forming in his mind. "You've certainty got everything worked out alright."

When Alan had left, old Bob sat amongst the bits and pieces of his adopted trade. The tools he used constantly, and the left over bits of discarded watches he'd found came in useful on various repair jobs over the years. He cannibalised the parts if they fitted or could be adapted to fit another watch. Cogs, gears, springs, casings, faces and glass fronts surrounded him. The bench was strewn with clamps and minute screwdrivers, and other small instruments needing a keen eye and a steady hand as well as the know-how to use them. Above all, Bob knew that the main requirements were ones that couldn't be seen in his toolbox, but were essential all the same; they were his determination and persistence. It was these qualities that had kept the repairer working at the Westminster's large face, attempting to remove the pointers.

Although an accomplished and skilled watch repairer, Bob's real interest was in electronics. He loved to play around with and rebuild old radios and televisions. He could build a new set from spare parts, or repair almost anything electrical from tape recorders to table lamps.

He tried every trick he knew, or had heard of, to remove the clock's pointers without damaging them, but to no avail. It was a painstaking task requiring endless patience, but he didn't mind, he was sure he'd succeed sooner or later. Anyway, he had nothing else to do; he didn't need to sleep much during the day, so he had all the time in the world. Apart from his hobby, reading filled in most of his spare time. Spy novels, particularly those which dealt with intelligence gathering, surveillance and the like, fascinated him.

He hadn't always been a lowly night watchman. Oh no; when he was younger he'd been a time-served tradesman in the shipyards. He'd been a shipwright, one of the elite, a skilled craftsman who'd helped to build some of the finest ships in the world. He'd been good at his job, made excellent money, and was expecting to be made foreman as soon as there was a vacancy. That had all ended with the accident. He'd been working on a partly constructed ship, when a strop suspending a metal plate that was being lifted onto the ship's hull, had snapped above him. The plate had fallen twenty feet and he'd been unable to get out of its way fast enough. Luckily, the plate didn't fall directly on him, but he'd been trapped under it for nearly an hour while they tried to lift it off him.

Rushed to hospital with multiple injuries, it had taken months of constant care and treatment before he was allowed home again. He'd lost his leg, his livelihood and his self-respect, all at the same time. There weren't any huge compensation packages in those days. He'd only received a small lump sum from the yard, and a smaller one from the union, and had been dependent on state benefits until a friend had recommended him for the night watchman's job at Yule's.

The watch and electrical repairs had began as a way to fill in his time during the day, and keep his mind occupied, and had gradually escalated over the years as people got to know about his expertise. He liked to keep his hand in even though he wasn't dependent on the extra few pounds it brought in. He prided himself that there wasn't a much that he couldn't repair, but this clock certainly had him stumped.

Time for some unconventional tactics, he thought, scrabbling about in his toolbox for his secret weapon. This had to work otherwise he was sunk. It was the last resort. It took him a while to locate the implement, but he did eventually find it. It was hiding underneath a large piece of sandpaper right at the bottom of the box. Elated, he returned to the clock and sprung open the glass front, exposing the face again. Grasping the mole-grip pliers firmly in both hands, he gripped the small securing nut positioned directly on the front of the spindle and with the pliers; he gently but firmly turned his hands, taut on the handles of the mole-grips, anticlockwise.

He increased pressure on both handles, gripping them tighter together and forcing them into the turn, but the nut refused to move at all. Fearing that he'd damage the thread, he stopped and released the pressure. Shaking his head yet again, he rested for a minute, regaining his breath and the strength in his hands and fingers, allowing the blood to flow into them again, and causing them to tingle slightly.

Absolutely convinced now that it must be a left-hand thread, he picked up the pliers and again gripped the nut firmly and resolutely. This time he tried to turn the nut clockwise, twisting his arms, hands and fingers, his arm muscles shaking with the pressure. But the nut steadfastly, and resolutely, refused to budge.

Finally giving up, the old man threw the pliers back into the toolbox in disgust. They embedded themselves point down in an oily rag, handles sticking up in the air vaguely obscenely, like a pair of open legs. He turned his back on the clock and filled an electric kettle from the tap at the kitchen sink. Plugging the kettle into its socket and switching on the power, he sat down and waited for it to boil. He purposely sat with his back to the clock, blocking it from his vision, and his consciousness, tired of it and now resigned to failure. It's no good, he thought. I'm useless. If I can't even do a simple thing like take the pointers off a clock, then I've had enough for tonight, I'll have another go tomorrow. He threw the rest of his tools into the toolbox with disgust and took a couple of Aspirins, washing them down with a mouthful of hot, fresh tea.

9

The following day a small group of three men made their way on foot slowly up the steep bank. The December afternoon sky was full of threatening clouds, and the wind suddenly increased its ferocious bite that they all felt right through their clothing. The three men quickened their pace up the hill towards the allotments.

"This is going to be a long job," Alan said.

"You think so?" asked Richie, using his finger to push his spectacles into a more secure position further back along his nose.

"Oh aye. Once these bastards get a bee in their bonnet they're bloody hard to shift."

"It's going to be a bastard of a Christmas for us, then," Joe said.

"Aye. Nowt surer."

"It's wrong, you know. Just because they've served their time and got a trade doesn't make them better then us, just luckier," Richie said, somewhat naïvely.

"That's right enough. You don't have to be a brain surgeon to be able to weld two plates together, do you?" Alan said.

"The tacker dilutees proved that. They didn't need a six or seven year apprenticeship," Joe said.

"Most of the time the apprentices only mess about and make the tea anyway," Alan observed.

"Well, I've said it before and I'll say it again now, there's only one way to make sure that you can survive and that's to always keep your three days of sick time in, and get paid sick money right away. Otherwise you have to sign on three days for nowt every time. Plus, if you keep your three days in, then, after six months, you get onto invalidity benefit automatically, which is a lot more money," Joe said.

"But you shouldn't have to do that to be able to survive," Richie said.

"Of course you shouldn't, but he's just being realistic isn't he? You've got to use your loaf, man," Alan said.

"What about that job you mentioned earlier?" Richie asked.

"Which one? I've got more than one planned, you know. In fact I've got a real big, juicy job in the pipeline that'll set me up for life," Alan bragged.

"The yard one, you know, nicking the cable."

"Oh, that one. Aye, the more that I think about it the more I like it. Wednesday night's favourite. No moon," he added, to forestall Ricky's inevitable query, and because it made him appear to be a thorough professional, who had prepared extensively.

The others were suitably impressed.

"It'll be easier getting in than I first thought. Apparently the night watchman takes off his false leg after twelve o'clock and gets his head down until about five. Doesn't do any rounds or anything until then," Alan said.

"How do you know that he takes his leg off?" Richie asked.

"Never you mind. Let's just say that a little bird told me, eh?"

"So, how do we get in then?"

"Easy. We go in through the front gate."

"And how are we supposed to manage that? It's just stupid."

"Easy. Old Bob's mate, the second night watchman, goes home at twelve and doesn't come back until about half six in the morning. The cheeky bugger gets paid for sleeping with their lass five nights a week."

"He should be paid for sleeping with her, have you seen her?" Joe put in.

"Anyway, he leaves the gate unlocked. I've heard that there's only one key between them since he lost his key three months ago, and it's the third one that he's lost and they're made of brass, very expensive to replace and he got a bollocking last time and a warning. A little bird told me that as well," he said by way of explanation.

"Probably that little bird with the miniskirt that works in the office?" Joe put in.

"Aye, that's right," Alan admitted. "She told Trev that night he took her out a few months ago."

"They haven't reported the loss of the key, and share the one key between them?" Joe asked, incredulous.

"That's right, they daren't mention it, not for a while yet, anyway."

"So is it just going to be the two of us?" Richie asked.

"No, we need three at least, to make it worthwhile. There's enough welding cable lying around in the yard for a dozen men, but three would be enough."

"Who else is going then?"

"Well, there's you and me for sure, and probably Harry. The others wouldn't touch it with a barge pole. Mickey's still running for Pope. I've told him that he can always do the raid and then go to confession and be forgiven afterwards, but he won't have it. And, that famous star of stage and screen, Trev, is too far up his own arse to be bothered. Anyway Trev's performing at a club on Wednesday and Mickey's helping him."

Alan paused and nodded towards Joe. "Honest Joe here doesn't seem to be too keen, probably thinks that he's too bleeding honest."

"I've told you that I don't want to get involved with anything dishonest," Joe said defensively. "I'd rather starve than steal something that doesn't belong to me."

"Of course you would, but everybody isn't putting up for canonisation, and it isn't exactly the great train robbery, is it?

Pinching a bit of welding cable for the copper is a perk of the job, for God's sake. Working at the yard doesn't have a lot going for it, but that's one of the few advantages. Some people have no other choice but to bend the rules a bit, the way things are. It's the only way that some people will be able to have a reasonable Christmas."

"Is Mickey singing with Trev, then?" Richie asked, peering through his round, national health glasses, owl-like.

"No, he's not singing with him, you nugget. He's just helping him to carry his gear in, the amplifiers and things," Alan finished vaguely, not exactly sure himself of Mickey's duties.

"I just don't think that it's right to steal from your employer. It must cost the company a small fortune every year the amount of copper cable that goes missing."

"Look, Mr Honest Joe, you claim sick money when you're not sick, don't you?"

"Yes, but that's different. The sick money I get is a pittance anyway. It just helps us to keep our heads above water."

"It's different alright, but it's still stealing, isn't it? You're claiming money that you shouldn't have by telling your doctor lies, aren't you?"

"But everybody does it," Joe said defensively.

"No, they don't. I don't for one, and neither does Richie here, do you, cousin?"

"Okay, it might not be one hundred per cent honest, but I do really have stomach trouble, I've got an ulcer, and all I do is exaggerate the symptoms a bit. It's better than breaking into places and stealing things that don't belong to you. Anyway, you and Richie don't have wives and kids to consider."

"You don't have kids either," Richie said defensively.

"Maybe not, but Brenda's sister is a much bigger problem than looking after a couple of kids," Joe said with feeling.

Alan gave up trying to reason with Joe, and contented himself with a silent shake of his head, to indicate his disagreement.

The trio arrived at the large allotment on the summit of the steep hill just as the first drops of rain started to fall. Harry and Joe were partners in the project. For the past six years they had shared the work, and the expense of the garden, and produced quite a great deal of fresh vegetables for their own consumption during the season. The considerable surplus of vegetables that they grew, they gave away to friends and relatives. The allotment was rented from the local council for a small yearly rent, and was a useful and frequently visited safe refuge for the men, particularly now, during the lockout, it provided a secure refuge from the hard realities and frustrations of life, and from the harsh tongues of their wives. It was a place where they could voice their frustrations and share their worries. They could spend time together reading the newspapers or playing cards. Where they could sit around and indulge in idle gossip, philosophise, and put the world to rights.

There were fifty separate gardens on the exposed hilltop, each with its boundaries fenced off, meticulously maintained and jealously guarded. The allotment holders prided themselves on their gardening expertise and skill at producing the largest and best show vegetables every year. The culmination of the season's work was the annual leek and vegetable shows at the local workmen's clubs. Harry and Joe had been the undisputed leek club champions for the past six years, and covetously shielded the secrets of the prize leek feed formula from their always-inquisitive neighbours. Harry was even known to sleep in the shed in the garden on nights leading up to the shows to prevent suspected, but yet to actually materialize, attempts at sabotage to his prize leeks. Along one side, the gardens were adjoined by brightly coloured pigeon crees, and rumour had it that part of Harry and Joe's success at winning the contests regularly was the use of the bird droppings as an ingredient in a special secret fertilizer.

Joe shoved open the wooden gate and the hinges squeaked agonizingly in protest, as he entered the allotment, followed by Alan and Richie.

Harry was busy in the greenhouse as the trio approached. Seeing them, he stopped what he was doing, left the greenhouse and walked out into the lightly falling rain to welcome the new arrivals, wiping his grubby hands on a damp cloth.

"Hello lads. You certainly haven't brought the sun with you

today. Bloody weather's terrible," said Harry, looking cheerfully skywards towards the large formation of black, rain-laden clouds.

"The birds seem to be happy enough. They don't seem to mind a bit of rain and that's a fact," Alan observed, looking across the allotment to the red and yellow coloured pigeon cree next door. He'd always had a sneaking admiration for the birds, and could imagine himself flying high in the sky, soaring far above the ground, above the people and the houses, free as a bird. He'd stashed away most of his ill-gotten proceeds from his various petty thieving escapades with a half thought out plan of buying a flock of top-class racing pigeons and spending all his time with them. Of course, he'd also have to have enough money to live off, so he wouldn't have to work. He hadn't accumulated anywhere near enough money as yet, and had made no move to actually buy any birds. In fact he knew nothing at all about them, but it remained a sort of vague, idealistic dream. Like most young men of his age, he'd not given much conscious planning or thought to the reasoning behind his aspiration.

"They'll all soon be back in if it gets any worse," Joe said.

"There can't be much more rain up there now, not after the soaking we've had during the last few days," Harry put in optimistically.

"Can't get the ground dug over properly," Joe complained. "The allotment has gone to pot. It doesn't seem to ease off for long enough to get anything worthwhile done. It's enough to last us for the rest of the year, even if we see no more."

"Anyway, let's get inside and I'll put the kettle on," Harry said, leading the way towards the doorway of a rickety shed.

The rain started in earnest as the men reached the refuge of the shed. It was large enough to accommodate them all comfortably and they sat on the three available chairs, and the large, battered sofa. The wooden shed smelled strongly of paraffin wafting from an old heater in the corner. There was also a distinct smell of creosote, and damp earth, and tobacco smoke.

"Regular home from home you've got here, lads. All mod cons," Alan said indicating the kettle, sofa and radio.

"Aye why, it's no good having nowt and looking poor, is it?" Harry replied, trimming the excess tobacco from the ends of a cigarette and lighting up with a cough. "I blame the government for the weather," he went on, not that anybody was showing the slightest interest in what he had to say, Richie was looking around the shed and Joe and Alan were occupied lighting up their own cigarettes.

Disappointed at not getting the reaction he'd hoped for, he continued anyway. "Aye, I blame the government. All them space rockets and satellites they send up must interfere with something up there. Think about it. After every big battle in history when guns were used, not handguns mind you, but those big cannon and field guns. Well, after every one of those battles it poured down with rain. Now, that's a well known, recognised fact and is very well documented in all the history books." He paused again.

Again there was no spark of interest from his colleagues. He drew heavily on his cigarette and ploughed on. "So, if those cannon balls and shells caused it to rain when they was fired up into the air, just think what effect those rockets must be having on the weather. Just imagine those sputniks and satellites going around the world time after time, day in and day out, week in and week out for years and years."

The kettle whistled, announcing its job was complete and Harry broke off his account to make the tea. He passed a hot mug of the liquid to each of them and sat down again.

A pigeon fluttered onto the roof of the shed, then flew twenty yards and dropped onto the opening of the cree next door. The men watched the bird through the old and imperfect window glass. The pigeon's wavy distorted image was like that through a mirror in an amusement arcade, as it hovered on the threshold for an instant and then walked through into the nesting boxes.

A sense of pleasant torpor descended softly and gradually on the group of men. A vague sense of stupefaction, a comfortable, contented feeling akin to the sensation of warm, drowsy, satisfaction after eating a large and gratifying meal.

"How are your new teeth?" Joe asked Harry in an attempt to

break the settling spell.

"Don't talk to me about the bloody teeth," Harry replied, placing his mug on the widow sill. "I had that old set for nigh on forty years. Champion they were. Trouble was that I had them so long that they'd just about worn away. I couldn't eat anything with them, they couldn't cut through butter."

"The new ones alright then?" Joe asked innocently.

"No they're bloody not."

"You should have got proper new ones, not second hand," Alan said.

"They are new, you cheeky git. Cost me a fortune, these did."

"What's wrong with them then? Don't they fit properly? Why don't you take them back?" Alan asked.

"They fit alright, it's just that they're a lot bigger than the old ones…"

"That's 'cos they're forty years younger," Alan put in.

"…and they get in the way of my mouth, like."

"What do you mean, they get in the way of your mouth?" Alan asked incredulously.

"Well, I keep biting myself. My lips, cheeks, tongue. I'm sore with all the bites."

The men started to laugh.

"It's alright for you lot to laugh. I thought that I was turning into a cannibal. I take them out now when I'm eating. It's the only way I can eat anything without cutting myself to pieces." The men laughed even louder.

"This happened to me once before, years ago it was. Our lass and me used to put our teeth in the same glass when we went to bed, dead romantic eh? Anyway, when I got up on Monday morning, late for work, day shift at the time I was, I put her teeth in instead of mine. I had a terrible hangover and never noticed until dinner time when I nearly bit myself to death." This brought more howls of laughter from the others, and tears streamed down their faces.

It took some time before they regained their composure. Alan, wiping his eyes with his sleeve, looked out of the rain-covered window. The distortion caused by the rainwater outside, and the imperfections in the old glass, made the scene outside look blurred and dreamlike. From here, high up on the hill, he could see right across the valley to the busy road in the built-up, highly congested area on the other side. The soft hissing sound of the stream of vehicles drifted across to them. Far below them at the bottom of the slope the swollen river flowed wide, deep and swift. The men sipped their hot tea.

"Germany. That's where all the jobs are now. You've got to go abroad to get anything decent," Joe said, fiddling with his mug.

"It's just tradesmen they want, mate. Not ten-a-penny labourers like us," Harry said.

"How did cannonballs make it rain then?" Richie asked self-consciously adjusting his specs.

"Well," Harry started a little uncertainly, putting out his cigarette on the floor by standing on the stub. He was unprepared, and had thought that no one had bitten on that one, and wasn't expecting so late a challenge. He made a mental note to allow extra time for Richie's thought process to catch up in future. "Well, it stands to reason doesn't it, a big nasty cannonball ripping through the nice calm atmosphere, crashing through all those clouds and things, it's sure to cause a lot of disturbance up there and make it rain, isn't it?"

His audience didn't seem entirely convinced, so he tried to consolidate his position.

"They can even make it rain now by just dropping a few bits of aluminium or something from airplanes. They drop bits of them like streamers in the air, and it seeds the clouds or something," he said somewhat uncertainly. "I'm sure I read that somewhere in a newspaper, or a magazine. You read about that, Joe?" Harry asked, trying to enlist some help.

Joe shook his head and took a gulp of his tea. He was no help at all.

"Those space rockets are an awful lot bigger than those old cannonballs, so they must have a bigger effect on the atmosphere, it stands to reason." This was Harry's standard phrase when he didn't have any evidence to back up one of his theories. He paused and waited, but there was nothing, no interest or reaction at all. He tried again. "Then there's that phoney moon landing."

"Phoney moon landing?" Richie asked with interest.

"What the hell are you on about now?" Alan asked with a smile.

"I'm telling you. That moon landing we saw on the television was a fake. It stands to reason man, they're not going to send anybody all the way up there, and waste all that money for nowt, are they?"

"But they did. It was on the television and everything," Richie protested.

"Phoney. All of it was just a big swizz."

"I thought that they brought earth back, I mean er, moon soil, back to Earth to be analysed?" Joe said thoughtfully.

"Aye, but all that was just window dressing that's all that was. It was just ordinary soil dug up from somebody's garden. Not real stuff from the moon."

"But they tracked the spacecraft from all over the world. Even the Russians tracked it didn't they?" Alan commented, drawn into the conversation despite himself.

"Aye well, they might have said that, but they're in on it as well."

"You really serious about this?" Joe asked.

"Of course I'm really bloody serious. All that they showed us on TV was just hype. We were all conned, man. They didn't go anywhere near space, and certainly not to the moon. All those pictures were sent from a hangar somewhere in the Arizona desert. There's nothing at all up there. The moon's just a lump of barren rock, that's all. There's nothing there that is any earthly use to us."

"I don't know about that, mind. If it was true what you say, then what's to stop one of them that was in on it from blackmailing the American government, they could demand millions of dollars to keep their mouths shut?" Alan said.

"They wouldn't dare do that, man. The government would have them bumped off straight away," Harry retorted.

"You think so?"

"Why-aye, man, straight away."

There was a lull in the conversation for a minute or two while the group considered the prospect of the US government bumping off anyone stupid enough to blackmail them.

Again the pleasant sensation of languor settled over the group.

More pigeons found their way back home, landing on the roof of the cree and then settling into their nesting boxes, safe from the worsening storm outside.

"What really made the difference though is double British Summer Time," Harry said. He'd been keeping this, his best effort, back until the right time. Now the bombshell had been dropped. It lay like a hand grenade amongst the men. They all waited for the explosion. It came quickly.

"Double British Summertime, what the bloody hell is that?" Richie had bitten quickly this time, and risen to the bait immediately. "I think you just make all these things up as you go along," he said suspiciously.

"And how does it affect the weather?" Alan asked hesitantly.

Harry, happy now that he had their undivided attention again, continued with the assumed authority of an expert. "Double British Summer Time was brought in by the British government during the Second World War, in the 1940s," he announced knowingly. "They added an extra hour on to British Summer Time, you know, when you put the clocks forward one hour, that's British Summer Time, well instead, during the war, they used to put them forward two hours not one."

His audience looked at him quizzically, digesting this little gem while he continued. "The idea was that it gave us two hours of extra daylight in the summer and so helped the farmers reaping their crops, you see."

The group continued to look at him steadily for some time, still trying to absorb this knowledge so generously and freely imparted to them by their friend.

"How did it help the farmers?" asked Richie.

"Well, it meant they had more daylight hours, I've just told you, haven't I?"

"But there's only twenty-four hours in a day, so if you add a couple of hours on at night where're they coming from?" Richie contributed.

"They don't come from anywhere. They're there all the time, you just have to rearrange them a bit to give you more light at night."

"Yes, but if it's lighter at night, then it must be darker in the mornings, mustn't it?" Richie maintained.

This stumped Harry for a few moments. He was desperately trying to think ahead of Richie's reasoning, but this piece of logic had come out of the blue. "Yes," he said slowly, giving himself time to think. "Yes, that's right. It would be darker in the mornings if you put the clocks on an hour or two."

"Well, why didn't the farmers get their crops in on the morning and just leave the hours alone?" Richie persisted.

"Because the government said they had to put the clocks on two hours in the summer, that's why," Harry retorted, getting a bit flustered now. Richie's reasoning was unexpected and totally uncharacteristic. The logic of the lad's argument was getting beyond him. "And anyway, that's why the weather's like it is to day. It stands to reason, doesn't it?"

The group was silent again, but all their minds were racing, he really had them going.

Joe was the first to crack this time. "How did that affect the weather then?" he asked hesitantly.

"Why, isn't it obvious?" Harry responded eagerly. "All those extra hours that they added on, they were never taken off again. You add all those hours up over the summer months, all through the war years, and it amounts to a lot of time. It runs into months. No wonder the bloody weather's all to cock."

There was a full half-minute of complete silence. Harry could sense that his well thought out reasoning hadn't convinced them. He tried again to consolidate his case.

"For argument's sake, let's say all those hours added on, amount to three months, that's a whole bloody season, isn't it? Then that means it's actually autumn when it should be summer, or winter when it should be autumn, can't you see? It's obvious, man."

The small group of men thought about this for a while. They looked at each other thoughtfully. Richie opened his mouth to speak, but thought better of it and held his tongue. Outside of the window the heavily laden storm clouds lay very low, the sky almost black.

10

Harry nodded his head towards the gate, as its familiar piercing squeak filled the air. "Look who's just arrived. Well, better late than never."

Trev and Mickey walked into the shed. "That gate needs a bit of oil, mind," Trev said as he squeezed himself on the old sofa with Joe and Richie, while Mickey, unhappy with the cigarette smoke, pulled the last unoccupied wooden chair near the open door.

"Aye, it does that, but we never seem to get the time to do it," Harry said with a smile.

"Well, you're going to have quite a bit of time now, 'cos there's no way that we'll be back to work until after the new year." Trev said.

"Yes, the new year," Joe agreed.

"Mickey here's got some information about that Yank," Trev said.

Mickey lost no time in passing on the news about Chisholm's meeting with the McKennas. The others listened attentively to the details.

"So, the plot thickens. What we've got to figure out is, why are Morgan and Skinner so determined to keep the welders out on strike, because that certainly seems to be what they're doing? And what has this American and the McKennas got to do with it?" Harry said thoughtfully.

"Those welders certainly seem to have a death wish. They'll not be happy until the yard's closed down and we're all out of work permanently," Trev said.

"I reckon Skinner and Morgan are trying to bankrupt the company so that this American takeover will go ahead," Joe said. "And this Yank, what's his name, Chisholm? is the American syndicate's man."

"That would explain the welders' excessive walkouts ordered by Morgan," Harry said thoughtfully. "And it would explain Skinner and Morgan receiving a big pay-off from the Yank, that Joe overheard them talking about at the races."

"But what about the McKennas? Where do they fit in all this?" Trev asked.

"We should go to the yard management, or the police," Richie suggested uncertainly. "They'll be able to do something about it."

"I don't think that's a good idea. Skinner's management isn't he? How do we know that all of the others aren't in on it as well?" Joe said hesitantly.

"And just what are we supposed to tell them anyway? We've got no proof that any of them are doing anything wrong, or illegal. In fact we've got no proof that they're doing anything at all," Harry said.

"It is only circumstantial evidence," Alan agreed.

"I think that we should turn up mob-handed and demand to know exactly what is going on," Trev said.

"What, you mean confront them?" Joe asked warily. "Those McKennas are supposed to be right hard bastards."

"Well, maybe the best thing to do is for us to keep our eyes and ears open for more info and wait our time, that's all." Harry said.

The group fell silent as they digested what had been said.

"What about this raid on the yard then? Anybody up for it?" Alan asked.

"I've told you that I'm not interested," Joe stated.

Mickey shook his head.

"What about you then, Trev?" Alan asked, his tone of voice implying that he already knew what the answer would be.

"No thanks. I'd rather make money honestly," Trev said stiffly.

"Pinching welding cable isn't dishonest, man. It's a perk of the job," Alan said. He shook his head in disgust. "Well, that leaves me and Richie. What about you, Harry, are you in?"

Harry nodded enthusiastically. "I'm in. I've got to get some money from somewhere and that's as good a place as any. Like you say Alan, it's not really stealing is it?" Harry looked at the disapproving faces of Trev, Joe and Mickey.

"Come on, you can't tell me that none of you haven't taken a bit of firewood home from the yard now and again. Or never had some govvie job done by a welder or asked a burner to knock you up something for home? It's just the same, so don't look down your noses at me."

"It's not quite the same, Harry," Joe said. "You're actually going to break into the yard to steal cable."

"We're not breaking in, actually," Alan put in. "We're going to walk right in because the gate will be open."

There was a brief lapse in the conversation.

"Look lads, I've got an idea," Harry said. "Why don't we take a look in Skinner's office while we're inside the yard?"

"After we get the cable?" Alan said.

"Yes. We'll get the cable first and then take a look in his office. It shouldn't take long and there could be all sorts of incriminating evidence lying about in there. You'll be able to get us in there, won't you, Alan?"

"Oh aye, I'll get us in there alright."

"If you do find something to link Skinner to keeping the welders out, or the takeover, or anything else, then we'll have something to take to the police," Trev said.

"Oh, so suddenly you're all for it, eh? It's all different now isn't it?"

"The motive's different," Trev said, defensively.

"I can't see as how it makes any difference. We're still breaking into the yard, aren't we?"

"It is different. Entirely different," Trev said.

"Right then. If it's entirely different, then no doubt you be wanting to come with us now then, do you?" Alan said.

"No," Trev replied.

"What about you two then?" Alan asked Joe and Mickey.

They both shook their heads.

"But you'll want to know if we find out anything about Skinner won't you? Bloody hypocrites!" Alan spat the words at them and walked out of the shed. Richie followed without a word. The gate screeched open moments later. There followed a period of uneasy silence.

Harry broke the spell by getting up and lighting the gas ring to boil the kettle. "Time for another cuppa," he said cheerfully, getting up and filling the kettle with water.

All of the birds had now returned to the cree. Some, the most hardy, or most stupid, stood on the roof and shook their feathers in the rain, leaving behind slowly descending downy pieces in the wet air, before finally retreating into the dry warmth of the nesting boxes. The late afternoon light was almost entirely gone now, the dark rain clouds prematurely bringing nightfall. The inside of the shed was now almost completely in darkness. Harry switched on the single bare bulb hanging from the wooden roof. He'd rigged up the light himself, powering it with a 12-volt car battery. The naked bulb illuminated the small space with its uncertain, flickering dim light, and cheered the occupants.

11

Elsie could hardly carry all the clothes and toys. Her arms were full of plastic carrier bags displaying the names and logos of large chain stores and small select boutiques on the sides. She was tired and hungry, having only managed a rushed sandwich all day. She hated Christmas, well, not so much Christmas itself, but the run up to it. The streets and stores were crammed with shoppers wandering about as if waiting for inspiration to strike and tell them to buy for Uncle Fred or Aunt Alice. She couldn't stand such amateurs and avoided them whenever possible. The stores were as hot as greenhouses, the central heating turned right up, so that it was sometimes very uncomfortable inside the hot store while wearing warm outdoor winter clothing.

The orders had almost all been filled now. There were only the last few remaining items to find. It was always difficult to find what at first seemed to be the simplest of requests, and she had spent inordinately large amounts of time on very simple orders such as earrings or gloves.

Most of the current orders were important because they were to be worn at the forthcoming wedding, and everybody wanted to look smart for that. Even though most of the men were laid off because of the strike at the yard, the ladies still were determined to look their very best and had taken various measures to ensure that they got their clothes for the special occasion from somewhere, strike or no strike. She got very few orders from the men, and had often wondered about their mentality, they were just not interested in planning or making arrangements beforehand and saving money.

She walked into the large, brightly lit store and looked around. Margaret, her friend, who could be mistaken for her brunette twin, walked in behind her. Totally ignoring each other, the women strolled around the store touching and examining various types of clothes.

The man watched the monitor screen closely. He'd had his eyes on the plumpish, middle-aged blonde woman for about ten minutes, and was almost sure that she was up to no good. She'd been in the changing room four times, which wasn't in itself odd, he'd seen genuine shoppers, women of course, try up to a dozen items on and still leave without buying any of them. But there was something about this one that set off warning bells inside his head.

He rechecked the photograph file of known shoplifters, but couldn't see any that resembled her among them. He'd give it another couple of minutes, he thought, and continued to watch her, switching cameras and angles, as she made her way around the store. From the corner of his eye he spotted another woman, a brunette of similar age, on another monitor. He was almost sure that he knew this one. He thought that she was definitely on the known list and he reached for the photographs without taking his eyes from the screen.

Elsie looked hurriedly at her scribbled list again. Yes, she was finished now. The blouse was the right size and colour, but she was sure that the customer would manage to find something wrong with it, she was never satisfied that one. Checking the list again, she made sure that the blouse was indeed the last item, it was, and now she could go home, she thought with relief, her shoes were killing her.

She looked nonchalantly around the store, looking calm and serene, but she wasn't happy at all. The blouse that she was trying to steal just wouldn't stay where she put it, inside her own blouse. The shopping bag on her arm was already crammed to the top, full of stolen items, and she was relying on a tried and tested tactic to enable her and Margaret to escape from the store without being stopped and searched by store detectives. She finally managed to get the item to remain inside her blouse by the simple expedient of nipping her elbow into her side and trapping the rebellious article between it and her body.

She nodded to Margaret who was browsing through a line of dresses and then followed her as she made her way towards the exit, keeping a decent distance behind her, but not too far behind so that she wouldn't be able to take advantage of the diversion. As she approached the exit she saw a large, dark-haired woman hovering near the doorway, trying to be inconspicuous and beside her a large, hard-looking man, dressed in casual clothes, who just had to be a security guard.

Margaret, who was just in front of Elsie, also saw the pair, but didn't hesitate. She walked directly towards them, seemingly unconcerned that she had quite a lot of stolen property about her person, she strode confidently towards the door. It happened as she neared the exit. The female store detective stepped forward as if to stop her from leaving the store, with the large security guard behind her, when there was a sudden flash of light, closely followed by an almighty bang that came from inside the store. Everybody stopped what they were doing and looked to the other end of the store to see what had caused the explosion. A surprising amount of dust, violently dislodged from the suspended light fittings, floated above their heads before slowly descending, like a hazy cloud.

The security guard and the female store detective stared with open-mouthed astonishment at the plume of black smoke that was billowing upwards towards the ceiling from one of the ladies' changing cubicles, like a small mushroom-cloud. The pair at the door, and all the other customers and staff turned to watch the spectacle with astonishment. Everybody was totally spellbound for at least ten seconds. Everybody but Elsie and Margaret, who continued to walk calmly out of the store, turned in opposite directions and disappeared into the bustling hoards of shoppers in the street.

They'd planned to meet up later at Elsie's house, where they normally sorted the goods in their respective shopping bags for delivery to their customers. Elsie was surprised that she'd arrived home first, having had great difficulty getting on a bus in the town. When she did finally manage to board one, she couldn't get a seat, and was forced to stand all the way home. She'd glared at the men sitting, and mentally bemoaned the fact that gentlemanly good manners were now obsolete.

"You've only yourselves to blame, Mother," Alan said when he came home. "You all wanted women's liberation, didn't you? And now that you've got it, you still want men to open doors for you and give up their seats on the bus."

"I didn't want any bloody women's lib. And I do think that men should give up their seat if there's a woman standing. Don't forget that I've been to work as well, bloody hard graft shoplifting is. All mental strain and brainwork it is."

"Come on then, let's see what you've got," Alan said, rummaging through the shopping bag.

"You keep out of there," Elsie said, rapping his knuckles with one of her shoes that she'd just taken off to ease her aching feet. "All those are ordered. They're already spoken for, there's nothing spare at all."

"Business must be good, eh? Orders coming in fast and furious?"

"You can say that again. I'm running myself into the ground. I'll be happy when the Christmas rush is over and I can get back to the normal, steady work. I'm getting too old for all this pressure and fuss. We had to use another one of those fireworks this afternoon. The store security was circling us like sharks. Try to be inconspicuous they do, but you can always spot them a mile off. They never wear coats for a start, too warm for them wandering around all day inside the store, so you know straight away that they're not shoppers."

"I told you to be careful with those things, Mam. They can be bloody dangerous, especially in a confined space."

"I won't tell you again about your language, Alan. And I made sure that there was nobody anywhere near the thing when it went off. And anyway, what was I supposed to do, just walk up to the store detective and surrender?"

"Just be careful with them, that's all. How many have you got left?"

"That was the last one. I must say that they have come in very handy. Can you get some more?"

"No, Mam, I can't. There's no way that I'm going back to that quarry. No way. I nearly got myself killed in there the last time."

Margaret, Elsie's friend and accomplice, let herself in through the front door, and squeezed into the room with her bags. She dropped them all onto the floor and dropped her tired body into a well-upholstered armchair, kicking off her shoes with obvious relief. "Bloody mad down there, it is. I only just managed to get on a bus because our Renee's Tommy was the conductor. He's only been working on the buses for a couple of months. Doesn't like it, wants to go back to sea. Canny lad he is, wouldn't take my fare and he had to turn somebody off the bus to let me on. Already on the platform this bloke was and not too happy about having to get off, but our Renee's Tommy's a big lad and he didn't argue, just pushed him off the bus."

"Go and put the kettle on, Alan, can't you see that me and Margaret are beat. Been out all day we have, filling all these orders," Elsie said, lighting a cigarette.

"And what do you think I've been doing then? I've had a busy day as well."

"No you haven't, you lazy sod, you've been wasting your time and money down at that snooker hall, that's where you've been all day. I'll bet you've been in there since you got out of bed," his mother said.

"I've been planning things, important things, and meeting important contacts down there," Alan answered, but went into the kitchen to comply with her request anyway.

Elsie looked at her friend and smiled. "He thinks that he's really getting into the big time now. I saw him with some of those villains from the Westwood estate, that's who he was with."

"He wants to be careful with those. They get up to all sorts of bother they do."

"Well, he's big enough and daft enough to look after himself now. He's not a bad lad really," Elsie said, "but he does tend to get carried away, you know, romances about things instead of just keeping them simple. Simple and quick, that's the way to steal, eh Margaret?"

Margaret laughed. "That's right and we've proved it over and over. The amount of stuff that's gone through our hands over the years." Margaret looked keenly at her friend. "Have you told him yet?"

"No, not yet. I'll tell him today."

"How do you think he'll take it?"

"I don't know, but he'll just have to get used to the idea. I tried my very best to stop his father coming here, but he made it very plain that if I refused him, then he'd make my life a misery. And he would too. Eddy doesn't make idle threats."

Alan returned to the room with the tea. "Here you are then," he said, placing a tray containing two cups and saucers, a teapot and the other requisites needed to make a proper cup of tea onto the small occasional table. "And I've even put some biscuits out as well."

"Oh thanks, Alan, you're a real good lad, you are," said Margaret.

"Right then, that's my good deed for today. I'll see you later, I'm going to have a wash and a shave, then I've got to meet somebody," he said as he left the room.

"And just you be careful what you get up to when you're out. I don't want any trouble with the police over Christmas, mind. I don't want to be trailing across to the cop shop on Boxing Day again this year."

The women waited until they were sure that Alan was upstairs, and then they resumed their conversation.

"Is he still on bail, then?"

"Yes, that's why he went back to work at the yard really. His probation officer told him that the court would be probably be more lenient if they know that he was working and holding down a steady job."

"When's he up again?"

"He's been up, but the judge wants more probation reports before sentencing him. He's due back in the middle of February."

The women drank the tea and ate the biscuits as they examined the clothes that they'd so recently stolen. They didn't consider it theft of course, and genuinely thought that they were involved in a sort of Robin Hood operation rather than organised shoplifting. It was their opinion that if they could help friends to obtain some good quality clothes at a reasonable cost, and make a few pounds for themselves while doing it, then what's the harm? The stores could claim the loss from their insurance companies, and they made massive profits by charging hugely inflated prices for their goods anyway. The women charged their customers, who were all their friends and acquaintances, only a quarter of the store prices, and there was no shortage of takers.

The customers generally did their own selections, browsing the clothes shops for the particular goods they wanted, picking the exact style, colour and sizes. If the right size or colour wasn't in stock then they'd ask the store to order it in, then they'd notify Elsie or Margaret, who would then go and steal the item for them. They'd begun to get some weird and wonderful requests as their fame grew in the district. They were often asked to get television sets, and these requests they passed on to Alan. Twice they were asked to obtain cars, and another customer wanted them to steal a horse. Again Alan was able to oblige. Reluctantly, but necessarily, they eventually had to restrict orders to clothes or toys, the latter a special concession only allowed in the months immediately before Christmas.

This year had been particularly busy one for them. The cumulative effects of lost work because of strikes throughout the year, and previous years, plus the current yard lockout taking place at the worst possible time, meant that their unique services were very much in demand by their customers, quite a few of which were the wives of shipyard workers.

Elsie wouldn't take any money from some of the worse-off families, and provided their clothes free of charge, considering herself to be a sort of cross between a female Santa Claus and a fairy godmother to the struggling families. She actually was the very embodied essence of the motherly figure, loving, warm and kind. She couldn't bear the thought of children doing without clothes or toys at Christmas, and took it upon herself to provide them. She didn't tell Margaret about this, and so was totally unaware that her friend had also come to the same conclusion, and had made similar arrangements herself for certain of her customers. They were quite probably among the best shoplifters in the country, but almost certainly the worst at turning a profit, preferring a warm heart to a bulging purse.

After about half an hour her friend left the house and Alan came downstairs, dressed to go out.

"You're not going to that snooker hall again are you?"

"No, Mam."

"Sit down, son, I've got something to tell you."

Puzzled by his mother's serious expression, Alan sat on the edge of the settee. "What's the matter?"

"It's your father. He's coming out soon."

"I know."

"No son, listen. He's coming here, tomorrow."

Alan sat back on the settee, a look of incomprehension on his face. "He's coming home tomorrow? You mean he's coming here, to live with us?"

"Yes. That's what he wants to do. I've told him that he can stay here for a few weeks until he finds somewhere permanent to live, but that's all. He's got to get out then." She paused and lit a cigarette. "I don't want him here, but he's a right bastard and will make trouble for me if he doesn't get his own way, so I thought that it would be best if I let him stay here for a little while."

"Aren't you being a bit hard on him, Mam? This is his home."

"His home? His home? This is our home. I've provided

everything in this house and don't you forget it. What has he ever done for us? For you, or for me? Nothing. Not a bloody thing except cause us grief."

"But Mam…"

"Look, your father is a bad man, not just a thief, but a real bad man. You don't know him like I do, and I'm telling you to stay as far away from him as you can." She paused and looked at Alan keenly.

"He's being released today and he should be here early tomorrow morning. He can sleep in the spare room, but he'll have to fend for himself, I'm not cooking any meals for him. I want you to be polite to the man, but not too friendly with him. Do as I say and stay as far away from him as you possibly can. He won't be here for long."

"Okay Mam, but I still think that you are being too hard on him."

"You can think what you like. I know the bastard and you don't. He's a nasty, violent man, Alan. Even in prison he couldn't stop hurting other people. Why do you think he's lost so much remission and spent so long inside? Just do as I tell you and keep your distance from him, alright?"

"Alright Mam."

"Good. That's settled then. Now then you little shit, where's the clock?" his mother said.

"What clock?"

"Don't give me any of that rubbish. Who do you think you're talking to? I'll take the side of your face off if you don't tell me." She raised her hand in a threatening manner.

"What clock? Oh that clock."

"Where is it, you little thieving git?"

"I took it to get repaired, didn't I? I wanted it to be a surprise present for you for Christmas. You know that I wouldn't steal from you, Mam, or from anybody that I know."

"I'm not so sure about that," she said. "When you were a kid you were always taking money out of my purse."

"All kids do that, Mam. Look, when I did the pub over, I took everything that wasn't nailed down. But I never touched a penny of the lads' club money, did I?"

"Only because they would have bloody killed you if you had. Anyway where's the clock?"

"I took it around to old Bob a couple of days ago. You know the one that works on the gate at the yard? Somebody said that he was good at mending clocks and things."

Elsie knew old Bob and his wife. They were her friend Margaret's in-laws, and Bob's wife was a regular customer. "And has he fixed it yet?" she asked impatiently.

"Not yet, Mam. He's having a problem with the pointers."

"Why? What's wrong with the pointers then?"

"It's just that he can't seem to get them off the spindle."

"No? Well he won't, will he?"

"What do you mean? Why won't he?"

"Because your grandmother had a lot trouble with them when the clock was working. They were very slack, and they kept falling down to half past six."

"So?"

"So she super-glued them on to the spindle. No, he won't ever get them off."

12

Harry sat looking out of the bus window as it travelled through the brightly lit streets. The shop windows were throwing out light, showing off their imaginative Christmas displays, each trying to outdo the others in attracting customers. The journey to the hospital took forty minutes and involved changing buses in the town centre. Harry had made the same journey for weeks now and knew the bus timetable by heart. He lit a cigarette, coughed a rasping smoker's cough and glanced down at the local evening newspaper on his knees. The headline proclaimed Yule's denies takeover talks. Harry shook his head sadly. "Where there's smoke there's fire," he muttered to himself.

The hospital depressed him as usual, and the familiar feeling of dread increased the nearer he got to the entrance. His gait slowed considerably, it always did, as he walked the green-painted, antiseptic-smelling corridors toward the Women's Surgical Ward. As always, he could detect a definite smell of urine under the thick, acrid odour of the disinfectant.

Visitors were only just tolerated and definitely not encouraged in any way by the strict ward sister who looked upon them all as distracting intrusions into her perfectly organised routine. They were allowed to stand outside the wards, downstairs in the corridor until the sister gave permission to open the doors exactly on the stroke of 7.30. At 8.30 they were all expected to be out of the ward again, and were reminded by warning bells five minutes before and then exactly at the end of visiting time.

Harry stood with the other visitors, half-listening to their chatter but remaining silent himself. He nodded, acknowledging one or two familiar faces in the crush, regular visitors he recognised from his previous trips. At the appointed time the doors were opened and Harry was carried along with the waiting visitors as they streamed into the ward.

He strode up the middle of the ward keeping his eyes fixed on the approximate position of Olive's bed, trying to ignore the tubes going into and coming out of some the other patients as he passed. Hospital was not Harry's favourite place and like most healthy men, he tried to avoid it if he possibly could. Olive was sitting up in a bed on one side of the long dormitory ward. This part of the hospital was originally the Victorian Workhouse and still held forty beds, twenty on each side. The beds all faced towards the centre, leaving a space of about ten feet or so in the middle of the ward for passing nurses, doctors and visitors. Olive was watching the approaching crowd, eagerly scanning the sea of faces and smiled when she saw Harry.

"You're looking well," Harry lied as he kissed her and then sat uneasily on the hard plastic chair at the side of the bed.

Olive had obviously made an effort with her appearance. She wore a little makeup and was even wearing the National Health wig to disguise her hair loss, but it couldn't disguise her gauntness. She looked really ill.

"I feel fine now, love."

"You had any more of that radium treatment today?"

"Yes, and I'm sure that it must be working because I feel a lot better than I did."

Harry nodded and smiled at her, keeping up the pretence. He pulled a paper bag from his overcoat pocket and handed it to her.

"Here, I've brought you some of those sweets you like."

She nodded and opening the bag offered it to Harry. "No thanks, Olive, You have them. I bought them for you, love."

"I'll try one later," she said and closing the bag pushed it into her bedside locker. As she did so Harry noticed the other small treats that he'd brought her over the past week still lying in there untouched.

"You eating alright?" he asked quietly.

"Oh yes, the food's fine and they give you a lot of choice." She looked around and indicated a large woman a couple of beds away. "She always asks for seconds and gets them as well," Olive said, shaking her head. "I don't know where she gets her appetite from, being stuck in here all day."

Harry watched the large woman eating fruit, which her visitors had brought in for her. He'd brought fruit in for Olive but she couldn't eat it, and it looked like she hadn't touched any of the other stuff he thought she might like. He looked past the large woman and watched the patient in the adjacent bed, an old lady who was sitting up as bright as a button and appeared to be giving her visitor a telling off.

Olive saw him watching. "The old girl is ninety-three, she looks good for that age doesn't she? That's her son, he's seventy-four and she still tells him off. Just like a kid." She laughed and shook her head and Harry smiled. Serious again, she nodded to a bed on the other side of the ward, behind Harry. "They brought a young girl in during the night. Only twelve years old. In a terrible state she was, I thought she was dying."

Harry turned around slightly to see behind him. A slight figure lay prone under the covers, tubes disappearing into various parts of her body. Two visitors sat silently, one on either side of her bed. Leaning against the wall was a child-sized artificial leg.

Turning back to Olive, Harry said quietly, "She doesn't look well."

"Terrible isn't it? Twelve years old and she's already lost a leg. She's got bone cancer apparently. It's something you don't appreciate until you've lost it. Your health."

"Aye, that's a fact," Harry agreed wholeheartedly.

Olive asked him a list of questions about what he was eating, what bills he had and had not paid, and he based his answers according to what he thought would please her most, rather than on strict factual accuracy. He tried to anticipate her questions before she asked them so as to prepare his answers.

He glanced nonchalantly at the clock on the wall at the end of the ward and was dismayed to see that it said 7.37. Surely he'd been in here for more than seven minutes? It felt more like twenty and he was dying for a smoke.

Harry tried to lift his mood by reminding Olive how much they would enjoy Christmas. The prospect of seeing their daughter and grandchildren cheered them both and Olive could think of nothing else since she'd learned of their visit. She assumed the money to pay for the flights had came from Harry's successful gambling on horses, and if she had any suspicions at all she didn't voice them.

Harry endured the remainder of visiting time but even to a casual observer he showed signs of acute and increasing agitation.

"You don't have to stay until 8.30, you know. You can go early if you like," Olive said, as she always did, knowing how much he hated hospitals. But of course he never would leave early, considering it his duty to remain with his wife for the full hour allowed. At last the allotted time came, the bell was rung, and Harry gratefully kissed his wife and, his duty done, made his way out of the ward. The ninety-three-year-old lady waved goodbye to her seventy-four-year-old son and shouting down the ward after him, warned him to watch the roads and reminded him to cross only at proper zebra crossings.

As soon as Brenda opened the door she felt a stab of dread in her chest. "Oh, it's you."

"Aren't you going to ask me in then?" the collector asked, licking his thin lips.

William Morton was a small, thin, narrow-shouldered wimp of a man. He'd worked for a number of credit companies for the past thirty years, ever since he'd left school and he loved the work. He particularly liked calling on young attractive housewives, especially if they were behind in their payments.

"But I told you on Friday, I can't pay you this week." Brenda didn't like the tallyman. She thought that he was a creep and she'd heard tales about him making propositions to women who got behind with their payments.

"That's why I'm here," he said, stepping into the kitchen uninvited. "I waited until I saw Joe go out with your sister, we don't want them getting worried about repossessions, do we?"

"Repossessions?" said Brenda alarmed.

"Well, last Friday wasn't the only time you've missed, not by a long way and if you can't pay, then I'll have to notify the office and you know what that means, don't you?"

"What?"

"They'll send in the bailiffs and remove goods to the value of what you owe, plus all the extra costs of course. Costs always add a lot to the bill, sometimes they add up to more than the original amount owing." He smiled showing crooked, discoloured teeth and sat down uninvited at the kitchen table. "Can you imagine what the bailiffs coming in would do to your application to the social services? They'd have Sharon in a home before the bailiffs' van drove away."

"Look, I'll pay up the arrears when things get back to normal at the yard, or when they sort out the bairn's benefits. It can't be much longer."

"And what am I supposed to do until then, whistle for my money? Do you know how much you owe me?"

"I've told you that I'll pay you in full just as soon as I can."

He opened his ledger on the table and tapped a grubby, nail-bitten finger on the total written at the bottom of the page. "And I've told you that I want the money. Unless you pay up the full outstanding amount by next Friday, I'll notify the office."

"But I'll never be able to get the money by then."

"Then we're going to have to come to some little arrangement," he said with a leer, his meaning unmistakable.

She shook her head. "Get out you bastard. Get out of my house now."

He stood up. "Your house. Your house is it? I'll bet it's not your house for much longer. Never mind the social services, as soon as the Building Society finds out that we've sent the bailiffs in, they'll be demanding their money as well. You'll be evicted and they'll repossess the house. You'll be out on your pretty little ear, darling, just you wait and see." He stepped around the table and touched her shoulder. He was so close that Brenda could smell his fetid breath. He smiled conspiratorially. "Look, why don't you be sensible, all I want…"

The back door opened suddenly and Elsie walked in without knocking, as she usually did, her arms full of carrier bags. "Sorry Bren, I didn't know that you had company. Oh, it's you, Mister Morton, I wasn't expecting to see you here."

"That's alright, Elsie. Come in. Mister Morton was just leaving," Brenda said coldly.

"Right," Morton said stiffly. He walked towards the door and past Elsie without acknowledging her. "But you think about what I said. I'll see you on Friday."

The women watched as he closed the door behind him. "You want to watch that one, love," Elsie said, sensing the highly charged atmosphere in the room.

"I'm finding that out. The creep was coming on to me, threatening to bring the bailiffs in if I didn't go along." Brenda filled the kettle at the tap, her hands shaking with anger.

Elsie nodded. "I've heard that he's tried the same thing with a few others. Never tried anything with me, though. I don't know whether to be relieved or insulted." They both laughed. "It wouldn't be so bad if he was a bit better looking, eh Bren?"

Brenda laughed again, but shivered. "He really gives me the creeps. My Joe's not a violent man, but if he knew what that bastard had said, he'd kill him." She sat down and covered her face with her hands. The tension flowing from her, her shoulders shook as the sobs racked her body.

Elsie put her arm around her shoulders and comforted her. "Don't you take on so, Bren. That little creep isn't worth getting upset about. He won't do anything about the arrears, you'll see. He just likes to threaten women and see what he can get." She pulled a handkerchief from her pocket and handed it to Brenda. "Anyway, there's lots of folk got arrears around here, what with the lockout and one thing and another, so don't you get yourself upset about it."

Pulling herself together with a conscious effort, Brenda wiped her eyes with the handkerchief and, sniffing, shook her head. "It's not just owing the money Elsie, it's the social services. If they find out that we've got such serious financial problems they'll not let us keep Sharon. God, Elsie, I don't know what I'm going to do. It's not just that bastard Morton, we owe money everywhere. We haven't got two halfpennies to rub together, we're behind with the mortgage, electricity and gas, the catalogue, everything."

"Don't you worry, love. Everything will be okay. Just you wait, something will turn up, it always does, believe me. Anyway, I just called around with a few things for your sister." She indicated the bags she'd dropped onto the table. "I think they'll fit her, oh, and there's a couple of tops and a skirt in there for you as well. They cost me nowt so you can have them for nothing."

Brenda smiled gratefully. She knew that the items were stolen, but needs must, and pushing her money worries to the back of her mind, she examined the clothes with as much enthusiasm as she could generate. "I hear that your old man is coming out?" she said hesitantly.

"That he is. Due home tomorrow. Alan's looking forward to seeing him but I just wish he were locked away forever. He's nothing but bloody trouble that man. Do you know what he said to me when I tried to stop him coming here?"

"What?"

"I asked him why he was so determined to come back, and he said he wanted to see Alan, his son. His son? The lad has never had a father. I told him that everything he touches turns rotten and that he would spoil the lad's life coming here, and he said Alan's already making a good job of spoiling it himself."

"He said that?"

"Yes. Anyway, I said he could stay for a few weeks until he finds somewhere else, but I wish the bastard would just disappear and leave us in peace."

Alan's father's arrival at the family home was something of an anti-climax. Alan wasn't sure what to expect. He experienced a number of mixed emotions as the stranger walked through the front door; expectation, fear, anxiety and happiness all mixed up together. He certainly wasn't what Alan had imagined. He appeared to be thinner, older and harder-faced than he was expecting. They exchanged muted greetings, no handshake was offered or accepted, and they merely nodded to each other as Eddy dumped his bag on the floor.

"I don't suppose your mother's in?"

Alan shook his head.

"No, she wouldn't be. She doesn't want me here you know? Wants me out as soon as possible."

"You want a cup of tea or something?" Alan asked.

The man shook his head. "You got any money?"

Alan nodded.

"Then why don't we go out and get a proper drink?"

After three pints each in the local pub, Alan and his father made their way to the snooker hall and sat waiting for a game, as all the tables were in use. Alan liked the smokey atmosphere of the place; it reminded him of scenes from countless gangster films he had seen. The men around the tables holding the long cues in the dimly lit room had a slightly sinister appearance. Only fully visible when they leaned over the illuminated snooker table to take a shot, the rest of the time being only shadows on the periphery of the light. There was definitely something about playing snooker that was conducive to conspiracies and crime.

The McKenna brothers were playing at the table nearest him. They had acknowledged the newcomer's presence. Alan felt that he had really arrived now. For these two to speak to him, however briefly, was a sign that he was accepted. To his surprise, his father walked across to the pair and was greeted like a long lost brother. After a lot of backslapping and handshaking his father beckoned

Alan over to the group. "This is my lad, Alan," he introduced him to the brothers.

They were invited to join the McKennas in a game of snooker, and took a pound from each of the brothers by winning the game. Alan couldn't believe he was actually here in the snooker hall, playing with his father against the two hardest and most notorious men in the area and had even taken money off them.

Later, in a pub with an atmosphere so smokey that it was difficult to see the bar from where they were sitting, the brothers discussed their various prison experiences and swapped tales with Alan's father, who they seemed to regard with something like awe. Apparently he was in the upper echelons of the criminal fraternity, an armed robber. The McKennas had been in the same prison as him for some time. Listening to the conversation, Alan gathered that his father had been something of a modern day bandit; stealing payrolls from a number of armoured cars during his criminal career, and had even been involved in a failed attempt to hold up a bank.

Alan was proud to be seen in the men's company and really happy that his father was home. After the McKennas had left, Alan and Eddy decided to have another couple of drinks before returning home for something to eat.

"I didn't know that you knew the McKennas, Dad."

"Don't call me Dad. Call me Eddy." He drank some of his beer. Eddy was in a talkative mood, the unaccustomed alcohol loosening his tongue.

"Aye, I've known those two for quite a while. I could tell you some stories about that pair and no mistake. The bastards will cut your throat for a couple of pence. Don't trust them. Never, ever, trust anybody. You hear, son? Never trust anybody."

Mickey was arrested at the youth club. In front of the astonished stares of the youngsters, and a baffled Father Gallagher, who tried, unsuccessfully, to intervene while a total of five policemen barged into the hut, handcuffed the stupefied Mickey, and escorted him to a police van.

At the police station a bored looking, middle-aged detective sergeant and a keen young detective constable interviewed him at length before he was released pending further investigations. He was warned that he could possibly face charges of GBH and actual bodily harm.

He left the police station in a daze. The arrest had come totally out of the blue. Apparently, the two youths who had attacked Chisholm outside the Blue Angel alleged that he'd assaulted them for no reason.

As he walked home, Mickey gradually came to realise that if he was charged and found guilty of unprovoked violence, then he's almost certainly lose his ABA licence and wouldn't be able to train the lads at the club.

13

Trev had dusted off his guitar and amplifiers with anticipation. He'd always liked a wide variety of music and knew the words to dozens of numbers. After a few practice sessions he felt that he was ready for his solo début, and that the Northeastern club circuit was in for a treat. After leaving school he'd played in a pop group for a couple of years. The group had been well received in the clubs, but had performed only at weekends as all the players had full-time jobs, most of them being apprentice shipwrights. The band had broken up after arguments amongst the various members and Trev hadn't played seriously since.

Within a week of being registered with an agency, that charged him seven and a half per cent of his fee for the privilege, he'd got a booking at the local Royal Naval Club. Trev practised a selection of current popular hit songs and some older ballads, which he thought would go down well with a predominantly middle-aged audience.

He arrived at the club in Mickey's old white Escort van, the Capri still requiring vital, expensive repairs.

Mickey helped Trev unload the van at the door of the club, placing the equipment carefully on the stone steps.

"Look, you get yourself away now, Mickey, I can manage from here. I'm not totally useless, you know."

"I'll just help you get them inside, you don't want to leave them lying about out here, they'll get nicked," Mickey said as he carried the guitar through the club doors and into the foyer.

"Look, just go will you," Trev said affably.

"Well, if you're sure you don't mind, Trev. I want to get back as quickly as possible, what with Tracy not being well."

"That's fine. You just go home and see to Tracy and the kids. And don't worry. I'm sure that she will be fine after a lie down. She really suffers badly from those headaches of hers doesn't she?"

"Yes so does. The doctor says it's migraine, but I think she's worried about me going to court. She worries a lot, you know. The tablets the doc's given her just knock her right out, and there's nobody else to mind the bairns until her mother comes around at nine."

"Okay then, off you go, and thanks for the lift and everything."

"No bother, Trev, I'll come back for you about half ten, alright?"

"Yeah okay, and Mickey,"

Mickey turned around. "Yes?"

"Don't you worry about that assault charge, mate. It'll never get off the ground."

"I hope you're right. I really do."

Trev watched Mickey drive the van away, and turning, picked up one of the two amplifiers and walked up the steps and through the double doors into the club.

"Hey! You can't go in there without signing in." The command came from behind. Trev turned around, and looked over the top of his amplifier. He identified the disembodied voice as coming from a small figure ensconced in a sentry box-like cubbyhole that was located just inside and to the left of, the front door. He walked back with difficulty, and steadied the heavy loudspeaker awkwardly on one knee as he balanced precariously on the other leg. The small wizened face peered at him from over the top of a counter that protected him from the public. The little old man waved a pen at Trev. "You a member?"

"No," Trev said, over the top of the amplifier.

"What?" the old man cupped a hand to his ear.

"No, I'm not a member," Trev said shaking his head.

"Didn't think so. You CIU affiliated then?"

Trev shook his head again.

"What?" the doorman asked, turning one ear towards Trev. "Are you a member of another CIU club? You know, the Club Institute and Union."

"No," Trev replied, "I'm the artist."

"The what? Oh, the turn. Why didn't you say so? You've still got to sign in though. I'll get a member to countersign you in as a guest."

Trev was still tying to balance the amplifier on his knee, and was having tremendous difficulty maintaining his equilibrium. "Okay. I'll just put this in the concert room first, and then sign in, okay? Is this it here?" he asked the old man, and indicated a set of double doors opposite to the front door.

"You can't go in there until someone signs you in first," the doorman insisted.

"But I just want to be able to park this," Trev said. "It's bloody heavy you know, and I've got another one just like it outside."

"Well lucky you, and there's no need to use language like that. Not in here. Club rules; no profane or blasphemous language will be uttered within the perimeters of the club premises," the old man said as if reading from the club rulebook.

"What bloody profane language?" Trev asked mystified.

"You've just gone and used it again. Trying to be clever, are you, sonny?"

Trev shook his head; amazed that such a mild expletive had brought such a fervent response. "But this is the Royal Naval Club," Trev said with surprise. "If you can't swear in here, where can you? Anyway, old sailors like yourselves must have heard it all before, surely?"

"That's got nothing to do with it. There's no profane or

blasphemous language will be uttered within the perimeters of..."

"The club premises, I know," Trev finished off for the old man. He heard that alright, the old bastard's got selective deafness, he thought. The amplifier was getting really heavy now and Trev didn't think that he could hold it for much longer. "Look," he said, exasperated, but determined to have one more try at reasoning with the old man. "I'll just go in there and put this amplifier on the edge of the stage and then I'll come straight back out and sign the blood..." he decided against his choice of words, not wishing to inflame the situation, "...sign the visitors' book for you, is that alright?"

The old man looked Trev straight between the eyes. "Look, son, if you don't sign in first, then you don't go anywhere in this club. It's against the rules. Do you understand that, or have you got difficulty with your intellect, as well as with your hearing? You youngsters seem to think that any rules that you don't like, only apply to other people, not to you. I know that the current education system isn't as good as when I went to school, but I didn't think that it was as bad as all that."

Trev stared at the man with mild astonishment. The old codger looked as if he couldn't string two words together, was obviously as deaf as a post, and yet had come out with that little lot and put him right in his place. Trev conceded defeat and placed the amplifier on the edge of the counter, so that he could leave at least one hand free to sign the book with.

The old man had other ideas. "You can't put that thing on there," he said with determination.

"It's just until I sign in," Trev said with disbelief and waved his empty right hand about in the air in a mimed impression of writing his signature.

"You can't put that thing on there." The old man was adamant.

"For God's sake," Trev said as he half-turned and placed the amplifier as gently as he could on the carpeted floor of the foyer.

"I've already told you that the use of profane, or blasphemous language will..."

"Not be uttered within the perimeters of the club premises. I know, but it just slipped out," Trev said, thinking that the old git definitely had selective deafness.

"I won't tell you again. One more time and you're barred."

"How can you bar me when I'm not a member, and I can't even get into the club?"

"If you sign in and are countersigned by a member then you can be allowed in as a temporary member just for tonight."

So you can bar me then, thought Trev. "Okay, I'll sign in right now, alright? Just give me the pen."

The old man passed the pen to Trev and indicated to him where he should sign. Trev completed the task and handed the pen back to the old man. "Now what?"

"Now you need a full member of the club to countersign your signature and vouch that you are an honest and upright person, and as such should be allowed in here to enjoy the hospitality of our club, and engage in the continuance of social intercourse."

Trev wasn't one hundred per cent about the last bit, but he let it go, now more impatient than ever to get all of his gear inside and set up for his performance. He hated the thought of his expensive equipment just lying outside inviting attention from rogues, thieves and vagabonds. "But I don't know any of the club members, and they don't know me," he said desperately.

"Oh, that's alright, son, I'll sign you in," the old man said amiably, and countersigned with a flourish of his wrist. "That'll be five pence, please," he said and waved a wooden box with a slot in the top under Trev's nose.

Trev searched his pockets and finally came up with a coin. It was a fifty pence piece, all the money that he had in the world. "I've only got a fifty pence piece," he said. The old man shrugged his shoulders and pointedly continued to wave the old, varnished box under Trev's nose. Trev reluctantly and hesitantly placed the fifty pence piece into the slot and listened as it fell into the box, clattering on the wooden bottom.

The front door opened and the foyer was suddenly full of people, obviously members, who nodded to the doorman as they walked straight through the double doors without signing in. Trev looked through the briefly open doors, and saw the stage at the other end of the long room. "Right then. I'll just get my gear in there then."

"Aye, you'd better hurry up because you haven't got much time before the entertainment starts. You don't want to be late, do you? Good comedian on tonight there is," the doorman said with a straight face.

"There's a good comedian right here on the door," Trev muttered as he walked outside and picked up the other amplifier and the bag containing his stage clothes. He left the first amplifier on the floor of the foyer, and pushed his way through the doors into the concert room, struggling to the stage with the loudspeaker.

He got about halfway down the long room when he found his way barred by a portly old gent, wearing a new navy blue blazer with a large, golden Royal Navy badge sewn on the breast pocket. Trev tried to edge around the man, but the aisle wasn't wide enough.

"Excuse me," Trev said politely, "could I just squeeze through there?"

"Where do you think that you are going with that thing?" the blazer-clad man asked.

"I'm trying to put it on the stage. I'm the artist, and I'm setting up my gear," Trev said, trying to keep his temper. All he wanted to do was to set his gear up, go on stage and do his numbers and then get out with the money.

"You'll have to report to the concert chairman first, son. No one gets onto the stage without the concert chairman's express permission."

"I'm not going on the stage," Trev said as if explaining it to a child. "I'm just going to leave the amplifiers on the side of the stage until it's my turn to go on."

"Nobody puts anything on that stage unless he first clears it with the concert chairman," the man insisted.

Trev placed the heavy amplifier on the top of a nearby vacant table. He rubbed his arms, encouraging the circulation to get going again. "Alright," he said exasperated, "I never thought that there would be so much trouble getting set up in a club. You can't do this. You can't do that. The concert chairman says this, and the concert chairman says that. Okay, I'll go and see the concert chairman, what's his name by the way, Adolf Hitler? I'll get his express permission to set up my gear on the stage." He looked around the rapidly filling room. "Where is the bloody concert chairman?"

"I'm the concert chairman," the man with the blazer said. "And I'll tell you just once, that if you so much as think about swearing in here again tonight then you'll be thrown out of the club. It is not permissible for profane or blasphemous language to be uttered within the perimeters of the club premises. It's one of the club rules. And another one of the club's rules is that you can't put that," he indicated the amplifier with a slight nod of his head, "on there," again he used his head to indicate the table.

"Yes, alright, of course you are the concert chairman. I might have guessed," Trev, said quietly, now almost totally defeated. He was nearly at the point of quitting, even before he'd got to the stage, but took deep breaths in an effort to calm himself down. "Look, is it okay for me to set up my gear now, or what?" He asked resignedly as he lifted the amplifier off the table.

"These rules all have a purpose you know. We can't have just anybody wandering in here and putting strange boxes down everywhere now can we? For all I know you could be an IRA bomber, couldn't you? You could be coming in here to plant explosives in the concert room, couldn't you? They could be concealed in that big amplifier, couldn't they? Royal Naval Club this is you know, son, not just any old workingmen's club. We could quite easily be a target for terrorists, all our members are ex-servicemen you know, fought for Queen and country, they did."

Trev was somewhat taken aback by the rebuke, and although he was still annoyed at the rigmarole to get into the club, he had to concede that they did have a point about the bomb threat, but not a very strong one. "Okay, I take your point, but can I set my gear up now, please?"

The chairman nodded slowly. "Yes, you can, you have my official permission, but I'm warning you again, no swearing or blaspheming, and make sure that your songs' lyrics are suitable for family entertainment. We don't want any filth in here. This is a very upright and morally decent club, and we are determined to keep it that way."

Trev assured the concert chairman that his act was famed for its completely family orientated entertainment, and now that he was finally given the go-ahead to complete his setting up, wasted no time in doing so. He retrieved the other amplifier and set both up on the stage. He used the small dressing room at the side of the stage to change into his stage gear. He'd borrowed a stage suit and invested in a new shirt. He was admiring himself in the mirror when the door opened, and a tall, thin man, entered.

"Howdy fucking do, partner," the man said. "My handle's Al Fonso, best fucking comedian in the west. Well, the best in the north-fucking-east anyway." He stuck out his hand for Trev to shake.

Trev introduced himself. "You performed at this club before?" he asked, wondering how the comedian he ever got past the doorman or the concert chairman using language like that.

"Not this one, but I've done quite a few others in this area. They're all the fucking same, start off a bit slow, and it's only in the second half that they get warmed up and really start laughing when they've had a few drinks down their necks. What about you, have you been here before?"

"No, I haven't. This is my first gig here. In fact it's my first gig anywhere on my own."

"Really? Well fuck me gently. Fancy fucking that. Your first gig, eh? I can remember my first time that I performed. I was scared shitless. Terrified. Club over in Gateshead it was. Rough as fuck the audience was. The doormen asked if you were carrying any weapons when you went in, and gave you some if you said no, you know? The sort of place where you wipe your feet on the way out." He shook his head as if to clear it of the memory. "I was booked with a handful of strippers, and what a fucking handful they were? Fucking hell, a couple of them were okay, but the others were real dogs.

Anyway, I was first on, so up I steps on to the stage fucking shitting myself, I didn't know that adrenaline was brown, did you?

Up I get and start to go through my routine, but they weren't interested in me at all. Most of the audience just talked amongst themselves the entire time that I was on stage. A few laughs were all I got, and a little bit of applause at the end when I came off. I could have been reading aloud straight from the telephone directory for all the notice they took."

Trev, who was more than a trifle nervous himself at the moment, made some sympathetic noises.

"But I wasn't worried at all. No, not a fucking bit. I was so pleased just to get off the stage. It turned out to be a good night after all. I took one of the strippers home after the show, she was one of the dogs, but a good shag, and got my leg over in my van. Broke the fucking suspension, one of the shock absorbers went. I was just about on the vinegar stroke and fucking bang, the van nearly tipped right over in the car park. She thought that I was a marvellous lover, the best she'd ever had she said, and I couldn't fucking get rid of her. She kept following me around for months. The earth must have really moved for her, eh? The van certainly did. She couldn't get over it. It was a great night."

There was the sound of music from outside. The backing musicians, consisting of an organist and drummer, were warming up by playing a melody of recent hit tunes.

"Here we fucking go then, these jokers will be on for about ten minutes while the audience get their bingo books in, then it'll be eyes down for a fucking line then a full fucking house, and then fuck me, they'll have a jackpot on for a shout of under fifty numbers. You buying any tickets? I'll get them if you like, I always like to have a game. Try my luck like. If I knock the jackpot off I won't go down very well. I can tell you. I once did that very thing you know, at a club in Killingworth. Not bingo, but a bandit. I won one hundred and twenty-three pounds on a fucking one-armed bandit jackpot. Fucking livid the members were. The fucking thing hadn't paid out for months, and then I walk away with the fucking jackpot the first and only time I'd set foot inside the club. They weren't pleased at all. I went down like a lead balloon there, I can tell you, but I didn't give a shit, you can't have everything, can you?" He paused and looked at Trev. "Well?"

Trev had been so immersed in the man's continuous speech that he'd forgotten what he was on about. "Well what?"

"Well, do you want me to get some bingo books for us or what?"

"Oh, no thanks, mate. I've come out without any money, and anyway I don't like playing the game."

"That's alright mate, I've got money. You at the yards, are you? Thought so. I had a bit of that myself a few years ago. Fucking terrible it was, always out on strike for something or other. They're in and out faster than a fucking fiddler's elbow they are. You take a tip from me and stick to the clubs. You can make good money doing the clubs, and it's a lot easier than working at the fucking dirty old shipyards, believe me. Look, I'll pay for the bingo books, and we'll share if we win, okay? Anyway it'll calm your nerves, take your mind off going on stage, eh?" He disappeared through the door, and Trev, at a loss what to do, followed him out.

The bingo books were on sale at the top of the room near to the bar, and Trev stood near the bar while Al joined the bingo queue. "Here Trev, you might as well get a couple of drinks in for us," Al said and passed him a five-pound note.

"Sure, what do you want?"

"Just get me a diet Coke, I need to lose some weight, no I'm only kidding, make it a whisky and lemonade, alright, mate?"

Trev bought the drinks, and came from the bar just as Al walked from the queue carrying the bingo cards. "Right, now we need somewhere to sit," Al said looking around the room. All the seats were occupied and no one gave the slightest indication on shoving up to make room for them on the long leather side seats. "Well, just have to stand at the bar and rest the books on the counter," Al said.

They stood to one side of the bar, and tried to keep out of the way of the customers, as there were still people waiting to be served. After a few minutes the music tailed off, the lights dimmed, and the concert chairman, still resplendent in his new blazer, walked centre stage with a microphone. "Good evening, ladies and gents. We've got some great entertainment for you all tonight." He walked up and down the entire length of the large stage as he talked, and Trev found that he was slightly hypnotized by the man's soft smooth voice and his slow backwards and forwards movement. The stage lights reflected off the top of his bald pate and shone into Trev's eyes, and he had to make an effort to stay awake. "First of all there's the bingo. Tonight we're playing for big money." He emphasized the last two words, and there was an answering whispering echo of 'biggg moneyyy' from the audience.

"Fucking hopeless," Al said, shaking his head. "That's all most of them are in here for, the fucking bingo. You watch, they're just not interested in the turns."

The concert chairman noticed the pair at the bar. "Could I remind everyone that the club rules forbid anyone standing at, or near to the bar. Thank you," he finished as if they'd already complied with his directive, and had moved away from the forbidden place. The pair slowly and with obvious resentment, moved away from the counter, as the chairman continued to stare pointedly at them. They inched a few paces further down the room to a position that was marginally further away from the bar, as if every single inch was costing them money and causing them considerable pain.

"Miserable, old, fucking nit-picking bastard," Al muttered.

The concert chairman, apparently satisfied with the pair's new position, and thankfully being too far away to hear Al's comment, went on. "Yes, very big money tonight, ladies and gents. We're playing for twenty pounds a line, and forty for a full house. That's not all, of course, because we're also got a huge roll-over jackpot of…" he waited for a few seconds allowing the tension to build up. "…sixty-five pounds on the last house." The whispered words sixty-five pounds could be heard going around the audience. "The jackpot will be paid if there is a call on fifty or less numbers."

"Some jackpot, eh?" Al said.

"Aye it is," said Trev. He could do a lot with that sort of money, he thought, or even half of that, as he remembered that he'd have to split it with Al if he won. Still thirty pounds would sort out a few of his problems. It would go towards getting the Capri repaired for a start. The preparations all ready, the first game began. Trev kept looking up to the numbers board to check that he was hearing the called numbers correctly. He didn't have a single one. He still didn't have a single number when someone at the front shouted for the line. The numbers were checked, and as there was only the one shout, the winner received the whole twenty pounds.

"Lucky bugger," Al said as he prepared to play the rest of the game for the house.

"Will you play my books for me while I go to the toilet?" Trev asked.

"Of course I fucking will," Al said, taking Trev's bingo books.

Trev didn't need to go to the toilet; he just wanted to get out of the tension-filled room for a few minutes. He was really nervous about going on stage and the nearer the time came, the worse he felt. His palms were sweating, his hands shaking, and he was starting to get a headache.

The first house was won while he was away. Two correct shouts, giving the winners twenty pounds each.

Trev was back in his original position as the next house started. The line was won quickly after only six or so numbers had been called and he'd only managed to mark one number off on his card. The house seemed to be won just as quickly, and Trev shook his head in disgust. "I'm not doing very well at all on here, how's yours?"

"Not so bad. I was only waiting for two there for the house, and only wanted one for the fucking line."

The last house started with even more tension filling the air. There was no movement around the room and nobody asked their neighbour to mark their books while they went to the toilet or the bar. In fact nobody bought drinks at the bar, which was just as well because even the barmaids were playing. This was very serious money.

Trev, lost in his thoughts, was nudged sharply in the ribs by Al. "Come on, look lively, you've got number five there and you haven't marked it off. Trev realised that Al was right; he'd missed the number completely. He marked it off immediately, and got another two in quick succession. He realised with a start that he only needed one more number for the line, number ten. As soon as he realised that he needed the number, it came out. Trev was momentarily struck dumb. He tried to shout but nothing came out of his mouth. Finally he managed a slight croak, which although wasn't a proper shout of 'House', was loud enough to halt the proceedings, and brought the usual murmur, of 'I was only waiting for one,' from some members of the audience.

"Was that a shout for the line?" the concert chairman asked.

"Yes, here," replied Trev, holding his bingo card up high, with a shaking hand.

The checker, one of the committee men, also sporting a snazzy new blazer, checked off the numbers on Trev's card and declared him a winner, and handed him two new, crisp, ten-pound notes. Trev's hand was still shaking as he passed them on to Al who gave one back to Trev, saying, "we're sharing, remember."

"But you bought the cards, and the drinks," Trev protested.

"Fucking shite," replied Al, and shoved one of the notes into Trev's shirt pocket. "All we've got to do now is to knock the jackpot off as well."

Trev couldn't believe his good luck. He was a tenner to the good straight off, even before he set foot on the stage. With the tenner he'd be able...

He was again nudged by Al. "Come on, wake up, this house is for sixty-five pounds and there's only forty-one numbers out."

The next few numbers came out as if in a dream, Trev watched his partner marking them off, one straight after another.

"I only want one now," Al said, "number twenty-three. Come on twenty-three."

The concentration in the room was total and absolute. The tension in the air was tangible. Trev noticed that his hands were shaking again.

"Twenty-three, " the concert chairman called. Al stood rooted to the spot for a fraction of a second and then shouted as loud as he possibly could, "HOUSE-YOU-FUCKER!"

The reaction in the room was amazing. There wasn't a sound. You could have heard a fly fart, as Al put it later. Trev went beetroot red, embarrassed by his colleague's exclamation. Al, on the other hand, didn't give his choice of words a second thought. All he was concerned with was collecting his winnings.

There was much discussion amongst a very concerned and enraged group of committeemen, which went into a huddle near the stage with Al's winning bingo card. The blazer-clad group looked like a male voice church choir without the charity, and were at first reluctant to pay out owing to his 'utterance of profane language within the perimeters of the club premises'. Trev could imagine the rule being repeated again and again. He thought about telling Al about the rule but decided that it might not be the most appropriate time to do so. Al couldn't understand what all the fuss was about, or, 'all the fucking fuss,' as he expressed it to Trev.

"What the fuck's the matter with the bastards? Have they spent all of the fucking jackpot money on new blazers or what?" was one of his typical comments that just about summed up his opinion of the committee collectively and individually.

The general consensus of opinion around the room, as far as Trev could gauge it, was to not pay Al out at all, and continue with the game. There were some very loud arguments for this course of action, mainly from people who were waiting for only one or two numbers when Al had shouted.

Eventually, the committee reluctantly decided that they would pay Al, and he was duly given the money, six crisp new ten-pound notes and a fiver. Al immediately gave thirty pounds to Trev, insisting that he accept it and again pushing the money into his pocket.

Al came on stage after the bingo to a somewhat muted introduction from the concert chairman. Not even a token smatter of applause came from the obviously resentful audience, most of whom now seemed to be busily engaged in unwrapping and eating their sandwiches which had been produced as if by magic from ladies' handbags all over the concert room.

Al, standing confidently on stage, seeming unaware or perhaps unconcerned at the audience's muted response, looked around and started his routine. "The committee hasn't spent much on the

Christmas decorations this year, have they? Still, they've all got to get their Christmas presents out of the club's money, haven't they?" His supposedly humorous remarks were met by silence. He tried another tack. "Last time I won a game of bingo was in the Catholic Club. Anybody been in there? They know what to do with fiddling committeemen. It's the only club I know of where they've got a committee man nailed to the wall." Al went down like a lead balloon. He performed less than another minute of his routine; the first word of his next joke was 'fuck', and the murmur of disapproval that buzzed around the room had the concert chairman running to the side of the stage beckoning Al off, as the curtains were rapidly closed in front of him. They paid him off immediately, giving him half the money agreed on. Al took the rejection, and the pay-off philosophically, pocketing the money happily and waving cheerily to Trev as he left the club.

Trev was really nervous now, and his legs shook as he walked on stage. He prayed that he'd be able to keep control of them and wouldn't fall down. He need not have worried. The chairman gave him a good build up; perhaps because now he was the only entertainment they had left for the evening. His songs went over very well, the sandwiches now all eaten and the alcohol starting to take effect. Some of the older ladies at the front of the room even joined in singing some of their favourites, and he got a good round of applause as he came off. Apparently his winning the £20 line was considered to be only a misdemeanour, and quickly forgiven by the members. Not like the grievous, capital crime, the stealing of the jackpot by that foul-mouthed, so-called comedian.

Trev had another drink at the bar during his break and then went on again for the last half-hour. He went down a treat, and even had them dancing in the aisles at the front of the room. The chairman turned a Nelson-like blind eye to this minor breach of the club rules, and Trev was even promised another booking for early in the New Year. He was paid the agreed money, plus the half that had been kept back from Al. He walked out of the club on a high. He'd earned more in a few hours that he'd earn in a fifty-hour week night shift at the yard, cash in hand, no off-takes, and on top of than he'd won a total of forty pounds on the bingo, thanks to Al. This is the life for me from now on, he thought, they can stuff the yards.

14

Trev, still very much elated, was waiting for Mickey in the club car park, surrounded by his equipment, when he saw the girl come out of the club alone. He couldn't take his eyes off her. She was beautiful; tall, blonde, slender, and moved with the grace of a gazelle. He was thunderstruck. He watched her walk out of the door of the club and she smiled as she passed him.

"You've got a good guitar there."

Her voice was like music to Trev's ears and it was a few moments before he realised that she was speaking to him. "Er, yes," he cleared his throat noisily, gathering his wits about him and regaining some control of his brain. "Yes, I've been appearing here tonight," Trev, said, a little more loudly than he intended.

"I know. I caught your last few numbers from just inside the door. You play the guitar well," she said, indicating the guitar case and amplifiers.

"Thank you. It did seem to go down very well tonight."

"I play the guitar myself," she said. "Classical guitar, actually."

"Really? Classical guitar?" Trev was impressed. "You with an orchestra then?"

"Yes, the Northern Philharmonic."

They were interrupted by a group of people emerging from the club door. She indicated toward them, "I'm here to pick up my mother and father, they are always in the club Wednesday nights." She turned to walk towards them.

"Er, how about meeting me for a drink one evening?" Trev asked, pumped so full of adrenaline that he was brimming with confidence.

She turned and looked at him for a long moment, as if considering his offer. "Yes, alright."

"Tomorrow, half seven at the door here?"

"Yes, that sounds fine. I'll look forward to it," she said, and smiled at him as she walked to meet her parents.

It wasn't until she'd driven away with a smile and a wave that he realised that he hadn't asked her name.

The adrenaline was still surging through his body and Trev felt as high as a kite when Mickey turned up and helped him to put the equipment into the van. Trev was full of plans for his singing and for his date tomorrow night and didn't stop talking all the way home in the van. He gave an astonished Mickey a tenner for his trouble.

"Thanks, Trev, I'm pleased that you went down so well, and won on the bingo, but you haven't forgotten that we're going for sea coal tomorrow, have you?"

Trev, with the excitement of the evening's events, had indeed forgotten all about the next day's planned trip to get sea coal, but he was still up for it, and assured his friend that he'd be there bright and early.

Trev met Mickey with the van on the main road near his home early next morning as arranged. Both men were still half-asleep, and not in the best of humour at being out of their beds at half past five on a cold, dark, wet winter's morning. Trev wound down his window and lit up half a cigarette that he had left over from last night. He deliberately blew the smoke out of the window, and not in Mickey's direction.

Mickey's nose wrinkled with disgust, as he smelled the smoke. He had always detested cigarette smoke. His dedication to keeping fit meant that he abhorred anything but clean fresh air. His hatred of smoking grew to almost obsessive proportions after his mother contracted, and subsequently died of, throat cancer. She had smoked heavily all her life, and although medical opinion was still divided regarding the dangers of smoking, Mickey was convinced that it had killed her.

It was too cold to leave the window open for long, and Trev was relieved when he'd finished the cigarette and threw the butt out of the window, where it flashed backwards in the van's slipstream. He wound up the window and the blast of freezing air receded. "Bloody cold out there," he said, coughing cheerfully, and rubbing his hands together to generate some feeling into them. He was starting to come fully awake now that he'd had his smoke. "I hope this turns out to be a good idea. Going out to work this early in the morning is worse than night shift."

"We'll do alright. That lad was telling me that the only thing that you have to worry about is the tides. If the tide comes in too fast, then the van gets stuck and we're knackered," Mickey said.

Trev's mind was still full of his success at the club the previous evening. He re-ran the evening again and again in his mind. He was sure that he'd found the right career for himself. And the girl he was taking out tonight was more than just the usual type of date; he really felt that she was something special. "I really enjoyed last night you know, Mickey. Why don't you be my road manager when I get more club bookings?"

"I couldn't be a manager," Mickey said.

"Not that type of manager. It'll be a doddle. All you have to do is drive me to the clubs, then help me get the amplifiers inside and set up on stage."

"That's all I'd have to do, set up the gear on stage?"

"That's all, and I'll pay you cash in hand. How about it?"

"That sounds alright to me. There's only one thing, though."

"What's that then?"

"The smoke. I couldn't stay in the concert room all night, not with all that cigarette smoke."

"That's no problem. You could just leave after setting the gear up and come back later. That sound alright?"

Mickey nodded.

"Good. When I'm a famous singer, you'll be that busy running me about that you won't have time to go to work at the yard, believe me."

"That'd suit me fine," Mickey said with feeling. "It'd be nice to have money coming in regularly."

Trev looked at his friend appraisingly. "How's Tracy?"

"Still the same. She was still asleep when I left, but she'll be alright. Her mother stayed the night."

They drove for a few minutes in silence, each silent with his thoughts. The two were comfortable with each other having known each other since they'd started school at five years old. They were both descended from Irish Catholic families, part of the mass exodus to England to escape the Irish potato famines in the mid-nineteenth century. Both boys had survived the ordeals of the strict Catholic education, endless scrapes with authority and countless fights with other kids. They were both thoroughly ingrained with the terrible guilt such a religious upbringing guaranteed. But, whereas Trev had successfully suppressed his culpability and hadn't seen the inside of a church since he'd left school, Mickey was still a regular churchgoer and chose to take his religious traditions seriously, attending mass and the sacraments and being busily involved in parish activities. Tracy was from a similar Catholic background and took her religious duties even more seriously than Mickey, if that were possible.

Mickey was the one to break the silence. "I saw Harry cleaning the inside of his windows last night."

"Well, seeing as you live opposite him, that's hardly surprising, is it?" Trev answered shortly, still a bit grumpy from lack of sleep.

"No. He wasn't just cleaning the windows; he was hiding behind the curtains and just pushing his hand out with the wash-leather. If anybody went by the house, he'd wait until they'd walked by and then start again. He did the whole front of the house, upstairs and down like that, making sure that nobody could see him."

"Olive's home now, isn't she?" Trev asked.

"No, she's still in hospital, but she's due home this week sometime. That's probably why he's cleaning up a bit."

"It must be a bit rough on Harry, you know. He thinks the world of Olive and he hasn't been the same since she took ill."

"He always seems cheerful enough though," Mickey said.

"That's true, but that's just for show, mate. He's really cut up inside and that's the only way he can handle it, by pretending to be cheerful like. He must be really upset to have gone and nicked the lads' holiday money like that. He's really gone to the dogs a bit since Olive's been ill. He looks like a bag of shit most of the time, doesn't shave or try to iron his shirts."

"I've always liked Harry," Mickey said with feeling.

"You like everybody, you do, you big Christian you. I'll bet you got Tracy to go round and offer to cook Harry's meals and do his ironing for him when Olive went into hospital, but he wouldn't have it."

"How did you know that?"

"Just a guess, mate. Just a guess." Trev coughed and changed the subject. "This lad that you were talking to, how much did he say that we could get for a bag of coal?"

"Well, he's got regular customers that pay seventy-five pence a bag, and most take two or three bags a week in the winter. Say, they only take one bag each, and multiply that by say, fifty customers a week and that's thirty-seven pounds and fifty pence."

Trev smiled. Mickey had never been any good with figures, so Trev guessed that he'd done the sums previously, probably with the help of a pocket calculator.

"That's eighteen pounds seventy-five each, for a couple of mornings' work. Not bad eh? Better pay than a week's night shift at the yard."

They arrived at the coast, and turned down a narrow lane that ran along the top of a cliff. After travelling for about a half-mile or so, Mickey drove down a dirt track that descended steeply to the shore. They had come down a couple of days ago in daylight, to reconnoitre and plan their route. The van's suspension rocked and bounced, squeaked and squealed its protest as the vehicle came down the steep gradient and ran slowly down to the sandy beach. It was still pitch black, and they were amazed to see a multitude of other stationary headlights along the sand, their beams cutting through the blackness.

"What going on?" Trev muttered.

"Looks like we're not the only ones with the same idea," Mickey said. "Will you look at those lights, there must be dozens of them."

Trev did a quick count. There were twelve sets of headlights not counting their own, and still more vehicles had come down behind them.

"This is going to be a free for all, this is," Trev said.

As they got nearer they could see that the vehicles were an assorted collection. From the big fifteen ton ex-British Army trucks, right down to Escort size vans the same size as theirs. The men with the vehicles were all waiting patiently until the receding tide was at a particular level and would reveal the sea coal lying in the wet sand.

"Trev?"

"What?"

"This coal, this sea coal?"

"What about it?"

"Well, where does if come from?"

"Come from? From the sea of course."

"Yes, but how does it get into the sea to start with?"

"Oh, I see what you mean," Trev said. "Well, some people say that sea coal is not a natural phenomenon, but the result of us dumping colliery slag into the sea. After the miners dig the coal out of the ground, the stuff is passed through a washer and separated from the waste, which is dumped into the sea." He paused. "You taking all this in?"

"Yes, go on, it's interesting," Mickey said.

"Well, intermingled with the dumped waste there is always a fair quantity of good coal that has slipped through, and not been separated from the slag during the washing process. This coal is lighter than the slag and washed ashore by the tides. It remains here, on the beach waiting to be taken totally free of charge by anyone like us who is thick enough to take on the backbreaking task," he paused and looked at Mickey.

"Then again, other people say that it's the result of the tidal movement exposing coal seams near to the surface of the seabed and the coal is washed ashore. So take your pick, mate. It could even be a mixture of the two."

Mickey was still digesting these facts when the other trucks started to move. The pair took their lead from the others, who on some imperceptible cue, had all driven as far into the sea as they dared, and begun to fill sacks with the round, water-smoothed coal. Trev drove as far out as the other vehicles, and stopped the van. Leaving the headlights on so they could see what they were doing, they carried the empty sacks and shovels to the very edge of the lapping water.

"You bring a torch?" Trev asked.

"Of course," Mickey replied as if mortally offended at the question. "You don't think that I'm going to come down here in the total darkness and not bring a torch do you?" he said indignantly, producing a small plastic child's torch from a pocket.

Trev looked at the object without enthusiasm. "That the bairn's is it? One of his Christmas stocking fillers?"

"I got it for him last Christmas," Mickey said defensively. "Why? What's wrong with it?"

"Well, it's hardly a bloody searchlight is it? I mean just look at the beam."

Mickey looked at the narrow, weak beam of light that the torch emitted. "Well, I suppose I should have got some new batteries for it," he admitted.

"We'll get some later today when we get paid for some of this coal," Trev said. "In fact we'll buy a brand new flashlight."

"Best start here I suppose then," Mickey said, dropping the sacks and starting to shovel the dark pieces of coal into a sack. Trev did the same, and the two men were soon sweating with their exertions, even in the freezing cold North Sea air. The coal was soaking wet, and very heavy. Shovelling it up put a tremendous amount of pressure on their lower backs, as they pulled each shovelful from the wet sand, which seemed determined to hang on to each piece. After a while they devised a routine, Mickey shovelling the smaller pieces and Trev picking the larger ones and bagging them with his hands.

"I'll put some holes through these shovels tomorrow, to let the water run through. That should make them a bit easier to lift then." Mickey said, leaning backwards to ease his aching muscles.

"We should have thought of that today," Trev said. "It would have made the job a lot easier."

It took them the best part of twenty minutes to fill the first two sacks. They had to stop for frequent breathers, and to ease their aching backs. Two hours later, after filling five sacks each they'd both just about had enough.

"How many sacks did we bring with us?" Trev asked, wiping the sweat from his face.

"There are about twenty I think," Mickey replied.

"Twenty. We'll never fill them all. Not the way I'm feeling. I think I've done my back in, and I can't get my breath."

Mickey resisted the urge to tell him to stop smoking, and instead just nodded sympathetically; despite regular gym workouts and road training he wasn't feeling too good himself at the moment. He looked around the beach. Although nowhere near daylight yet, the darkness had receded somewhat, and he could make out the other figures digging in the gloom. "Let's get these full ones to the van first anyway, before we fill any more," he said to the tired Trev.

They dragged the sacks, one at a time, to the back of the van. When all ten were there, Trev opened the double doors, and they lifted each sack into the back. The lift was a good three feet, and the bags were hard to grip in their wet, freezing hands. They eventually hit upon an effective method of getting them inside. Both men grasped a corner and lifted in unison. The last of the ten sacks aboard, the men realised that there wasn't going to be much room for many more in the van anyway. Another four would be enough they estimated.

Filling the last four bags seemed to take as long as the previous ten. The men were dead tired, and the results of the unaccustomed backbreaking work and the early hour was taking its toll on them. They finally achieved their target, and dragged the bags back to the van. Loading them in the back proved to be almost as tiring a filling them, but finally they were all safely stowed away in the back, and the doors firmly closed behind them.

They were the first of the vehicles to leave, and Mickey started the van's engine, glad to be able to get the heater going to thaw out their numb hands. The engine started without hesitation, and putting the van into first gear, he released the handbrake and pressed his foot down on the accelerator. Nothing happened. He tried again, and again the van didn't move an inch. The engine revved noisily and sand flew from the spinning back wheels.

"Bollocks," Trev said, and stated the obvious. "We're stuck."

The tired men climbed out of the van and using the small torch Mickey had brought, examined the wheels. The back wheels had dug themselves into the sand to a depth of about four inches.

"It's hopeless, we'll never get out of here," Trev said.

"Oh yes we will. We just need something to put under the back wheels so they'll grip, that's all," Mickey said optimistically. They tried the empty coal sacks, but the spinning wheels simply shot them high into the air behind the van. The two men looked around the beach with the help of the fading torch beam, and finally, after a few minutes search, found part of an old lobster pot that had been washed up further along the beach. Placed under the rear wheels, the collapsed pot should have helped the van get enough solid grip to be able to climb out of the depression it had spun itself into to. But it didn't. They tried repeatedly, and only succeeded in driving the wheels deeper into the sand. They then tried another tack, placing a couple of the empty sacks underneath the pot, and tried reversing out. This worked much better, and with Trev's sustained pushing, the van eventually backed out of the soft sand. Relieved and almost completely worn out, Trev gratefully jumped into the passenger seat. "Okay, let's go, I'm freezing, soaked right through, and I just want to go home," he said wearily.

Mickey obliged, and the van started to move slowly towards the exit point. "There's something wrong with the steering," Mickey said, with concern. The last thing that they needed right at this moment was another problem with their transport.

"It's probably just with the heavy load in the back," Trev said unconvincingly. They made slow progress along the beach, but the van was becoming more and more difficult to control. It veered way off course, slipped and skidded, and the steering wheel was almost jerked from Mickey's hands.

"We'll have to stop and have a look," Mickey said finally. "The thing's not going anywhere where I want it to."

Both men got out of the van and walked around it. The problem was immediately obvious to them both, even in the faint and flickering torch light. All the four tyres were flat as pancakes. "Shit!" Trev said predictably. How the bloody hell has that happened?"

"Probably one of those gents let them down," Mickey said, pointing to where a small group of men were watching them with interest. They heard one of the men make a comment and the others laughed. "I thought that the tyres looked a bit flat when they were stuck in the sand, but I thought that it was just the weight of the coal in the back, but they've all been deliberately let down."

"Bastards," muttered Trev. "What do we do now?"

Mickey bent down and examined the tyres closely. "There doesn't seem to be any cuts or slashes in the rubber. They probably just let the air out with a matchstick," he said with disgust.

"Shit," said Trev again. "You got a foot pump?"

Mickey shook his head. "It broke. Didn't get a new one, couldn't afford it. I'll go and see if I can borrow one from one of those trucks. You stay here with the coal, we don't want any nicked," Mickey said, and walked off in the direction of the nearest truck.

The group of men watched his approach. There were six of them, and they worked three to a truck. They were all talking and laughing, but grew quiet as he drew closer. The nearer Mickey got the bigger the truck grew. It was one of the old ex-army fifteen tonners, which seemed to be the preferred vehicle for the job.

"You got problems, mate?" one of the men asked as he approached.

"You can say that again. We've got four flats and we haven't got a foot pump. Any chance of borrowing yours?"

"Well, to tell the truth, I don't think that we've got one between us," a large powerfully built man said, as he scratched the top of his head, seemingly deep in thought. The others smirked at his remark, but remained silent and watchful.

"That's a pity," Mickey said. He was almost certain that one or more of these men had let the air out of the tyres, but there wasn't much that he could do about it right now. He nodded, and made as if to walk away towards the next truck.

"I wouldn't bother asking them, they haven't got one either."

Mickey was sure now that these men had sabotaged the van. "That right? How come you're so sure?"

"'Cos we work with them all the time. We're down here every day. It's our job. Every day of the week. It's how we make our living. We're not part-timers who just come down for beer money, or to make a few bob when they're on strike. We've been doing it for years. We've got regular customers who rely on us for their coal every week. Now, if some part-timers come in and take our coal, then our customers are going to be left without fuel for the worst of the winter, aren't they? Tell you what. You won't be able to get the van off the beach before the tide comes in, not with four flat tyres, so I'll do you a favour. I'll buy all those bags of coal you've got in the van for two pounds. It's better than nothing, and you just might be able to push the empty van up high enough on the sand to keep it above the high tide mark. What do you say?"

Mickey said nothing, and walked away. He didn't bother asking any of the other men with the large trucks, but walked to a group working near to a van that was about the same size as theirs. These men were a lot friendlier, and they did have a foot pump that they were prepared to lend him.

Back at the van it took him and Trev another half hour or so to pump all the tyres up before Mickey could gratefully return the foot pump to its owners.

The two laden fifteen tonners rumbled past their van, the men in the cabs shouting and gesticulating obscenely at Trev and Mickey as they prepared to leave.

Most of the other trucks had left the beach by the time that they'd got the van mobile again. Trev had visions of them being marooned in the van and surrounded by the sea. The Air Sea Rescue service would probably have to be called out for them. He could almost hear the clattering sound of the approaching bright orange coloured, Sea King helicopter, its winch wire already descending to pick him up. It was his worst nightmare, and he was very relieved when they finally drove off the beach, and struggled up the narrow twisting track up to the cliff top in first gear.

They arrived home exhausted, just as dawn broke and cast its weak light across the town. The pair dried off and gratefully warmed themselves by the fire, their clothes steaming in the heat. After something to eat provided by Tracy, the pair sat down with a welcome cup of tea each.

"Only the easy bit to do now," Mickey said rubbing his hands together in anticipation. "How much will we get for a bag again, seventy-five pence times fourteen bags, that's what?"

"Ten pounds and fifty pence between us," Trev said immediately, having worked it out during the miserable drive back.

"That doesn't seem to be much for all that hard work that we put in this morning, does it?" Mickey said.

"That's because it isn't."

"Well we could only get fourteen bags in the van, couldn't we, and that was only our first attempt. We'll get better at it as we get used to it."

"I'm not sure that I want to get used to that. It's not exactly easy money, is it?"

"You'll feel differently when we sell the bags. You'll see. Where shall we start?"

"What do you mean, where will we start? How do I know, you're the one with the list of customers, aren't you?"

"What list? I haven't got any list," Mickey said.

"But you were the one that was saying all about how easy it was, and how much we could get for a bag, and how we'd build up a base of regular customers," Trev said incredulously. "You mean to say that you haven't even approached any potential customers?"

"Not exactly."

"What do you mean, not exactly? How many have you got exactly?"

"Well none. I suppose that we'll have to start from scratch and find some customers, won't we?"

"You mean that we haven't got any? That we've got to start walking around in this weather knocking on doors? If I'd have wanted to do that I'd have joined the Jehovah's Witnesses, wouldn't I?"

"It shouldn't take long," Mickey said with characteristic optimism. "Look, you write out a list of all the people that you can think of that might be short of money, and need coal."

"But that's just about everybody I know."

"Come on then, Trev, write down everyone you know that'll want coal."

"Then what?"

"Then we call around and see them and ask if they want to buy some coal cheap. They'll all jump at the chance, price of the stuff today, and then we'll carry a bag up the path and tip it in their coalhouse, get the money and away to the next one. Easy."

The pair wrote out a list of names each. Trev got about twenty and Mickey about half that.

"Give me your list then," Trev said impatiently. "Let's see who you've got down. Mrs Johnson, shit, I've got her as well." He scanned the list to the bottom. "Bloody hell, Mickey, you've got virtually the same names as me." He counted them. "There's only three that aren't already on my list." He threw the piece of paper onto the table. "This is going to take for ever, mate."

Mickey picked up the papers and compared the names. "We've still got over twenty names to go at. Come on, let's get round and see them. The quicker we get started the quicker we'll get back home."

They set off on foot to visit their first prospective customer who lived in the next street. The old lady opened the door, and smiled as she recognised the men.

"Oh it's you two, come on in, I haven't seen the pair of you for ages, you're so much bigger now than when I saw you last."

She insisted that they have a cup of tea, and asked after Mickey's wife and children. "Fancy you being married with children of your own now, Michael. It just seems like yesterday when you were knocking on my door asking for a drink of water in the summer school holidays, can you remember that?"

Trev realised that this wasn't going to be a simple in and out job. They were stuck there for quite a while before they even got in a mention of the coal. "It's nice and warm in here, Mrs Johnson, you can't beat a real coal fire can you?" Trev said, skilfully bringing the topic of the conversation around to coal at last.

"No you can't," the old lady jumped in, "I was just saying to Mrs Forster across the road yesterday, or was it Monday? Anyway, I was just saying to her how you couldn't beat a real fire. Those gas things don't throw the heat out like these do." She paused for breath, but restarted before either of the men could get a word in edgeways. "Yes, she was saying that she once thought about getting one of those, what do you call them, them there Park Ray fires, but she changed her mind. He sister Alice had a one once and it didn't throw much heat out at all, she said. Mind you, Alice would cause trouble anywhere. She'd start an argument in a telephone box, that one. I was at school with her husband you know, lovely man Billy Thompson, he used to play football…"

"Would you like to buy some cheap coal, Mrs Johnson?" Trev interrupted. He didn't like to be rude to the old dear, but if he didn't assert himself then they'd be here all day.

"Cheap coal?" Mrs Johnson diverted her mind from what she was about to say, and focused in on a subject that was obviously very near to her heart. "Cheap coal?" She repeated. "Certainly I'd like to buy some cheap coal. That man I get my coal from robs me blind. Charges the earth for a small bag he does. I can't afford to pay out money like that, can I? My pension doesn't go far as it is, what with one thing and another nowadays. Why, only yesterday the Co-op wanted to charge an extra tuppence for a bag of flour. Well, I told them that it was just too much to pay and I put it right back on the…"

"So you'd be interested then?" Trev cut her off again in mid flow.

"Why yes, of course I would. I was just saying to…"

Trev held up his hand palm towards Mrs Johnson, and it had the desired effect, which was to shut her up. "So if we dropped a bag or two off for you this morning could you pay us today?"

"Well, I couldn't pay you now, but I could pay you on Friday when I get my pension," she offered. "That's what I do with the man who brings my coal now. He brings the coal on Mondays. And calls back on Fridays for the money. If you can do that then I'll give you all my business and he can go and take a running jump at himself. It's a disgrace what he charges, I don't know how he has the brass neck to come and ask for the money from poor pensioners that are trying to scrape by on a pittance."

"Alright then, Mrs Johnson, we'll drop the coal off in about twenty minutes and then call on Friday for the money," Trev said and looked at Mickey for his agreement.

Mickey nodded slowly, but he seemed concerned.

"What do you think then Mickey?" Trev asked, curious as to why his friend seemed so hesitant.

"That sounds okay," Mickey said, nodding. "Er, as a matter of interest, just how much does your coalman charge for a bag, Mrs Johnson?"

"That robber, he's obviously got no thought for anyone but himself. He's definitely out to get rich quick, he is. Charges me fifty pence a bag. Fifty pence," she repeated, a lot louder for emphasis.

Trev and Mickey exchanged despairing looks. They'd committed themselves to supplying the coal to Mrs Johnson now and couldn't very well renege on the agreement. Mickey shrugged philosophically. "Right then, Mrs Johnson, we'll drop the coal off for you shortly."

"Lovely. I always did like you two lads. I promise that I'll give you all my business. I'll always get my coal just from you two every weeks from now on. And I'll ask around my friends. A lot of them get coal from that robber and will be more than happy to give you their business instead if it's cheaper."

"No, please don't do that, Mrs Johnson," Trev said quickly. "We've got all the customers we can handle at the moment."

Trev and Mickey walked dejectedly away from Mrs Johnson's bungalow. She stood in the doorway and waved to them until they turned the corner.

"Well, we certainly talked ourselves into that one, didn't we?" Trev said with disgust. "It's going to cost us money giving her the coal cheaper than fifty pence a bag, we'll never get our petrol money back, never mind make a profit. And she was going to get us more customers at forty pence a bag. We should have refused and charged her more."

"Well, she's a canny old soul, and she hasn't got much money, and we can't see her without a fire this weather now, can we?"

"No, I suppose not. But we'll have to make sure that every other customer that we get is paying enough to make it worthwhile for us, otherwise there's just no point in doing it, is there?"

The pair spent the rest of the day visiting potential customers, and offering to supply them with coal on a regular basis. They found to their acute disappointment that most of the people they approached, already had arrangements with the same man who supplied old Mrs Johnson, and were only prepared to risk losing that guaranteed supply if they could buy the coal cheaper from Trev and Mickey. None were prepared to pay more, or even the same money, and risk their existing guaranteed supply of fuel. The pair at first resolutely refused point blank to accept less than seventy-five pence a bag, but soon realised that if they held out for that, then they wouldn't sell any at all. They were eventually forced to accept the prevailing and unyielding market conditions, and only a paltry forty pence a bag for their coal. Every new customer that they took on insisted that the pair would guarantee to supply them regularly at the same price, for the rest of the winter at least, and they were obliged to give those unconditional guarantees.

They delivered all the coal the next day, and then retreated to the pub. "Well, that was a big mistake wasn't it?" Trev said, counting out the money from the few customers who had paid that day. "We've got one pound sixty here, and another four pounds to come in on Friday. That's a grand total of five pounds and sixty pence. I ask you? Five pounds sixty between two of us, that's two pounds and eighty pence each," Trev said with disgust.

"Two pounds, eighty pence," Mickey repeated.

"For a hard day's real graft, I've done me back in, we could have got beaten up, and drowned, it's just not worth it."

"It's not a lot, is it?" Mickey agreed.

"And what's even worse is that we've now given an undertaking to provide a bag at the same price, to each of those pensioners every week until next March. They really are hard old bastards."

"We'll never get rich," agreed Mickey.

"What are we going to do then? You want to go back tomorrow and get another van full or what?"

"No. I think that we should ask around first, try and get at least some customers who would be prepared to pay seventy-five pence or thereabouts, before we lumber ourselves with more coal," Mickey said.

Trev nodded. "That's what we should have done first, instead of diving in at the deep end, getting the stuff and then trying to sell it."

They did ask around over the next day or so, but heard the same story from everyone they spoke to. No one was prepared to pay more than forty pence a bag for sea coal. They agreed between themselves to go out only one day every week until March, at whatever time the tide dictated to get fourteen bags, no more or less, deliver them to their existing customers, and to stop and do no more when those verbal contracts ran out. They would ensure that their customers were given ample warning that they would lose the coal at a specific date in March, so that they could make other arrangements. It was a very hard lesson that they never forgot. As Trev succinctly put it, "Always research the market first."

15

Trev paced nervously backwards and forwards outside of the club. He'd really made an effort, dressed in his best suit and had even polished his boots. He looked again at his hands that were still ingrained with coal despite repeated scrubbings. His fingernails were broken, ragged and torn by the wet bags that morning, and the muscles in his arms, legs and back ached.

Despite this he felt elated. He couldn't understand it. He had never felt this way about any girl before. Okay, he rationalised, lots of times he'd been very keen to take girls out, but that generally was for a specific reason, he wanted to get into their knickers. But, this one was different somehow. She was very attractive and he was drawn to her, but in a different way to all the others. He gave up trying to analysis his emotions as he was beginning to get a headache.

She arrived. Stopping her car near Trev, she wound down the window and smiled at him. "Shall we use my car?"

"Er, yes, that'll be great," Trev said, and climbed stiffly into the passenger seat.

"You hurt yourself?"

"Just a bit stiff. Nice car," he said as she pulled out of the club car park and into the flow of traffic.

"Yes, it's not mine really, it's my dad's, but he lets me use it whenever I like." She half turned and smiled again. "What did you have in mind for this evening?"

"Er, I thought we could maybe go for a drink somewhere," Trev said hesitantly. He realised that he hadn't really given the matter much thought, assuming that they'd just do what he normally did when he took girls out, go to a club or pub for a few drinks and a chat before he took them home and tried his luck.

"What about if we go to a little Italian restaurant I know for a pizza and a glass of wine?" she suggested, sensing his uncertainty.

"Okay, that sounds nice," Trev agreed hesitantly. He hadn't expected to go for a meal, but he'd brought enough money with him, so why not?

She drove to the coast and along the seafront, stopping outside a brightly lit restaurant facing the blackness of the sea.

"This is the place, I've been here lots of times with my family," she said as she got out of the car.

Although later Trev would be hard-pressed to give an exact account of what Fiona was wearing that night, he knew that the overall impression was of classic good taste. She wore nothing cheap or flashy and looked like a million dollars.

"Ah, Signorina Fiona, it is nice to see you again, good evening, Signor," the waiter greeted them at the door. "A table for two? Please follow me."

Seated in a secluded dimly lit area of the small restaurant, they made themselves comfortable while the waiter fussed around them, lighting the candle on the table, bringing bread, a carafe of water and the menus.

Trev looked at her while she studied the menu. So now he knew her name, Fiona. It suited her. As he watched her he knew that she couldn't be called anything else. She was glorious. Her long eyelashes and blue eyes enchanted him and he couldn't stop admiring her. She looked up at him and flushed slightly, her cheeks turning pink.

"I'm sorry," he said, "it's just that you look so lovely."

"I'll bet you say that to all the girls," she said with a smile, recovering her poise.

"By the way, my name's Trev," he said feeling slightly stupid as he offered her his hand.

"Fiona. Pleased to meet you, Trevor," she answered shaking his offered hand and smiling. Trev felt an electric shock run down his fingers and into his arms as their hands touched.

"Your hand is very rough," Fiona said, turning his hand over and examining his palm. "Let me see the other one."

Trev proffered his left hand.

"They're both cut and scraped. What happened? How on earth did you manage to get them in this state?" she said with concern.

"Well, me and Mickey, that's my mate, we went for sea coal this morning, to make a bit of money and it was a lot harder than we were expecting." He told her about their outing and the amount of money they'd made. He also told her why it was necessary to try to earn the extra money because of the welders' strike and the lockout.

"I only did it because Mickey wanted to go. I'd made enough last night at the club to see me alright for a while."

He'd thought about lying about his work, he generally did as a matter of course with other girls, so as to impress them, but decided to tell Fiona the truth. He liked her, wanted to see a lot more of her and reasoned that she'd find out sooner or later, so they may as well start on a firm foundation from the very beginning.

Fiona was amazed that they should be in such dire straights through no fault of their own. "I think that's really nice. Your loyalty to your friend. I've always admired practical people who work with their hands and are able to produce something useful. It must give you real satisfaction to achieve something like that. To be able to build great big ships and to see them launched and sail away to all parts of the world."

Trev had really never given the matter any thought at all. "Well, I don't really have that much to do with it. It's the tradesman who actually build the things, the shipwrights, welders and platers, we labourers just help them to do it."

"But they couldn't do it without your help could they?"

"No, I suppose not, but they can replace a labourer a lot easier than any of the skilled workers. It takes years to train a shipwright."

"Even so, I still admire anyone who works with their hands and can help to build a ship."

Trev could count on the fingers of one hand the number of times he'd been inside a restaurant, and had never felt particularly comfortable. He was always afraid of making a mistake with the cutlery, using the wrong knife and fork, or committing some other social gaffe that he wasn't even aware of, but tonight, with Fiona, none of that mattered, in fact no doubts entered his mind at all. Another thing that worried him about restaurants was the cost, but he had plenty of money from last night, and anyway, he noticed that Fiona chose carefully from the menu and didn't go for the most expensive items that most girls he'd dated would have done.

He hadn't a clue about wines and so left the selection to her. She suggested the inexpensive, but adequate, house red. They talked about music, especially guitar music. Trev learned that Fiona also played the cello and piano. She'd studied music since she was five years old and played seriously since she was seven. Last year, at nineteen, she'd been invited to play with the Northern Philharmonic on a permanent basis and had travelled all over the country with them. She was now giving solo performances as a regular part of their appearances. Trev didn't know a lot about classical music, but was impressed. He knew enough to realise that she must have an outstanding talent to be playing with such illustrious musicians.

She was very interested in his music. "Why don't you try to get on Opportunity Knocks or something?" she suggested. "Once you get your face on television you'll be made."

"I've thought of doing that myself. I might even get around to writing to them."

She laughed at all his jokes, and they were all clean, as Trev was on his very best behaviour. They touched each other a lot, held hands, and offered each other tit-bits of food. They got on like a house on fire. The meal was satisfying and the wine sweet. Trev couldn't remember when he'd enjoyed himself so much.

But, all too soon the meal was over and the restaurant staff waiting to close up. Trev and Fiona were totally wrapped up in each other and the last to leave, still happily chatting to each other. She insisted that they go Dutch and tried to shove money into Trev's suit jacket's top pocket despite his protestations. She had difficulty in pushing the note into the pocket and eventually removed her hand still holding the folded five-pound note. Also between her fingers was something else that she teased from his pocket like a conjurer.

Trev realised with horror that they were a frilly pair of lacy knickers that he had last seen on Mandy, the barmaid in Harrogate.

Trev grabbed the panties and shoving them into a trouser pocket, garbling something about them being part of his stage props.

Fiona didn't seem totally convinced at his hurried explanation and obvious embarrassment, but she didn't make any comment and seemed to be vaguely amused by his obvious confusion.

Sitting in the car, they looked out across the vast black expanse of the North Sea. A passing ship's lights were visible some distance offshore and looked small and isolated in the darkness. There was a full moon casting its silver light over the not so smooth waters.

"It's very romantic isn't it?" Fiona sighed.

"I suppose it is really," Trev said. He didn't really have any idea what romantic was, but he knew that he didn't want this evening to end. They watched the sea moving in the moonlight for half an hour or so, the waves crashing onto the beach. They sat quietly, holding hands like a couple of kids, content with each other's company.

It was late when Fiona drove them home. Trev asked her to drop him off where they'd met, at the club. They arranged to meet again at the weekend, and she drove off after giving Trev a kiss on the cheek. He stood in a dazed state and watched her drive away. He whistled all the way home.

Alan slowly opened the door and slid his hand stealthily through the narrow gap. He grasped the artificial leg, pulling it through the opening and silently closed the door of the gatehouse. Old Bob, the sleeping, one-legged night watchman, spy novel open and face down on his lap, stirred slightly as the door closed but he didn't wake up.

"Bloody hell, Alan, you'll get us hung, you daft bugger," Harry said, half-admiringly. Harry had been amazed at the difference in Alan's demeanour, as they had approached the yard. His whole being was more alert and alive. He obviously thrived on the adrenaline rush that the impending raid was producing in his body, unlike Harry, who was terrified. "It's bad enough us being in here thieving without you playing daft games."

"Who's playing daft games?" Alan asked indignantly, his face deadpan, but his eyes alive with excitement. "He can't chase us if I've got his leg under my arm now, can he? Anyway, when he wakes up he'll be hopping mad."

The three men doubled up with laughter, smothering their hysterical hilarity by covering their mouths with their hands to muffle the guffaws. It took them all of thirty seconds to regain their composure. They made 'whisht' noises at each other, which only made the situation worse, bringing renewed waves of laughter from first one, and then the others.

Their nervousness made them laugh. It was a way of releasing the tension that had built up in them. Finally, they calmed down and shivering in the cold night air, walked towards the river, their minds again focused on the welding cable they had come to steal. Keeping to the shadows, the three walked quickly past the shipbuilding sheds, through the berths and climbed up the wooden staging onto the partly constructed boat. The ship's keel with its rib-like protrusions, some partly covered with steel plates, gave it a slightly sinister skeletal appearance in the dark, like a large dead, and partially devoured sea monster.

"Bleeding hell," Harry whispered as they rounded a deck housing. "Listen. What's that noise?"

The men stood stock still, their ears turned slightly towards the berths.

"That's it again," hissed Harry. "Somebody's over there. That's it, all bets are off, let's go home, it's too risky."

"No way," replied Alan. "I'm not leaving without the cable."

"Neither am I," Richie said nervously, taking Alan's side, as he always did.

The men ducked into a deck housing where they couldn't be seen from the berths, and listened intently. Alan could hear slight sounds some distance away near to the berths. The sounds were familiar, a faint scurrying. He knew what the sounds were. He strained his ears until he was absolutely sure. "It's alright, lads," Alan said confidently. "It's only the rats." Alan's favourite pastime was hunting rats on the berths, and he spent countless hours chasing, and trying to spear them with welding rods.

Finding the cable was easier said than done.

"They've locked the stuff away," complained Harry.

"That's because there are lots of thieving bastards around," reasoned Alan.

"Can't trust anybody nowadays," agreed Richie with genuine indignation, peering around short-sightedly.

"Ah, there they are," Alan said quietly, pointing to where a pile of welding masks lay on a large steel box. "We've found the bastards."

The cables had been locked, but not very securely, in the box near to the main office building. One of Alan's homemade, foot-long crowbars made short work of the padlock and the men pulled out the cables. They worked quickly, gathering the cables and cutting them into manageable lengths with their knives.

"We still going to try and get into Skinner's office then?" Harry asked.

"We might as well, seeing as how we're already inside the yard," Alan said.

With as much cable as they could carry wrapped around their bodies, the easiest way to carry it, they began to make their way to the office block.

As the small group rounded a corner of the building, Alan held up a warning hand and the men stopped. "There's someone over there in the doorway," Alan whispered.

The men strained their eyes towards the door and sure enough they could see the glowing end of a cigarette in the shadows, as a smoker drew heavily on the cigarette. They waited impatiently, but quietly, until the man had finished his smoke and flicked the stub away into the darkness, where it sent a cascade of sparks across the ground when it landed.

As soon as the man had disappeared inside, Alan did a quick recce around the back of the building and returned to the others.

"Skinner, the McKennas, and another guy are in an office at the side, you can see the lights," he indicated towards the other side of the building. "There doesn't seem to be anyone else around so I think we should sneak in and try to find out what they're doing."

Harry and Richie agreed.

Alan entered a window at the back of the building and, opening a door, let the others in. They made their way as quietly as possible through the darkened building, careful not to make any noise. The interior was a large engineering workshop containing centre lathes, milling machines and other assorted equipment. A row of glass-fronted offices on a raised gantry stood along one side of the workshop. They could see a light in one of the offices and they headed for that. Climbing up awkwardly onto the top of a stack of wooden packing cases, greatly encumbered by the stolen cable they carried, they could see into the lighted interior. Seated around a table were both McKenna brothers, their large muscular build contrasting sharply with the diminutive shape of Skinner. The fourth man, standing up and facing the others, was tall, distinguished looking, and had an American accent. The interlopers could just about hear what the conspirators were saying, and deduced, rightly, that the fourth man was Chisholm. The group in the office seemed to be talking about a future meeting when the American would make an initial payment to the others.

"...and don't forget that this is just for starters," Chisholm told Skinner and the twins. "When things are up and running and the stuff is coming in on a regular basis, then you'll be raking it in. You guys will have so much money that you won't know what to spend it on."

"So let's get this straight," Skinner said slowly, sitting up straight and squaring his shoulders. "The Friday before Christmas you'll give me," he indicated himself, "£5,000 in cash?"

"That's right, and my friends the McKennas here will get a similar amount at the same time, as will Morgan. A nice Christmas present, I'm sure you will agree."

"And all we've got to do is to keep the welders out for as long as possible?"

"Exactly. The yard is losing money hand over fist because of the strikes and lockouts, and the penalty clause will soon kick in, isn't that so?"

Skinner nodded his agreement. "That's right. Another week or so of these layoffs and the yard will never be able to complete the ship on time. Then the penalty clauses will kick in. If this ship is so much as a day late coming off the blocks, it'll cost the company a fortune, and it'll go bust."

"Then, my friends will be able to buy the show for a knockdown price and we can start bringing in serious amounts of the happy stuff that everybody wants. That's when we start making some real serious money."

"So why do you need the yard to bring in the stuff?" one of the McKennas asked.

"Because it's the ideal cover for it, that's why. And with Skinner here and Morgan running the yard, we can bring anything in we like with the materials we'll be importing from all over the world. You two guys are going to be very busy organising the distribution and selling of the stuff."

"What about the drugs, do they stay at the warehouse for another week or what?" the other McKenna asked.

"Yes. I was hoping that we could have sold them sooner, but the buyer can't take them until next week. They'll be okay where they are for the time being, that old church is the last place anyone will look for cannabis." He looked around. "Everyone happy?"

They all nodded their agreement.

"Okay then. Now I want to go through the details of the yard's penalty clauses. You bring them like I asked, Skinner?"

The eavesdroppers slowly backed away from the window as the men in the office gathered around and examined the papers that Skinner placed on the table.

As they backed away, Richie backed into a cleaner's discarded bucket, sending it clattering across the floor.

The interlopers froze. They stood stock still in the darkness as the men in the office came to the window. They could see Skinner holding his hand at an angle against the glass pane, shielding his eyes against the reflected light of the office bulbs. Not satisfied, he turned towards the door, gesturing urgently to the McKennas.

"Come on, let's get out of here before they put the lights on," Alan hissed.

The three men moved through the building as fast and as quietly as they could, encumbered as they were by the cable wrapped around their bodies. They reached the door just as the large overhead lights illuminated the whole place.

"Get out! Get out!" Alan said urgently, shoving Richie through the door. Harry followed the other two outside and into the pitch darkness of the yard.

As they ran away from the building they could hear shouting behind them and men running. Turning, Alan could see the McKennas twins running inside the illuminated building towards the door, fast. Skinner remained framed in the office doorway. The American was nowhere to be seen.

"Split up," Alan commanded, and took off towards the river, as the outer door to the office block spilled brilliant light and running men, out into the darkness.

Harry ran towards the main shed, and Richie, after a moment's hesitation, ran as fast as he could towards the fence.

16

"Three pints of Best Scotch please, Betty," Harry shouted to the barmaid as they entered the Mason's Arms. The building was old, solidly Victorian. The vault-like interior had somehow kept most of its character despite the worst attempts by trendy design consultants employed by the brewery to update it. Although repeatedly redecorated according to the latest style, the structure and most of the original fittings had remained virtually untouched.

The men were happier than they'd been for a while. They'd weighed in the copper at the scrapyard that morning and been paid the going rate.

"Not enough, the robbing bastard," Alan moaned, but he'd taken the money anyway. Reasonably happy with the reward for their efforts, they'd headed for the Mason's to celebrate.

After a long swallow of their beer they found a table by the window and sat down. Harry indicated a corner table. "I see Morgan and his mates are in." He shook his head. "Well, I suppose that they've got to spend their time somewhere when they're not at work." He winced as he gripped his glass. He'd cut his finger with an old cut-throat razor while stripping the rubber covering from the cable, and sat with it heavily bandaged with an off-white, none too clean, piece of linen.

"Why man, that's nowt at all, is it, Richie?" Alan stated. "Tell him about that accident that you had when you were working day shift in the store."

"What do you mean?" Harry asked. "What accident?"

"Richie here got his dick caught in his zip, didn't you, cousin?"

"Shut up, Alan," Richie said, his face reddening and obviously embarrassed.

"Go on, man, tell him what happened," Alan said laughing.

"I'm going to the toilet," Richie said and disappeared towards the back of the pub.

"Alright, I'll tell him then," Alan said to the back of Richie's retreating figure. "Richie goes into work one Monday morning, he worked in the store for a while, until they found out that he couldn't read the labels on the boxes, old George covered up for him but it was no good. Anyway, Richie gets to work and he says to old George the storeman 'Do you think I should let the first aid man have a look at this?' and showed George his prick. Well, old George nearly collapsed. The thing was all swollen and enlarged, mangled and twisted. It was a terrible sight, all discoloured and bloody. George says he'd seen nowt like it since his honeymoon. It was caught tight in the lad's trouser zip and it wouldn't budge at all. Been like that since the previous Saturday morning, Richie told him. Two days and nights. Terrible. Just imagine it."

"No thanks," said Harry shuddering. "It doesn't bear thinking about."

"Puts your little scratch into perspective, don't it?" smiled Alan.

"What happened to him then?" asked Harry.

"They got the medical attendant to look at it and he called an ambulance right away. He'd never seen anything like it either. Terrible mess. They had to cut his jeans off and sedate him to remove the zip," Alan mused. "It took seven stitches to patch him up."

"Seven?"

"Aye, he's a big lad. Anyway, it was no wonder he got it caught, waving a thing like that about, bloody dangerous. He was off work for a fortnight. Still, as long as it's okay for the wedding night."

"Oh aye, the lad's getting married soon isn't he? Silly bugger," said Harry again and laughed.

"Whose turn is it?" asked Alan, his eyes darting from Harry to the bar and back to Harry again.

Harry remained silent.

"Then it must be mine, I suppose," Alan said, as he got up and walked to the bar still chuckling.

Richie returned from the toilet and sat down, hoping that the topic of conversation had moved on from his private parts. But Harry wasn't finished with him.

"Your chopper fully recovered, has it? It'll be alright on the night, eh? You know, on the wedding night, lad? It's not long now is it? The wedding I mean, not your chopper," Harry said smiling.

"Aye, that's right, not long now," Richie said uncertainly, adjusting the position of his spectacles on his nose with a finger.

"Does your future bride know what she's letting herself in for then?"

"What do you mean?" Richie asked, his face again turning the colour of a turkey cock.

"Well, you should warn her about that thing, if it's as big as Alan says it is, then you might very well do her an injury with it," Harry said winking at Alan who had returned with the pints.

"Get lost, Harry," Richie said. "It's not that big."

"Still, I suppose she's already seen it, eh?"

Richie's face coloured even more as Harry went on, "Aye, it's only natural like, I suppose. Two young people getting married shortly, they're sure to be at it like rabbits, eh?"

Richie, his face a bright scarlet, headed for the toilets again, and Harry and Alan laughed.

"You and the rest of the lads are all invited to the wedding you know, and your wives," Alan said. "Julie and Richie sent all the invitations out ages ago."

"Aye, our lass has been shopping for an outfit for weeks. And, she's got Elsie looking all over the town for something suitable. Still, it keeps her mind occupied, I suppose," Harry said. "Julie, is that her name?"

"Aye, that's what they call his bride to be. She's alright, a good lass, but she's not much brighter than Richie."

Harry nodded. "I suppose they'll want a wedding present? So that's the rest of the cable money gone."

"Don't worry, Harry. I've another couple of little jobs lined up that'll make us more money. Then, I've got this very big one in the pipeline. Now that one is going to make me very rich, and I'll see you alright, so don't you worry about anything."

Harry nodded silently. He'd known Alan for a number of years and had lost count of the 'big jobs' that he was going to pull. They all were bound to make him rich and set him up for life. All rubbish of course. Pie in the sky.

Harry and Alan watched Morgan and his friends drink off their beer and make their way out, noisily shouting their goodbyes to their acquaintances around the room, when Joe, Mickey and Trev entered the bar.

As usual, the obnoxious shop steward couldn't keep his mouth shut.

"They let anybody in here now, don't they, lads? The place has really gone down market. Anyway, what are you lot doing in here, I thought you were all skint?"

The three ignored the remarks and pushed past Morgan and his friends.

"Hey, I hear that you've got a new girlfriend, is that right?" Morgan said to Trev.

"Take no notice," Joe said nervously and tried to push Trev to the bar after Mickey, who was halfway to the counter.

"A musician eh? Must be posh. I've heard that they're the worst. Those posh birds. Plays with an orchestra does she?" He looked around to make sure that his friends could hear. "She play with them all together, or just one at a time?" Morgan said with a leer. "I'll bet they keep her busy eh? She good at blowing a horn, is she?" His friends laughed.

Trev looked steadily at Morgan. "Actually she plays the classical guitar, cello and the piano."

"The cello eh? Well, her legs will be the right shape for you then, won't they? Wide open like."

Trev made a determined lunge for Morgan, but was prevented from reaching him by Mickey, who had seen what was happening and had decided to intervene. He held Trev back by the shoulders.

"Don't let him get to you Trev, you'll only do something you'll regret, just calm down a bit," Mickey cautioned.

"The fat bastard's not worth the bother," Joe said under his breath.

Morgan turned to face them. "Turning into a right den of thieves this place is," he said loudly to his friends. "I think we're going to have to find somewhere else to drink until they do something about the clientele."

Harry, seeing what was happening, stood up and shouted in anger "Instead of finding somewhere else to drink, maybe you, Skinner, and the Yank should do something about getting the welders back to work."

Morgan's venomous eyes fixed on Harry's, as he allowed himself to be shoved through the bar door by his friends.

The trio made their way to the bar and bought drinks. Trev gradually calmed down and they joined the others at the table.

"You shouldn't have said that about the Yank," Alan said.

Harry nodded. "No. It wasn't very clever, me letting him know that we're on to them, but he made me mad. The big-mouthed bastard."

Alan, Richie and Harry lost no time in passing on to the others what they'd learned at Skinner's office the night before, and how they'd made their escape after being discovered. With their knowledge of the yard's layout, the McKennas had no real chance of catching them in the dark.

"You mean they want to disrupt the yard so that they can buy it for a song and then smuggle drugs into the country?" Trev said incredulously.

"That's right. If the deadline for the launch of this current ship isn't met, then the penalty clauses will kick in and the yard will go bust. This American syndicate will buy it for a song, and then set it up as an oil rig supply and repair yard. They'll bring drugs in with the legitimate materials that they'll be importing," Harry said, pulling his old Golden Virginia tin from his pocket.

"It's not a bad plan actually. A oil rig supply yard is ideal for the purpose," Alan said. "The American's got things organised very well, the McKennas will distribute the drugs while Morgan and Skinner run the yard and make sure that nobody gets too noscy."

"So, what can we do about it then?" Joe asked uncertainly.

"I think that we should go to the police," Harry said, rolling a cigarette.

"They won't believe us," Alan said.

"They will when they find the drugs," Harry said.

"But there's no link from the drugs to Chisholm or the McKennas. It'll be impossible to pin that on them unless they're caught with the stuff red-handed," Alan said.

"What about contacting this American syndicate and telling them what's going on?" Richie suggested.

"They're probably in on the deal," Alan said.

"Let's get this straight," Trev said. "They are going to sell the stash of drugs they've already got, and use the money for the initial pay-off to Skinner, Morgan and the McKennas. It's their payment for causing the strikes and setting up the takeover, is that right?"

The others affirmed that that was the plan.

"Right then, all we've got to do is to take the drugs and then they can't sell them. And if they can't sell them, then they've got no money for the pay-off."

The others sat in silence for a few moments digesting Trev's thesis.

"They'll just bring more in, or find money from somewhere else for the pay-off," Joe said.

"Well, if it doesn't stop the takeover then at least it'll slow it down. I think Trev's right, we should nick the stuff," Alan said.

"What the hell do we do with the drugs then?" Harry asked.

"We could destroy them, or just hide them for the time being and keep them out of Chisholm's reach," Mickey said.

"How are we going to do that? We don't even know where the bloody warehouse is," Harry said.

"I've been thinking about that," Alan put in. "When I was playing snooker with the McKennas the other day, they mentioned something about an old church used as a warehouse in a village in Durham. I'll bet that's where the stuff is kept and I think we should have a look at it." He paused. "The only thing is though, if the drugs are there, then all of us have to do it."

"Do what?" Joe asked.

"Break into the warehouse and steal the stuff."

"I don't know about that," Joe said.

"Me neither. I don't want to get involved in a break-in." Mickey said.

Alan looked at Trev challengingly. "And I suppose you don't want to get your lily white hands dirty either, do you?"

Trev didn't answer.

"Well, either we all do it, or it's a no-go. I don't see why some of us should take all the risks, while you others just sit back and benefit."

None of the others wanted to be responsible for abandoning the idea to save the yard, and none could find a flaw in Alan's argument, so they reluctantly agreed to go along. Although they all had grave doubts about the theft, they were relieved to have agreed a solution, however vague and half-baked. With the decision made, the tension caused by the uncertainty dissolved and they began the real drinking.

"How did you get on at the doc's then, Joe?" Trev asked.

"Signed me off, hasn't she?"

"Signed you off?"

"Yes, I'm fit for work again. The results came back from the hospital. She said that the X-ray was negative. It showed no abnormalities, so I've not got an ulcer, just a nervous stomach. She's told me to stop smoking and drinking and avoid greasy foods. Stop drinking, I ask you? I wouldn't care, but my stomach really is playing me up now."

The others commiserated with him.

"What do you think about giving Alan here money to put on this dog then?" Joe asked the company in general, changing the subject, as he put a couple of stomach pills in his mouth and washed them down with beer.

"Well, I don't really know. It could very well be a bit of a con, couldn't it?" Trev said, looking at Alan.

"Come on, lads, you know that I wouldn't rob you."

"You're the biggest thief in town, why should we trust you with our money?" Trev said.

"When is this dog running, anyway?"

"Next week. Don't worry, I'll let you know well in advance so that you can scrape up the stake money."

"You're asking an awful lot you know, Alan," Harry said earnestly.

"What do you mean?"

"Well, you're asking us to hand money over to you without us knowing which dog you're going to put it on."

"So?"

"What do you mean, so? Your reputation isn't exactly one hundred per cent unblemished around here now, is it? And you expect us to trust you with our money?"

"I'm not the only one that has a bad reputation where money is concerned," Alan replied, and Harry, realising he was referring to him, looked down at the floor sheepishly.

"And at least I wouldn't steal from you guys, you're my mates." Alan finished indignantly.

There was something in the way that Alan had said that sentence that they instinctively recognised as genuine. Trev nodded his head. "Okay then Alan, I believe you this time. The lads are going to trust you with the money. Just don't let us down alright?"

Alan nodded. "Don't worry, you'll all get your stake back plus a lot more besides, believe me."

"And you lads will all get your money back that I borrowed from the holiday fund," Harry put in quickly.

"Look Harry, I didn't mean what I said just now. We all know why you took that money; to give your lass a holiday when you found out that she was ill, so don't worry about it. There's not a man working in the yard that would have done any different," Alan said.

"You'll all get your money back," insisted Harry.

The yard raiders were spending, and drinking, freely now and the mood was well and truly set. They threw the remainder of their ill-gotten gains into the centre of the table and declared that it was to be used as a general kitty for all their drinks, including the newcomers. A lot more drinks followed, bought by the newly, and very temporarily, wealthy group.

Most of the men's social contact with each other was generally associated with drinking alcohol. Traditionally the bars of the workingmen's clubs and the pubs were places where men could meet, relax, socialise and indulge in their shared favourite pastimes of dominoes, darts, gambling and smoking. They could discuss work, football, horse and dog racing and swear profusely without fear of offending any female ears. Any man who temporarily couldn't drink because he was taking medication, or had medical problems that forbade it, would still turn out with his mates and drink pints of orange juice, which was generally considered to be an acceptable substitute. A man who didn't drink was looked upon as a bit odd, and generally became something of an outcast, an outsider, tolerated, but definitely not one of the lads.

The men, their tongues loosened by the alcohol, told stories of the various yards they'd worked in and the characters they'd worked with. Every story growing in exaggeration.

Underneath the humour there was a hint of anger. The anger of an underclass being exploited by the fat cats. Not only were they exploited by their bosses, but also by their workmates. The tradesmen got the lion's share of the wage bill, while they were paid buttons. The labourers also had a sneaking suspicion that the union was exploiting them for its own devious political reasons. The conversation turned to the current dispute and previous ones. The general consensus of opinion was that the tradesmen earned far too much money and were prepared to walk out for very little reason at the drop of a hat.

Some, but by no means all, of the men would take advantage of any weakness or flaw they could find, getting away with as much as they possibly could. Work was a necessary chore they had to do to keep a roof over their heads and food on the table. If they could, they would leave work early. They would not turn in at all if they could get someone else to clock their time cards for them. If someone clocked them in and out so that they still got paid without working, then that was fine. It was one small way they could redress the balance of fate that always seemed to be stacked against them.

If they could they would pilfer the copper in the welding cables, the tallow soaked wood for firewood, or the paint meant for a completed ship. Good waterproof paint was always in demand, even if sometimes the colours were a bit drab. The paint was robust, strong and long lasting. The outside of the Mason's Arms was at that very moment covered in a rich navy blue waterproof paint that would last virtually for ever. The general consensus was that brickwork would go before the paint, as the paint wasn't originally intended to be used on the Mason's Arms or any other pub or building, but for the hull of a private yacht, which happened to be in the yard for a refit when the Mason's needed repainting.

The day wore on and the drink took its toll on the men's intellect and speech, which was now noticeably slurred. They'd all done their fair share of night shift and were telling stories of dark deeds committed on that gloomy shift. Harry was recounting a tale about a whole deck unit that was built in the shed, under cover because of the bad weather.

"It was complete and ready to be moved outside onto the berth and fitted onto the boat. The cranes were ready and lifted the unit onto a low loader for transportation. All went well, it was lifted on, settled, secured and ready to move. The low loader with its huge burden trundled slowly out of the shed."

Harry could be quite eloquent with his words, thought Trev. Out loud he said, "Away man, hurry up, we haven't got all day."

"It moved smoothly and quietly and all seemed well when there was an almighty crash. The low loader ground to a halt. At first nobody realised what had happened, but it soon became obvious, the top of the unit had hit the top of the door. It was too bloody big to get out. A full eight foot had to be cut off the top to be able to get the thing out of the shed. The burner was on the job a good three hours. He didn't want to bugger it altogether, just take enough off the top so it could get out. They did it eventually, but there was hell to pay the next day when the day shift came in and the general manager found out."

They all laughed.

As Harry drank deeply from his pint glass he became aware that Mickey was somewhat subdued, and although laughing in the right places wasn't really enjoying himself and not taking any part in the conversation, in fact he'd said very little since he came in. The others were entirely engrossed in a story Joe was relating.

"What's wrong Mickey? You look a bit down, mate," Harry asked quietly.

Mickey was taken by surprise. "Oh. It's nothing, just this assault charge and the lack of money, you know? Tracy's making herself ill with worry. What with Christmas nearly here and the kids wanting this, that and the other. Now that I've chucked that doorman's job I'm feeling the pinch more than ever."

"You did the right thing packing that in, mate. But don't you worry, you'll always manage somehow. Olive and me had the same trouble year after year at Christmas, the kids wanting toys and stuff. Then it's school uniforms and school trips here, there and every bloody where. Somebody is always coming with their hand out asking for more money."

Mickey nodded his agreement.

"The thing is though, son, they soon grow up, and that's when your troubles really start. The teenage years are the worst. Nowt but trouble they are when they're at that sort of age. I suppose it's all those hormones and things changing in their bodies that affect them. Then, just when get a bit of sense, when they're old enough to look

161

after themselves, they bugger off and leave you, don't they? Me and Olive haven't seen Debbie for seven years since she moved out to Australia, and Jim went to sea when he was seventeen and we haven't seen much of him since, just the odd week at home when he gets a bit of leave and a postcard from Singapore or wherever now and again."

He took another long drink of his beer, leaving the inside of the glass froth covered. "You spent all those years looking after them, working all the hours that God sends to earn enough to keep them, you spend all your money buying them clothes and toys, bikes and the like, and then they just up and off without a second thought about you." Drinking again, he almost emptied his glass completely. "I know that it's the right and natural thing for them to do, didn't I do the exact same thing myself? It's just that for years they are the centre of your life and they leave a bloody big vacuum when they're gone."

Mickey sat silently, surprised by Harry's emotional response. His kids leaving home had obviously affected him quite considerably. Mickey cleared his throat; naturally he hadn't given the subject any thought at all, his children being so young, and felt uncomfortable with the lengthening silence, and wanted to fill it. "Well, at least it gives you the chance to spend more time with your lass, to get out and have a drink and that." As soon as he had opened his mouth, he knew that he'd said the wrong thing, and he desperately tried to compensate. "When she's fully recovered that is…"

Harry smiled. "It's alright, Mickey, I know what you mean."

"I'll get the drinks in, thirsty work all this talking," Mickey said, as he picked up the empty glasses and money from the table, and headed gratefully for the bar.

"Hang on, I'll give you a hand," Alan said and followed him.

"How is she, then?" Trev asked Harry.

"Not too clever. The drugs are affecting her more and more, and she needs bigger and bigger amounts. I want to make sure that she has one good last Christmas, because she won't see another one. In fact I don't think that she'll see much of next year. It will really cheer Olive up when the family are over here for Christmas." Harry made a deliberate and noticeable effort to shake himself out of the maudlin mood. He sat upright in the seat, squared his shoulders, and rubbed the palms of his hands together briskly. "Right then. How are we going to get the money to make sure that we all have a good Christmas then?"

"Well, Alan, the master criminal, keeps going on about this dog scam being a sure thing, and then there's this big job that he's got lined up. I don't know if it's all bullshit or what, but he certainly seems to think that it's going to set him up with a lot of money alright," Trev said.

Mickey and Alan returned from the bar and distributed the drinks. Alan picked his pint up and went and sat down in the corner. Harry walked across and sat next to him. Trev watched as the duo talked earnestly and furtively, looking around frequently to make sure that there was no one within hearing distance. Alan produced a piece of paper and a pen and Harry looked on with great interest as he drew a diagram on the paper.

Joe moved over to where Richie was sitting. "You still on for that thing we talked about then?" he asked, "the rabbit hunt?"

Richie nodded. "Why-aye it's still on. I've arranged to borrow the bike and the dog and everything, but we'll have to leave early tomorrow morning."

"I'm really looking forward to getting out into the countryside. I fancy a nice rabbit stew, and if we catch a lot of them we might make a few pounds selling them around the doors."

"Great," Richie said enthusiastically.

"Your dad alright about it, is he?"

"Oh aye. He hardly uses the bike now, and doesn't bother with the dog at all. Won't even take it for a walk. It'll be alright, but we'll have to get an early start."

"What time is early?"

"Well, we'll have to be long gone before it gets light. Say about six o'clock."

"Alright then. I'll bring some sandwiches and a flask of tea. Our lass makes great sarnies."

"You'd better put a lot of warm clothes on as well. It'll be freezing on the back of that bike."

"I thought it had a sidecar?"

"It has."

"Well, I'll sit in the sidecar then. It'll be a lot warmer in there, surely?"

"Oh aye it's a lot warmer alright, but the dog will be sitting in there, won't she? Can't let the dog get cold, that's a valuable animal, that is."

"The dog's in the side car while I'm freezing my bollocks off on the back of the bike? That's not right, is it?"

"'Course it is. If the dog gets cold she won't be able to catch us any rabbits, will she? Then that'll cost us a lot of money. Anyway, the dog can't very well sit on the pillion seat, can she? She'd fall off."

"Well, I've heard everything now. The dog gets pampered in the sidecar and I'm relegated to the pillion seat," Joe said, shaking his head.

17

Joe and Richie both had bad hangovers from the alcohol that they'd drunk the day before, but they were up early and met at the prearranged time. Joe had had a lot more to drink than he'd planned, but to his surprise his stomach was alright and not giving him any trouble.

Soon they were out of the city and travelling on country roads without the benefit of street lighting. The morning was cold and overcast and there was a strong breeze. The old motorcycle chugged gamely down the country lane, interspersing the clouds of thick black smoke from its exhaust with the occasional backfire for variety. These sudden, loud and unexpected noises sent the alarmed crows squawking from their trees, screeching their displeasure at being so rudely disturbed.

The riders were well muffled up against the cold December air, the driver with a crash helmet and thick goggles covering his eyes and an imitation leather, waterproof, ankle-length, coat protected him from the worst of the elements. His passenger, perched uncomfortably on the pillion, also wore a crash helmet pulled down tightly, and with much difficulty, over a multicoloured, knitted woollen hat.

Joe was almost entirely encased chin to toe, in a thick woollen greatcoat that his dad had been issued with during the Second World War. Brenda had said that he looked very smart in it, but she'd had that look on her face, and Joe had a very strong suspicion that she was making fun of him. It was a light khaki colour, and still had the original brass buttons right down the front, although they would have benefited from a good polish. Despite the fact that the pockets had been removed sometime in the past to patch another similar coloured garment, he looked very soldierly and regimental. The coat was warm and the ideal colour for camouflage out in the bleak winter countryside.

The dog, a grey-blue coloured whippet, completed the party and had the best seat on the contraption, in the open sidecar. Richie had taken the obvious precaution of placing goggles on the dog's head to protect its eyes, giving it a permanently surprised appearance. The addition of an old, thick, woollen scarf wrapped tightly around its neck, seemed to Joe to be a trifle over the top, making the animal look like a Biggles impersonator on a bad day. There had been a heated discussion between Joe and Richie about who should wear the second set of goggles, and the dog had won. "If it gets something in its eye then it can't see, can it? And if it can't see, then it can't catch rabbits," Richie had reasoned without fear of contradiction.

The bike was a much sought after (so Richie's father said) old Triumph Tiger Cub of uncertain age, but certainly more than fifteen years old. It was well past its best, hadn't been looked after properly, didn't have a particularly powerful engine, and certainly wasn't the ideal machine to be pulling the extra weight of a sidecar attachment and the passengers.

The game old machine's less than ideal nature soon became apparent. When negotiating steep hills it was necessary for Joe to dismount and push the struggling machine up the hill, helping its ancient, labouring engine on its way and then jump back on before it got up too much speed at the top.

They got lost a couple of times and on each occasion it took them quite a while to get back on their intended course. Then the old Triumph broke down, coming to a sudden stop with much shuddering and smoke. It took a prolonged and sustained effort on Richie's part to get the machine mobile again. They finally arrived at where they thought that they had the best chance of catching rabbits, around lunchtime, and parked the machine at the side of the lane. Joe rechecked his map, and declared that they were in exactly the place that they should be, although Richie wasn't entirely convinced.

Finding a spot sheltered from the cold wind, they made themselves as comfortable as they could beside a drystone wall and opened the packet containing the sandwiches.

"Not long now for the wedding," Joe said, his mouth almost full of corned beef, onion, and bread.

"No."

"You looking forward to it then?"

"Suppose so," Rickie said hesitantly.

"Just suppose so?"

"Well, it's a lot of responsibility, isn't it, getting married?"

"'Course it is, but it's got a lot of advantages hasn't it? Otherwise no one would get married, would they?"

"What advantages?" Richie asked, munching contentedly.

"Well, it's nice being in a loving relationship. Looking after each other. Having kids, bringing them up. Each of you has a part to play in the relationship and you just, I don't know, work together, I suppose."

Richie nodded his head, but Joe wasn't sure that he understood.

"I mean, Brenda, she's the sensible one. She takes care of the money side of things. She makes sure that all the bills are paid and everything. And, that's not easy, things being like they are at work recently. She's also great looking after her sister, and that's a full-time job, believe me."

Richie was still nodding his head.

"Whereas me, well, I'm not much good with money, but I'm a good worker, and I take the money home. When the welders aren't out on strike I do anyway."

They ate half of their sandwiches and decided to save the rest for later. Joe gave the map and the remaining sandwiches to Richie to carry, as he had large pockets in his heavy leather overcoat.

"Julie's like your Brenda. She's good with money. Trouble is she wants to put a deposit down on a house and I don't fancy lumbering myself with a mortgage for the next twenty-five years of my life. She'll have to stop working soon anyway, what with being pregnant."

"I didn't know she was pregnant, Richie. You kept that quiet. Congratulations, you must be really proud to be an expectant father."

"Thanks. You and Brenda not having any kids, Joe?" Richie asked innocently.

Joe paused. "I'm not sure that I can have any, mate. We've been trying for years, but nothing has happened. Brenda keeps going on at me for us both to have tests done to see if there's a medical reason, but I'm not too happy about that."

"Why not? At least you'd know then."

"That's what I'm worried about. What if it's me?" Joe paused "But, about taking on a mortgage, I'd think long and hard first. It might be best to wait until things are sorted out at work before taking on something like that. It's no joke lying awake at night worrying about how you're going to make the monthly repayments."

The men lapsed into a period of silence, each with their own thoughts. Sheep were baaing in the distance and crows cried raucously, high in the trees.

"Thanks for spending time to show me how to write my name properly Joe," Richie said sincerely, breaking the stillness.

"That's okay, mate. Happy to help."

"I'd have felt a right prick at the wedding if I couldn't sign the register, what with everybody watching."

"Well, that's one thing that you don't have to worry about now, do you?"

"No. Thanks again Joe. It means a lot to me."

After drinking all the refreshing, hot tea from Joe's vacuum flask, the men set off purposefully over the fields in pursuit of their hopping game. They hadn't gone far before the first of a series of disasters struck. After walking only a few minutes they were all almost knee deep in dung. The sludge-like stuff had settled at the bottom corner edge of the field, and formed a sort of lake of liquid manure. The effluent lay just under the surface of a seemingly dry area of short grass and reeds, and the unsuspecting party had wandered right into the middle of it.

They extricated themselves as best they could. The men were covered in the dark stinking stuff up to the knees, and the dog was covered up to her stomach and absolutely caked in it. They squelched onwards, unhappy, smelly and soaked, but not bowed. They covered the five or six fields adjacent to a river's edge without seeing, or even finding a trace of an animal. There were no burrows, scrapings, or droppings, not a single sign of a rabbit. Then they got lucky, or thought they had. The dog caught sight of something away to the right and stiffened, straight as a ramrod, nose pointing and twitching, ears pricked alertly, and eyes staring at some point near a stone wall.

Richie slipped the dog's lead and it took off towards the wall like an arrow. The men ran after it and followed the animal up the hill. There was a narrow gap between the wall and a wooden gatepost, and the dog, intent on pursuing its prey, squeezed through the gap and turning right, disappeared from their view behind the inside of the wall. Joe reached the gap before Richie, and squeezed himself through sideways, as eager as the dog was to capture the prey.

He got through the narrow gap with difficulty, and turning right, was just in time to see the dog, tail between its legs, running back the way it had come, towards him. It ran as fast as it possibly could and was being chased by an enormous black bull. The bull had its head down and its yellowy-white, large, and noticeably very pointed horns, were in a primed position right behind the dog's backside. For a fraction of a second Joe stared in total disbelief at the drama being played out before his eyes, then he turned and dived for the gap through which he'd so recently entered.

He made to squeeze himself back through the gap the same way that he'd come in, but was somewhat thwarted in his attempt by Richie, who was coming the other way, trying to get into the field. The two men pushed and shoved for a brief second, until it became obvious that Joe was not going to be able to force his way through past Richie before the bull was upon him. Joe was too startled to say anything, even to begin to try to explain what was behind him, and anyway there was not enough time. Too full of fear to speak, and without the time to explain his predicament, he simply backed off a step from the wall, gripped the top of the gate, and with a tremendous lunge, vaulted over the gate.

Richie was surprised by his friend's actions. First Joe had tried to push him bodily out of his way, then when that didn't work he'd retreated back into the field, and thrown himself over the six bar gate, landing in a heap on the other side of the very muddy and manure covered gateway, where he now lay face down. Richie tried to make sense of all this as he stepped out into the field, finally free of the restraints of the narrow gap. He stood in the field and pulled his coat around him, and then he became aware of the dog. It shot straight through his legs and exited the field through the gap that he'd only recently vacated. Almost simultaneously he became aware of the reason for the above actions by Joe and the dog.

The instant he saw the bull Richie knew that he was a dead man. He let out a funny sort of high-pitched scream. He knew instinctively that there wasn't time to struggle back through the narrow gap, and so he set off across the field as fast as his legs would carry him with the angry, snorting animal in hot pursuit. Richie could almost feel the hot, moist breath of the beast on his neck as it chased him down the field. He felt the vibrations on the ground through his feet as the heavy animal charged behind him. He ran until he thought that his lungs would burst, and his legs would fall off. He ran like he'd never run before, because he was terrified like he'd never been terrified before.

He ran in a sort of tight circle, reasoning, as far as he could reason, (probably a more accurate description would be an instinctive knowledge gained in his desperate state of near panic), that he might shake off the bull by this manoeuvre, or at least make it back to the gap in the wall and get through it before being gored to death by his mad pursuer. In a sort of very limited way the manoeuvre worked quite well, but not well enough. The bull, with its head down so that it was almost touching the ground, had a very limited view of his quarry, and could only change direction very slowly, in a gradual turn. Sudden, abrupt turns were not possible for the large beast, and he managed to stay behind Richie only with the utmost difficulty, but stay with him he did.

Richie became aware of another sound that gradually entered his consciousness, above that of the bull's thundering hooves. At first he couldn't identify the sound, it was familiar, but eluded his recognition. Then he realised what it was, it was cheering. Joe, who from the safety of his vantage point behind the gate, was obviously sufficiently recovered from his recent dive into the effluent, and was cheering him on. The shouts got louder as Richie neared the gate. He was extremely aware of the bull right behind him, and put on an extra spurt to save his life. He thought that he might just make it. He could see Joe waving frantically at him, and the dog staring from beneath the bottom bar of the gate with wide eyes. He was only a yard or so from the gate, when the bull caught him.

Caught him is perhaps not the most accurate of descriptions in one way, but is perhaps quite adequate in another. The bull caught Richie with its head. The massive piece of bone and gristle hit him squarely in his backside. This assault, added to Richie's own momentum, had the startling and immediate effect of catapulting him high into the atmosphere, his legs still pummelling away in mid-air, as he flew in a soaring arc right over Joe and the dog and landed with an audible crunch six feet inside the gate.

The bull, now on a collision course with a quarry that was no longer there, had no time to stop, or even to think about changing direction, and hit the corner of the drystone wall, which crumbled like cardboard. After clipping the wall, the bull hit the gate with a resounding crash. The wooden bars splintered, and the gate disintegrated into matchwood. Splinters flew in all directions, and a large piece hit Joe, who had leaped to one side to get out of the way of the approaching beast, in the right buttock. It penetrated his thick overcoat and trousers and embedded itself a full half-inch into his flesh. Joe was only vaguely aware of this wound, as his whole concentration was centred on the bull, which was now, having smashed its way through the gate, in the same field with them.

The extremely annoyed beast stood towering over the inert figure of Richie. It pawed the ground with its front hoof and bellowed loudly. The sound was a primeval bellow of victory, the noise that an animal would make over its vanquished rival. The sound those sent shivers down Joe's spine and made his blood run cold.

"Bloody hell," he said out loud. "What do I do now?"

He debated whether to do the right thing and go to the rescue of Richie, who would surely be killed by the beast if he didn't, if he wasn't already dead that is, he thought warily, or to take his lead from the dog, who had made her own mind up as to the best and very necessary course of action. She had taken to her heels and now ran like an arrow towards a clump of trees at the bottom of the field.

The decision was taken for him, although he was sure that he would have chosen the right course of action anyway and rescued his friend, had he been given the time to come to a decision. The bull caught the movement of the dog out of the corner of its eye and took off after her down the field, much to Joe's relief. He forced himself out of the total terrified inertia that seemed to have paralysed him, and took a step towards where Richie lay in a heap. It was then that he became acutely aware of the splinter of wood embedded in his backside. The sharp pain caused him to come to a sudden halt, and he grimaced as he reached back with an investigative hand to explore the reason for the pain. Discovering the cause of his discomfort he grasped the protruding wood determinedly, and pulled it from his flesh. It came out cleanly, and left only a small wound that although painful, wasn't serious.

More or less mobile again, Joe reached Richie, and was relieved to find that his friend was still alive, and moaning. He helped the dazed man to his feet, and leaning on each other for support, they started to walk in the opposite direction from the one taken by the dog and the bull. They put the relative safety of the stone wall between them and the animals, and set off in what they hoped was the right direction to take them back to where they'd left the motorbike.

Every now and then they would call out for the dog, more in hope than expectation, Their efforts were eventually rewarded however, when the dog turned up, wagging her tail, and made it obvious that she was very pleased to be reunited with her human companions. She was in a terrible state, and Joe checked over her body for any sort of wound. He found no blood and she seemed to be free of any sort of injury, but was absolutely caked in dirt of the very worst sort, dung, mud and other, rankly smelling but unidentifiable mire.

They had travelled perhaps a quarter of a mile, keeping to hedges at the sides of the fields, when they became aware of sounds from behind them. Turning, they were astonished to see a figure, that they assumed was a farmer, running towards them. Not only was he running towards them, but also he appeared to be very angry, and waved a shotgun in the air as he shouted raucously and waved his fist, the one not holding the gun, in their direction.

The trio, assuming the worst, that the farmer was chasing them to demand payment for the damages to his gate, wall, bull, or all of the above, took off in double quick time, the dog leading, and ran into a large wood.

They ran deep into the wood and kept going even when it was obvious that they weren't being pursued. Stopping for a rest, and to get their bearings, they stood breathing heavily while they took stock of their surroundings and realised that they were totally lost.

"You've gone and done it this time," Joe said to Richie.

"What do you mean? It was you who came this way, not me."

"I didn't hear you arguing with me, did I?"

"Well; I thought that you knew which way you were going, didn't I. I'm not the map reader, am I?"

"The map!" Joe exclaimed. "Where's the map?"

"I don't know, you had the bloody thing, didn't you. You wouldn't let me even have a look at it."

Joe was sure that he'd given the map to Richie, but nevertheless he searched his inside pockets, and insisted that Richie do the same, but there was no map. It was lost. As an added bonus, they also realised that the sandwiches left over from lunch and also placed in Richie's pocket, had disappeared. "Great. That's all we need," he said, somewhat annoyed.

"Do we really need the map, Joe?"

"Of course we need the map. How else am I going to find our way out of this lot and back to the bike, without the map?"

"Well, we didn't use the map to get us in here, now did we?" Richie said with undeniable logic.

Joe knew that there was flaw in Richie's reasoning somewhere, but couldn't be bothered at that precise moment to look for it through the mysterious, weird and wonderful fairyland that passed for reason in Richie's tiny mind. Instead, he rubbed his chin ruminatively, and pondered what their next move should be. He took stock. They were lost in the deepest wilds of the English countryside, without the faintest idea of where they were. They'd lost their map, and didn't have any food, having lost that also. There was a wild farmer whose main intent at this precise moment was to kill them with a shotgun, after relieving them of monetary reimbursement for damages to his wall, gate, and livestock. He couldn't immediately think of anything else to add to their list of troubles. He looked at Richie, and Richie looked back at him, searching his face for some sign of hope. "We're done for, Richie lad," Joe declared. Richie believed him.

They finally found their way out of the wood very late in the afternoon. They'd made many stops to get their breath, bearings, and to listen for any sign of the farmer, and the weak sun was low on the horizon when they emerged from the trees within sight of a rutted farm track.

"Which way's the farm, that's the problem." Joe said. "We don't want to go trotting up the wrong way and arriving at the farmhouse to be greeted by John Wayne shooting from the hip, now do we?"

Richie readily agreed that they didn't want that at all. Joe didn't waste time trying to make a decision; he simply tossed a mental coin, checked which way up it fell, and walked off in that direction, ignoring the other route entirely. The track went up a hill and disappeared into another clump of trees and they unhesitatingly followed it.

It was definitely getting darker now, and the shadows lengthened as they pushed on up the track, further into the dense woodland. They stopped, exhausted and hungry, and almost at the point of despair.

"I don't think that we've got much choice now, Richie. We'll have to go back the way we've come and chance running into the farmer."

Richie had no option but to agree. He had no wish to be stuck out in the wood, or even the open countryside for the night. The very thought of it was causing him some mental distress already. They stood, brushed off the worst of the muck from their clothes as best as they could, and prepared to set off back down the track, when they heard a sound. It was faint at first, but then it repeated itself and seemed to get louder. Joe strained his ears toward the direction it seemed to come from. The sound was repeated.

"That sounds just like…" Richie said, amazed.

"I does, doesn't it, but it can't be? Can it?"

They both listened patiently and were again rewarded with the same sound. "It is. It's an ice cream van's chimes," Joe said as he started to run in the direction the chimes. Turning a corner of the track, they were both astounded to enter a cleared picnic area, complete with swings and a slide for children, wooden picnic tables, a pink-coloured ice cream van, and even toilet facilities. The only thing missing was fairground rides. In the distance, above the treetops, they could see the roof and chimneys of a large house.

"Well; I'll be…" Joe said under his breath. "Can you believe this?"

There were a few kids still in the play area, but the light was fading fast and their parents were in the process of rounding them up. The bedraggled pair made their way across the car park to the ice cream van.

"Any chance of a bag of crisps or something?" Joe asked, more in hope than expectation.

"Any chance of you paying for it?" The vendor replied, looking down at the pair with disdain. "No, I didn't think so."

"Look mate, we've got money you know, but it's just that we're temporarily financially embarrassed," Joe said.

"Aye, well, I'm also financially embarrassed, but permanently, not temporarily, 'cos I give stuff to people like you who can't pay. Now sod right off," he replied with finality.

"Okay. Forget the crisps. Can you direct us? How do we get back to the road that runs alongside the river?" Joe asked.

"The river road? That's easy. Walk out of the car park by that gate over there," he pointed the gate out to them, "and then turn left. Go about two hundred yards along the road and you come to a T-junction. That's the riverside road."

"By the way, what are you doing out here in the middle of winter selling ice cream?" Richie asked.

"Well, that's a story and a half that is." The man sighed loudly. "I'm supposed to be here selling hot-bleedin'-dogs and burgers and chips to the visitors attending the county house auction sale," he motioned his head sideways indicating the large building that they'd seen through the trees. "Only the bleedin' burger van broke down didn't it? And rather than lose the concession here, which I'd already paid for, I thought that I'd turn up with my ice cream van instead." He sighed loudly again. "Of course I was hoping for some good weather, perhaps a bit of sun, and maybe sell some ice cream and crisps, or even cigarettes, you know, it would have been better than nothing wouldn't it? But it never materialized, did it? There's only been a dozen people here all day, and it's been bleedin' freezing."

"You haven't sold a lot of ice cream then?" Richie asked quite needlessly.

"No, I haven't sold a lot of bleedin' ice cream, but I've had quite a few clever bastards asking me why I'm here in the middle of bleedin' winter selling bleedin' ice cream," the vendor said with surprising venom.

"Probably just as well then really," Richie said innocently. "It would have made your hands all cold serving freezing ice cream, wouldn't it?"

Joe, realising that the man was becoming dangerously angry, pulled Richie, who was preparing to ask the man another question, away from the van. "Right then, Richie, let's get back to the motorbike, eh?"

The pair set off immediately, and they were soon heading for the riverside road, which they could see plainly right ahead of them. They were overtaken by the ice cream van as they neared the bridge, and the driver gave them a peal of his chimes as he passed. Greensleeves faded into the distance with the noise of the van's engine, leaving only a smell of burnt oil and a smokey trail from its leaking exhaust, hanging, and slowly dispersing, in the cold evening air. The pair were left in the hush of the darkening countryside. A blackbird sang its evening territorial song in preparation for the oncoming darkness.

They reached the T-junction and looked up and down the road. "Which way?" asked Richie.

"Well, It's a good bet that van's heading back to town, and we didn't pass this turn-off on the bike, did we? So I'd guess that that's the way the bike is," Joe said, nodding in the direction the van had taken.

They trudged up the road, now in almost total darkness. "It's creepy, this is," Richie said with feeling, looking around at the darkening hedgerows.

"There's a lot to be said for city life alright, the old street lights and regular buses," Joe said.

"At least you can see where you're going."

They walked for almost half an hour without incident, except for a bat, or a bird or something scaring them half to death by flying silently just above their heads. Both men were startled by the flying thing, but concealed their nervousness from their companion, and eventually regained their composures. A light mist began to rise eerily from the ground.

A little further on they literally stumbled over the bike. It was where they'd left it parked on the grass verge. The two were absolutely overjoyed to find their only means of transport out of the wilderness. They were both freezing, cold through to the bone. Their lower legs and feet were still sodden with the effluent that they'd found themselves in earlier, and they were ravenously hungry, not having eaten since the couple of sandwiches they'd had at lunchtime.

"Thank God for that!" Joe exclaimed with heartfelt relief, as he sat exhausted on the pillion seat of the motorcycle. Richie almost fell as he straddled the bike, and there were tears in his eyes as he pulled on his helmet and leather cycling gloves. The dog needed no encouragement, and jumped straight into the open sidecar. Richie began the starting process, switching on the fuel switch, and pulling down the kick-start handle, when a figure loomed suddenly out of the darkness in front of him.

"Oh!" Richie exclaimed, jumping involuntarily.

"What?" Joe began, when he too saw the figure emerge from the mist. "Bloody hell, it's the farmer."

"That's right. I thought that you two would be back for the bike sooner or later. But I expected you back a lot earlier than this. I've gone and missed my tea now, because of you two conniving robbers."

"Now you look here," Joe started, but he was forced to shut up when the farmer pushed the large, long barrelled shotgun towards him.

"You just keep your mouth shut. You town folk think you own the whole country. You come here and run riot across my land, scaring my stock, and damaging walls and gates. You know that the bull injured itself chasing you two, eh? That beast is worth a fortune, it is, and if any lasting damage has been done to it you'll be paying for it. I want your names and addresses and proof that you are who you say you are before you leave here." He was getting more and more irate, and started to wave the gun about in a wild manner.

Joe swallowed hard. "Look mister, we didn't mean to do any harm to your bull, or to anything else, it just happened that way. The beast chased after us, that's all."

"Don't you tell me lies, you sly thieving criminals! I've seen the likes of you on the television. Think that you're clever, do you?

Well, I've got something here that will make you think different."
The farmer pushed the gun nearer to Joe's face.

Joe, intimidated by the gun in his face and the irate farmer's
threats, decided not to wait and see whether he was bluffing or not.
He grabbed the gun barrel, pushing it up and away from his face.
The farmer tried to pull back the gun from Joe's grasp, and it went
off.

There was an ear-splitting explosion, and a brilliant flash of light
that lit up the struggling men. Luckily the barrel had been pointing
skywards and the shot fired off harmlessly into the night air, sending
nestling pigeons flapping heavily skywards in alarm. Joe was
momentarily stunned, and almost deafened, but didn't relinquish his
hold. The men staggered backwards and forwards, wrestling for
possession of the firearm.

Richie, looking on, almost blinded and deafened by the
explosion, still hadn't fully recovered his wits when the second
barrel went off. This time the majority of the shot hit the sidecar. It
went in at the front, low, and blew the front panel clean off the
machine, leaving a wide gaping hole in the fuselage.

The dog, startled by the nearness of the explosion, leaped out of
the sidecar and took off down the road as if the demons of hell
themselves were chasing her, disappearing from sight in the mist.

The second discharge of the shotgun seemed to quiet the farmer
immediately, and the fight went right out of him. Joe pushed him to
the ground, and pulling the gun away from the shocked man, he
threw it by the barrel as far as he could over a wall and into a field.

"You stupid bastard, you could have killed us all with that thing!"
he shouted at the cowering man. Joe's hands were shaking so badly
that he put them in his pockets in an attempt to steady them.

Richie walked to the front of the sidecar and examined the
damage. "My dad will go spare when he sees this, Joe. He'll kill
me."

"If we don't get away from here fast, this mad bastard might kill
you before Jackie does." Joe said, jumping on the bike. "Come on,
let's get out of here fast, before the twat finds that gun."

"But what about the dog?"

"She'll have to look out for herself. It's through her that we're in this pickle anyway."

The bike started first time, and Richie lost no time in releasing the clutch, and accelerating away from the still muttering farmer.

The dog was standing trembling about a half a mile up the road. Richie could quite easily have knocked her over, but saw the terrified animal, captured in the headlight, just in time. She jumped into the damaged sidecar, not waiting until the machine had stopped moving, and they were off again, heading back to the town. Joe leaned over and retrieving the items from the floor of the sidecar, put on her goggles, and wound the thick woollen scarf around her neck.

The bike didn't let them down and they didn't stop until they reached the outskirts of the town, where the streetlights banished the darkness. They inspected the sidecar, which was a sorry mess. The damage would entail a major repair job. The hole in the front was wide and surrounded by numerous other smaller holes where the shot had spread.

"The dog must be freezing," Richie said. The dog did indeed look perished, even wrapped up in the scarf.

"We'll take the sidecar off the bike, and take it into the yard to get welded when we're back to work," Joe said. "Jackie doesn't use the bike that much, does he? He won't miss it for a while. I'm surprised that he lent it to us really." He looked closely at Richie. "He does know that we've borrowed it, doesn't he?"

"Well, not exactly."

"What do you mean, not exactly?"

"Well, I was going to tell him, but I somehow never quite got round to it, you know?" Richie added lamely.

They drove to the road where Jackie lived, and dismantled the sidecar from the motorcycle, leaving the cycle propped up against a small wooden box of about the right height at the back of the garage, so that Jackie would believe that everything was as it should be if he gave only a cursory look inside.

Richie disappeared inside, taking the dog with him. He borrowed some money for a fish supper and then rejoined Joe. They walked to the nearby shop for fish and chips. They were probably the best that the friends had ever tasted in their lives, and they made short work of them, eating them with their dirty fingers, from greaseproof paper wrapped in old newspapers, and drenched in salt and vinegar.

18

As almost all of the men's money-making schemes had come to nothing, they were putting all their faith, and the little money they had left, into Alan's much awaited greyhound scam. They hoped that their investment would prove to be financially rewarding and that Alan's integrity to his friends would be proven. Some of the group were almost inclined to ensure the latter by following him closely at the dog track after handing over their money to him, but they thought better of it.

Julie polished the glasses absent-mindedly. She'd worked as a barmaid at the dog track for over three years now and was seriously considering a change of employment. She was sick and tired of the sight, sound, and smell of the bar, the customers and the dogs. She looked at the clock above the bar. Half past seven. She automatically started to fill a pint glass with lager. Richie saw her there five nights a week, which was the number of nights she worked. He generally went straight to work from the track at about half past eight, and changed into his overalls at the yard, but due to the lockout, he was now staying until closing time. As the amber liquid settled into the glass Richie walked into the bar. He held a copy of the local evening paper open at the greyhound section, which he was studying with interest as he crossed to the counter.

"I expect you'll want the usual?" Julie asked.

"Yes, please," Richie said, straddling a barstool, still engrossed in the paper. As he could really only read with difficulty, he found his way around the racing page slowly. He could understand the runner's names and numbers, the distances they'd run over previously, and the abbreviated form symbols, but he couldn't read a sentence of news, even news about greyhounds.

"Did you get it?" Julie asked, placing the drink on the bar in front of Richie, wiping up the excess liquid form the bar surface, and ignoring the money he proffered.

"Er, no. Not exactly." Richie said, looking at her over his glasses somewhat sheepishly. He picked up the glass and drank some of the lager.

"What do you mean, not exactly?" Julie demanded.

"Well I didn't have time, I'll get it next week."

"But the wedding is only two weeks away."

"Saturday. I'll call in and get it during the week. I promise."

"You promised me faithfully that you'd get it today."

"I know, but I didn't have time. I had to give Alan a hand, didn't I? And the shop closed at half five," Richie explained hurriedly.

"Oh yes, you haven't got time to collect your new suit, but you'll always find time for Alan."

"It was pouring down. He'd have been absolutely soaked if I hadn't helped him."

"I'm not getting married to you if you look like a tramp in your old clothes, just because Alan didn't want to get wet."

"I've told you I'll call in and get the suit during the week. It'll still be there, don't worry."

Julie was decidedly not happy, as she moved away to serve someone else; she kept her disapproving eyes on Richie as he removed a race card from his pocket and ran his practised eye down the list of runners for the first race, comparing the details with those printed in the evening paper. Julie returned and resumed her confrontational position directly in front of Richie.

"The dress I picked looks beautiful," she said, a dreamy smile on her face.

"The number three looks good in the first race," Richie said, scanning the form.

"I ordered it from the catalogue this morning. It's sort of off-white colour, with ivory lace bits and everything," Julie continued. "I wish that we were getting married in a church with a long white wedding dress and everything instead of the registry office at the civic."

"That number five might be a danger though, it was second last time out," Richie mused.

"I'll look really lovely with it on. I showed the catalogue to Kate this morning," Julie persisted. "She was dead jealous, you could tell, but she had to say that it looked really lovely."

"It'd be a better price than the favourite anyway," Richie said, seemingly oblivious to Julie's comments, obvious exasperation, and growing annoyance.

"The bridesmaids' dresses looked really lovely as well."

"I think I'll take a chance on it," Richie said, drinking the remaining amber liquid from the pint glass.

"They're all in pink, the four of them."

"Same again please," Richie said, placing his empty glass on the bar counter, the froth still clinging to the sides. "And anyway, I thought that we'd agreed that a registry wedding was better, no fuss and expense?"

Julie walked to the pump, and refilled the glass. She returned and placed it in front of Richie, who had again turned his attention back to the race card.

"We can't afford any expense. We can't really even afford to hire the club for the reception," he said.

"We can. Dad got the club cheap 'cos he knows the steward. And anyway, just because we're getting married in a registry office doesn't mean I can't have bridesmaids."

"Hmm."

"Kate and Simon are buying a house on that new estate when they get married next year." This remark was evidently serious enough to evoke a response from the taciturn Richie.

"Cost a fortune them houses and that place is out in the wilds," he said dismissively, shaking his head. His whole demeanour suggesting that living there, three miles outside of the town was at the ends of the earth, and that anyone who even considered living in such an out of the way place was absolutely crazy.

"They're lovely houses."

"Too far away, they're at the back of beyond."

"There will be a lovely view from the back windows when they're built. They'll be able to see right over all the fields and everything. There's even a small wood right outside of where the back gardens will be. There'll be trees and flowers, and everything."

"Too handy. That's just what the burglars like. It's ideal for them to get in and out quick. Then they're off through the wood and over the fields. Criminal's paradise that place will be."

"Well, your cousin would like that then, wouldn't he?" She said, and was about to add more, but Richie gained a brief respite as Julie was called away to serve someone else. However, she soon returned.

"All Simon's friends from work will be at our wedding," she said, changing tack.

"Hmm."

"They all work in offices."

"I couldn't work inside an office all the time," Richie said, standing up straight and squaring his shoulders, as if he'd often had the opportunity. "That's not proper work, anyway. They don't make anything, do they? Not like building ships, or making engines now, is it?"

"They go to work in suits and ties."

"I always feel restricted when I've got a tie on."

"They always look very smart though."

"Hmm," Richie said, apparently losing interest.

"And they're never on strike or laid off or anything."

"That's 'cos they do nowt," Richie said irrationally.

"I wish that I could get a better job than this," Julie sighed, looking around despondently.

"What's wrong with working here, then?" Richie asked, looking somewhat shocked,

"What's wrong with working here, in a dingy, dirty, smelly bar in a dog track?" Julie asked incredulously. "Nothing at all, if you like this sort of place, I suppose. But sometimes it can be just a little bit boring," she said with more than just a touch of sarcasm.

"Boring?" exclaimed Richie, her sarcasm going right over his head. "How can anyone possibly be bored in here? There are all these races going on every night. The excitement, the different dogs, the chance to win money." He shook his head in wonder. "How can you ever be bored?"

"I'm sick of the sight of this bar and greyhounds. Kate says that there's a vacancy coming up soon at her place. The money would be better, and it's nice and clean. The office is high up on the top floor, and she says that she can see right across the town from her desk."

"Speaking of money, you see your Uncle Tom today?" Richie asked, suddenly conspiratorial.

"Yes."

"Well?" Richie said impatiently.

"Well what?" Julie asked, confused.

"Well, did you get the tablets?" Richie asked, dropping his voice, and looking around furtively like a pantomime character during a performance.

"Oh, the tablets, yes I got them. He gave me three and a tenner to put on the dog," Julie said, taking her purse from her handbag, which she'd retrieved from under the bar counter.

"Great. Pass them over. Alan's coming in soon."

"They'll not hurt it, will they?"

"Of course not. They don't hurt your Uncle Tom do they, when he takes them?" Richie said, examining the small red pills in his hand.

"No, but greyhounds are different."

"The pills will just speed it up a bit that's all. Just like they do for your Uncle Tom's heart."

"How are you going to get the dog to take them?" asked Julie.

"Don't you worry about that. Alan will know what to do. He's done it before, loads of times."

"How will Uncle Tom know which dog his money is on?"

"He won't know silly. Only Alan knows. Tom gave you the stake money, you gave it to me, and I'll give it to Alan, and he'll put the bet on for him, along with our money."

"Don't you trust Uncle Tom then?"

"Of course we do. No, it's not that, but we don't want word getting out about this. The more people that know about it, then the more people will bet on that particular dog. That'll affect the odds, and bring the price down," Richie explained.

"Are you sure these little tablets will make it win?" Julie said, looking at the pills doubtfully.

"Of course I am. You don't think that I'd bet all that money of ours on it if I thought that there was even a faint chance that it might lose, would I?"

"How do you know that Alan will put the money on for us, if we don't even know what the name of the dog is? He could just tell us that it had lost and we'd be none the wiser."

"Because he's my cousin and my mate, that's why."

"How much money do you think we'll win?"

"I don't know exactly. It depends on how much we can scrape together to bet on the dog. The more we put on the more we'll win."

"It would be nice to win enough to buy a house like Kate's," mused Julie.

"Then it depends on what the odds are. It'll be an outsider so it should be a very good price."

"I could see us living next door to her and Simon."

"The longer the odds are, then the more we'll win," enthused Richie.

"It's really not that expensive," Julie maintained.

"If we put say £20 on, and it comes in at 20 to 1, that would make us £400." Richie might not be able to read and write properly, but he could certainly count money and reckon the odds.

"How much would we get back if we put £100 on?" Julie asked, suddenly very interested.

"Don't be silly. Where would we get £100? It's cost us everything that we've saved to pay for the wedding. Have you got money tucked away somewhere that I don't know about?"

"I might have," Julie said defensively. "If we did put the £100 on, how much would we get back?"

"Well, at that sort of price, 20 to 1, say, £100 would give us, let's see now, £2,000."

"£2,000?" Julie said, her eyes wide.

"Yes. And we'd get the stake money back as well, if we paid the tax, so it would be £2,100 all together,"

"Kate's deposit on the house was only £1,000."

"Even if we had that sort of money, we couldn't bet that much on a dog. That would be too risky," Richie said, suddenly aware of the way the conversation was going. The last thing he wanted was to lumber himself with a mortgage, and have a millstone around his neck for the rest of his life. He'd seen what that sort of huge debt had done to Joe, and to others, and had no intention of taking such a commitment on at his age. He also had no desire to live next door to Kate and bloody Simon, or anyone even remotely like them.

"But they didn't pay out all of that money themselves, their families helped a lot."

"Anyway, those tablets aren't guaranteed to work, you know. Things can sometimes go wrong."

"Her father paid for most of it anyway."

"There's always a chance that the dog will lose the race, then all that money would be lost."

"£1,000 or so would be a tidy deposit on a nice house."

"Anything can happen in these races, and we can't afford to lose £20, never mind £100."

"If we won £2,000 then there'd even be enough left over to buy the furniture."

"These races can be fixed, you know," Richie said without a trace if irony. "Some of the dogs might even be drugged. Anyway, we haven't got anywhere near £100, have we?" Richie looked relieved when Alan, who had just arrived, joined him at the bar.

"Got the tablets?" Alan asked.

Richie gave the pills to him.

"Good, now what about the money? How much do you want on?"

"Well, I've got £20, and Julie's uncle has a tenner to bet." Richie said.

"Good, give me the money now, and I'll let you know the result tomorrow night, okay? The other lads have raised a few quid to go on as well, we'll all do very nicely out of this, cousin."

"Er, Alan," Richie said hesitantly.

"What?"

"Er, this is going to win isn't it? I mean that's all the money we've got, and the wedding's in a few weeks, you know."

"Look, don't worry. This has always worked just fine until now, and there's no reason to think that it won't work tonight, is there? Just sit tight and I'll bring you the winnings back tomorrow," he reassured Richie, tapping him lightly on the cheek with his open palm. "Just don't you forget to pass Uncle Tom's share of the winnings along to him."

The drugged dog did win, but at nowhere near the high odds that they were expecting. Alan duly paid out the winnings to all the lads, his reputation and integrity still intact, but with a faint question mark above it. It was generally suspected that he'd put the money on the drugged dog and then selected a much lower prices winner at the same meeting and told the lads it was the dog he'd put the money on. But, of course, they couldn't prove any of it.

Julie's Uncle Tom also duly received his winnings. Although not as high as expected, the money was gratefully received by everyone and put to very good use.

19

"I'm really worried about her, Trev."

"Is it her headaches again?"

"Aye, she's always got a headache, but now she's talking about ending it all. I've had to hide the tranquillisers in case she takes too many."

"Is her mother there?"

"Aye, but I can't leave her there on her own all night, I'll have to go back after I drop you off."

Trev and Mickey arrived at the club in good time, despite getting lost a couple of times on their way there. Mickey helped to carry in the gear and then immediately left for home, promising to come back for Trev later.

The club was one of the biggest and most popular in the region, and was full to the rafters. The concert chairman was much in evidence, and in a state of high excitement, probably because of the expected arrival of the strippers. He pointed out where Trev could change into his stage gear.

"I don't mind sharing a dressing room with the strippers," Trev joked to the man.

"I'm sure you wouldn't. But dream on, bonny lad. You'll either have to get changed in the gents' toilet or outside in the car park. There's nowhere else," he said officiously.

"What about the committee room, or one of those others, surely there's one of them free for a few minutes?" Trev said, slightly mesmerized by the glinting metal badges in the lapels of the man's jacket.

"'Fraid not, son, monthly Leek Club meeting in there tonight, they have a one every..."

"Yeah, every month."

The chairman ignored the remark and nodded towards the committee room. "And the committee has to sort the share-out ready for the weekend. Got to get the pint tickets calculated, you know."

"Work out the fiddle more like," Trev said.

"There's no need to take that attitude. Two-bit turn. Who the fuck do you think you are, Frank fucking Sinatra?"

"If I was Frank Sinatra what would I be doing a flea-bitten club like this?"

"Look smart arse, we've had top turns in this club. Bobby Thompson was booked here a couple of months ago."

"How did he go down?" Trev asked.

"We'll never know, he never turned up, did he?" the man said. "Anyway, if you want paying, then get yourself changed in the gents, do your turn, and then you can fuck off and don't come back."

Trev didn't reply to this remark with a response of his own, not from any sense of propriety, but simply because he couldn't think of an appropriate one. He walked to the gents and, locking a cubicle door behind him, changed in the confined space as quickly as he could. Encouraged by the success of his first solo club appearance, he'd invested in more stage clothes. He came back out into the concert room resplendent in his tasselled cowboy shirt, held at the neck by a thin black string tie fastened with a silver bull's head. Faded blue jeans held at the waist with a wide studded leather belt boasting a Bull Durham Tobacco logo buckle. The outfit was completed with high-heeled, brown, tooled leather cowboy boots, with pointed silver toe covers. Tonight he was billed as a country and western extravaganza.

He was told that he'd be on after the comedian, and before the first of the five strippers. Not that anyone of the audience minded in what order the turns were to perform. They were here for the strippers and the bingo. The vast majority of the crowd was made up of men. It was definitely a man's night and the few women in evidence were intently playing the bandits in the foyer, waiting patiently for the bingo to start.

He walked across the concert room to the bar and stood sipping lemonade and looked around at his prospective audience. The club was in the middle of the Durham and Northumberland coalfield and most of the customers were typical miners. Their unique and distinctive accent and vocabulary was referred to locally as pitmatic. Many of those sitting at the table were playing cards. A card game called Napoleon, or Nap for short, and it looked to Trev as if it was a regular pastime for the members.

He listened to the good-natured banter going on around him amongst the crowd, struggling sometimes to understand the broad accents. His stomach was uneasy, and felt like there was a large cold stone lodged in it. He always felt nervous before a performance, and particularly so tonight. It must be the pie and chips he'd had for tea, he reasoned.

"Look at this prick, lads. It's the fucking nine-stone cowboy. I hope you're the turn, coming in here dressed like that..." the loud voice was familiar.

Trev half-turned to face the speaker, a big pot-bellied man, accompanied by six or seven others, most of them similarly overweight, who looked around their spokesman's bulk at Trev with amusement. Trev looked hard at the man's face. It was none other than Morgan.

"...'Cos they don't let puffs in here." This second remark from Morgan brought an appreciative laugh from the group of men as they seated themselves with their drinks at a nearby vacant table.

"They must if they let welders in," Trev retorted quickly.

Morgan's entourage laughed despite the thunder-like expression on the welder's face. "Oh, it's you. You doing the clubs now then, are you? Suits you better than an overall, that big girl's rig-out does." Morgan looked around the room. "Where are your thieving mates, they going to do the club when it's shut, I suppose?" The group of men laughed again and Morgan made for their table.

"Arsehole," Trev muttered under his breath. He smiled directly at the man and out loud he said," Don't you worry, ducky, I'll not touch any of your boyfriends."

The fat man, so recently seated, started to stand up again, his piggy eyes narrowing dangerously as he stared hard at Trev. In his haste to get up he caught the edge of the table, and knocked over his almost full pint glass, the spilled beer soaking the front of his trousers. "Bastard!" he shouted, swiftly moving himself away from the still flowing liquid running from the tabletop.

"Testing one two, testing... Order please gents." The lights dimmed, and then went out completely, as the concert chairman appeared on stage with a radio mike in his hand. Trev took the opportunity to remove his presence from the bar to the foyer where he watched the rest of the introduction.

"Good evening, gentlemen. Before I announce the entertainment for this evening, I've got to remind the Leek Club members that it is their monthly meeting tonight. As always, the Jolly Boy's raffle tickets are on sale, Tony's coming round with them now. Buy plenty because the prizes are fantastic, aren't they, Tony? Well worth winning. Now then lads, we've got some really great entertainment for you tonight. A first class comedian, a country and western singer, and five, yes five gorgeous strippers."

"Best of order now for the first turn. First up tonight is a comedian so well known that he needs no introduction..." The compère looked behind him as if seeking inspiration. He looked to the side of the stage and walked sideways like a crab, his hand cupped to his ear. "Aye, that's right, now please give a big hand for... What was it again? That's right, got it now. A big hand for Charlie Chase."

The comedian walked on stage shaking his head. "Fucking good start that eh? Calls himself a concert chairman? Good job he's on the committee, and doesn't have to work for a living. He wouldn't last two minutes in a shipyard. And what are the fucking badges for eh? Fucking knots and needlecraft or what?" Who does he think he is, a fucking boy scout?

There was a shouted response from the audience. A few catcalls from the front of the room near to the stage. But most were continuing their conversations amongst themselves. The comedian told a dozen fast jokes, all blue, with a deadpan face and rapid delivery. He didn't go down very well, few people laughed. He was being tolerated, Trev realised. They were prepared to put up with him, until the time came for the strippers and the bingo. Trev made his way backstage, determined to just go through the motions tonight because there was no way he was going to get across to this crowd.

The comedian came off the stage to a deafening silence, shaking his head the same way he had when he'd gone on. "Fucking ignorant bastards," he said disgustedly. "Just whiz through your songs son and get off quick," he advised Trev.

"I intend to, mate."

The compère stood centre stage waving his mike around again. "I forgot to mention this earlier on, but there's a special committee meeting next Monday night to discuss the complaints about the cost of this year's Christmas decorations…"

The announcement was greeted with shouts of 'about time', and 'it's a disgrace', from the audience.

"…We all know what happened last year, and it won't happen again. I want to stress that all the receipts are here and available to be scrutinised by any interested club member." He paused and waited for the murmur of discontent to subside. "Also, we've had lots of complaints about letting women in for the bingo tonight. Alright, they are only associated members, but the committee has agreed to let them in." He raised his hand to stem the protests from the audience. "They are entitled to come in for the bingo if they want to. Because of this, the bingo will start as soon as the next turn has finished. The women will go out of the concert room straight after the bingo's finished, and the strippers will come on then. The raffles will be drawn after the first three strippers."

There was more protest from the floor of the room, but the concert chairman was adamant. "Look, there's nothing we can do about it. We've taken legal advice and they are entitled to come in here for the bingo regardless of what entertainment has been booked. If anyone makes any trouble they'll be banned from the club, sine die." He strode to the edge of the stage and appeared to be addressing a specific person in the audience. "You hear that Bobby Johnson? Be warned." He walked up and down the stage waiting for the mutterings of disapproval to diminish. He tapped on the top of the mike to command attention, while trying, with great difficulty, to maintain his dignity. He clumsily unfolded a piece of paper that he'd retrieved from an inside pocket. "Also, I've been asked to clarify the result of last Sunday night's raffle, as there seems to be a bit of confusion about it in some quarters. The winning ticket was 34 green. That's 34 green, and the prize is a divan suite. That's a divan suite, and not a diving suit as the compère announced. Thank you."

He walked off the stage quickly to uproarious laughter, totally forgetting, or perhaps too embarrassed to hang about and introduce Trev, who simply walked on stage himself behind the drummer and organist. The backing duo took their places at the back of the stage, each of them carrying a pint in each hand, which they placed carefully on the floor near their seats. Trev hadn't even had a chance to go through his repertoire of songs with them.

He started off a bit shakily, but the backing soon caught up with him, and he had to admit that they weren't bad; in fact they jammed very well. There wasn't any noticeable response from the audience at the end of his first number, even from Morgan and his mates, so he ploughed straight on and completed the whole range as quickly as possible, and got off stage. It was the fastest that he'd ever performed, and it was a relief to leave the stage.

The concert chairman pushed an envelope into his hand as he left the stage, and Trev shoved it into his jeans pocket without counting it. All he wanted to do was to get out of there and go home. He opened the door leading to the foyer and had to stand aside as three of the strippers came in. They walked past him without acknowledging him. They were all very attractive, obviously well made up and smelled of heady perfume. Trev was disturbed by their nearness as they passed. The last of the three looked vaguely familiar, and Trev's forehead creased in a frown, as he tried to remember where he'd seen her before. He studied the back of her head as the door closed behind her; she was definitely familiar but he couldn't place her.

He started to change as quickly as he could, half expecting Morgan and his friends to corner him in the gents. He hoped that they were occupied getting their bingo tickets. He didn't want any trouble with them or they'd most likely kill him, he thought as he changed.

Back in his street clothes he made for the door and carried his gear back to the van. He had intended to go straight home, but the brief sight of the strippers had unsettled him and he decided to hang around a bit and watch the show. He found Mickey outside, waiting in the van.

"After we get the gear in the van do you fancy coming in for the bingo, Mickey? It's good money, and we might as well, while we're here, eh? Come on, I'll buy the tickets."

Mickey thought about the proposition for a moment and then agreed. "Okay then, as long as we go when the strippers start."

They quickly removed the equipment from the side door of the club and stowed it safely in the back of the van.

They returned to the club and made their way to the foyer where the bingo tickets were on sale. As Trev waited in the queue to buy the tickets, he noticed that quite a few people in front of him weren't paying the full amount for the bingo books they bought. The committee man selling them simply handed over the tickets with a knowing wink and took half the proper price. Trev realised that they must be working a fiddle. Probably the committee man giving the books away at half-price would be in for a share of the prize money should any of his discounted price friends win. The seller obviously didn't rate Trev's chances of winning though, as he took the correct money from him. Trev found a spot at the edge of the bar where he and Mickey could watch the proceedings and mark their bingo cards without being interrupted.

The bingo, like everything else this evening was a farce. The concert chairman, who was displaying every indication of having suddenly developed acute and advanced dyslexia, was calling out the numbers. He'd apparently had trouble with the bingo machine in the past because he referred to the 'bother we had last week'. They'd had the machine overhauled and repaired, he said, and he hoped that there wouldn't be a repeat performance. But of course there was.

The concert chairman managed to get through the first game without any major disastrous incident, despite twitching nervously every time a ball appeared at the end of the tube. He lifted them all out as if they were bombs that might explode at any minute. He developed a pronounced stutter in the course of the first game, and his voice shook as he called the numbers out into the microphone. The first game complete, the books checked, there were two claims, and the caller started to relax a little and even attempted to crack a few jokes. This was tempting fate too far.

The second game was more sedate as everyone had now settled down and was concentrating on the game, instead of watching for something untoward to happen to the caller. Trev found he was only waiting for one number when someone called house. It was woman's voice from the back of the room, and a angry murmur went up from the men.

"The bloody professionals are in again!" someone shouted.

"Why don't you get yourselves to the bingo hall," another added.

The shout was genuine, and despite the-ill feeling from most of the participants, the woman was paid out.

"Now gents… and ladies of course," the caller corrected himself. "Now we come to the highlight of the night, the rollover jackpot. The prize for the house is £25 and the jackpot stands at £120. This will be paid out on a house along with the £25, if less that fifty numbers are called. If house is called after fifty numbers, then the £25 will be paid out, and £120 will be carried forward to next week."

There was a deathly hush in the room as he started to call out the numbers. He had regained his poise and confidence and grasped the balls firmly as they emerged from the end of the tube. Trev, caught up in the excitement, and with an eye on the £120 jackpot, was concentrating on the game, but couldn't help himself from mentally calculating the number of balls called. Twenty balls out and Trev had half his numbers crossed through. Forty numbers out and he was only waiting for two, twenty and forty-eight.

Trev glanced at Mickey's card and saw that he only had a few numbers crossed off. No good. He looked around and saw by the whispers and nudges going on at the other tables that a lot of other players weren't waiting for many numbers. The tension in the air was tangible. Trev was now waiting for one number, twenty, and he could feel the sweat forming on his brow. What he could do with £145. His eyes were drawn to the blower tube, as he tried to read the number of the next ball out through the narrow clear plastic tube. People around him were doing the same, and obviously were also waiting for only one number.

That's when it happened. The mechanism that held the ball in place at the top of the tube malfunctioned. Instead of holding the ball in place until it was required, it just spat the waiting ball into the air. The other balls, as they reached the top of the tube were also unceremoniously ejected with a force that was surprising in its velocity. The caller caught the first two ejected balls, but dropped them while trying to catch the other balls following them out of the tube. They were thrown high into the air, to bounce and ricochet from ceiling, walls, concert chairman, and the other committee men who ran on to the stage to try and contain the missiles.

The balls shot out into the audience and hit quite a number of people sitting near to the front. The committee men's amusingly acrobatic, but clumsy attempts to catch the balls only made things worse, as they inadvertently assisted the renegade missiles' trajectories as they tried to grab them, enabling them to achieve almost impossible distances around the room, which caused a great deal of consternation in the audience.

The whole room erupted, some people laughing uproariously at the absurdity of the situation, thinking it was the funniest thing they'd seen in years. Others, who were waiting for only one or two numbers, weren't so amused and made their complaints vociferously evident.

The situation was finally brought under control, not by someone turning off the compressed air box, which was the obvious thing to do, but because the box ran out of balls. The whole lot of them were now bouncing across the floor of the concert room, chased by a lot of people in various stages of high, but completely differing emotions.

The comedian went on for his second spot and shook his head disgustedly as he passed Trev. "What fucking chance have I got of getting a laugh up here with a concert chairman like that? You couldn't fucking make him up. He's a fucking accident waiting to happen he is. He's got more laughs tonight unintentionally than I've had in the whole of my last two gigs. He'd make a fucking fortune if he went professional. The man's a fucking master of slapstick comedy, and I've got no fucking chance here, man, I'm telling you. Fancy having to follow that prick on stage, eh?"

Trev and Mickey couldn't help but laugh, and had to agree that the man was a walking disaster, and could spoil the show for any comedian. The comedian did his spot and went down surprisingly well. Now that the bingo was out of the way, he only had the audience's natural apathy to contend with, plus a couple of raffle ticket draws, of course.

Trev and Mickey made their way to the bar in the semi-darkness of the concert room as the first stripper started. Ordering drinks at the bar, Trev turned and watched as she slowly stripped off until she was absolutely naked for a brief instant before the curtains closed in front of her. Her magnificent body, large round breasts, and hourglass figure were hugely appreciated by the audience, which shouted and yelled their approval and encouragement as she stripped.

"Come on, Trev, I thought we were going?" Mickey said.

"We can't go yet, mate. I've just got these in, and it's against my principles to leave any drinks unfinished." Trev was determined to remain at the bar and watch the other strippers perform before going home. "Anyway, if the first stripper was anything to go by, then we're in for a treat."

The second was even better than the first. "At this rate the last one should be like Marilyn Monroe," Trev said to Mickey, who was somewhat preoccupied watching the men sitting at the table in front of them.

"Here, you know you said that some fat bloke was giving you aggro, earlier?"

"Yes, it was Morgan," Trev said, his eyes and thoughts on the stripper.

"I thought he looked familiar. That him over there at that table?"

Trev looked around briefly dragging his eyes from the nearly naked woman on the stage. "That's him alright. Why?"

"They've all been looking over here and making comments. They're all laughing at something."

"They're real jolly souls, aren't they," Trev said, turning back to the stage. "Forget it, just watch the show and enjoy yourself. I don't think that he's seen you yet, mate."

Mickey returned his attention to the stripper, but glanced at the table every now and again.

The woman finished her performance totally naked and walked off-stage, this time without the benefit of any drawn curtains. The concert chairman, or whoever was operating the curtains seemed to be totally preoccupied and forgot what he was supposed to do. The resounding applause and cheers from the audience quieted as the next woman walked on stage. She strode on wearing a sort of sexy nurse's uniform with a ridiculously short skirt, fishnet stockings and six-inch stiletto heeled shoes. First off was her little white hat, which was closely followed by her flimsy apron which barely covered her lap. The audience was totally silent as she performed and again was hugely appreciative when she finished.

The concert chairmen came onto the stage and announced that there would now be a short break before the last strippers came on to allow the meat draw and the gardening club raffles to be drawn. There was a mad scramble from the seats as some men made for the toilets, including Mickey, while others, including Trev, made for the bar to order more drinks. The raffles were drawn and the lucky winners received their respective prizes.

Morgan walked to the bar and brushed past Trev as he did so. Trev had an idea that that was his intention, and so braced himself before the contact, and the fat man was knocked slightly off balance. He reacted by shoving Trev bodily out of the way, pushing him forcibly to one side. Trev, as he was shoved sideways, inadvertently spilled some beer from his glass onto a seated man's head.

The startled and angry man jumped up cursing, and turned to face Trev, who held up his free hand, the one without the glass in, in a gesture of surrender, palm out, facing the man. "Sorry mate, I couldn't help it," he said innocently, as the man wiped the moisture from his head with a handkerchief. The man muttered something intelligible and sat down again. Trev turned to the bar and could see the welder smirking at him.

"You should be more careful and look where you're going, cowboy," Morgan shouted, as the men around him at the bar laughed. The fat man turned to the bar and ordered his drinks still laughing and shook his head as he indicated over his shoulder toward Trev with his thumb. The lights dimmed again and the backing duo took their seats at the organ and the drums, as the concert chairman make a reappearance to introduce the last two strippers.

"Right then, lads, best of order for the girl now, I give you tonight's ultimate exotic dancer, Salome," he said, as he backed off stage holding his arms out to the figure that had appeared in the wings at the opposite side of the stage, as if drawing her forward. She did come forward, swaying to the music. Most strippers brought their own backing music on tape but this one didn't have any, and relied totally on the club backing duo. She was dressed as a harem dancer, and her body, including her face, was covered pretty comprehensively with quite a number of variously coloured veils.

Morgan walked past Trev carrying his drinks and smirked. "Where's your partner, Tonto, gone? Doesn't he like women, then?"

Trev couldn't ignore the remark. Morgan couldn't know that it was Mickey with him; otherwise he'd be more respectful. "Why don't you ask him yourself when he comes back, if you're so interested in him?" he said.

"I might just do that, Roy fucking Rodgers, I might just do that," Morgan said as he pushed past Trev and took his seat.

Trev watched the dancer. She was good, he thought, and was exciting the audience with her swivelling hips and provocative gestures. Mickey returned from the toilet and the pair watched totally enthralled, as did the entire audience, the room was in absolute silence, except for the music coming from the stage.

"She reminds me of somebody," Mickey said after a couple of minutes.

"Yes?" Trev said, realising that she was the same one that he thought that he recognised earlier.

"Aye, the way she moves and her figure, she definitely puts me in mind of somebody."

"Marilyn Monroe," said Trev.

"No, not her. Somebody else. Not a film star. It'll come to me," Mickey said.

The dancer was down to her last couple of veils, and hesitated provocatively before removing the one covering her face, teasing the men at the front of the audience and playing hard to get. She finally removed the veil, and almost immediately afterwards took off another one that covered one of her breasts. The effect on the audience was electrifying; the men stared at her perfectly rounded breast as if enthralled. They'd already seen three other women totally naked tonight but it was the way that this one moved, teased and gyrated that held them spellbound. Trev couldn't take his eyes from the voluptuous figure as she moved sensuously across the stage, preparing to remove another veil.

Mickey shoved him sharply in the ribs. "Trev," he said in a harsh whisper.

"What, man?" Trev replied, his eyes still glued on the woman.

"I know who it is that she reminds me of now."

"Who?"

"Brenda. That's who it is. Brenda."

"Brenda? Brenda who?" Trev asked still completely immersed in the woman's movements.

"Joe's Brenda."

20

"Joe's Brenda?" Trev said half to himself, his eyes still totally focused on the dancer. "Good God!" he said as realisation finally hit him. "It is Brenda." He stood rooted to the spot. Now dumbstruck, his mouth half-open, he could only gesture ineffectually with one hand towards the stage, astounded by the knowledge that it was their friend's wife up there, dancing naked in front of all these men. "It is, it's…"

"It is definitely Brenda," confirmed Mickey again, as if talking to a four-year-old child.

"But that impossible, she's…she's…" Trev stuttered as he watched the dancer finally remove the last veil and she stood there completely naked before the hugely appreciative audience. The men stood up and cheered, clapped and whistled as she walked off stage, and it was some time before the appreciative hum died down.

The last dancer came on after a brief introduction by the chairman. She had brought her own backing music, and so the disappointed backing duo was reluctantly forced to give up their choice seats on stage and retreated to the wings, taking their pints with them.

Trev and Mickey looked at each other in total shock. "What do we do about this?" Trev asked, totally at a loss. "Joe must be ashamed of Brenda stripping or he would have said something about it. Do we let on that we know about it or what?"

"He can't know anything about it or he would have told us," Mickey said.

"You're right. Joe can't know anything about her stripping. He wouldn't allow it. He'll go barmy when he hears about this."

"If he hears about it," Mickey said.

"What, you mean that we don't tell him?"

"She'll tell him if she wants him to know, won't she?"

"But we can't have a mate not knowing that his wife is stripping around the clubs, man. If anybody else finds out, and somebody's sure to, then he'll be a laughing stock. We've got to tell him before somebody else does."

The final stripper had finished her dance routine, and got off stage quickly.

"She must be in a hurry for the last bus," Morgan's voice shouted loudly above the din from the audience, and was answered by someone else at the same table who said, "I'd run her home for a small consideration."

"It's your small consideration that she'd better watch out for," another of the group said, and they all laughed.

"Morgan knows Brenda, doesn't he? He'll tell Joe for sure, he couldn't keep his mouth shut about something like this, the big bastard," said Trev.

The strippers were now fully dressed and were indeed in a hurry to leave. They walked through the room together ignoring the comments from the audience as they passed. As they reached the bar, Trev and Mickey turned their heads away, so that Brenda wouldn't see them. They could see behind them through the mirror on the wall behind the bar and watched as the women passed. They heard Morgan's loud and crude comments as the women passed his table, and the raucous, appreciative laughter that the comments drew from his equally obnoxious mates.

Morgan was making mock attempts to grab the women as they passed, and then actually got a hold of one and pulled her to him, trying to make her sit on his lap. The woman pulled away from him as he held her coat and slapped him hard across the face. His mates laughed as the blow knocked his head sideways with a great deal of force. He stood up, but the woman who had hit him was now gone. He turned his attention towards the next one to pass him. It was Brenda. He grabbed her and pulled her to him, holding both her hands in one of his, and holding her close to his body.

"Hey, I know this one. She's married to some prick of a labourer at the yard."

She struggled desperately as he held her, and he started to paw her breasts with his free hand. "Look at the size of these beauties, lads," he shouted, and lifted up her jumper to reveal her breasts straining against her bra. "They're wasted on that prick of a husband she's got." His mates laughed again as he rubbed his face between her breasts, ignoring her shouted protests. Tears were now running down Brenda's face as she struggled helplessly against her assailant.

Trev, seeing this through the mirror, acted. He moved quickly across the room and grabbed Morgan by the neck from behind. He tried to pull the man away from Brenda but his opponent was bull necked and very strong. Morgan shook Trev off like a fly and turning around, kicked him savagely between the legs. Trev fell to the floor writhing in agony and Morgan turned his attention back to Brenda.

Through watering eyes Trev saw Mickey stride across from the bar and reach the struggling pair. The fat man had now pushed the struggling Brenda on top of the table as he tried to put his hand up her skirt.

Mickey grabbed Morgan by the shoulder and spun him around so that he was facing him. Mickey's fist moved in a blur, only covering a distance of about a foot. It connected with the point of the fat man's chin, and sent him flying backwards as if propelled by a giant catapult.

The welder fell over a neighbouring table, his legs going right over his head, knocking the drinks onto the floor, and covering the seated figures with the spilled alcohol. The men at the table jumped up and those nearest Mickey made a grab for him.

Mickey pulled the sobbing Brenda out of the men's way, and pushed her behind him where Trev, now back on his feet, took her in his arms. Mickey then turned and gave his complete attention to the group of men coming at him. He hit the nearest one who quickly followed the route already taken by Morgan, and disappeared over the table.

The next one obligingly stepped forward at just the right time, and Mickey caught him with a perfect punch to the nose. The force of the blow spread the man's nose across the right side of his face as if by magic, and splattered the others with the blood.

The remaining men now rushed Mickey. He headbutted one, and kicked another squarely between the legs. They went down like sacks of potatoes, one unconscious and the other writhing around the floor in agony. Trev, still half-doubled up in pain and holding the sobbing Brenda, could only look on and shout encouragement to Mickey.

When one of the assailants tried to creep up and attack his friend from behind, Trev stepped forward, and catching the man off balance, pushed him across a neighbouring table and sent him flying to the floor.

Mickey was laying about himself now with a vengeance, totally immersed in the fight. He was like a well-maintained machine. He hit out right, left and centre and the area around him looked like a disaster zone.

Bodies littered the floor, lying amongst the broken glass; chairs and the remains of the tables overturned during the fracas. Mickey's one-man war continued, and more bodies joined those already on the floor.

A committee man tried to intervene and he too joined the other casualties on the floor. Finally the big guns arrived in the form of no less than the concert chairman, who walked straight up behind Mickey and placed a restraining hand on his shoulder.

Trev tried to shout a warning to the man, but it was too late. Mickey turned instinctively and without any attempt to identify his perceived assailant, punched the chairman squarely in the face.

The stunned man fell backwards as stiff as a ramrod, and the back of his head hit the floor with a resounding crack.

Mickey was only now starting to become aware of what was happening outside of the immediate vicinity of the fracas. His eyes slowly refocused as Trev, still tottering on unsteady legs, beckoned to him. It was time to get out of the club.

Mickey started to walk towards Trev, but a man picked himself up from the floor and jumped on his back, holding Mickey around the neck, and wrapping his legs around his body. Mickey struggled this way and that with the man clinging to him. Eventually he jammed his unwanted passenger against the bar counter a couple of times and the man fell to the ground where he lay groaning.

Mickey finally reached Trev and together they helped the still weeping Brenda from the club, and into the van. Mickey climbed into the back nursing his bleeding knuckles, leaving the front passenger seat for Brenda, and the driving to Trev. There was a wailing of sirens and a police car with flashing lights, raced into the club car park as they drove out.

Brenda was inconsolable and cried throughout the journey. Mickey dabbed at the cuts on his knuckles with a handkerchief as Trev, trying to ignore the discomfort in his testicles, concentrated on his driving, unsure of what to say to the sobbing woman. Eventually Brenda's tears dried up long enough for her to talk.

"Joe doesn't know," she sobbed.

"We'd figured that out for ourselves, Brenda," Trev said quietly.

"Oh God, he'll go mad when he finds out."

"Would you rather we didn't tell him then?" Trev asked.

"You'd be better off telling him yourself, Brenda," Mickey said from the back of the van, before she could answer.

She sat quietly for some time before speaking. "You're right, Mickey. I'll have to tell him myself. I was only doing it to get some money for Christmas. This strike's got us right on the bottom. I had to give up my job to look after my sister, and it was the only way that I could think of to earn some money."

"We figured that out for ourselves as well," Trev said, as he stopped the van at the corner of the street where Joe and Brenda lived. "I'd better drop you off here okay, love?"

"You don't have to tell Joe that we were there, you know," Mickey said. "He doesn't have to know that we..." He searched for the right words, the least embarrassing words. "... were in the audience like," he finished hesitantly, not sure if he was helping the situation or making her feel worse.

"Thanks, Mickey, but I'll tell him everything. That Morgan will make sure that everybody hears about this and Joe will find out. Anyway, I've told too many lies as it is." She got out of the car.

Mickey leaned forward, and pushed down the front passenger seat, and climbed out, intending to take her vacant seat.

"Look," he said to her as she prepared to walk the hundred or so yards to her home, "regardless of what you tell Joe, or don't tell him, we won't say anything to anybody, alright."

She kissed Mickey on the cheek, thanked them both and walked hurriedly away.

Joe was sitting in front of the switched-off television reading a two-day-old newspaper, when Brenda entered the house.

"Hello love. Want a cup of tea? I'll put the kettle on," he said, putting down the newspaper and getting up from the chair.

"Yes. Yes please. That'd be nice," Brenda said quietly. "Sharon asleep?"

"Yes, she's been in bed since eight o'clock."

Joe made the tea and brought two cups into the living room. "Everything alright? You seem a bit quiet?" he said, offering the cup to her.

"Joe," she began, placing her cup onto the coffee table. "Joe, I've got something to tell you."

"What is it, pet?" he asked, concerned.

Brenda didn't know how to begin to tell him. How to tell him without making it seem too explicitly dirty and grimy. She took a deep breath as she realised that there was no easy way to do it. "I've had a job on the side to make a few extra pounds for Christmas. For Sharon's sake, to buy toys, clothes and things. And for us as well of course, I'm sick of having to make do with second best all the time," she finished lamely. "I wanted to make enough for us to have a good Christmas this year. So we could maybe have a night out at the club if we wanted and plenty of nice things to eat, you know?"

"I know, you told me that you'd got a start doing part-time casual at the jeans factory with Sylvia," Joe said slightly puzzled.

"The thing is Joe, I haven't been working there."

"No? Where have you been working then?"

She took another deep breath, her chest felt like it was about to explode, and she wondered if she was having a heart attack. She didn't care, she deserved to have one, and she deserved to die. "I've been stripping," she said finally with a faltering voice. "On the clubs."

"What? You've been what?" Joe jumped from the armchair and slammed his cup down onto the coffee table with such force that the tea splashed up the wallpaper behind. He turned and strode across the room, and then swung back. He stood above her bowed head, his arms on his hips, and shook his head as he tried to come to grips with this bombshell that had just shattered his existence.

Numerous thoughts raced across his mind as he fought to keep control, and prevent himself from yelling. "You mean to say that I've been stuck in here minding your sister night after night, while you've been out flaunting yourself naked in front of leering men? A right mug you've made out of me then, haven't you? What are the family and the neighbours going to think about you?" Another thought hit him. "And what am I supposed to say to the lads at work? What are they going to think of me, when you go and do something like that? They'll think that I'm not much better than a bloody ponce, letting my wife prance around with no clothes on for money, that's what they'll think of me."

Brenda began to speak again, the flood of words came tumbling out, but at first he was so angry that he couldn't take in what she was saying.

"I only did it to try and get us out of the mess we're always in because we've got no money. We've had no steady money coming in for ages, and this year has been absolutely terrible. Even your sick money was stopped when they signed you off. Everything was just getting out of hand. I owe money on the mortgage, we're behind with the gas and electricity, and they're threatening to cut us off next week if we don't pay, and the tallyman's being funny because I can't pay the weekly money, I've even had to cash in the insurance policies."

She stood up and grabbed his shoulders. "Oh Joe, I didn't want you to find out. I wanted you just to think that I'd got the money from the factory work, and I was going to pack it in after a few weeks when I'd got enough money to tide us over."

"But stripping, Brenda, how could you?"

"How could I? Because that's the only way that we are going to have a half-decent Christmas like most other people have, with enough to eat, and some decent presents, that's why. And so we've got some decent clothes like our friends have. We haven't had any new gear for ages, and always have to rely on handouts from the family and on Elsie's lifted clothes. Have you any idea how I feel, with me having to walk around looking like a refugee. I wear hand-me-downs from my family that are so old that the styles are years out of fashion and they look terrible. Even Sharon's beginning to notice what she's wearing now, and it's a crying match every morning, she's not going to wear this, and wouldn't be seen dead in that." She paused to regain her breath. "You remember that birthday party she was invited to last month? Little Michele's who lives down the road. It was her thirteenth? Sharon was so pleased to be invited and got all excited. She'd never been to a party before and was looking forward to it all week."

Joe nodded.

"Well, the only party frock that I could find that would fit her, that I could afford, was a big flouncy old-fashioned thing that looked like it had come straight out of Mary Poppins. She did look nice in it, mind, but when she got to the party all the other girls had modern gear, short fashionable skirts, and most were wearing a bit of makeup. You know how young girls like to dress up. Anyway, she came home all upset, crying her eyes out. Because she's a bit slow it makes it a lot worse for her. Some of the other kids laugh at her as

211

it is, and she knows they do. I vowed then and there that I would never, ever, put the kid in that sort of position ever again, no matter what it took. I promised myself that from now on she'd only get the best. The best presents and food, and the best clothes that money can buy. Clothes that she'll feel comfortable in, and will be proud to wear. Clothes that make her feel, and look, good."

Joe opened his mouth as if about to speak, but Brenda was in full flow now and started again before he could begin. "And don't say that I should have told you. What good would that have done? All I ever get out of you is 'We'll wait and see'. Wait and see? I've been waiting all this year and still haven't seen anything that will get us out of the situation that we're in. I just got tired of waiting Joe, and decided to do something about it myself. Not like you, sitting about and waiting for something to happen.

"I wish that you had a bit more go in you, Joe. I love you dearly but I know for sure that if I left things to you we would still be living in a council house and never get anywhere. You'll always do what your union tells you to do, rather than think for yourself and get another job out of the yards, somewhere with a steady decent income and some prospects for the future. But no, you'll not do that. Not you. You'd rather stay where you are and follow the other sheep. You seem unable to do anything to keep your family properly. Whenever I've mentioned money in the past you've never wanted to know. You've always left that side of things to me. Well, that was great when there was money to go around, but there hasn't been any for quite a while, and every time I've brought the subject up, you still didn't want to know. Well, you know all about it now, don't you?"

Joe stood still; shoulders slumped, his mind still trying to process the reams of bewildering information that had been given to him so suddenly, forcefully and so unexpectedly. There was a faint cry from the bedroom, and Brenda gave his shoulders a loving squeeze before leaving him to see to Sharon. In the bedroom, she sat beside the crying child and hushed and patted the girl to soothe her back to sleep. She heard the front door slam, and his footsteps on the front path outside and started to cry, as she realised that Joe had walked out of the house.

He left the house in a daze, turning blindly along the pavement without seeing where he was going. His head was full of negative, nasty and suspicious thoughts that refused to go away. How could this happen? How could his wife, not some mini-skirted good-time girl, out for what she could get, but Brenda, do something like this to him? He shook his head frequently as he walked the dark wet streets, losing all sense of time and direction as he struggled with the tumbling thoughts and violently troubling emotions within him. Her words regarding the money and his inability to provide for the family stung him like wasp stings, and hurt him again and again as he heard them repeated in his mind. He struggled to come to terms with her opinion of him.

Both Trev and Mickey were arrested in the small hours of the next morning.

Mickey was handcuffed roughly after an altercation at the front door of his home after he'd been too slow to cooperate with the arresting officers. It turned out that one of the people assaulted by Mickey at the club was an off-duty policeman, a well-liked and respected local bobby and the arresting officers weren't too inclined to be patient, polite or gentle.

Mickey's concern for his wife was his main consideration, and when the police barged into his home, he reacted automatically, as they expected that he would. They were prepared, and beat him with their truncheons until he was bloody and subdued. Then they dragged him from the house and threw him into a police van.

Tracy was absolutely distraught at the appearance of the police in her home at that time of the night, and the barbaric treatment of her husband that she witnessed. The children had started screaming uncontrollably and Tracy sank to the floor with her head held in her hands. Her mother was sent for. There were no WPCs in attendance at the arrest, and a considerable delay was experienced while they waited for Tracy's mother to arrive to take care of the distraught children and hysterical woman.

Mickey was dazed and seemed unable to comprehend what was happening to him. He was taken to the central police station and interviewed at length.

The detectives interviewing him gave him a hard time. They both knew the policeman who was injured during the fight at the club and were in no mood to pander to his assailant.

"So, then, you're the hard man are you? You think you're tough, eh?" the senior officer of the two, a detective sergeant goaded him.

Mickey remained silent, stunned by the evening's events.

"He's the strong silent type, he is," the detective constable put in.

"Well, you have really gone and done it now, haven't you? Grievous Bodily Harm, Actual Bodily Harm, assaulting a police officer in the course of his duties. Attempted murder."

Mickey looked up at his tormentors in bewilderment and then bowed his head again.

"You know that two of the people that you assaulted last night are in intensive care at the General? They could both die. Then you're for it and no mistake!" The DS, leaning over the desk, shouted at the prisoner's bowed head.

Mickey was interviewed at length, held in police cells overnight and charged the next morning with a number of counts of Assault and GBH. After appearing before a magistrate, he was remanded in custody to Durham Gaol.

Trev was also interviewed extensively. He was eventually released without charge early the next morning.

Joe returned to the house sometime later. Brenda was sitting in a chair staring at the wall, her eyes puffed and swollen. Joe sat down opposite her. He cleared his throat.

"How much do we owe altogether?"

Brenda looked at him. "So you want to know about it now, do you?"

"Just tell me how much we owe."

She got up, and took a piece of paper from a drawer. She held it out to him. "That's the list, the total's at the bottom."

"Good God," Joe said as he saw the total. He sat back in the chair, while Brenda got up and went into the kitchen. He looked at the figures again taking in the individual amounts. The list was a long one, and he shook his head in despair. "Good God," he said again quietly.

Brenda returned with freshly brewed tea. He accepted a cup from her as he continued to analyse the list. It was pretty comprehensive. Gas and electricity were the most pressing, he reasoned, as they were threatening to cut them off. The mortgage arrears were high, and the catalogue arrears were up there, too. There was even a slate run up at the corner shop and at the butchers. Joe sighed and ran his fingers through his hair. "For God's sake, Brenda, why didn't you tell me?" he asked meekly, swallowing two aspirins with the help of a mouthful of tea.

"I did tell you, but you didn't really want to know, did you? Look Joe, I didn't mean a lot of what I said before. I was just getting in my retaliation first, you know? I thought that you would blame me, I suppose. The few times that I did try to mention it to you, you seemed to take it as if I were getting at you, blaming you for not being able to provide. Your pride was hurt, I suppose. Anyway, we were both brought up to accept that the running of the home and the managing of the family's finances were the wife's responsibility and that a good wife should be able to manage on next to nothing. God knows that's what our parents had to do in the thirties and forties, what with strikes, world wars, rationing and all that. I felt that I'd failed you just because I couldn't manage. I just kept on trying to manage, and it kept getting worse not better."

Joe nodded his head. He was beginning to understand now. "It's not your fault, Brenda, we're both to blame." He paused and looked at her tear-stained face. "Well, what do we do about it, then?"

She smiled with relief. She leaped up from her chair and sat on his knee, throwing her arms around his neck, and kissing him on the lips. "Oh Joe, I thought that you'd go absolutely mad and throw me out."

"Throw you out, why would I do that? It's not your fault. And don't worry, I'll take care of all the money that's owed." He looked at her seriously, and repeated it slowly and meaningfully. "I'll take care of all the money that we owe. When you first told me I think I really could have killed you, do you know that? Then when I had a chance to calm down and think it through, I realised that I was only concerned about myself, I was worried about how other people would react. What they would think of me, and you as my wife, and that's wrong, completely wrong. I know that you did it for the right reasons and that you didn't want to hurt me. You were concerned about me, and all I was worried about was myself. I love you, Brenda, and we'll work this thing through together. I've always left you to manage all the household expenses, because I thought that was a woman's job. And as you just said, when things are going well, that's fine, it probably works better that way, but now that I'm not earning anything, I've got to pull my weight and take the responsibility."

Brenda hugged Joe, her arms tight around his neck, and tears rolled down her cheeks. "But how will we repay that much, Joe? Where will you get that all that money?"

"Just let me worry about that for the time being. It'll get sorted, believe me, and soon."

Incredibly, Brenda believed him.

"Look, first thing to do is to get rid of the stripping job," he said.

She nodded. "Alright. I hated it anyway."

"Anybody else know about it?"

"The club I was at tonight…Trev was in there performing, Mickey was with him, and that horrible welder, Morgan, he was there as well. Oh Joe, there was a terrible fight…"

Joe shook his head ruefully. "They saw you?"

"Yes."

"That's why you've told me tonight." It was a statement not a question.

Brenda dropped her eyes and nodded. She felt ashamed to have lied to her husband but she could have hardly told him the truth. "The lads promised not to tell anybody, Joe, and you can trust those two, they're not like the others, but Morgan's a different kettle of fish. Anyway, I thought that it wasn't right them knowing and not you. I always hated telling you lies"

He nodded. "Anybody else know about it?"

"No, nobody else, only Sylvia, it was her that got me interested. She'd been doing it for months. She won't say anything to anybody."

"Does her husband know?"

"No, he'd kill her if he found out."

"Right then," Joe said. "First thing to do is to cancel the stripping. From now on I'll take care of the bills, all of them. First priority on the list is that we've got to sort out the gas and electricity. I'll go down first thing in the morning and see them, I'll explain the situation, and tell them that we'll pay off a bit extra every week, get one of those payment book things. That'll hold them until I get the money to pay them off in full."

"I've already tried that, Joe. They want all the money before the end of the month or they'll cut us off."

"Right then, I'll get the money before the end of the month. That'll be no problem," he said unconvincingly. He studied the list again. The catalogue will have to wait. What about this club man, you said he'd been funny?"

Brenda hadn't meant to mention that. It had slipped out in the heat of the moment. Joe looked at her steadily. "Come on, Brenda, what did you mean? How is he being funny, has he been trying it on with you?"

"Oh nothing like that, Joe. He just wanted his money that's all, and got a bit…" she hesitated; if she told Joe the truth she knew that he'd kill him. "He was just a bit nasty like."

"What sort of nasty? Did he threaten you? He didn't try to come on to you or anything, did he?"

"No, no. Nothing like that," Brenda lied quickly. "He was just asking for payment, and keeps threatening to send the bailiffs in, that's all."

"Okay. I'll sort him out the next time he calls. I'll give him something to be going on with, and he'll have to make do with that for the time being, and wait for the rest."

"Where are you going to get the money from, Joe?" she asked again.

"Don't worry, some of the lads have a few casual jobs lined up, and they've asked me to help them, that's all, nothing to it. We'll be rolling in the money by Christmas, don't you worry about it."

"You'll not have anything to do with that Alan will you? He's a wrong one. Promise me that you won't have anything to do with him. He'll get you jailed, some of the things that he gets up to."

"I'll not get into trouble, but I will pay off these bills, all of them, I promise, so don't you worry about anything."

Tracy sobbed uncontrollably in her bedroom. She'd been inconsolable since being told that Mickey was being held in prison. Tears streamed down her face as she swallowed the prescription tablets, one after another, washing each one down with hot, sweet, tea.

21

Elsie pushed the front door closed behind her with her foot. The door slammed shut, the bang startling Alan, who was almost asleep in an armchair in front of the fire.

"It's alright for some," she said, looking at him as she dropped her packages onto the kitchen table. "Toasting themselves like a dog in front of the fire. I wish I had the time to do that."

Alan rubbed his eyes with his knuckles, then stretched and yawned. "I'm off out in a minute. Got to see somebody about a job."

"Oh aye? Well you be careful what you are doing. The police seem to be working overtime lately. I've just heard that those fine friends of yours the McKenna brothers have been lifted. If that pair go down again it'll be for a very long stretch."

Alan was immediately alert at the mention of the name of McKenna. "Who told you they've been picked up?"

"Never you mind who told me. The police raided the house at six o'clock this morning and took them both away in handcuffs. Gave them a good going over from all accounts. They had the whole street awake they did, banging and yelling."

They parked the van in a side street near the old church and turned off the lights. Trev stayed in the driver's seat ready for a quick getaway, Harry took up his allocated lookout position in the bushes near the main road while Alan led Richie and Joe towards the rear of building.

The flash of forked lightning lit up the sky with a crackling charge of electricity. Thunder rumbled almost immediately afterwards as the storm raged right above their heads. The tall, dark building was illuminated for an instant in the lightning flash, as it towered menacingly above them.

"You said it was a warehouse?" Joe said accusingly.

"It is a warehouse," Alan said quickly.

"No it's not. It's a church."

"It's an old church being used as a warehouse. Look, I've got it all sussed out. The alarm is a doddle. I can fix it in a couple of minutes. The window at the back can be opened with a penknife, we'll be inside the place in two minutes flat."

"It doesn't seem right somehow, breaking into a church," Joe maintained.

"Look Joe, I'm pleased that you have decided to come into this thing with us, but how many times do I have to tell you? It's not a church."

"It's got stained glass windows," put in Richie unhelpfully.

"That's because it used to be a church. For God's sake, what does it matter? It's just a building, that's all." Alan always enjoyed these escapades but the others' constant complaining was starting to annoy him now, and it showed.

The old building was situated right in the middle of a colliery village. The houses that surrounded it were mainly occupied by pensioners, and Alan had warned the lads to keep it as quiet as possible. Pensioners were notoriously nosey and slept lightly so it was imperative that they keep the noise level right down. The small group of burglars began to make their way around the back of the building, hoping that the thunderstorm would cover any unusual noise they might make.

"Just let's get around the back. The sooner we're in, then the sooner we'll be out again." Joe said, anxiously.

Alan took longer than he'd promised to disable the wires of the alarm system, but opened the window lock with a practised flick of his penknife, pushed open the window and then disappeared inside, wriggling headfirst through the small opening. The pair outside were soaked through in minutes as the heavens opened and torrential rain fell like stair rods. They stood as close to the old church wall as possible, in a forlorn attempt to shelter from the downpour. It seemed like an age to them until Alan opened the back door and let them inside. It was dark inside, and they needed the torches they'd brought with them to find their way around and to avoid falling over boxes of tinned carrots, peas, green beans and other various consumables, which were piled in high, untidy stacks on the floor.

The place was a veritable Aladdin's cave. All sorts of foodstuffs were stacked high in the makeshift warehouse. There were hundreds of cartons containing Heinz baked beans and soups. Large, rough, wooden cases containing catering size, 6lb, tins of an obscure brand of corned beef, were stacked twenty high from the ground. The intruders gazed around awestruck at the extent and variety of goods as they walked down the aisles between the stacks.

Alan stopped suddenly and the others walked into him in the dim light.

"Steady on, give me a bit of space." He looked around and pointed. "That looks like the safe," Alan whispered, his voice hardly audible above the thunder and falling rain drumming onto the roof of the building, as he led them further into the building. "Here we are then," he whispered. He turned around and jumped as he bumped into Richie who was right behind him. "I said, give me some space, will you?"

He'd stopped in front of a large steel structure, about six feet by ten feet long and ten feet high. One side had a pair of large steel doors that were secured by means of two large bars across the front, held together with two very large, brass padlocks.

"It's like Fort Knox," Joe said, also in a whisper.

"Why are you two whispering?" Richie asked.

Alan ignored Richie's question altogether. "Stop moaning will you, Joe? It'll only take me a couple of minutes to get into this tin can, so stop worrying."

"What's that?" Richie asked quietly.

"What's what?" Alan asked impatiently.

"That. That red light thing, there."

Alan and Joe took a step to one side to where they could see what Richie was pointing at.

"It's a laser beam," Joe said loudly. "Alan, the place is alive with beams. It's got more ray guns than Dan Dare. Come on let's get out of here before the police turn up."

"Wait a minute Joe, don't panic," Alan said calmly. "Let's just have a look at this thing."

"Who's Dan Dare?" Richie asked predictably.

"Never mind who Dan Dare is, what are we going to do now?"

Alan stroked his chin and looked ruefully at the red light. "It's one of those magic alarm beams, and it runs about a foot off the floor to that other red light over there, on the wall." He took his time to examine the whole area they'd already covered from the back window and door.

"There aren't any more beams, only this one in front of the safe. They must be worried that that's what any burglars would be after," he pronounced with great insight.

"Then they're right aren't they?" Joe said impatiently.

"Take it easy," Alan said, "I'll nip back to the van and get the oxy cutter. It's a good job I came prepared isn't it? Good planning that is. Joe, just keep quiet and climb on top of the safe so you can see out of that window up there. If you see Harry waving, let us know and we'll scarper."

"And just how am I going to get up there?"

"You can climb up on top of those boxes there. If you get onto the top of that stack you'll be able to reach the window alright."

Alan helped Joe to begin his climb before he disappeared into the gloom of the building taking the torch with him.

"Hey, give me the torch, will you? I can't see a thing up here,"

Joe whispered hoarsely. Alan duly returned and handed the torch to Richie, who proceeded to shine it directly into Joe's eyes.

"Point the thing the other way, that's right, point it towards the safe," Joe hissed as he started his unsteady climb, clambering precariously on a stack of Persil soap powder boxes. Placing his feet in the small gaps between the boxes he was able, with considerable difficulty, to reach the top of the pile, which was about fifteen feet from the floor. From his unsteady perch the floor looked a great deal more than fifteen feet away, it looked to him like a good forty feet or more.

Steadying himself as best he could with a tenuous grip on a windowsill he peered out of the grimy window. He could make out Harry's dark form in the bushes near the road. Joe turned and looked down at the steel roof of the safe, which was now below him. The surface was covered in dust, and was strewn with a collection of various items of rubbish. All along one side of the roof, empty biscuit tins were stacked precariously five or six high, one on top of the other. He renewed his grip on the windowsill and hung on for dear life.

Alan returned from the van carrying the portable oxyacetylene torch and bottle. "Good job I brought this along," he said to Richie and Joe. "No, please don't you all congratulate me on my professionalism at once," he said sarcastically, as he lit the torch and began to cut a hole in the side of the safe.

The noise from the cutting torch seemed extraordinarily loud and the intense luminosity threw strange flickering shadows up onto the walls, much to Joe's alarm. He scanned anxiously from his lofty perch, convinced that the light would be seen from outside.

The metal of the safe wall was thin and it didn't take Alan long to cut a hole large enough for him to crawl through. He passed a number of holdall type bags out through the hole to Richie, who placed them on the floor. When they were all removed from the safe, Alan climbed back out through the hole.

"I'll take the oxy bottle back and then we can start carrying these bags out," Alan said, walking away into the dark, carrying the cutting equipment.

Joe heard a sound from below him, looked down, and saw Richie gesturing. He was whispering something, but Joe couldn't hear what the lad was saying, so, bending almost double, but still retaining a firm grip on the windowsill with his left hand, he leaned out and downwards. "What?" he asked as loudly as he dared.

Again there was a muffled sound from Ritchie standing below. "I can't hear a word you're saying," Joe whispered a bit louder. "Speak up, man."

"You want to be careful because those boxes at the bottom are starting to buckle."

Joe, bent double on the top of the stack, felt a distinct movement below him as the boxes moved. He felt a slight, but definite lurch to the left. Joe immediately cast around him for a way to get down safely. The boxes were trembling now and his weight was causing the slide to the left to become even more pronounced. They were collapsing.

Joe saw what he thought was a glimmer of hope, a literal lifeline. A piece of rope hung down from the darkness of the upper reaches of the building and was draped casually over the windowsill that he gripped so determinedly. Joe immediately sprang into action. He let go his tight grip on the windowsill, and trusted his weight, and his life, to the rope that he perceived to be his salvation. Grasping the rope in both hands he abandoned the tottering stack, or rather it abandoned him as it slowly slid away from under him. Without any further deliberation, or option, Joe launched himself optimistically out into the void and away from the leaning tower of Persil. As his feet left the relative solidity of the boxes, a fleeting thought, more like a prayer, raced through Joe's mind. It went something along the lines of, I hope that this thing holds my weight.

The rope did hold Joe's weight. The rope also held something else. Far up in the roof of the old church, attached to the other end of the rope was a large metal bell. The bell used to be used for funerals. It didn't chime or peal, or anything fancy, as a set of proper church bells is normally expected to do. It just tolled. A single mournful sound, a sound which heralded a deceased parishioner's passage from this life to the next. The bell had remained up there, forgotten in the dim recesses of the church's dusty rafters, quiet and silent for a number of years since the building's conversion to a warehouse. Released from its restraints and years of inactivity and galvanized into action by the weight of Joe's body below, it now performed as it was intended, and burst into mournful but very loud tolling.

The bell struck a single, very loud note, which was more than enough to scare the living daylights out of the men below. Joe particularly, was absolutely terrified by the sudden piercing and thunderous noise above him. He didn't have any idea of its source and automatically and instinctively let go of the rope. This spontaneous action had three unforeseen but natural repercussions. The first was that Joe fell the five or six feet that separated him from the top of the safe, hitting the top of the structure heavily with a thump that knocked all the air right out of him. The steel roof had a fair bit of give in it, and vibrated up and down with resonance, making a sound not unlike a large kettle drum. Joe was literally like a pea on a drum, and bounced up and down continuously until the momentum lessened. The resulting thunderous percussion effect resounded around the building, to accompany the still echoing clang of the bell.

Joe's fall also had repercussions on, and directly affected, the stacked empty biscuit tins on the edge of the safe roof. They tottered, leaned precariously, and then fell, one or two at a time, onto the hard concrete floor below. Each fall was accompanied by a tremendous and resounding crashing as the empty tins hit the ground. The third of the repercussions was that the rope, so recently released by the shocked Joe, now swung freely and loosely in the air unburdened by Joe's attachment. This freedom, and the weight of the bell, plus the unstoppable effects of gravity, caused the bell to swing back to its original position again and again to replicate its toll, which it did proudly, loudly, and repeatedly.

The noise from the bell, plus the reverberation of the percussion-like safe roof, and the crashing of the empty biscuit tins, had the ears of the men ringing, in fact it affected their hearing for quite some time. Joe was, in his terrified state, quite oblivious to what had actually happened. In his fevered imagination the thundering sound from above was the vengeance of a disgruntled God who was decidedly not happy about his church, his home, being broken into. The collapsing boxes, the almighty crashing above his head, his drop from the leaning tower and his subsequent fall onto the steel roof of the safe, all convinced him that he was justly on the receiving end of the wrath of God himself.

Richie was too confused to understand exactly what was happening, but he knew more or less instinctively that they shouldn't be creating this sort of noise in a secret and covert operation such as they were currently engaged in. He jumped up and down trying to see over the top of the roof, to see if Joe was alright and not dead. "You alright up there, Joe?" he shouted with consternation. "Joe, Joe!" he cried out even louder, competing with the dissonance of percussion around him. "Are you alright?"

Joe groaned quietly, and struggled to sit up, holding his hands over his ears. "Shut up, Richie. There's enough noise, isn't there?"

"Thank God you're alright, Joe. You had me worried there for a minute." His words were partially drowned by the still ringing bell above them.

"See if you can get hold of that rope and stop that bell clanging, will you, Richie?" Alan said.

The sound of Alan's voice made both Richie and Joe start. Richie actually jumped entirely off the ground an inch or so, totally involuntarily. "You shouldn't sneak upon people like that, Alan," Richie said reproachfully. "You gave me a shock, you did."

"I gave you a shock? I gave you a fucking shock? You ringing that fucking bell gave me such a shock that I dropped the oxy bottle on my foot and I think it's broke. You've given the whole fucking neighbourhood a shock. I bet there are lights going on all over the place. We'll have to get out of here double quick before the police get here."

"Is it alright then?" asked Richie.

"Is what alright?" Alan said impatiently.

"The oxy bottle, you said you think it's broke."

"My fucking foot, you daft twat, not the fucking bottle. I nearly broke my fucking foot by dropping the fucking bottle on it. God Almighty!" Alan screamed, clasping a hand to his forehead. He made a visible effort to control himself, taking deeps breaths and closing his eyes. "Get up there and grab that bell rope," he hissed at Richie between clenched teeth.

While the lad tried to reach the rope, Alan pulled one of the cartons from the collapsed Persil stack, and standing it on end, stepped up onto it and peered over the edge of the safe appraisingly at Joe, who was sitting on the still vibrating roof of the safe. "Do you think that you can get down yourself, Joe?" he asked.

"What? What happened?" Joe moaned.

"Just slide yourself over here will you?" Alan said, beckoning to Joe with his hand. "Hurry up, man, some time this week would be nice."

Joe slid to the edge of the roof, knocking off the few remaining biscuit tins as he did so, which resulted in even more noise as they crashed to the ground.

"What the fuck, it doesn't fucking matter, the whole fucking place is wide awake by now," Alan said with disgust. "Hurry it up, grab one of these bags each, we've got to get out of here fast."

Richie, still trying unsuccessfully to get a hold of the swinging rope, which remained a tantalizing few inches out of his reach, now started to climb down from the ruins of the Persil stack, and jumping the last three feet, landed heavily on Alan's foot. Alan let out an unearthly yell and hopped around on one foot, grasping his injured toes in both of his hands.

"Shush," Richie said.

"I'll fucking well shush you, you fucking useless daft git."

"There's no need to say things like that," Richie said genuinely shocked. "I thought you said that we should keep the noise down, and you shouting and bawling like that. I was only doing what you told me to…"

"Will you shut up!" Alan screamed at him. Alan had now lost his composure altogether and was gripping Richie by the lapels of his coat. He shook the lad backwards and forwards for about ten seconds until he gradually regained his senses and composure.

"Look, just get outside and get into the van with Trev. That's if the fucking van is still there, and we're not surrounded by the whole fucking police force." He held up a single finger to his lips as Richie began to say something else. "Just get out now."

Richie, grasping one of the bags in each hand and mumbling incoherently to himself, made his way towards the door they'd come in through, what seemed to be like a lifetime ago, but in reality must only have been about ten or fifteen minutes. Joe, also carrying a couple of the bags, but still in a confused and dazed state, and supported by a still seething Alan, followed about twenty feet behind. On reaching the door, Richie walked through and made his way to the van. The others followed and found the van still standing where it had been before, its engine now running impatiently. Trev beckoned furiously from the open window to them. "Hurry up, come on, the whole place is awake," he said in a loud stage whisper.

The three loaded the bags and the cutting gear into the back of the van, climbed in after them, and Trev drove off before they'd even closed the doors. He paused briefly to let Harry scramble aboard at the main road.

"What were you daft bastards doing in there to make all that noise? I'll bet that they could hear you all the way over in Consett," Trev complained.

"Give it a rest eh? We've had enough for tonight," Alan said.

"You've had enough? Who was it stuck out here in the cold, not knowing what was going on? Eh? I'll tell you. It was daft Harry here, the fall guy, that's who," Harry complained.

"Alright Harry, that'll do, I think that we've all had a bad night." Joe's reassuring tone calmed Harry down to somewhere near normal.

Although the break-in had been successful, the unexpected finale and subsequent fear of capture had seriously frightened the lads. Richie had been chosen to keep the bags. He'd decided to store them in his father's garage for the time being, until they decided what to do next.

22

Money was in desperately short supply, but the entire fore-end squad and other labourers from Yule's managed, one way or another, to find the money to join Richie for his stag night drink.

On Friday night they made an early start, making their way across town where they were to meet the rest of the lads in the Beehive. The Beehive had a reputation for being a bit rough, but the lads knew from experience that it was generally quiet enough at this time in the evening. It was near closing time that it got a bit lively. They met up in the pub, Richie was already there waiting for them, smart as a pin in his new suit.

The group moved on to the next pub after a quick half, and started the serious drinking. It was halves for everybody from now on. It was universally accepted that you could drink more beer when drinking halves. And anyway, if they didn't like the look of the place for whatever reason, then a half pint was always easier to drink quickly, and then they could move on to somewhere else. A pint was not so easily manageable, especially later in the night when they'd had a fair bit to drink.

They were all suited and booted in Burton's or Jacksons the Tailor's best made-to-measure suits, and various coloured shirts and ties. Their outfits were topped off with short overcoats with belts, which most of the lads tied at the back of their coats. The walks between the pubs weren't long. There were a lot of public houses close together within a few streets of each other in the town centre and by eight o'clock most of the places were filling up and it was becoming more and more difficult to get served. The lads, there were about twelve of them in the party now, crowded into the bar of the Oak Tree, and Joe, who was trusted with the kitty, struggled through the crush, waving a fiver in his hand, and tried to catch the elusive barman's eye.

There was a skill to getting served in crowded pubs. More of an art really, Joe had discovered. He manoeuvred himself behind someone who was already being served, and waited patiently until the drinks were being paid for. At this precise moment, when the barman's attention was focused entirely on the existing customer, Joe struck. "Twelve halves of best please, mate," he shouted, adding an understanding, "when you get a minute."

This strategy nearly always worked. Joe had given it a bit of thought and reckoned that it was when the barman or barmaid was at their most receptive. They were drawing to an end of one relationship, so to speak, with the previous customer, and therefore more receptive to another order. Previous to this specific point in time, the server's whole attention and concentration was focused on that customer's order. Joe had deliberately experimented with the timing, and found that if he spoke just a second too soon or too late, then the effect was lost and someone else had grabbed the server's attention. It worked perfectly tonight. Joe had spoken a fraction of a second before a big, ugly-looking bloke, who had pushed his way unceremoniously to the front of the crowd at the bar at the other end of the room. Joe caught his malevolent eye, and gave a rueful smile and a 'better luck next time, mate', shrug of his shoulders. This matey interaction didn't go down too well with the giant, who stared at Joe intimidatingly.

"It was my turn then, you bastard," he growled nastily.

"Really?" Joe said a bit hesitantly. He felt that he had to give the aggrieved hulk a reply, and couldn't decide whether a joking or conciliatory reply would go down better. He decided on the conciliatory, considering the circumstances and the size of the man. "Sorry mate, I didn't see you there." He felt a hand on his shoulder.

"This man bothering you, darling?" Alan asked, staring aggressively at the big man.

"Give over, Alan." Joe whispered.

"You getting served yet?"

"Yeah, he's filling them now."

The barman arrived right on cue, with a tray full of overflowing, foaming, half-pint glasses in his hand, which he placed on the bar in front of them. "Twelve halves, there you go." He took the fiver, and brought back the change.

Alan continued to give the big guy the evil eye, to which he couldn't really respond effectively, as he was now engaged in giving the barman his order.

"Do me a favour and leave it, Alan. No trouble tonight, okay?" Joe pleaded.

They transferred the glasses from the tray to the bar counter between the two of them. The others came across and grabbed a glass each, and they moved away from the bar to a less crowded part of the room. Trev produced some cigarettes and passed the packet of twenty Embassy around and they all took one and lit up. When he got the packet back the coupon was missing.

"Come on, which thieving bastard has nicked my coupons?"

"You save them, Trev?" Alan asked.

"Yes, I bloody do." Trev wasn't happy.

"What you saving them for? I'll bet it's a sheepskin coat? All the showbiz stars wear them. Isn't that right, Trev? A nice, thick sheepskin overcoat to keep you warm in the nasty cold weather?"

"Never mind what I'm saving them for. Just give them here," Trev said, holding out his hand.

"How do you know that I've got them, eh? You doing a mind reading turn now as well?"

"Just pass them over, Alan." Joe butted in, "I saw you take them

231

out of the packet. Hand them over. Come on now, we don't want to spoil the lad's stag night now, do we?"

Alan reluctantly handed the coupons over to Joe, who passed them straight to Trev.

"Can't you take a joke or what?" Alan tried a strained laugh that didn't quite come off.

"Bleedin' hell, it's not half past eight yet and there's already been two possible punch ups. What's wrong with everybody tonight?" Joe asked.

"It must be the heat," Harry said, and they all laughed.

At nine o'clock they went onto the shorts and things got a bit confused after that. Joe had his best suit on. It was a light grey colour and the sky blue lining that had cost him a pound extra. He'd had a account at Burton the Tailors since he'd left school and started work, and had bought a new suit every six months or so until he got married. It was a good two years since he'd bought this one. So he was rather annoyed when a big blonde lass wearing a leopard skin swagger-style coat, while attempting to squeeze herself past him, inadvertently knocked her glass of Mackeson Sweet Stout all over his leg. The effect was startling. As well as being soaked by the liquid, one of the legs of his suit was a normal, light grey colour, while the other was now a distinctly darker colour as a result of the deluge of Mackeson.

"You look just like a black and white minstrel," Trev said flatteringly.

The blonde was profusely apologetic, but Joe said that it didn't matter and that it would soon dry out, and that he needed a new one anyway. He was almost drunk now, and the accident didn't have the same effect on him as it would have if he'd been entirely sober. It took days for the suit leg to dry out, and Joe had it dry cleaned as soon as he could afford it, but it was never the same again after that.

The kitty was all gone now, and they all had to contribute another fiver each. All agreed readily except Alan, who maintained that there should still be money left, and it couldn't have all been spent, not on the amount of drink they'd had up to now.

"A thief always thinks that everybody else is a thief," Harry said philosophically.

"You go and fuck yourself," Alan said viciously.

Joe had to restrain Trev from attacking Alan, but his resolve was weakening, and Trev wasn't going to be compliant for very much longer.

By closing time the entire group was well and truly drunk. Joe's speech was slurred, and he kept dropping his cigarette. In doing so, he inadvertently dropped the lighted cigarette onto the back of a young girl's coat. She and her friends didn't even notice, and he diplomatically didn't bring the fact to her attention, he just covertly brushed it off her clothing, leaving a singed mark on her coat.

At closing time, the oldest member of the group, Harry, to shouts of derision from the others, said his goodbyes and made for the bus home. He'd had enough to drink and was wise enough to know that he wasn't missing anything by not going clubbing and drinking even more.

The queue for fish and chips was long. It snaked out of the doorway and into the street. "Why don't we get something to eat in the nightclub?" Alan asked.

"'Cos we can't afford the prices in a nightclub. It's alright for you, you're probably rolling in money, but we're not all burglars, you know," Joe said.

"Listen who's talking. You should be able to afford a meal surely, what with all the money your…"

"Shut up, Alan," Trev said, shoving him violently into the road, and away from Joe. He gripped Alan by the lapels of his coat and shook him like a rat. "Shut your mouth. You mention Brenda and I'll kill you," he hissed.

Alan pulled himself away and readjusted his coat, shrugging his shoulders. "Well, he shouldn't keep having a go at me. He's always so high and fucking mighty. At least I've got enough money to buy myself something to eat."

If Joe had noticed anything untoward he didn't mention it, and probably took it to be the drink talking. They stood in the queue until they were served, then walked back towards the town centre, eating the fish and chips from the newspapers they were wrapped in, as they went.

"You getting on alright with your dad?" Richie asked his cousin, more to try and change Alan's mood after the argument with Trev, than from genuine curiosity.

"Aye. He's not such a bad bloke once you get to know him. My mam still hates him, but I think he's alright." Alan had become really friendly with Eddy and spent a lot of time drinking and playing snooker with him and the McKennas. They got on so well that Alan had even told him about his plan to save his money and buy a flock of top-class racing pigeons, something that he'd never mentioned to anyone else, not even his mother. He'd never told anyone else because he felt that he should have higher aspirations than just a flock of racing pigeons. He should be setting his sights higher, and aiming for something more worthwhile. And he would, as he got older and more worldly wise, but at the moment he really didn't have any idea of what else he should be aiming for.

They had just about finished their suppers when they reached the door of the Sands Nightclub. The sound of loud dance music bellowed from the club's brilliantly lit doorway.

"You can't come in here with that," the big doorman said aggressively.

"No bother," Trev said, crumpling the newspaper up and dropping it in a nearby waste bin.

The rest of the group followed suit and started to file past the grim-faced doormen. One put out his hand and pushed Alan backwards.

"I know your face. You're barred, aren't you?"

"No, not me mate. You must be mistaken."

The other bouncer came across having a look. "No, he's alright. You're Alan Spencer, aren't you?"

"Aye, that's right."

"I know you from Durham. You were in on remand on D wing

about a year ago, burglary, right?"

Alan nodded. "That's right."

"Thought so. I'm good with faces I am. Go on get yourself in, but no trouble mind."

"Sure. Thanks mate," Alan said, as he followed the others up the stairs towards the source of the music.

They paid their entrance money to the bored blonde behind the desk, got cloakroom tickets for their overcoats, passed the small groups of bouncers who were watching the male customers, watching the girls on the dance floor, and joined the revellers. The place was heaving, and the noise almost deafening. Pushing their way through the throng to the bar, they eventually ordered drinks after managing to catch the eye of the barmaid. Joe was into explaining his well-thought-out philosophical theory in obtaining the attention of the barmaid in situations such as this one to Trev, but his audience was well beyond any sort of sensible participation in the discussion.

Trev was actually giving most of his attention to a couple of girls standing near to them. The girls were both blonde, attractive and as they were making obvious to Trev, available.

"You should try your luck there, mate," Joe said to Trev, giving up on trying to explain his theory.

"No. Not me. I'm courting now. She's a lovely lass is Fiona. She's entirely different from any other girl I've known. Wait until you meet her tomorrow at the wedding." He stayed with the others at the bar and continued to drink, paying over the odds for the alcohol they were served.

A couple of the other lads tried to break up the two girls on the dance floor, but were soon given their marching orders as the females made it obvious that their attentions weren't appreciated.

The night wore on. At closing time in the early hours of Saturday morning, one of the stag night group came out of the club alone after being separated from the others and was involved in an altercation outside of the club with a bouncer. As a result he needed hospital treatment and was taken to the A&E department by ambulance. Xrays confirmed that he had a hairline fracture of the skull, and concussion. He was kept in hospital for observation. The police commenced an investigation into a possible assault charge against the doorman, as witnesses stated that he'd punched and kicked the injured man repeatedly and without justification.

Another of the party, who also became separated from the group and while walking home, was set upon by three men. He was drunker than they were and weighing up the odds against him, quickly decided that discretion was the better part of valour. The three chased him for a hundred yards or so and then lost interest, but he didn't realise this, and thinking they were still pursuing him, vaulted over a three-foot high wall, planning to make good his escape through a neighbouring housing estate. Unfortunately, the drop on the other side of the wall was a bit more than the three foot he'd vaulted over, and fell away in a sheer drop of twenty-five feet to a disused railway line beneath. He hit the ground standing upright, and as a result broke almost every bone in both of his legs. He passed out immediately and didn't know anything else until he woke up in hospital twelve hours later. He could quite easily have lain there for a couple of days, but a workman taking a shortcut on his way home from his shift at the local glass works, spotted him and phoned for an ambulance.

The main body of the group left the club together at about half past two. They were too drunk to sing or make a fuss, and saved their depleted energy resources for the long walk ahead of them to reach home, not having any money to waste on such luxuries as taxis. The cold December night air, coupled with the unaccustomed, copious amount of alcohol that Richie had drunk took its toll. He passed out, and fell backwards as though pole-axed, stiff as a board, to the ground.

Luckily, he was at the front of the little procession, so the others saw him fall, and he wasn't left behind, as so easily could have happened had he been at the rear. After a brief but expressive discussion, in which various suggestions were put forward to resolve the problem, including leaving him there to sleep it off, rolling him home along the ground, and dragging him by his feet, they came to a consensus.

The lads hoisted him up onto their shoulders and began to carry him homewards. All went well, despite the obvious difficulties. As Richie's dead weight was spread pretty evenly across their shoulders they could carry him well enough and they made fairly good progress in the right direction. That is until the police arrived. The little crocodile of bearers had just reached a building site, and someone suggested that they have a break for a fag, when the panda car pulled up alongside them. The crocodile was stationary, still balancing the prone body on their shoulders. Some of the more optimistic amongst the group thought that this was an opportunity for the boys in blue to come to the rescue and offer them a lift home. They were soon proved to be wrong, of course.

"Right then," the extremely tall and overweight sergeant, who had just unfurled himself from the restraining confines of the extremely small panda car, said, as he stretched his arms way over the top of his head, yarned luxuriously, and broke wind loudly. "What have we got here then?"

His companion, the driver, an equally tall, but very thin constable, emulated his superior's exaggerated body movements but didn't speak, or fart.

One of the body carriers at the front of the crocodile, supporting Richie's feet, was nearest to the policemen and tried to answer, but, because of a combination of the excessive alcohol consumption, his weariness, and the freezing cold night air, couldn't get his mouth to form the correct words that he was trying to express. It came out something resembling, "Jushhh…"

Decidedly unimpressed, the sergeant said, "Oh aye." His suspicious eyes took in the lifeless body balanced precariously on the shoulders of this line of obviously drunken men.

"I'll bet money that this lot have been up to no good," he said to the constable.

The now stationary bearers, having to constantly readjust and reposition their hold on their unwieldy heavy burden, swayed unsteadily. .

"Is he okay, do you think?" the sergeant asked the inebriated stutterer at the front, indicating Richie's prone form with a nod of his head.

Again the drunken, weary, and very cold man was unable to respond intelligibly, but that didn't matter now because something was happening, something was stirring, it was Richie.

"Oh, it's alright, he isn't dead at all." The sergeant said in mock surprise, as the future bridegroom came to life before their eyes.

Richie did indeed come to life. He opened his eyes and could see nothing but the black night sky high above. He could see the stars twinkling up there, but just at this precise moment wasn't in any mood to appreciate the undoubted beauty of the scene. All that he was aware of was being afloat, seemingly unsupported in the ether. He was also aware of things trying to grasp at him from below, claw-like, disembodied hands that grasped and groped at him. His overcoat was wide open, as was his jacket, and due to the constantly moving supporting hands, his shirt had also come open, the buttons coming adrift from their restraining button holes. Richie, unaware of what was happening to him, did what anyone would have done in the same situation, he struggled, twisted, turned and screwed himself in all directions in a desperate attempt to escape these claw-like creatures.

The sergeant watched with growing amusement as the crocodile of drunks lurched first one way, then the other, trying to maintain their balance and retain the wriggling figure still held, now even more precariously, aloft. They couldn't maintain it for long of course, and the laws of gravity inexorably intervened with the inevitable effect.

The crocodile, together with the still struggling Richie, toppled into a mud-filled ditch at the side of the building site. They went down like the Titanic, brave but doomed, still holding Richie on their shoulders like pallbearers at a funeral, and disappeared entirely from the view of the two policemen, who stared open-mouthed in wonder at the spectacle. They soon recovered their professional bearing, if not their composure, and were still laughing heartily as they pulled the men out of the mud hole, like drowned rats, one at a time.

23

The groom was resplendent in his uncle's old, shocking-electric-blue, crushed-velvet three-quarter jacket that reached to his knees. It was fashionably trimmed with black fur at the cuffs and collar. His wedding suit was completed with faded blue, denim drainpipe jeans, and one-inch thick crepe-soled, black brothel creeper shoes which sported large silver buckles. He had also borrowed Trev's tasselled cowboy stage shirt, complete with bootlace tie held with the silver horned steer's head grip.

The overall natty effect was somewhat marred by the thick white thread stitching that held the seams together along the whole length of the back of the jacket. It was the best that his friends and family could rustle up at such short notice, and infinitely better than the new suit he'd worn the night before which was now just a pile of unserviceable rags at the bottom of the dustbin. The clothes belonging to everybody that had fallen into the ditch were unwearable, and the male wedding guests involved had turned up in a variety of sometimes-unbelievable combinations of jackets and trousers.

Joe had also borrowed an old suit from Trev that was a size or two too small for him, and its concerned owner spent most of the ceremony anxiously watching the bulging seams as if willing them to hold every time that Joe bent over slightly or sat down.

The bride looked her very best in an off-white two-piece suit that was going back to Great Universal first thing on Monday morning. The four bridesmaids, all friends of Julie, were similarly attired but in pink. In fact their outfits had been ordered by the mother of the bride from exactly the same catalogue.

Alan, the best man, was also rather exotically dressed in a pair of faded blue jeans, an old leather bomber jacket and black suede shoes. The shoes were scraped, scuffed and definitely well past their best, but were all that he could obtain in his size, at such short notice.

The groom and Alan, on the pretext of 'getting some fresh air', had fortified themselves in the local pub as soon as it had opened, forty minutes before the taxis were due to arrive. They managed two pints each. The first was simply a mender, or a 'hair of the dog', hangover cure. They'd ordered and drunk the second pint simply because they were feeling a lot better now, and they still had ten minutes before they had to go back home to get the taxi to the civic centre.

The civil ceremony went fairly smoothly with only two of the wedding guests getting into trouble with the security staff at the Civic Centre. One of them was Julie's Aunt Mary who was 87 years old. She had a disagreement with Great Aunt Alice. The trouble between them had been going on for donkey's years now, and stemmed from an alleged affair Uncle Arthur, Aunt Mary's husband, supposedly had with Sally, Great Aunt Alice's daughter. A number of relations became embroiled in the fracas, which at one time got so bad that it threatened to halt the wedding, as the security guards threatened to throw them out of the building. However, things gradually settled down again, and the ceremony went ahead.

Richie was obviously as proud as punch and Julie looked radiant. Some of the guests took photographs after the ceremony and Richie was particularly insistent that they got photographs of him signing the register.

Safely back in the local club, where a room had been booked for the day, the celebrations began in earnest. The bride's mother had made the sandwiches with her own fair hands. In fact she had arranged all the catering.

Richie and the bride's father made brief, nervous speeches and then sat down again relieved that their oral ordeal was over. Alan, as best man surprised everybody, not least himself, with his verbal skills.

Alan's speech was full of jokes and innuendoes, but was received well enough. "Richie and Julie have known each other for three years. They met at the dog track one Friday evening. Richie hadn't picked a winner at all that night." Alan paused to allow the laughter to subside. "They have a lot in common, and really are ideally suited. Richie likes to drink and gamble on the dogs, and Julie is a barmaid working at the dog track. Julie claims that she is only a little bit pregnant, can't understand how it happened and is barely five months gone. The bump is a bit conspicuous, but she says that it's handy as she can rest her drink on it while sitting down." He continued in similar vein, mentioning Richie's supposed attendance at a VD clinic and his treatment for premature ejaculation - "it was touch and go for a while". He ended on a serious and sincere note, wishing his cousin a long and happy marriage, and asking everyone to toast the good health and future married life of the couple.

When the club closed at three, all the guests repaired to the mother of the bride's house where more refreshments were available.

The evening's celebrations resumed early back at the club, and were in full swing by eight o'clock. Couples were up dancing to the mobile disco, which was blasting out the latest top ten chart hit for the third time in twenty minutes.

Harry and Olive had, after due deliberation, ensconced themselves at the rear of the room in prime seats that were positioned near to both the bar and to the toilets. Trev, who was uncertain that he had done the right thing in bringing Fiona, had managed to secure seats nearby, within easy socialising distance. He was concerned that she would think his friends a bit beneath her, but his fears turned out to be groundless, as Fiona proved to be a big hit with everyone who met her. Fiona seemed to be enjoying the evening, telling Trev that she considered his friends and the other wedding guests to be lovely. Trev wanted to leave after a couple of drinks and go somewhere where they could be alone, but she was enjoying herself and insisted that they stay, despite Trev's protestations.

Brenda didn't accompany Joe to the wedding. They couldn't get anyone to look after Sharon for the day, and Joe guessed that she didn't really want to face the other wives, who would all know about her stripping escapade by now. Somehow Joe found himself separated from his friends and was tightly sandwiched between the bride's Aunt Mary, and another, unidentified, elderly female relative. The two women talked across Joe as if he wasn't there, and although he offered to move seats on a number of occasions, he was told by them to stay where he was and enjoy himself. Despite himself, he was beginning to become enthralled in their conversation, which seemed to centre on an unidentified relative's wedding. Aunt Mary had obviously been interested in the subject for quite some time, and was clearly making the most of this golden opportunity to cross-examine the other lady who appeared to be a key witness. Joe's interest started as a few snatched overheard words of the conversation, and he gradually became drawn into the drama of the thing until he couldn't wait for the next disclosure to be made.

"Didn't she ever go back then?"

"No. Never. That was the last that we ever saw of her. She left all of her clothes and everything. One of the neighbours, that Mrs Jones from number 23, her with the dirty nets, she reckoned she once saw her in Woolworths, that was a few months after, but she never spoke, just walked right past her."

"And what about him, did he ever…?"

"No. Never."

"And she just went like that, eh?"

"Aye. Through the window. She just upped and went and climbed through the bedroom window on their wedding night. Can you credit it?"

"And he never, you know, said anything about why she did it?"

"No. It's not the sort of thing that you can bring into polite conversation, can you really? but I did try and get to the bottom of it."

"And did you?"

"No. Well not really. He was very cagey after that."

"I mean it's not as if they didn't know each other very well or anything."

"Oh no, they'd been courting for twelve years, on and off like."

"Aye, more on than off, eh?" The women both laughed dirtily.

Joe, who had finished his drink some time ago, but was reluctant to go to the bar in case he missed an important piece of the evidence, could finally wait no longer, and excused himself as he squeezed past the still gossiping women. The bar was crowded with people waiting to be served, and the psychological theory regarding the best way to get served that had seemed so plausible early the previous evening, now deserted him, and he waved his empty glass helplessly in the direction of the barmaids in the vague hope that this would produce a response. Luckily a man next to him had just been served and was paying the barmaid; Joe caught the barmaid's eye and ordered his drink.

The man was reorganising the drinks on the large tray in front of him on the bar counter, preparing to carrying them to the table where his company were sitting. It was Richie's father, Jackie. "Put that brandy in the snowball glass, that's for your mother."

"But she doesn't drink brandy, she only drinks advocaat." His assistant was Richie's younger sister Karen.

"No, she thinks that she only drinks advocaat, but I always put a brandy in it for her. Why do you think that she always ends up singing?" Turning his head, he recognised Joe. "You having a good time, Joe eh, enjoying yourself?"

"Yes thanks, Jackie. Everybody is." Joe gestured around the room expansively with his hand. "And no trouble to spoil things."

"Aye, I asked Fingers and Sid to sit near to the door so as to stop any gatecrashers," Jackie said, proud that his foresight and planning had worked so well. The two aforementioned local notables weren't really doorman material. Neither was more than average in 'using himself', but they certainly looked the part, both being large, muscular, and having the facial features of failed heavyweight boxers. One look at the pair would deter all but the most determined gatecrasher from attempting to enter without an invitation.

"You want a drink? Go on have a short," the inebriated parent said to Joe.

The happy parent apparently was on the shorts himself now and the tray contained large quantities of whisky, rum, brandy, vodka and tonics, port and lemons, brandy and Babychams, plus of course the aforementioned 'snowball' for members of his company. "Do you want a drink then or what?"

Joe, remembering the problems he'd had with his stomach the last time he'd drunk spirits, decided to stay off the shorts for a while longer. "Thanks, Jackie, I'll have a pint."

Joe stood at the bar with his lager, happy to watch everyone else's antics as they danced and cavorted on the dance floor. People danced at weddings who never normally took to the floor, and it showed. One couple in particular caught his eye; they were some distant relation through marriage to Julie's family and could hardly stand up straight, never mind dance. Joe guessed that they were doing some version of Rock and Roll, as the music was in that vein, but they looked more like they were doing the Twist. He watched enthralled as they bent and rose, twisted and cavorted, their antics becoming more and more eccentric. He felt almost certain that they would crash to the floor very soon and couldn't take his eyes from the couple in case he missed the grand finale.

"You alright?" The voice came from behind Joe, and he turned to find Alan standing with a pint in his hand.

"Yes, champion thanks. You?"

Alan nodded, or attempted to nod while taking a drink. "Good night. I think that most of these will be flat out by closing time though." He indicated the revellers in the room. He moved closer to

Joe. "The McKennas have been arrested, nothing to do with the drugs thing, they got lifted for a robbery they pulled last year." He looked around furtively. "Apparently there's another Yank on his way over with more money for the pay-off. This one is one of the Mob's button men. Guy named Scaretti."

"Button men?"

"Aye, you know, a hit man," Alan's voice was strained.

"A hit man?"

"Aye, a hit man. You gone deaf or something? They're not happy because it was their drugs that went missing and they think that Chisholm and the McKennas might be ripping them off. Apparently the whole set-up is their idea. The yard takeover, bringing the stuff in etc. It's all theirs, the Mafia."

"Bleedin' hell, what happens if they find out it was us?" asked Joe, disconcerted.

"Doesn't bear thinking about."

"How come you know all this anyway?"

"Me mother told me." Alan thought for a moment, anticipating the next question. "She must have got it from me dad, I suppose, he knows the McKennas, did a stretch with them."

"Look Alan, this is something else this is. I don't like the sound of this Scaretti. This is big time, man, it's way, way out of our league," Joe said.

"You're right there, mate. But look, think this through, Scaretti's going to bring more money with him for the pay-off."

"So?"

"So, assuming that he doesn't shoot them all, it means that the pay-off is going ahead as arranged."

"So?"

"So we've got to stop it haven't we?"

"Have you told the others?"

"Not yet."

Joe swallowed hard. He knew that they'd all agreed to stop the takeover, and they could only do that by stopping the pay-off, but now that the Mafia was involved, he was having second thoughts. "Stealing the stuff from that church was bad enough, but actually tackling a Mafia hit man is a bit too much. This is real big time crime. We're shipyard labourers man, not the bleedin' FBI. Don't you think this is all getting a bit too heavy for us, Alan?"

Alan did indeed think so but there was no way that he was going to show it. Their conversation was cut short by a commotion from the dance floor. They looked around quickly just in time to see the couple that had captured Joe's attention a few minutes ago fall with an almighty waving of limbs and land in a heap, taking a number of neighbouring dancers down with them. The prone couple lay helpless and winded as the other dancers helped the fallen to their feet. They rubbed their bruised and injured parts as they limped off the dance floor.

"Look, we'll talk this over later with the other lads, okay?" Alan said.

Joe, looking worried, agreed.

After closing time, huge quantities and varieties of bottled alcohol were bought, mostly on credit, from the club steward and carried carefully home to be consumed by the guests, The alcohol would never be wasted; if it wasn't drunk tonight then it would be consumed tomorrow, and would help to wash down the last of the now stale sandwiches, pies, and sausage rolls left over from lunchtime. With laden arms the group made their unsteady way back to a house where the celebrations continued well into the early hours of the following day.

Sunday morning was wet and cold. The allotment shed was cold and draughty. The paraffin heater was broken and the roof had started to leak in a couple of places. Rainwater dripped monotonously and loudly into the old buckets that Harry had strategically placed to catch the drips. The five men sat quietly nursing hangovers and listening intently as Alan told them all about the impending visitor from American organised crime. The news came as a bombshell to them all except Joe, who Alan had informed at the wedding.

Harry shook his head and blew smoke upwards, as if to plug the holes in the roof with it. "I don't like the sound of this," he said to the assembled company.

"You're not the only one," Joe said earnestly.

"This is getting really dangerous now," Trev said, lighting a cigarette and adding to the pollution.

"I think we should give it up for now. Just leave things and let events take their course," Harry said, putting into words what the others were thinking.

"There's not really much we can do now that the Mafia's involved," Trev agreed.

"We could all end up dead if we meddle in their business. They don't play around, these guys," Alan put in, as if he knew all about the workings of the Mob.

"So that's it then? We just let them get on with their plans to take over the yard?" Harry asked.

"Well, there's not much else we can do, is there?" Joe agreed.

"What about you then, cousin, what do you think?" Alan asked Richie.

"I don't know. I suppose we should just forget the whole thing. I don't want to end up dead, but…"

"But what?" Alan asked.

"But, I don't know, it just seems wrong to chicken out and not do anything," he said simply.

Richie's statement summed up the other men's feelings exactly. They all desperately wanted to stop the takeover, but were afraid to get involved with the Mafia. The men left the shed depressed and somewhat ashamed, having agreed not to get drawn into the dangerous dealings of the Mob.

24

The strike was over; or rather it was postponed until after the New Year. The strikers threatened that they would walk out again then if their demands weren't met in full. They'd agreed to go back to work for the last two weeks before Christmas to allow themselves and the other workers to receive at least one week's pay before the festivities arrived.

The yard didn't take long to get back to normal. Within an hour of starting work, the night shift was in full production and there might never have been a stoppage. However, it was to be a shift that would be long remembered by the workers.

Skinner strode up to Joe who was standing in A bay.

"Give your mate up there," he indicated the overhead crane, "a shout and tell him that I want him in the crane in C Bay for a lift in ten minutes." The manager then strutted off to the other end of the shed.

Joe duly whistled to attract Harry's attention and indicated that he should come down.

Harry gave him the thumbs up sign and started the crane moving. Joe watched as his friend moved the crane to the end of the bay and come to a stop at the supporting stanchion. Harry squeezed awkwardly out of the narrow doorway, and climbed carefully down the sixty-foot-high steel ladders.

"What does he want now?" Harry asked. "I saw him pointing at me."

"The squad in C Bay need a lift in a few minutes and he wants you to go over there."

"Albert's not been replaced then?"

"No. I heard that he's started work in a some factory over the river," Joe replied.

"Bloody hell, so I've got to do his job as well now, have I?" Harry grumbled as he made his way towards C Bay.

Harry reached the bottom of the ladders and started to climb slowly, one step at a time, ensuring that he moved only one arm or leg at any one time. This meant that he always had at least three of his limbs attached to the ladders and so reduced the chance of him falling. He took his time and ascended gradually and without undue effort. The ladder was made up of four, fifteen-foot sections, which were bolted to the concrete stanchion that supported the overhead crane tracks. Three quarters of the way up he paused, hooked his arms around the ladder and rested for a few minutes.

The squad below, ready to commence their lift shouted and catcalled to him good-naturedly.

"Get a move on, you old git. Me granny could move a lot quicker than that," the plater shouted.

"Aye, is that right? Well why don't you get her to come up here and do it then?" Harry replied, giving him a two-fingered salute.

"Come on, get a move on, we need this double bottom turned tonight," the plater complained.

"Aye, right then, don't get your knickers in a twist. You're a right nag. Worse than our lass, you are," Harry said, but started to climb again.

He reached the final ten-foot section of the ladder, and as he got higher, within a few feet of the top, he felt the metal move. He automatically grasped the sides of the ladder more tightly, but the movement continued, and he looked around, puzzled, trying to figure out why. Looking up, he realised too late what was causing the movement. The top of the ladder was coming away from the stanchion. He stared horrified, as if transfixed, as the ladders swung out and away from the stanchion.

He could see the top of the ladder, just a few feet above him. The two ten-inch long bolts that should have held the ladder in place were loose and ineffective. In fact, he realised with horror, one was missing altogether. He hung on helplessly as the ladder tilted towards him and the one remaining bolt fell out of the hole, narrowly missed his head, and fell to the floor below.

All he could do was to hold even tighter to the collapsing piece of steel as it took him outwards into the yawning void.

Harry held onto the steel ladders for dear life. They swayed out terrifyingly into space, taking him with them. Then, suddenly they stopped with a jerk as the one remaining bolt in the bottom of the ladders became wedged fast in its hole. It was only the angle of the ladders, and his weight on them, which kept the bolt in position, preventing the ladders, and him, from falling.

Harry, with an agility that surprised the onlookers on the ground, wrapped his legs around the outside of the ladders and slid down to the safety of the lower set, which he grasped tightly. His weight removed, the jammed bolt at the bottom slackened, fell out, and the ladders slid away from the stanchion. They fell to the ground, where they landed with a bang. They lay on the floor, shaking and vibrating for some time before finally lying still.

The men working in C Bay ran across and formed a loose circle around the stanchion while Harry climbed slowly down to the ground.

Joe, alerted by the shouts and unusual activity, ran across to find out what had happened.

Skinner arrived, white-faced, as Harry reached the ground.

"You alright, mate?" Joe asked.

"Aye, just a bit shook up, that's all. Bastard things aren't safe," he indicated upwards with his head. "Those bolts have been loosened deliberately. The nuts have been removed. There's no way that they could come loose on their own, not all of them at the same time."

"That's impossible," Skinner snapped. "All the ladders were checked during the strike, there's no way they can be dangerous."

"Well, if you don't believe me, then just you go and have a look for yourself," Harry said angrily.

"I intend to do just that," Skinner said, and climbed the ladder slowly as if unwilling to reach the top and discover what he already knew was there. One of the platers followed him up, as if to give him moral support. The waiting men below watched as the pair examined the top of the ladders. Even by their cursory examination, it was obvious that the retaining bolts were conspicuous by their absence. The men climbed back down.

"Don't you think we should cordon the area off, Mr Skinner?" the plater asked.

Skinner looked at him blankly. "Cordon off?"

"For the investigation, you know."

"Oh, yes. The investigation. I suppose we should," Skinner said weakly.

The plater, with the help of a few others, cleared the men from the area and began to search for evidence that would be needed to establish the cause of the accident.

The fallen section of ladder's position was noted and recorded, as was the position of the two retaining bolts found. Despite an extensive and prolonged search they couldn't find any other bolts or their nuts.

Joe's colleagues came across and the details of the accident was recounted again and again. It had been a close thing, and Harry was very lucky that he hadn't been killed. After a few minutes, Harry went off to have a cup of tea.

"That was a close thing, Joe," said a voice behind him.

Joe turned to see Trev.

"Yes," Joe said noncommittally.

"It's a bastard when you've got to risk getting yourself killed to earn a few quid, isn't it? I've been talking to the shop steward and he says that the takeover has gone ahead. He reckons that it'll be all over the local papers tomorrow."

Joe nodded. "Well, there's not much we can do about it now. You don't mess with those types if you want to live to a ripe old age."

"You're right. I've been thinking about it long and hard, it's not worth the risk and there's no way we are going to get involved. I don't want my head blown off. But mind, I'm sick to death of bowing and scraping to make a few quid, when the likes of those," he indicated a welder with a nod of his head, "can afford to go to Spain three or four times a year. Why should they earn so much more that I do? They're no better than you or me, are they? They don't shit golden nuggets, anymore than you or I do, do they?" Trev said.

"The game's not straight," Joe agreed. "You working inside tonight then?"

"No such luck. The barmy plater wants us outside to berth two plates on the fore-end. In this weather, I ask you."

Outside on the slipway, Alan collected wood for the fire. He liked the night shift. The darkness suited him, and being awake when most other 'normal' people were asleep. He liked the strange feeling of power that it gave him. Being awake all night and seeing dawn break over the river and surrounding countryside, watching the salmon jump in the river and listening to the birds' dawn chorus, soothed and refreshed him. Although he had never given it any thought at all, and certainly never analysed his thoughts or emotions, had he done so, he would have been surprised at what he found. He may have discovered a link between these feelings of power and his nocturnal criminal activities, perhaps? But that should be perhaps more properly left to a future prison psychoanalyst's report.

The fire was well alight now. The tallow had made all the difference. The large oil drum with holes punched through the sides made an ideal brazier and once the flames had taken hold the wood was quickly engulfed in their greedy embrace. It was one of the labourer's jobs to keep the fire going all night. It was a focal point and somewhere that the squad could dry out if wet, or warm themselves if cold during the ten-hour shift.

Alan searched the berths for more wood to be used as fuel. He knew from experience that broken staging planks were amongst the best but they were scarce now, as other squads were also scavenging for fuel. At a push, planks of staging actually in use as platforms on the side of the hull, could be 'accidentally' broken. But he'd have to be very careful doing this as the foremen frowned upon such criminal waste. But, for unadulterated luxury, the real top of the range fuel was, without doubt, berthing blocks. Berthing blocks, especially the old ones, which were soaked right through with tallow were, with a little kindling of oily rags and wooden wedges, ideal material to keep the darkness and cold at bay. The blocks were used to support the hull of the ship while it was under construction on the slipway. At the launch the greasy tallow on the blocks ensured that there was no friction between the steel hull and the wooden blocks as the ship left its birthplace forever and slid smoothly down the slipway, and into the river. These tallow-saturated blocks would burn for hours on end with very little coaxing. Often just one of the blocks would be sufficient fuel for the entire night.

Once the fire was alight, and Alan was satisfied that it would burn for at least an hour or so, he engaged in his favourite sport of rat spearing. Carrying a cardboard box full of welding rods, he walked along the slipway and under the keel of the ship on the blocks. On reaching the water's edge he paused, stood perfectly still and waited. After only about thirty seconds he heard a slight rustling underneath the blocks, followed by scratching and squeaking. Holding his breath he slowly removed a welding rod from the box, and holding it by its tip, again paused, awaiting sight of his prey. He didn't have long to wait. After a couple of seconds a large brown rat scurried out from under the blocks and darted towards the river. Taking aim quickly, he threw the rod like a throwing knife, flicking it towards the running animal. The rod turned and somersaulted a number of times in mid-air before burying itself in the soft ground just in front of the rat. Alarmed, the rodent paused for a second before it changed direction and it was turning to the left, intending to run back under the blocks to safety, when the second missile embedded itself squarely in the back of its head, killing it instantly.

The riverside's population of rats was nowhere near equalled by the number of feral cats living in various overgrown corners of the shipyard and the felines had their work cut out trying to control the growing rodent population. Alan considered his nocturnal hunting expeditions as part pest control and part sport.

It was a successful night; the first rat he killed was the biggest he'd ever seen in the yards. It was a giant. Alan speared another two large rodents before returning to tend to the fire.

The edge of the huge steel plate hung over their heads like the sword of Damocles.

The plater waved frantically at the crane driver. He indicated that he wanted the plate lowered another four feet and moved to the left. Not that the driver could understand the signals, or even see them clearly, as he was forty feet higher than the plater, who was himself thirty feet from the ground and perched precariously on two planks of wood pushed together to form a crude piece of staging against the upturned hull of the fore-end. To make their position even more dangerous, the staging was covered in ice; it was a pitch-black night and it was snowing.

Trev could see that the driver didn't understand what they wanted him to do. He guessed that the man would have difficulty seeing them standing up here like pigeons on a telephone wire and the plater's indistinct hand signals were as good as nothing. He decided to intervene. "He can't see us from up there, man. We'd be better off packing it in and calling it a night." He nodded skywards. "The snow is worse now, and it's dangerous enough us just being up here without trying to berth these big awkward things."

"If they don't get berthed tonight the squad won't get their bonuses before Christmas," the plater said.

That's no skin off my nose, Trev thought to himself. Out loud he said, "That's all very well, but I'm not killing myself just so that you can have an even better Christmas than usual."

"It'll not take us long to get them tacked in, you'll see. Why doesn't he switch on his searchlight so he can see us?" the plater said, beginning to wave his arms frantically at the crane driver again.

Trev shook his head sadly. "If he turns that thing on it'll blind us. He can just about see us, but just doesn't know what you want him to do. Look, let me direct the crane, will you? You get inside the hull and pull the plate in when it gets near enough, okay?"

The plater agreed, happy to leave the crane directions to Trev, and scrambled inside the hull. Trev waved his arms over his head to catch the driver's attention and then, with his outstretched arms, he slowly, repeatedly and clearly indicated where he wanted the plate to go. The driver, now understanding exactly what was required, responded, and the large, inch-thick, steel plate swung slowly into position right over Trev's head. Luckily, there was very little wind, so the twenty-foot by fifteen-foot plate didn't swing around or deviate from its position at all. It simply hung there, in the night air, like a huge, dull, oblong gong, with snow falling softly around it.

Trev indicated again, with exaggerated arm signals and the plate dropped inch by inch towards him until it was almost level with his head. He reached up and pushed it towards the hull. The driver helped by swinging the jib of the crane a fraction closer, and the edge of the plate was soon almost balanced right on the rim of the plate already in position immediately below it. Trev indicated that the driver should hold it right there, which he did.

The plater shouted down for the tack welder to climb up.

The tacker was annoyed. The last thing he wanted was to be interrupted, as he was busily engaged in warming his backside by the brazier on the ground inside the hull. Reluctantly he made his way up the ladder, carrying his screen mask, gloves, and pulling the welding cable behind him. The men turned their heads away, shielding their eyes from the brilliant light, as the welder, looking like something out of a sci-fi film, his shield protecting his face, struck up an arc with a violent crackle of electricity, and got to work.

The fore-end of the ship, on which they were working, and the aft-end, which another squad constructed, were built upside-down, outside, near the berths. When fully assembled, they would be lifted into position and affixed to the rest of the ship's hull, which was being constructed on the slipway.

The lug welded in place on the suspended plate, a small winch was attached to it, and to a steel frame inside the hull at the other end and the plater began to ratchet the plate into position. The plate was very heavy, and as it was pulled inwards, the crane took up any slack on its strop or all its weight would fall onto the tack-welded lug, resulting in it breaking off. The plate was pulled inch by inch into place, the crane dropping the thing as smoothly as possible while it slowly moved into position.

A burner was required to burn off any excess pieces of plate so that it became a snug fit nestling against its mates already in position. Trev was sent off to find one. There had been a burner below, warming himself alongside the tacker at the fire when they'd started work, but he'd long ago disappeared. Trev had an idea where to find him and set off in the falling snow, which was slowly blunting the familiar sharp outlines in the yard with a blanket of cotton-wool-like softness.

The dark, disused shed was full of prone bodies. A stranger to the yard wouldn't have guessed that the piles of old overcoats, tarpaulins, and other assorted rags covered sleeping men, but Trev did. He lifted the various coverings and scanned the faces of the sleepers until he found the one he wanted.

"The plater wants you to burn-in a plate on the fore-end," he told the man, after shaking his shoulder to awaken him.

"What the fuck is he doing berthing plates in this weather? Daft bastard," the burner said, in a broad Scottish accent, rubbing the sleep from his eyes.

"Last shift for the plater's squad bonus, isn't it."

"Well whoopsy-fucking-do for their squad bonus. It doesn't get me any more money, does it?"

"I'm sure that they'll buy you a drink for Christmas," Trev said without conviction.

"Aye. That'll be right. Sure enough, pal. I won't hold my breath, by the way," he said sarcastically, pulling his coat collar up.

"Well, at least the platers are willing to work, the welders just seem to walk out at the drop of a hat."

"Aye, right enough. You're no wrong there. All the same, this barmy bastard plater should be locked up. He's got to be daft working out here in this. He'll get us all killed, he will."

The still grumbling burner walked with Trev back to the fore-end. The snow was increasing its efforts, and a strengthening breeze blew small, cold, stinging icicles into their faces as they walked.

At last, with a lot of banging and pulling, shouted directions from the plater and curses from the burner, the job was done and the plate safely secured. The tacker scuttled up and down the plate, tack welding the seam to hold it temporarily. The permanent welding would be completed tomorrow by the day shift.

The men took a well-earned break, and climbed down inside the hull to warm themselves at the brazier on the ground. They lit cigarettes and warmed their hands and backsides.

Most of the yard workers wore overalls under some sort of jacket or three-quarter topcoat that had once been worn for best. These old clothes, instead of being simply discarded, which would be considered to be a sinful waste of resources, were utilised for work, and so a ragtag array of work dress was the norm. They all wore flat cloth caps; no one except the foremen and managers wore the American-style hard safety hats. Indeed, any workers attempting to wear them would be ridiculed by their workmates. However, without exception, they all wore sturdy, steel toe-capped, safety boots, suggesting that they considered their feet were more essential than their heads. Most workers had a belt, or a piece of twine, tied around their waists outside of their coats to help keep cold draughts from reaching the top half of their bodies.

It was snug and warm on the inside of the hull, and the men were reluctant to venture outside into the cold night. There was just under an hour to go before the next meal break, so they decided, as a group, in an unspoken, but democratically assumed decision, to remain where they were until then.

They were toasting nicely when Skinner made an appearance. He looked around in apparent disbelief. "I wish I had time to stand around the fire warming my backside." His remark was to no one in particular; in fact it was seemingly addressed to the deckhead immediately above the men's heads. "I'd much prefer to be able to stand in the warm all night than work outside in the cold and the snow."

The burner melted away into the darkness and disappeared like snow in July. The tacker was making subtle efforts to do exactly the same and edging slowly towards the exit.

"We were just…" the plater began, but he was cut short by the foreman's interruption.

"I know. You were just going to move the fire outside and put it out, weren't you? You were going to move it outside so that it wouldn't buckle the hull with all the heat that it's throwing out, isn't that right?"

"Er, yes, that's right. Give me a hand to move the fire outside, will you, Trev?"

The plater and Trev used welding rods pushed through the holes of the brazier to lift the hot, glowing drum, gingerly and awkwardly outside. They dropped it a yard or so away from the hull, but a disapproving stare from Skinner made them reconsider, so they picked it up and moved it even further away.

Seemingly satisfied with the brazier's new position, Skinner kicked it over, spilling the flaming wood out onto the ground where it smouldered and spluttered impotently.

"Right then, I'll be off," Skinner said. "I'll come back later, you should have the other plate berthed by then," he said over his shoulder and disappeared into the night.

Skinner's appearance, and promised return, left them no option but to start the berthing process of the second plate, which they would have preferred to leave until after the break.

"It's probably just as well to get it done now, because that snow's starting to come down heavier, and the wind's getting up," the plater observed philosophically.

The second plate was too high and too far out for the men to reach, and they were forced to stand and watch helplessly as it turned slowly in the wind. The crane's cab and driver were now invisible to them in the swirling snow.

"You'd better get down and tell that crane driver to lower it a bit," the plater said, licking his lips nervously.

"A bit?" Trev replied. "How will he know what a bit is? Do you want it dropped ten feet or what?"

"Aye. Tell him ten feet. That should about do it," the plater said uncertainly.

Trev, muttering to himself, made his way along the two narrow, icy planks, and clambered down the wooden ladder, disappearing into the darkness below. He climbed down slowly, taking his time. He didn't intend to slip on the ice and fall the thirty or so feet to the ground.

"We shouldn't even be working up here tonight in all this weather," he muttered to himself. "How come we are working night shift when the day shift will probably only be allowed to work in the shed, because it's too cold for them to work outside?" He reached the bottom and made his way across the snow-covered ground towards the ghostly dark shadow that was the crane about fifty yards away.

The crane loomed out of the snow as he approached. It was a very large piece of machinery that ran on tracks like a train. He stepped carefully over the steel tracks, walked under the crane, and opened the yellow box attached to the side that held a telephone. It was a struggle to remove the handset from its vertical spring-held cradle, but he managed it and twirled the cranking handle furiously. The voice in his ear was faint. "What's up?"

"Hello, Frankie. Look mate, we can't see you at all from up on the fore-end now because of the snow. Can you drop the plate about ten feet so that we can get a grip on it?"

The reply from the disembodied voice was indecipherable.

"What? What did you say?" Trev shook the phone, and tried again. Nothing. "It's as good as nowt," he said to himself as he slammed the telephone hand piece back into the cradle.

He heard the hum of the machinery moving high above him as he hurried back to the fore-end and made his way up the ladder. At the top again, he walked the few feet to where the plater was reaching out to the slowly descending plate. The men watched carefully as the plate slowly came nearer and nearer. The whirring sound of the machinery stopped. The plate ceased its descent and hung suspended eerily above them, seemingly without support of any kind, even the steel strop attaching it to the crane's hook was hidden now by the thick, falling snow.

The strengthening wind was now starting to spin the large plate around like a giant helicopter blade, its speed increased noticeably as they watched. Nothing at all could now be seen of the crane, only the suspended plate, giving the appearance of a huge magician's illusion that had gone drastically wrong. Trev stared in amazement. He couldn't believe his eyes. The plater was actually jumping up and down on the narrow, icy staging, trying to grab the corner of the plate as it flashed by.

"Bloody nugget," Trev muttered. Then, louder, he shouted at the plater, "You'll kill yourself if you get a hold of that thing, it'll carry you right off the staging."

The wind increased its velocity even more, and the spinning plate took on a new and decidedly more dangerous aspect. It acquired a definite wobble to its uncontrollable spinning. Even the plater now backed away from this new, and frightening, gyrating phenomenon.

"I think that we should get off here now," Trev said loudly.

The plater said nothing, but continued to stare, enthralled, at the plate, which was still increasing the speed of its spin.

"Well, I'm getting off anyway, you can please yourself," Trev said, making for the ladder.

The plate wobbled, dropped slightly and hit the staging near to the men. There was a horrible crunching sound, as the wooden planks spit and fractured, the men were showered in flying splinters of wood, as the planks of the staging exploded and disintegrated outwards and downwards in the night air.

"Bloody hell!" Trev exclaimed, and jumped the last few feet to reach the ladder, his head and shoulders covered with some of the smaller pieces of the splintered wood. The plater was right behind him and they descended the ladder fast.

The plate, now completely out of control, was swinging and swaying as it rotated. The crane driver aware that something was drastically wrong, started to swing the crane's jib away from the upturned hull, but it was too late.

Trev and the plater were now almost at the bottom of the ladder and jumped the last few feet and ran away from the hull, their bodies bent double. They stopped when they considered they were far enough away, and looked back.

The plate was wobbling wildly in its orbit. The wobble was getting more and more violent as they watched and soon the inevitable happened, the thing broke loose from the crane. The men watched with open mouths as it took off and quivered, unrestrained in the air. The plate seemed to be defying every law of physics as it soared, following its own flight plan that involved violent changes of direction that would have given a jet fighter a problem. The thing changed altitude, speed and direction rapidly and speedily. It actually flew right over the watching men's heads at one point, like a huge flying carpet.

The crane driver had by now completely removed his jib, leaving the flight path clear for the object to manoeuvre freely and without interference. This aerial display held the men spellbound for at least twenty seconds before it came to an abrupt and violent conclusion. The wind abated suddenly, leaving the flying plate without support, and it dropped like a stone towards the ground. It fell, dart-like, corner foremost, and hit the ground with a shower of sparks that briefly lit up the area near the base of the crane. The plate then proceeded to bounce along the steel rails that carried the crane, balancing on its edge, defying gravity, sliding for some yards, before finally diving right into the gap running alongside the rails. The gap carried the electricity cable supplying the crane's power. The cable also carried most of the power to the neighbouring part of the city. There was an almighty explosion and a flash of light that illuminated the whole yard.

Despite the falling snow, Trev and the plater could now clearly see the crane, the shed and everything else in the yard. This brief illumination was closely followed by a display of sparks that leapt twenty feet into the air, and were accompanied by the crackling sound of a powerful electricity surge. Then, the sparks, and the crackling stopped and there was total silence, and darkness. There wasn't just total darkness in the yard, but as they watched, whole sections of lights outside the yard, the streetlights in the housing estates, all went out. Section by section the whole north part of the city was plunged into total darkness. Even the snowstorm eased in strength as if cowed by what had just happened.

"I don't believe that," Trev said quietly.

"Aye," the plater said, still looking at the plate in open-mouthed wonder. "We'd better go across and tell Skinner then, you reckon?"

"I suppose we'd better," Trev agreed reluctantly.

But the manager was already on his way across to see what had happened and met them halfway to the shed. The plater explained what had happened, and blamed the weather totally and without hesitation for the whole calamity. Trev nodded and made affirming noises when he thought that it was appropriate to do so.

Skinner nodded and tut-tutted, shook his head and sucked his teeth in disbelief. Then he stormed off to speak with the crane driver. Trev and the plater made themselves scarce.

25

The plater and Trev parted company when they reached the darkened shed. The emergency generator kicked in and the lights came on as they made their individual ways carefully to opposite ends of the building, to where they normally ate their sandwiches with their respective work colleagues.

Trev unpacked his sandwich box and flask. The other labourers joined him, and Trev related the story about the flying plate. The tale amused, but didn't surprise the men, most of whom had experienced similar mishaps. The men sat around the small gas fire and ate their sandwiches. Trev was a lot warmer now, even after only a few minutes under the cover of the shed's protective roof. As well as keeping the worst of the elements out, the shed keep a great deal of heat in.

Alan watched Richie unwrap his sandwiches. "What's this? Your lass is putting serviettes in with your bait for you now is she then? Hey lads, will you look at this."

"Make the most of it, mate, 'cos she'll soon get sick of that." Joe said, and shook his head reminiscently. "Brenda was the same when we were first married. But it'll not last long; she'll soon get tired of that. Chances are you'll be making your own sandwiches in a couple of weeks, just you wait and see."

"You managing okay?" Alan asked.

"Managing? What do you mean managing?" Richie asked, puzzled.

"Well, you know, shagging all night and everything? You look a bit pale. If I was you I'd give the nest a rest for a couple of nights and build your strength up."

Richie's face instantly reddened with embarrassment. "Shut up, Alan."

"Is Julie alright with your willy, then, Richie? She'll be a bit sore by now, is she?" Joe asked with apparent concern. Richie took his sandwiches and tea, and escaped his tormentors. He walked across the shed to another group seated at a neighbouring fire.

Swallowing the last of his cheese sandwiches, Trev crumpled the paper bag that had held them and threw it in a waste bin. "This is ridiculous," he said with obvious feeling. "Why can't we just work inside at night? Other yards work like that quite effectively."

"We're lucky to be working at all, the way things are at the minute. The welders have been out at least one night every week for the past few months. It seems like everybody is out on strike these days. Factories closed down, miners out. The gravediggers are even out in Liverpool. Bodies piling up in the streets they reckon," Joe said, busily engaged in shaking a bottle of white, chalk-like liquid.

"Never in the world?" Trev said, watching Joe drink straight from the bottle. "Your stomach playing up again?"

"Yes."

"A few years ago the newspapers were saying that we'd all be millionaires with all the North Sea oil pouring into the country. We'd be oil rich like the Saudis. No need to work and the only problem we'd have is how to fill all our spare time," Trev said.

"Well, they got the bit about not working right," Joe said. "Only they're not paying us for the time off."

"Even the council workers are on strike, the gardeners and such," put in Alan.

"Your uncle still working there?" Joe asked.

"No, he got the sack last winter," Alan said.

"How's that then?"

"Well, they couldn't work in the parks what with all the snow could they? So the gaffer puts them all to work in the town centre. They were supposed to be shovelling snow off the pavements. Well, Jackie soon gets tired of doing that, it was freezing, so him and a few others nipped into the pictures to see that new film that was on, the latest James Bond it was. So they're in there all warm and comfy and when they came out the gaffer's waiting in the foyer, isn't he? Paid them all off with a minute's notice."

"How did the gaffer know that they were inside, then?"

"Easy. The dozy bastards had left their shovels leaning against the wall in the foyer, hadn't they? Never was very bright, our Jackie."

The men laughed.

"I'm going to move to Jeopardy, there's loads of jobs going there," Trev put in. The others looked at him.

Alan was the one to bite. "Jeopardy, where the hell is Jeopardy?"

"I don't know, but it said on the news this morning that that's where all the jobs are, in jeopardy."

"Funny," Alan replied, obviously not amused at all. But the others laughed.

"It's probably near to Loggerheads. That's where the unions meet the management. It always says on the news that they're at loggerheads," Joe contributed, and again they all laughed.

The sound of metal banging on metal interrupted them. It was Skinner, who had a habit of throwing bits of scrap metal onto the metal plates purely to create a noise when he considered that the break was over. He made his encouraging way through the various part-constructed deck housings, bulkheads and double bottoms, in the different bays of the shed. The noise was supposed to instil a bit of urgency or perhaps energy into the men and to remind them that this was a shipyard and that similar sounds should be emanating from them as workers in the yard.

Skinner walked across to Trev. "You can't work outside now, the crane's out of action and I suppose it's not safe working up there anyway, not the way that the snow's coming down, and we don't want another accident tonight, do we? So you just tag along with the transporters and give them a hand for the rest of the shift."

Trev nodded, and followed the foreman across to where a small group of men stood beside a tractor attached to a large trailer. "Trev here will give you lads a hand for tonight. Just get on with loading these flanges onto the trailer, that should take you up to going home time." He was about to walk away, when one of the transporters, who was walking from the direction of the toilet, put a restraining hand on Skinner's arm.

"Come and see what some dirty bastard has done in the toilet, Mister Skinner."

The manager, always suspicious of practical jokes at his expense, peered closely at the speaker. The transporter's face appeared to be perfectly straight and serious, and there was no obvious sign of a twinkle in his eyes, so Skinner allowed himself to be guided towards the toilets. All the transporters and Trev followed him. Trev knew that it was some sort of wind-up, as one of the crew nudged him conspiratorially in the ribs with his elbow and winked.

The group entered the dimly lit toilets. A row of half a dozen cubicles, empty of any human occupants, lined one side of the bare, brick walled construction, and four porcelain urinals lined the opposite wall. The transporter hurried across to where a couple of pages of newspaper lay on the floor in a corner. Bending over the papers, he said disgustedly. "Look what they've done. The dirty buggers. Just look at that."

Skinner crouched down on his hunkers and the rest of the men formed a semi-circle around them.

Lying on the damp newspaper were what appeared to be two large turds. They were, in fact, pieces of ginger cake left over from someone's bait. Some time had been spent rolling and forming them into passable copies of turds and Trev had to admit that the colour and texture did look like remarkably realistic in the weak light of the small bulb in the toilet. To add even more realism to the art form, a few drops of hot water had been sprinkled over them. This enhanced, and dramatised the effect by not only giving the impression of steam rising upwards from the objects, but also added to their realistically rich, moist, appearance.

Skinner was known to be an absolute stickler for tidiness and cleanliness, and the men watched with interest as his face grew a sort of puce colour. There were many nudges and knowing winks within the group of watchers, but Skinner, in his rage, was oblivious to them all.

The transporter, deciding to add a little more to the pot, put his hand tentatively over the top of the 'turds', his palm just touching one of them. "They can't have been here for very long Mister Skinner. They're still warm, feel."

The manager stood up quickly. He had no intention of feeling the offending items. "Get the shed labourer in here to clean that…that…"

"Shit," put in the transporter helpfully.

"…up immediately. I want it cleaned up now. He looked around as if searching for the offender. "When I find out who done this… this…" again he searched in vain for the right word.

"Shit?" The word was offered again.

"…Obscenity. I'll sack him. He'll be out of here in double quick time. His feet won't touch the floor." The irate manager stormed off, and the men smiled at each other but didn't laugh out loud until they were sure that he was well out of earshot and then they all erupted in laughter.

26

The men started to drift away from the toilet now, as the shed was coming to life again, with platers and welders picking up their gear and moving towards their work places. Noise began to fill the air.

The plater Joe was working with walked across the bay and stood beside him. "We've got to turn this big bugger tonight," he said, kicking a large thick bulkhead plate that covered most of the bay floor area. Joe nodded and set off to find a couple of large lifting lugs. He located two, and dropped them approximately where the plater indicated, then the tacker came across and began to weld them to the plate. When both were secured to the top of the plate, Joe looked up, expecting to see the crane moving into position above them, ready to lift the plate, but the crane hadn't moved. Joe whistled, but there was still no response from Harry, high above their heads.

The plater, seeing that there was a delay, picked up his hammer and started to hit the steel upright support column that was nearest the crane. The noise was very loud, but drew no response at all from the crane driver.

"The old bugger is asleep again. He did one lift over an hour ago and must have dropped off again. You fancy climbing up there to wake him up?" the plater asked Joe.

Joe looked up, and calculated how far the crane was away from the edge of the column. "Aye, alright. I'll see if I can reach him by throwing scrap at the side of the crane." He climbed the ladder slowly, making sure that he had a good grip on the steel sides before moving one foot up at a time. Reaching the top, he stood grasping the column, and turned towards the crane. From here he could see Harry sitting slumped in his seat, his head back, apparently fast asleep. Joe pulled the various sized pieces of scrap from his pockets and looked down to make sure that there was no one underneath before he started to throw them. He threw one of the smallest pieces of metal first. It hit the side of the crane with a resounding bang, and then fell to the concrete floor of the shed far below. There was no response from the driver.

"Bloody hell," Joe muttered, "the old bugger is out cold." He tried again. This time he chose a bigger and heavier piece of scrap, and threw it at the crane harder. It hit bang on target just below the window. Joe thought that he saw Harry stir a little.

Angry now, annoyed that his friend wouldn't respond, he leaned out over the side, and looked down to answer the shouted enquiries from below. He shook his head. "I can't wake him," he shouted in reply. "I'll have another go."

This time he chose the biggest and heaviest pieces of metal that he'd carried up with him. He steadied himself against the column, adjusted his balance and threw the metal as hard as he could. He thought at first that his aim was off, as the metal seemed to be heading straight for the crane's window, but the metal turned in mid-air, wobbled, and hit the side of the crane with a noise loud enough to wake the dead. Joe was expecting to see Harry sit up suddenly with the shock of the noise, but there was no movement from him at all.

Joe shook his head. There must be something seriously wrong. There was no other option now, he'd have to climb across the ten or fifteen yards of rails, and reach the crane that way. He put a foot gingerly on the rails, which were slippery with grease. He held tightly onto the overhanging girder for support and inched his way slowly across. Shit, he thought, I'm getting too old to be climbing about like this. Sweat formed on his brow as he hesitantly made his way across. Finally, and with great relief, he reached the cabin of the crane. He could see Harry sitting in there, head back, and watched closely for any sign of movement, a slight rising and falling of the chest or twitching of the nose or mouth, but there was nothing.

Joe stepped onto the roof of the crane, a nasty feeling of dread in his chest. He leaned over the side and found that he could just reach the door handle. He turned it and the door swung open. Dropping into the opening, he hit his head on the side of the metal window bracket that hung open near to him. Cursing and rubbing his smarting head, he shook the prone figure still hoping that he was only in a deep sleep, but the figure was a dead weight and there was no response at all to his shaking. Joe slammed the door shut, and standing in front of Harry, operated the controls to move the crane back to the stanchion from where he could alight and climb down the ladders.

He clambered down to the small group of grim-faced men at the bottom. "I think he's dead," Joe said unnecessarily.

Skinner, who had just arrived on the scene, climbed the ladder slowly as if unwilling to reach the top and discover what he already knew was there. One of the platers again followed him up. The pair examined the figure in the crane, and then slowly descended again. "He's dead alright," Skinner said decisively. He turned to one of the labourers. "Go and telephone for an ambulance and a doctor from the gatehouse. Oh, and you'd better get the police as well, I suppose."

The man ran off.

The police arrived and took charge, cordoning the area off with tape. The doctor examined the body and officially pronounced Harry dead. The police then directed operations to lower the body down from the crane and into the care of the waiting coroner's men who were now hovering like hungry birds of prey.

The deed was finally done and the body was whisked away in an unmarked black van to the morgue. As the van departed it seemed to take with it the yard's bustle and noise. A strange silence descended after the activity and recent excitement.

Skinner, shaken and white-faced, called the men together and announced the news that everybody already knew, that their workmate was deceased. The men were in a sombre mood, and it was obvious that there wouldn't be any more work done tonight, so he told them that they could all go home and that they would be paid for the rest of the shift.

"You can all go home and catch your missus and the lodger at it," was his feeble attempt at humour, which didn't evoke any response at all.

The men dispersed, but most were reluctant to go straight home, and walked slowly together up the bank to the main gate as if their comrades' presence could keep the dark thoughts of their own eventual demise away from their consciousness.

Joe went with the police to break the news to Olive and the sky was just beginning to acknowledge the pre-dawn glow of light when he finally arrived home. The other fore-end men had made their way to Trev's flat, where they talked and smoked, reluctant to leave the comfort of each other's company. It was as if while they were still together Harry was still with them, and he hadn't died during the night. They spoke of the man and his ways, of his jokes and his wisdom. Each one of them brought different memories of the man forward to be enjoyed and appreciated by the others. Although none of the men would ever use the word love, or even consider associating that emotion with what they felt for their deceased friend, never mind expressing it, nevertheless it was exactly what they did feel for him.

Joe told Brenda what had happened when he got home. She was upset by the news, and put her hands on Joe's shoulders, knowing how he would be affected by his friend's death.

"That's terrible Joe. I'll call in and see Olive later. She'll be in an awful state. How long have they been married? Forty something years?"

"Something like that," Joe said.

"God. How bloody awful."

27

"Doesn't he look well?" asked Olive as the two men came downstairs.

"Er, yes, I suppose so," Richie said, looking a bit confused.

"Yes, he does that," said Trev.

"They did a good job on him at the undertakers, didn't they? He looks years younger now, and healthier," Olive went on. "He's got his best suit on and I put his old teeth in. He never liked them new ones you know, he kept biting himself."

The men nodded and smiled politely as Alan moved along the sofa, allowing the other two access to the seats. When seated, they were anything but comfortable. They waited, fidgeting uncomfortably while the widow poured them tea and offered biscuits. The room was full of the unmistakable odour of newly laid carpet.

"No thanks, no biscuits for me," said Trev. "No sugar either thank you," he said, waving away the offered bowl.

Sitting uncomfortably on the very edge of the sofa the men sipped their tea, their feet tapping impatiently on the carpeted floor.

The three were feeling acutely uneasy and had to consciously slow down, and not gulp their tea in their haste to be away outside for a smoke.

They'd miscalculated and arrived a bit earlier than the rest. Joe had assured the others that the cortège was leaving the house at ten o'clock, but it was in fact leaving at half past ten, so they were a full half an hour early and had to endure the small talk and the ritual of viewing the deceased's body lying in state in the bedroom upstairs.

"Are you sure you won't go up and see him, Alan?" Olive asked.

"Er, no thanks Olive. I'll remember him the way he was when I last saw him." This was his standard reply when requested to view any deceased relative or friend. He didn't like dead bodies at all and wouldn't go anywhere near one.

"He's going to be a miss," Olive said. "I don't know what I'm going to do without him."

"Oh, Mickey sends his condolences and his apologies. He's sorry that he can't be here," Trev said.

"I heard about him getting arrested. It's a disgrace him being locked up. Mickey wouldn't hurt a fly and him with those bairns and Christmas just a few weeks away. And Tracy, the poor lass. She's worked herself into the ground looking after those bairns, making herself ill. It's a crying shame, that's what it is. Tragic. Those poor bairns, their father in prison and their mother in a mental hospital. I'd have taken them in myself if their grandmother hadn't taken them. God love them. Terrible it is, they say she tried to commit suicide. Whatever was she thinking of, the poor lass?"

Olive, mistakenly under the impression that she had succeeded in making her guests feel at ease, left the men in their uneasy state, and glided around the room, flitting from one small group of muted mourners to another, as they patiently waited for the undertaker and his men to arrive.

Harry's daughter and her children had arrived from Australia only yesterday. They were naturally very shocked by Harry's sudden death and were still jet-lagged and tired from the long journey. None of the family had been able to contact Harry's son, who had apparently changed his employers a number of times since their last contact with him. However, Harry's two sour-faced sisters had condescended to grace the occasion with their attendance and looked regally down their noses at everybody while making inaudible sarcastic remarks to each other under their breath.

After a few minutes Olive returned with the same plate of biscuits, which the men again refused.

"What do you think of the new carpet? Thirty pence a square yard, that's six shillings in old money, not cheap stuff this you know. There's underlay and everything," she demonstrated by peeling back a loose corner and displaying the rough brown felt beneath. "Woven back wool texture," she proudly read from the attached label sewn onto the underside of the carpet. She paused momentarily to draw breath.

The pause gave Trev the chance to mutter, "It's very nice, I like the colour."

She continued, "I got it from Storey's in the high street, dealt with them for years you know, never any bother about the finance," she said the last word quietly, under her breath, as if it was slightly improper to utter it in polite company. "They came and measured up and laid the carpet in two days. I told them that it was urgent, that he was being buried today and that I wanted it down before the funeral." Her eye caught a photograph in an old-fashioned wooden frame on the sideboard and she gave a slight shake of her head. Tears started rolling down her cheeks. The photograph was a wedding portrait showing a young Harry in army dress uniform, standing proudly beside an equally young and radiant looking Olive. She blew her nose noisily into a handkerchief and then dabbed her eyes. The men looked away.

More mourners arrived. The room was crowded now. The three trapped men, seizing their chance, leaped from their seats and insisted that the newcomers sit down and take the weight off their feet. They forced the not too strongly protesting, newly arrived, female relatives into the freshly vacated seats, and escaped to the relative freedom of the kitchen which was awash with other busy female relatives preparing sausage rolls, pork pies, bacon and egg plate pies, ham, salmon and cheese sandwiches. The relieved men made directly for the back door where cold fresh air and the chance of a quick cigarette beckoned.

A group of men was already there, the gravity of the occasion was apparent in their manner. In their best suits and overcoats they braved the squally wind and light rain. The sky was dark and foreboding, promising more foul weather. The men stood, hands behind their backs, hiding half-smoked cigarettes in their cupped hands, their uncomfortable bearing and self-conscious stiffness obvious to any casual observer.

The three escapees formed a small knot just outside the back door. Joe detached himself from a group nearby and made his way across to them.

"I've heard that those ladders were definitely tampered with," Joe said quietly.

"Aye. I heard the same thing. They reckon two of the bolts were loose, one on the top and one on the bottom of the top section of ladders, the nuts removed, and the other two bolts were missing entirely. They did a fingertip search of the whole shed and couldn't find them," Alan said.

"That near fall caused Harry's death as surely as if he'd fell to the ground," Trev said. "Heart attack, my arse. Harry would still be here if those ladders hadn't been tampered with."

"Who would do a stupid thing like that?" Richie asked.

"Who had a motive?" Alan asked.

They looked at him without speaking.

"Come on. Think. Who had the motive and the opportunity?"

"Skinner," Joe said.

"Skinner and Morgan," Trev added.

"Right."

"You mean Skinner sent Harry up those ladders knowing he would fall?" Richie asked incredulously.

"Either that, or Morgan guessed Harry would be sent up there. Harry worked in the next bay, and often stood in for Albert when he'd been off in the past. So Harry was the obvious choice if they knew that Albert wasn't coming back," Alan said with conviction.

"But would Morgan deliberately try to kill Harry like that?"

Richie asked, shocked.

"I'm convinced that he did. Morgan's had it in for Harry for ages, ever since the holiday money went missing. And especially so since Harry opened his mouth and let slip about the Yank in the Mason's," Alan said.

"So they knew Harry knew about their plan?" Richie asked.

"They know something's up and it's too near completion, and their big pay-off, for them to back out now," Alan said.

"He's right," Trev said.

"I've been thinking along the same lines myself," Joe said.

"So what are we going to do about it?" Alan asked.

"I think that this changes everything. What we agreed before, about doing nothing, well that's out of the window now," Trev said determinedly.

"What, you mean we should stop the pay-off?" Alan asked.

"Keep your voices down. Let's meet at the allotment after the funeral and sort something out," Joe suggested.

The others agreed.

"It makes you laugh, doesn't it? The official investigation is going to come up with absolutely nothing. It's a rushed job and a complete whitewash. Skinner is in charge of the whole thing anyway. It's a disgrace. And, to top it all, I've heard that they're only paying Harry up until the estimated time of his death," Alan said.

"What? That's downright dishonest," Joe said.

"It's dishonest right enough. It makes you sick," Alan said disgustedly.

"But that's terrible. They're paying everybody else for the full shift, aren't they? Everybody that was sent home?" Trev put in.

"Oh aye. It's only Harry's pay that has been stopped. They said that it was company policy," Alan explained.

"Well they want to change the bloody company policy. This game's not worth being in now, and that's a fact," Trev said. "What's the Union doing about it?"

"The Union's demanding that he's paid for the whole shift, and Olive says that at least they've kicked in some money for the funeral. They're paying for it out of the hardship fund. There won't be enough for a headstone, though," Joe said.

"Well, that's something. It's about time they did something useful. They're quick enough to take our subs every week, aren't they?"

"It really makes you think, doesn't it?" Trev said, half to himself.

"Think about what?" asked Joe.

"Well, what's it all about? Life I mean. What's the point? There's old Harry there, worrying himself to death about Olive, trying to do his best for her, even nicking the lads' holiday money so she'd have a holiday. And stealing to pay for his daughter to fly from Australia, and then what happens? He drops dead." He shook his head.

"That's the way it goes, mate," Joe said philosophically. "It could be any one of us tomorrow, or even today come to that. We just don't know, do we?"

"But why do we bother? Why do we worry? Why do we keep trying to stay within the rules when it doesn't seem to matter a toss in the end? We all end up dead. We should just live for today and forget tomorrow because we might not even be here."

"I'll be glad when this is over with, I bloody hate funerals," Joe said changing the subject and searching his pockets for a Rennie. "They always set my stomach off."

"Which undertaker is it?" asked Alan.

"Urwins from the High Street," Joe said.

"Is that the one with the tomato plants in the window?" Richie asked.

"I think so."

A sudden thought struck Richie. "Why do they put tomato plants in the window, do you think?"

"What else can they put in the window, you nugget, dead bodies?" Alan answered a bit more harshly than he meant to.

There followed a general discussion regarding the merits of funerals against other forms of family get-togethers. The general consensus seemed to be that weddings were definitely the worst because there was nearly always a fight at the reception, or sometimes even before that. This it was generally agreed was because of the complete set of bastards that were invited, namely the other side's family, the in-laws. Weddings were followed closely by engagements and birthdays.

Christenings were considered to be not so bad, and funerals were voted the best. As was pointed out by Joe, funerals generally went off with great solemnity and ceremony. Any serious drinking came after the show was over and the outsiders or casual acquaintances had left, leaving only the close friends and relatives to set about seeing off the deceased in a traditional and proper manner, namely by having a bloody good drink in fond memory of the deceased. To their acute disappointment, that time-honoured tradition wouldn't be followed this time because of their shortage of funds.

At long last the hearse arrived. The undertaker was admitted though the front door and a respectful hush dropped on the room like the proverbial wet blanket. The black-clad imposing figure entered the house, important and clearly in command of the situation in his traditional dress, frock coat and top hat. He nodded to everyone present in a dignified manner, had a quiet word with the widow, then oversaw the removal of the flowers from their temporary position on the floor just inside of the front door. The flowers cleared from the house and placed in the hearse, the pallbearers went upstairs to start their unenvied task.

There had been no shortage of volunteers and Olive had sought out Joe's advice about whom to choose. Joe selected the three other men he thought that Harry knew the best, which were, Trev, Richie and Alan. The men waited until the coffin lid was secured for the last time and screwed down tight, Trev averting his eyes from the spectacle, and then they lifted the coffin waist high and manoeuvred it around the doorway, the landing at the top of the stairs, and then down the stairs themselves, being careful not to mark the walls or the paintwork. They were fully aware that Olive couldn't afford the money to buy new wallpaper and paint. Their grim task almost completed, they were now outside of the house and lifting the coffin shoulder high, carried it down the garden path to the waiting hearse where they slid it into the open back of the vehicle. The undertaker made sure that it was secure, and then he invited the waiting mourners to board the funeral cars.

The pallbearers brushed the faint traces of the wood dust from each other's shoulders and waited until all the close members of the family were aboard. They were careful to observe the strict and jealously guarded protocol demanded by the occasion, allowing the relatives to board the cars in order of seniority. The blustering wind mocked their attempts to constrain their hair and blew cold rain in their faces as they stood respectfully by the hearse.

When all the relatives were in the cars, the men took their places in vehicles at the rear of the cortège as the hearse began to move slowly off. The undertaker strode resolutely in front of the solemn procession, stepping out with his ornate, silver-topped walking stick swinging in his hand, until he reached the corner of the road, and then removing his top hat, climbed into the front passenger seat of the hearse and the procession quickened pace.

The neighbours were all out and Trev could see mothers with their children standing at their front doors, watching the spectacle and paying their last respects. The car windows were streaked with the rain and the image outside distorted and blurred. Trev had often thought that it was a bit ironic that the deceased, who had probably never travelled in such a luxurious limousine during his lifetime, was now being carried in sumptuous comfort when he wasn't here to appreciate it.

The church was only about a mile away, and they could see its spire visible high on top of the hill as soon as they turned the corner. The priest was standing at the church door to greet them, and waited until they all alighted from the cars, and the coffin once again aloft on the pallbearers' shoulders, before leading the sad procession into the cold, but dry, interior of the church. There was quite a crowd of people waiting for the cortège outside the church. Friends and work colleagues, who felt that they didn't warrant the title of close friends, but all the same, were eager to show their respects to their deceased colleague.

The mourners fell in behind the coffin as the procession entered deeper into the church, and taking seats on either side of the aisle, filled the church from the back pews, leaving the front pews for the relatives and close friends of the dead man.

The priest conducted the service with practised ease, and in a southern accent that many in the congregation found hard to understand. The hymns were sung not with gusto, but with great reserve, many of the mourners not fully opening their mouths. To the vast majority, the church, any church, was a foreign place, a place they associated with fear. A vague fear of all the unspoken awful things that they were most frightened of, God, death, judgment, and a possible afterlife of eternal damnation. It's hardly surprising that not many of them were prepared to sing. They sat half-on, and half-off the hard wooden pews, their heads bowed to avoid eye contact with the bellowing priest at the front. They were not sure of the words of the hymns, and didn't even open the hymnbooks so thoughtfully provided. They weren't sure of when to stand and when to kneel, and followed anyone's lead that looked as if they knew what they were doing. All they wanted to do was to get out of this cold, fearful and claustrophobic place and back to the fresh air outside.

Joe, still chewing the remnants of an anti-acid tablet, walked nervously and hesitantly to the front of the church and turned to face the mourners. He sincerely wished that he's never agreed to deliver a short eulogy, but Olive had insisted that he was Harry's best friend and it should come from him.

His hands trembled as he unfolded the crumpled scrap of paper he pulled from an inside pocket. He had difficulty focusing his eyes on the words he'd written on the paper and swallowing hard, licked his dry lips, coughed, cleared his throat and began.

"Olive has asked me to say a few words about Harry. I knew Harry for a long time." Joe's voice cracked with emotion as he scanned the sea of faces before him. "I'm not much good with words and have never been much of a talker and I didn't have a clue as to what to say, so, I've just put something down in my own words," he said, casting a quick, nervous look at the coffin. He began to read from the paper in his hand.

"Harry wasn't stuck-up or toffee-nosed, he had no airs or graces. He was a plain-speaking, working man." Joe looked up from his notes. "Harry was a good mate. He was reliable and wouldn't see anybody in trouble if he could help. He was an honest man." Joe glanced up and around the congregation as if daring anyone to contradict him. "He was honest," he repeated, "and always paid his debts. He didn't like to borrow money from anyone and would only do so if it was absolutely necessary." Joe looked up again.

Harry's workmates knew that he was referring to the holiday club money that Harry had 'borrowed', but Olive and the other family members didn't have a clue what he was referring to and were unaware of the situation.

Joe pressed on, gaining confidence now. "What else can I say about Harry? He was an ordinary working man who always tried to be cheerful. He liked his garden, his leeks. Him and me won the leek prize for the last six years running. He liked a bet and a pint. He did his best for his family and for his mates. He was one of us. One of the lads." Joe folded the paper and shoved it back into his pocket as he walked back to his seat with tears in his eyes.

The priest stood up, took over again and was soon well into another hymn. The mourners stirred, knowing instinctively that the end wasn't far off now. There were coughs and sneezes, shuffles and murmurings as the priest began his final address. He insisted on calling the deceased Henry, gave a long and wandering and, to some of Harry's old friends, bewildering potted account of his life and his many qualities. Most were surprised at the account of Harry's wartime experiences; they'd had no idea that he'd even been in the forces during the Second World War. Harry had never mentioned that part of his life.

At long last the final hymn was sung and the service over, and the mourners remained respectfully in their pews to allow the family to leave the church first. They followed the coffin out of the door, and waited patiently until it was safely ensconced in the back of the hearse again. This time there was an additional long line of private cars that joined the end of the cortège as it snaked downhill away from the church.

The cars now travelled at a faster, but still dignified speed across the town until reaching the ornate gates of the cemetery. The hearse slowly turned into the gates and drove smoothly down the narrow road to where the priest was already waiting patiently in the falling sleet, having somehow mysteriously arrived before them. The gravediggers stood discreetly a little distance away, sheltering from the downpour under a large tree.

The pallbearers carried Harry to his final resting place and thankfully laid down their burden, then stood back and allowed the priest and family members to move nearer the graveside. Joe and Trev stood behind the family members.

"I think Harry would have preferred to have been cremated, it would have been a lot warmer," Trev said quietly, attempting a joke.

Joe smiled and said, "Yes, he hated the cold."

"That's right, he'd have been looking forward to getting stuck into those pork pies and sausage rolls as well," Trev said.

The priest again said the words of comfort and hope of future resurrection, and then the widow and other family members threw clumps of soil into the grave and down onto the coffin. The symbolic gesture signifying an end to the ceremony and a start to the process of rebuilding their lives without their loved one. The mourners quietly dispersed after spending an appropriate amount of time admiring the wreaths and reading the attached cards.

The subdued and damp group returned to Olive's house, had a cup of tea, and politely ate a couple of ham sandwiches and a sausage roll or two each.

"That was a very nice eulogy you gave Joe, thank you," Olive said.

"I was pleased to be asked to say a few words, Olive," Joe replied.

"How's your stomach today?" she asked with concern.

"Oh, so-so, Olive," he replied, patting his stomach softly with his hand.

"You've had a lot of trouble with it lately, haven't you? I'm so glad that your stomach's back on its feet now. With Harry it was always his chest, you know. Always chesty he was. That was always his Achilles Heel, his chest," she replied, leaving Joe in a maze of tangled metaphors.

The four men offered their condolences again to the widow and other members of the family and left, relieved to be out and into the fresh air. They walked resolutely and purposefully up the hill to the allotment. They had plans to make.

28

The group ensconced themselves in the shed. It was again watertight and warm inside as Joe had repaired the roof and got the paraffin heater working.

"Right then, Alan, you're the expert, what are we going to do to stop this pay-off then?" Trev asked.

Alan was surprised that they'd all changed their minds and agreed to do something about the pay-off. Their change of heart had been the direct result of Harry's death and now they were determined to foil the takeover plan.

"Well, we're going to do something to put the game straight, aren't we? We'll show the bastards."

"I wasn't going to get involved. It just didn't sit right with me, you know? But I'm surprised now that I even hesitated for a minute," Trev said.

"And then there's the money," Alan said.

"Harry dying like that was the reason. Not the money," Trev maintained.

"There's more to it than just money, you know, Alan," Joe put in.

"What? You mean you're Robin Hood now then, are you? Robbing the rich to give to the poor? Come off it, man."

"No. What I meant is that there's very little we can do to influence our lives normally, is there? You know what I mean. We're always at the mercy of events. The welders or some other tradesmen walk out and that's our Christmas down the drain. The management stops the overtime and that's our holidays buggered up. The Mafia tells the Yank that it wants the yard and the Yank tells Skinner what he wants and he tells Morgan to call the welders out and we're laid off again," Joe said.

"The bleedin' Mafia is telling us what to do now. We're always at the bottom of the heap and always being pissed on by every other bastard that feels like it. Well, I've had just about enough of being a whipping boy for every other bastard. At least now we can stand up like men and have a go. If it doesn't come off and we're banged up, or shot, then at least we've tried. But we're not going to be caught, or shot, and I'm going to make sure that this Christmas is a good one," Trev put in.

Joe nodded. "That's right. At least we're doing something for ourselves."

Alan nodded. As confidently as he could he quickly outlined the bones of the plan, while the others listened in silence. He told them that he'd thought it through and was sure that nothing could go wrong. This brought a disbelieving cough from Trev.

"Straight up, Trev, this is going to work," Alan said earnestly.

"Come on then, master criminal, give us the full details," Trev said.

Alan explained his plan in detail.

The men digested the information in silence. None of them, including Alan, really wanted to get involved with anything as serious as this robbery, especially as it involved stealing from the Mafia, but they were all sick and tired of eking out an existence with very little money. More than that, they were tired of constantly making excuses for their lack of success and feelings of helplessness. At least this would be one way for them to reclaim their masculinity, and enable them to have some influence over their own destiny. Each one of them, after the initial shock of finding out what the plan was, knew deep down that they were capable of carrying it out. They were basically honest and upright but they had all had enough of living from hand to mouth and the problems that involved.

"I still don't understand how you know where this pay-off is going to happen," Joe said.

"Easy, the McKennas must have mentioned something about it to my dad, he told me mother and she told me. I put two and two together, and bingo."

The men digested this piece of information in silence.

"I want one thing clear from the start," Joe said. "There's got to be no violence, okay? I'm not getting mixed up with any rough stuff."

"But we've got to carry clubs or something or they will just laugh at us," Alan said, "and what are we going to do if one of them is armed?"

"Well then, you carry a club as long as nobody's hurt with it, but I'm not getting involved in any rough stuff." Joe was adamant.

The others nodded their agreement.

"Alright. No unnecessary violence," Alan said. "But I'm taking a two-by-two piece of timber or something, just in case."

Trev looked at the others, not believing that they were in this situation, planning a raid, not as a paper exercise or spoof but in all seriousness. He shook his head. "How much money are we talking about exactly?" he asked.

"£20,000," Alan said.

"That's £5,000 each, divided up four ways," Joe said.

"What about Olive, then? I thought that we were going to see her alright?" Trev said. "And what about Tracy? Mickey's wife and kids should get something."

Alan sighed, "Well, I suppose we should give them something…"

"We should give them a full share each," Trev said.

"That would be £3,333 for everybody then," Joe calculated after tapping numbers into a pocket calculator.

The men nodded, some of them somewhat reluctantly.

"Right then, that's settled," Alan said.

"Er, there's just one thing you didn't explain, Alan," Trev said.

"Aye? What's that then?"

"Who is going to hold the money until the share out?"

"I am of course, who else?"

"I'm not happy with you holding it," Trev said determinedly.

"Me neither," Joe put in.

"But I'm the only one that can hold it," Alan maintained.

"Shit. Why not let someone else have it?" Joe asked.

Alan, realising that he was outnumbered, tried to negotiate, but was cut short by Trev.

"Look, you've just told us that Richie will stash the money. He'll take it up-river in a boat, then to his flat on the motorbike, hide it there and then race back to the yard. He'll be back within twenty or thirty minutes, sneak through the sheds and join us back in the yard waiting to be paid. So if the lad's already got the money, then I say that he should keep it until the share out."

After a lot more heated discussion, it was finally decided that Richie would keep the money; the others unanimously elected him, despite his protestations, and Alan's objections.

Alan made his way home disappointed because the lads didn't trust him to hold the money until the share out, but alive with excitement thinking about the forthcoming raid.

He knew something was wrong when he saw his mother sitting on the stairs as he opened the front door. She held her face in her hands and was sobbing uncontrollably. "I tried to stop him, son, but he wouldn't listen."

Alan could see the bruising on her face and the wet steaks from her tears. He rushed upstairs throwing open his bedroom door so hard that it rebounded off the wall. He stared in amazement. Looking around the ransacked room he tried to make sense of the scene. His clothes had been pulled out of drawers and strewn across the floor. The bed upturned against the wall and the mattress ripped open spilling its foam stuffing onto the floor. The carpet had been pulled up and flung into the corner. The room was destroyed.

But it wasn't only the room that was destroyed. He knew instinctively what had happened. Alan walked quickly to the dresser and felt underneath with his hand. The envelope was gone. Desperately he searched further underneath with an increasing feeling of dread, but he knew that the money wasn't there. He sat in the chair and shook his head, anger rising, realisation dawning. He couldn't believe that he'd been robbed, that the money he'd stolen from others had now been stolen from him. The money that had been so difficult to get and taken so long to accumulate was gone. But that wasn't why he was angry. The thing that really maddened him was the fact that he'd been betrayed, and by his own father.

29

It was Friday, payday, the last payday before Christmas.

The three men waited silently and watched through the crack in the partly opened door as the car drove up to the gates. They could see Chisholm, Skinner and Morgan standing by the door of the loading bay in the deserted factory yard.

The car stopped outside the rusted factory gates and a man got out. The three would-be robbers were ensconced in a small storeroom at the side of a building that the American would have to pass with the money to reach Chisholm and his companions.

"Just wait a few more minutes and then we'll all be in the money," Alan whispered, rubbing his hands in anticipation, displaying a confidence he certainly didn't feel.

The men watched, on edge, as the American ducked through a gap in the fence near the gate and walked though the factory grounds towards them. Scaretti was big, very big, and he walked slowly, but with an agility that belied his bulk. He carried a briefcase that presumably held the money.

Chisholm, Skinner and Morgan began to walk towards Scaretti, eager to receive their long awaited pay-off.

The lads watched wide-eyed from their hiding place.

"Wait for it lads, wait for it," Alan said softly as the man approached. "Time to put your masks on." Alan pulled three masks out of a plastic carrier bag, and passed two of them to his accomplices.

"What are these?" Trev hissed.

"They look like kids' cardboard horror masks," Joe said incredulously.

"That's because they are," Trev said, examining the masks.

The masks were indeed scary monster facemasks. They were a great success with children, being aimed at the four to ten year old age ranges.

"I don't believe the stupid bastard bought these for us. I'll kill Richie when I see him," Trev hissed.

"He said they were all he could get. It's too late now. They'll have to do," Alan said with resignation.

The men reluctantly donned the masks, holding them precariously in place over their faces with the thin elastic threaded through each side of the masks. The masks and a pair of new overalls, which they each wore, were considered all the preparation required for the operation. Alan had also thoughtfully provided himself with a thick, four-foot long piece of wood.

They could now hear the sound of footsteps on the concrete path, as the American got closer.

Joe felt a sharp pain in his stomach. His heart was up somewhere in his throat, then it jumped back into his chest and was hammering in there until he was sure that the approaching man must be able to hear it. He felt dizzy and suddenly realised that he was breathing much too quickly. Making a determined effort, he took a slow breath in and held it for as long as he could, and then exhaled slowly and quietly. By the time he'd recovered his composure the man had reached their hiding place. Alan, who was in pole position, could see Scaretti, who was now fully visible to him through the gap in the door.

They waited a few seconds until the man has passed them.

"Now!" Alan hissed, and the three men surged towards the door.

Scaretti's sixth sense told him that something was wrong and he turned just as Alan pushed opened the door of the storeroom. Reacting quickly and instinctively, the American kicked at the door and slammed it back into Alan's face. Alan dropped the wooden club and staggered backwards into Joe and Trev, who were both knocked off balance. Morgan and Chisholm, seeing what was happening, increased their pace towards the hit man, a not so enthusiastic Skinner bringing up the rear.

Alan was momentarily stunned at this unexpected development. But recovered swiftly and, assisted by the weight of Trev and Joe, pushed the door open despite Scaretti's efforts to hold it closed. Bursting through the door, Alan headbutted the American, who, stunned by the blow, dropped the briefcase, and grabbed hold of his attacker. Trev leapt at the rushing Morgan, punching him squarely in the mouth before the big man collided with him. Despite the solid blow, Morgan's momentum carried them both the ground.

Joe similarly engaged Chisholm, jumping on his back and grabbing him tightly around the neck.

Alan and Scaretti struggled desperately and fell over discarded rubbish on the ground. Swinging his fists wildly, Scaretti managed to break free and, standing up, looked desperately around for a weapon. He picked up a long piece of angle bar and swung it back, ready to hit Alan with it. Swinging the bar back, he inadvertently caught Skinner, who had just arrived on the scene, a glancing blow to the head, causing a bloody wound. Skinner screamed and staggered away holding his hands to his head.

Alan, struggled to his feet, and surprised Scaretti with a deadly one-two combination punch. The American, distracted by the screaming Skinner, didn't see Alan coming, and dazed by the blows, was still upright, but swaying. Alan took the opportunity to hit him a well-aimed and forceful uppercut to the chin. The man fell backwards, as if poleaxed and his head hit the ground with a sickening crack.

Morgan, spitting teeth from his bloody mouth, broke away from Trev and picking up the discarded angle bar, swung wildly at Trev. He was aiming for the head, but caught him heavily on the shoulder. Trev faltered, staggering backwards. The pause gave Morgan the opportunity to grab the discarded briefcase and run towards the river.

Chisholm took this opportunity to shake himself free of Joe and flee towards the gate, a route already taken by the injured Skinner.

Trev, recovered from the blow, picked himself up from the ground and set off after Morgan.

Morgan reached the river and looked around him wildly, trying to decide his best way of escape. The tide was high and the river was flowing very fast.

Trev bore down upon Morgan at speed, Joe and Alan some way behind. The man knew that he couldn't outrun his pursuers, so he made a decision.

He turned to fight. Swinging the briefcase wildly, he caught Trev on the side of the head hard enough to slow him down, and halt his charge. The blow was also hard enough to dislodge the flimsy mask from his face.

"You!" Morgan shouted, recognising Trev. "Well, well. I did for that thieving mate of yours and now I'll do for you." He smiled nastily. "Mind you don't fall."

Trev quickly recovered and, adrenaline filling his body, he lunged at Morgan. He was glad to be able to give vent to the frustration and anger that had built up inside of him over the previous months. Harry's death, his helplessness over the lockouts. The anger surged inside him. Anger caused by the numerous insults that this man had heaped upon him and on his friends. Brenda's humiliation, Mickey's arrest and imprisonment. Tracy's breakdown and her suicide attempt. All these frustrations merged into one, identifiable thing, the man that was before him now, and he saw red.

The men grappled, pounding each other's bodies with their fists. Lashing out, Trev caught Morgan a lucky blow squarely on the chin with a fist. The big man stumbled backwards, losing his footing in the slippery mud on the riverside. Off balance, Trev fell beside him.

Morgan kicked Trev and held his face in the mud with his boot. Then he panicked. His other pursuers were now almost at the river's edge and he knew that he didn't have the strength to fight them too. He made a decision. The wrong decision.

Still gripping the briefcase, he waded out into the fast flowing river, the water gradually immersing his body up to his chest. Finally, with only his head above the water, he struggled to swim across the wide expanse of water and reach the relative safety of the other side.

Alan and Joe came to a halt on the muddy bank and pulled Trev from the muddy water. They watched helplessly as their prey swam away from them.

"Where's Richie with the boat?" Alan asked. But there was no boat in sight. The three watched helplessly as Morgan reached the shallows at the other side of the river. He emerged from the water exhausted, water dripping from his saturated clothes. Summoning strength from somewhere, he threw the briefcase onto the mud on the far riverbank, where it landed with a soft splat.

As he tried to clamber ashore through the mud, Morgan lost his balance and wobbled unsteadily in the swirling torrent. His feet sank into the treacherous muddy river bottom and he disappeared briefly from view. Quickly regaining his balance, he stood up straight and tried to reposition his legs against the force of the water, but it was too strong for him and his legs buckled and his upper body dipped under again. This time he didn't resurface and the men caught a glimpse of him as the terrible force of the water washed him quickly away downstream.

Just then a small boat came into sight around a bend in the river, its motor put-putting quietly. As it got nearer they could see a tiger-faced figure in a small boat.

"Bastard's kept the best mask for himself," Joe muttered. Out loud he shouted. "Get over here and hurry up!"

Richie manoeuvred the boat towards them and Trev pointed to the briefcase on the opposite bank.

"Over there, get the briefcase," he shouted. Pointing across the river.

Richie crossed to the other bank and rammed an oar into the muddy river bottom to hold the craft in position and prevent it from drifting away in the current. He lifted the case with the flat blade of another oar and transferred it to the boat without difficulty. The briefcase safely in the boat, he pulled across to where the others were waiting.

Quickly the three men pulled off their new, clean overalls to reveal their dirty, workclothes underneath. They threw the overalls into a sack along with their masks, and this was thrown into the boat. Richie turned the boat and headed up river against the tide, the outboard motor chugging furiously.

Alan looked back to where Scaretti was. The injured man was still lying where he'd fallen, obviously unconscious, but there was no sign of Chisholm or Skinner.

"The bastards didn't have much fight in them, they just ran off," he said to the others.

"What'll we do about him?" Joe asked concerned, indicating the prone man.

"Leave the bastard there," Alan said shortly. "Let Chisholm come back and look after him."

"But he might die or something," Joe persisted. "I think we should call an ambulance."

"Okay then. You do that." Alan feigned indifference.

The prone Scaretti started to move his head and moaned loudly.

"He's alright," Alan said, "come on, let's get out of here before he wakes up."

The operation complete and with now nothing to link them to the raid. The three raiders quickly made their way back towards the scrapyard, while the tiger-faced boatman steered the boat into the darkness of the upper river.

As the raiders ran towards the fence, they were surprised to hear the sound of sirens and could see the blue flashing lights of police cars racing to the factory gates.

"Someone must have seen something suspicious and rang the police," Alan said.

"Come on, let's get out of here," Joe whispered harshly.

They set off at a run, the men beginning to feel the strain of the unaccustomed exertions. The sweat was running down their faces and into their eyes, and they were puffing and panting like old steam trains.

They continued to run as fast as their legs would carry them, charging around the corner towards the fence. The three ran past the deserted workshops and made directly for the fence separating the empty factory from the scrapyard, reaching the fence out of breath and panting.

Running through the untidy rows of wrecked cars and scrap metal the three men scrambled through the small hole in the opposite fence and into the shipyard. Adrenaline filled them, and it was all they could do to contain their excitement as they sped through the deserted sheds to emerge at the office building where they joined the noisy crowd waiting outside the offices for their pay, which hadn't arrived yet. The three felt like shouting their exhilaration as they mixed in with the crowd that grumbled and moaned regarding the expected size of their last pay before Christmas. They were still excited and wound up, but so were most of the other night shift workers so they didn't stand out particularly.

Richie arrived back at the yard unnoticed thirty minutes later, entering the yard through a hole in the fence like the others.

30

Joe went home from the yard the next morning and gave his wife his unopened pay packet. He explained exactly what had happened at the factory and told her everything. The temptation to keep it from her had been very strong, but he knew that Brenda would never believe some half-baked excuse about where the money had come from and anyway, since their recent heart to heart he'd resolved not to keep anything from her.

Brenda was dismayed. "How could you be so stupid to get mixed up in something like this?"

"There wasn't much else we could do, love. We had to do something especially after what happened to Harry, for God's sake."

"But why didn't you tell me what you were planning something like this?"

"Because I knew that you'd worry about it and try to talk me out of it."

Brenda wasn't happy about what had happened, but understood why Joe had become involved. She realised that there wasn't anything she could do about it now except make the best of the situation.

Joe looked after Sharon while Brenda went to the town and bought the items required for them to enjoy the festive season. It was important that they didn't draw attention to themselves by spending more money that they should have, and they agreed that they were paying no debt off this week and that all his pay was to be used to buy extra nice things for them to eat at Christmas. He told her that he'd be able to give her a lot of extra money on Christmas Eve to buy presents, but they again agreed not to buy anything too flash. They agreed that even though there would be more than enough to pay off all their debts at once, they would do it gradually so as not to draw attention.

The men could hardly wait for the following Monday, Christmas Eve, to arrive. No child ever looked forward so eagerly to the arrival of Christmas. They looked forward to the share out with great anticipation. Joe and Trev arrived at the allotment on Monday morning and huddled inside the small shed, sipping hot sweet tea and warming themselves at the now repaired heater, while waiting for the others to arrive.

"You see this morning's paper?" Trev asked.

Joe nodded. "They seem to be suggesting that there's some doubt now about the takeover going ahead. It said that the police were investigating a possible link with organised crime."

"I've been thinking, Joe, the police turning up like that. How did they know what was happening last Friday night, and where it was taking place? And how did they find out about the Mob being involved?"

"They have their sources," Joe said vaguely. "Don't they have grasses and stuff?"

At about ten past twelve, Alan arrived, out of breath carrying a plastic bag, and a bombshell. They knew immediately from his expression that something was wrong.

He entered the shed, letting a draught of cold air into the cosy atmosphere. He closed the door behind him and sat down heavily without speaking.

"What's happened?" Joe asked, voicing their concern.

Alan shook his head. "You're never going to believe this," he said.

"Believe what?" Trev demanded. "What going on, man?"

"Richie. He's done off."

"Done off? What do you mean, done off?"

"He's done a runner. Gone."

"But where's the money, then?" Joe asked naïvely.

"Gone with Richie. Well, half of it has. He's done off with half the money."

"Half the money, are you sure?" Trev asked.

"I'm sure, alright. Julie's mother says that they haven't been seen since Saturday morning. They were supposed to go around for their dinner at lunchtime yesterday but they didn't turn up. I went to their flat and it's empty, no furniture or carpets, nothing. The woman downstairs says she hadn't seen them since last week. I let myself in with the front door key that they always left under the mat." He paused and shook his head, as if unable to believe the words he was saying. "This bag was left in the corner of the sitting room There was no note or anything. They've definitely done a runner. They must have left sometime on Saturday."

The men sat in silence for a minute while the implications of this bombshell slowly became apparent to them. "But that means that we've only got half of what we should have got," Joe said slowly.

"That's right." Alan upended the bag and tipped the contents out onto the floor.

There was an audible and involuntary gasp from the onlookers as he did so. The bag spilled out wads of used banknotes. Alan spread the money on the floor and started to count the five and ten pound notes, grouping them into different denominations to make it easier and quicker. He threw some to the others and they too started to count, but their excitement made them noisy and careless in the calculating. After a number of recounts of the used fivers and tenners it was finally established that there was exactly the expected £10,000 in the box.

"£2,000 per share, including Mickey and Olive." Joe calculated.

"I think we should give Olive and Tracy a lot less now that we've only got half of what we were expecting, it's enough for them seeing as they did nowt for it," Alan said.

"What, £500 each you mean?" Joe asked.

"Aye. That'd be enough for a good Christmas for them. In fact £250 would be enough. We don't want them flashing money all over the place do we? It'd attract attention to them. Anyway Harry still owes us the holiday money he nicked," Alan insisted.

Trev shook his head. "No. We give them a full share each just like we agreed. I'll tell you what though. If I ever get my hands on that bastard, Richie, I'll pull his head off."

"Well, I suppose it's only right that they get a full share. But who'd have thought it, eh? Fancy the lad doing this to his mates," Joe said, shaking his head. "Hey, I've just realised, he's probably got the drugs as well."

"Aye, he's taken them as well. I checked Jackie's garage. They're gone," Alan said.

"I can't see him not taking them," Trev put in. "Not after ripping his mates off for the money."

"I'd never have thought that Richie would do something like that, and Julie pregnant as well. I can't believe that he robbed his mates, and his own cousin. His own family, and blood's thicker than water, always has been. It must have been her made him do it. Her family are all funny ones and that's a fact," Alan said, obviously genuinely shocked by his cousin's betrayal.

"That's what happens when you get a bit of money, isn't it? Everything changes. At least he's left us half the money," Joe said philosophically.

"Him doing a runner like that might attract the police's attention," Trev said.

"That's a point, it might put him in the frame for the raid," Joe said. "What do you think, Alan?"

"No, I don't so. I don't think that they'll even connect him pissing off with the raid. Richie is hardly a prime suspect, is he? It'll be me that the bastards will be looking at if they're looking at anybody, not him."

The group had to content themselves with their reduced shares, which as Joe put it, 'was still a tidy sum', although nowhere near enough for them to retire on. They each had their own plans on what to do with the money, and were determined to spend a little at a time and not draw attention to themselves.

Brenda was beaming when Joe opened the door. "I've got some good news, love," she said. "In fact I've got some absolutely amazing news for you." Before he could respond she put her arms around his neck and kissed him on the forehead. "The social worker's manager has been around and told me that we can keep Sharon here. They've reconsidered the whole case and have now decided that their initial judgment was too harsh. They're making all the necessary arrangements and she can stay here, with us, permanently. We'll also get all the allowances backdated, but that'll take a while to sort out." She kissed Joe on the forehead again. "Oh Joe, I'm so happy."

31

Trev walked through the large metal doors between the threatening, high walls of the prison. Contrasting dramatically with the picturesque surroundings of Durham City, its Cathedral and Castle, narrow old English streets and quaint shops and pubs, the prison was bleak, depressing and unwelcoming.

In the visiting room he sat opposite a pale and miserable-looking Mickey. Trev was amazed at the change in his friend's appearance. He'd lost weight and had a grey pallor to his now hollow cheeks. But it was his attitude that really worried Trev.

"How's it going then?" Trev asked, aware of the utter ridiculousness of the remark, but feeling that he had to break the lengthening and uncomfortable silence.

Mickey shrugged and pulled down the corners of his mouth. "Alright, I suppose," he said quietly.

"The food okay is it?"

"Shite."

Trev looked around furtively and lowered his voice. "Look Mickey, we've sorted out that thing with Morgan, Skinner, and the

Yank. You know, the yard takeover and everything."

"Oh aye. Good," his friend answered blandly.

"Well, that's good news isn't it?"

"It's not going to get Tracy back to normal is it? Or me out of here, and it's not going to stop them revoking my licence."

"I'm pleased Tracy's back home with the kids anyway."

"Her mother's going to have to help her with the kids."

Trev remained silent, not knowing what to say. The silence lay between the men like a heavy weight.

After a while Trev coughed and cleared his throat. "Look mate, when we sorted that thing out we came into a bit of money." He looked around again to make sure that no one could overhear. "There's enough money to see Tracy and the kids okay for Christmas, and a lot left over, so don't worry about that."

"How much exactly?"

"£2,000."

"Really? That much? Well, that's a relief, Trev. Can you imagine what it's like for me being in here at Christmas and not being able to provide for my wife and kids?"

"Aye I can. And there's more good news, Brenda and her friend Sylvia are going to give evidence for you at your trial. Then there's my evidence, and a few more people in the club that have come forward saying that it wasn't your fault. Morgan's gone missing and he's not likely to come back, and he was the main prosecution witness."

"Morgan's gone missing?"

"Aye." Trev shrugged and didn't elaborate further. "So, with the weight of evidence for you, it's almost certain that you will be fully acquitted and then you can get back to normal."

"You think so?" There was a trace of hope in Mickey's voice.

Trev nodded vigorously, as if trying to convince himself. "Certain."

Joe and Trev delivered the dependants' money. Olive was very emotional, and tearful when they told her that all the lads had had a whip-round and came up with the money. They had in fact organised a whip-round at the yard, but had only managed to total about fifteen pounds. She thanked them profusely, and said that she knew that Harry was well-liked but hadn't realised just how well thought of he was at the yard.

Tracy was equally grateful for the money when Trev and Joe visited her. She was obviously under sedation, her speech slurred and indistinct. There was also a strange sort of stillness about her, as if she'd been hurt terribly, was now beyond pain and accepted everything without complaint.

The men could see that she was suspicious about where the money had come from, but she didn't query it and accepted it gratefully. "Thank you very much. It'll give the bairns a good Christmas," she said flatly. "I'll put the rest away for when Mickey comes out."

"I saw him yesterday and he seems a lot brighter," Trev said, at a loss and feeling embarrassed.

"You visited Mickey? How is he?"

"He seems a lot more cheerful," Trev said. "I told him that Brenda and Sylvia and some others were going to give evidence for him at the trial, and that Morgan's gone missing."

Tracy was only half-listening. "You know what has had the most effect on him? Losing his ABA licence and not being able to teach the lads at the club. He was very well thought of in the parish, had a really good name, but now he feels like an outcast."

Both men tried to reassure Tracy that Mickey would soon be back to normal after he'd been found not guilty and released after the trial, but they didn't really convince themselves.

There were tears in both men's eyes as they left, and Joe blew his nose noisily into a large white handkerchief as they walked away from the house.

"Do you really think that Mickey will ever be the same, even if he gets out next month?" Trev asked.

"No. The man's really changed. He's a lot harder mentally now, disillusioned and bitter. He'll never be the same and neither will Tracy."

"That's what I thought."

"Do you know something, Trev?" Joe said.

"What?"

"I really felt excited while we were doing that raid, you know, alive?"

"Aye, me too. That'll be the adrenaline."

"Well, whatever it was. I've been thinking about it a lot, just suppose that Alan had another job like that lined up, would you be interested?"

Trev smiled. "No thanks. I might have been tempted perhaps, but not after seeing the inside of that prison and the effect it's had on Mickey. And anyway, I don't think that Alan is all that keen on pursuing a criminal career now that he knows what it's like to be a victim."

32

It later transpired that an anonymous telephone caller to the local newspaper had made serious allegations regarding the takeover of the yard by the American syndicate. The police became involved and discovered links between Chisholm and organised crime in the United States. Questions arose regarding the validity of the American syndicate's takeover bid. Further enquiries in America raised grave doubts about the money behind the deal and it was called off.

Although there was insufficient evidence to link him with the takeover bid and Chisholm, Scaretti, after being interviewed by the police, was deported back to the US as an undesirable alien.

Morgan's body was recovered a few weeks later, when it was washed up, all but unrecognisable, further along the coast. An inquest jury brought in an open verdict.

Chisholm's body was found in a wood in Northumberland around Easter. He'd been killed, shot through the head with a single bullet. Police said it bore all the hallmarks of a professional 'hit' killing. No one was ever charged with his murder and the killing remains a mystery to this day.

Mickey stood trial in February and was acquitted after the jury heard evidence from Trev, Brenda, Sylvia, and other witnesses. He was released immediately, but went home a changed man, having lost a lot of his good-natured cheerfulness and optimism. However, he recovered somewhat when the youth club asked him to resume his coaching of the boxing team.

Alan received twelve months' probation for his burglary conviction and the judge expressed a wish that he shouldn't get into trouble with the police again. Alan mentally and earnestly expressed the same wish. He hadn't relished his experience of being on the receiving end of thievery.

Skinner went on the run and was never seen in the area again. The police still want to interview him.

The welders elected a new shop steward who didn't call the men out on unofficial strike, well not as often as Morgan did, anyway.

33

"Well, have you fixed it yet?" Elsie demanded.

"I have that," Old Bob replied proudly, placing the Westminster chiming clock onto the table. "Took a lot of time and effort but it's fixed alright. Good as new and without the superglue."

"You see this morning's paper?" Elsie asked nonchalantly, unfolding a copy of the Daily News, its five-inch banner headline proclaiming - YARD TAKEOVER OFF.

"Aye. That's a good job as well," Old Bob said, nodding his head and smiling. "There's a rumour going round that your Alan and his mates stopped it somehow?"

"But we know different though, Bob, don't we? That was a good idea of yours to put a microphone in Skinner's office so we could hear everything that went on. They'd have gotten away with it if you hadn't bugged the place. The newspaper and the police were very interested in the information we passed on."

"It's you who deserves the credit, Elsie. I wouldn't have bugged the place if you hadn't told me what you'd overheard your Alan and his mates talking about. And they wouldn't have been able to stop the takeover without you feeding them that information about Scaretti and the pay-off."

"We'll let the lads take the credit, eh Bob? Let them think that they were solely responsible for keeping the yard open. It gives them a sense of pride and achievement, doesn't it? You know what they're like. After all, they wouldn't believe us pair of old codgers anyway, would they?"

THE END

PRISONERS IN THE NORTH

The best selling book by
John Ruttley,

The book details the forgotten deaths at Harperley PoW Camp, which was used to incarcerate German Prisoners during the First World War. There were also PoWs held at Harperley during the Second World War. The camp near Crook was recently featured on BBC 2's popular Restoration programme hosted by Griff Rees Jones.

What the press said-

'Wonderful, fascinating, educational and informative-this book is all of those and more, but best of all, it is one of those books that you only come across occasionally. It is a book that once started, you can't put down until you've finished.'-Weardale Gazette.

'Wonderfully written, an enthralling and interesting read, a friendly but at times chilling tale, well worth reading.'-Teesdale Mercury.

'A fascinating tale of a strangely neglected episode of war.'- Durham Town & Country magazine.

The book is Perfect bound, has a laminated full colour cover. A 5 size, it contains 79 pages plus another 8 pages of colour photographs. It also contains a detailed plan of the camp with an index.

ISBN No 0-9543366-1-5,

Excellent value at only £6.50 -

Order Now:
John Ruttley
PO BOX 1180
Sunderland
SR5 9AP

Mowbray the people's Park

by John Ruttley.

Featuring Sunderland's award winning park and reproducing all-colour photographs of its many attractions and features. This gem of a book tells the fascinating stories behind the park's monuments. It includes accounts of the terrible Victoria Hall tragedy which cost the lives of 183 children, Jack Crawford's heroic nailing of the British colours to the Warship's mast at the battle of Camperdown and General Henry Havelock's brave lifting of the seige at Lucknow. Mowbray Park and the adjacent Museum and Winter Gardens are among Sunderland's leading Tourist Attractions, enchanting and fascinating hundreds of thousands of visitors to the city every year.

Great value at only £5.99.

ISBN 0-9543366-07

Order now:

John Ruttley
PO BOX 1180
Sunderland
SR5 9AP